CW01501693

With thanks to my Patrons on Patreon, who've been helping me with many aspects of both writing and other things I'm working on, and especially to the members of the Murder Tier who I get to slaughter in various ways within my books now.

Cheers guys, and I'm terribly sorry that a couple of you survived this book... I'll get you in the next one.

# HARVEST

An Odyssey Novel

Evan Currie

# CONTENTS

# PREFACE

READING ORDER
Some confusion has been shown in what order the books should be fead in this series. Here is the author's suggested reading order, however this book is intended to be read by a new reader as well as an experienced delver of the Odyssey universe.

Optional Prequel - Holy Ground
Main Series :
Odyssey One
Heart of Matter
Homeworld
Out of the Black
King of Thieves
Warrior King
Odysseus Awakening
Odysseus Ascendant
Archangel One
Archangel Rising
Imperial Gambit
King's Fall
The Seeds that were Sown

# Harvest (SOL Stands)

# CHAPTER ONE

*Gaian Destroyer Bug Hunt (Outer System, Imperial World Kazir)*

Marcus Reid glanced at the feed as the *Bug* plummeted in system, data from the local Imperial Subnet trickling through his screens.

"Looks like the Contractor was right," He said aloud. "Another Imperial world in revolt."

"Seems so, Skipper," Mac said from beside him.

The Chief wasn't on shift, but everyone wanted to see what was going on as they entered the system. The Starsbane Empire, a laughably pretentious name for a political entity if ever Reid had heard one, had been fractured by the end of the war with Earth. Earth may have been turned into a snowball, but the Empire had burned that day... and he wasn't sure that the fires had *ever* been properly put out in the three decades since.

The current bit of fighting had become common within the boundaries of the former Empire, growing more and more widespread as the Imperial Navy continued to move in to stamp out each incident... and largely only succeeded in scattering the embers about willy-nilly as a result.

*If someone in authority doesn't get their head out of their ass before long, the Empire will self-destruct from their attempts to save it.*

Not that Reid, or any of his people would shed any tears if and when that happened.

The crew of the *Bug Hunt* were all Terrans, running an ongoing deep cover mission that had started *thirty plus* years earlier. The original task had been to scout out Imperial weaknesses, feed that intel back to Earth, and generally make the Empire wonder why Murphy had taken a dislike to them.

They'd done that job, but it hadn't been quite enough.

So when Sol burned, well they kept doing it. Survivors from Earth's military had coalesced around the old Archangel team and the Gaian Mercenaries had become what they were.

A thorn in the side of the Empire that the Imperials didn't even know existed.

It was a dirty job, but they were just the ones lucky enough to draw the short straw.

Of course, sometimes, that meant making it look like they were on the Empire's side.

*Like now.*

"Alright, Mik, take us in. We've got some people who need their bacon pulled out of the fire," He said to the Helmsman.

"Aye Skipper, taking us in," Ensign Eric Michaels said calmly as he reached over and worked the controls to bring the warp fields up.

The Tin Can started moving, squeezed through spacetime by the combined pressures of the warp fields pushing from behind and pulling from ahead.

Technically the kid was supposed to be running Ops, but Reid had opted to ask a senior non-com to handle the slot for the duration of this run. It wasn't that he didn't trust the kid, but there was a time and place to be learning on the job skills... and the middle of a hot extraction wasn't one of them in his book.

The *Bug Hunt* was on the move, though, so he expected that learning opportunities would be aplenty no matter what he preferred.

*****

## Imperial World Kazir

The fighting had gotten closer through the night, the former governor of the planet noted with trepidation. The Imperial Navy had been keeping the rebels under control, but for reasons beyond his understanding they'd withdrawn their forces in recent weeks, leaving him at the mercy... a trait laughably missing in the rebels he knew too well... of the malcontents who were intent of tearing apart everything the Empire had built over the last *centuries* as thought none of it were worth *anything*.

"Where are they?" He growled, pacing the hard stone floors of the governor's tower.

Abandoned by the Empire, what else was he to do? He'd contracted with some mercenaries to fetch him off this backworld planet and take him back to civilization.

*If they would just get here!*

The concussion of a detonation in the distance made him jump, but it had been far out past the city limits. He could see the smoke rising into the skies, though, and it was closer than the fighting had been yet.

The governor stared, a thrill of fear rising up in him as he realized that the rebels were now within the defensive perimeter his militia had established through the night.

*They'll be in the city soon! Where are those blasted mercenaries!?*

The Gaians had earned a remarkable reputation over the decades since they'd appeared, easily carving out a place for themselves as soldiers for hire who were more than pirates and brigands. They didn't take jobs lightly, and refused to operate against the Empire… which was unsurprising as only the greatest of fools would willingly fight the force of the Imperial Navy… but rarely failed to accomplish a job once they did accept it.

Rarely didn't mean never, however, and he was feeling more than a little pressured in that moment as the worry that this might be one of their rare failures weighed heavily on his mind.

"Where are they?" He fretted, sweat beading on his face as he turned and paced back across the room.

He almost jumped clean out of his skin when his communications link snapped open.

"Governor Jarvin, Gaian Destroyer *Bug Hunt*."

"It's about time!" He snapped, grabbing up the device. "Where are you?"

"Approaching orbit. There is fighting over your balance points, Sir. Do you know which forces are friendly?"

He snorted, "If there were friendly forces in orbit, Captain, I would not have had to call you. The rebels are as fractured as they are foolish. At least three groups are trying to claim that they're the rightful representatives of the people here, and not one of them has any real claim to the title."

"Understood. Governor, we do not engage with Imperial military. All of the fighting forces are broadcasting Starsbane codes, and that puts us in a bit of a quandary."

The governor flushed, "None of them are Imperial military, Captain! You have my word."

"We will require your bonded statement as the governor of Kazir. Transmit with your authority, sir, or we will not attempt to breach the fighting lines."

The governor fumed, but he knew the Gaian's contract as well as anyone could. They were *adamant* about not conflicting with the Empire, and had more than once refused or invoked contract clauses to abandon tasks assigned to them when a client tried to put them into such a position.

"Fine. Transmitting now." He said, sending the codes of the Planetary Governor to the mercenary ship.

"Codes received, Governor... authenticating. Cleared. Very well, advise that you get to the top of your tower and wait for us, we're beginning our approach."

The signal went dead then and he slumped.

*I'm saved.*

*****

## Gaian Destroyer *Bug Hunt*

"Take us in, Ensign," Reid ordered.

"Yes Sir." Eric 'Mik' Michaels said calmly as the destroyer responded to his touch and they broke their orbit and began the plunge in toward the planet.

"Quinn, eyes on those ships," Reid ordered. "If they look like they're taking an interest in us instead of just beating the ever loving crap out of each other... light them up."

"Aye skipper," Beverly Quinn said with a feral grin. "With pleasure."

Reid noted that with some mild concern, but he would be lying if he said he didn't feel it just a little bit himself.

The Gaian rule of never taking a mission that engaged with the Empire had bought them trust within the Empire, and left the Gaians with a surprising level of access through Imperial space. It was something that they couldn't lose, as the results would be catastrophic to their efforts...

But, after what happened to Earth and Sol... well, any chance they got to fire on an Imperial ship without risking that access and trust? It was not a chance any man or woman in the fleet, nest, or prometheus itself would let slip from their grasp.

"Colonel," He said, after opening a commlink to the Marines down in the small launch bay. "Stand by for drop."

"Roger, Captain. We're ready to go."

"No doubt. We're entering the planet's gravity well... *now*. Drop in five."

"Oorah, Sir."

Reid closed the connection and sat back, forcing himself to relax. He'd done his part, for the moment at least. All he could do now was let his people have their fun too.

*****

The *Bug Hunt* was a prize ship, captured from a pirate crew that no longer had need of it when the Gaian Marines had finished with them. Built by one of the Free Stars polities, it was not a particularly impressive piece of kit... not when the prize crew took it over originally, at least, but in the intervening months a great deal of work had been done to bring it up to certain minimum standards by the Terran engineers who'd been let loose on her.

So, now, she was in as good a shape as she'd been when new... most likely better shape actually, but she was still just a tin can from a third rate polity that barely knew how to build a ship that could keep from leaking atmo into space.

Not an Archangel, and certainly not a Heroic, but her crew were as good as any that served... so far as Reid was concerned, and that made the little Destroyer a very dangerous ship indeed.

She came screaming out of the black, no announcement of her arrival was offered, and by the time anyone of the rebels fighting over the Lagrange stations even had a chance to notice her she was through their battlelines and plunging for the outer edge of Kazir's atmosphere.

There was a brief lull in the fighting as the *Bug Hunt* ripped past, the crews of the feuding rebels clearly wondering if they should be paying more attention to her, but the moment past and a shot scored off a rebel held station started the fighting up again as the leading edge of the destroyer bit into the atmosphere and pushed out a blazing trail of flame ahead of them as the friction lit the air itself afire.

*****

"Marines away, Sir," Mac said from Ops, the slight lurch in the decks the only tangible sign of the Marines' drop ship launching.

"Very good. Mik, how long for a tight orbit?"

"Fifteen minutes at the current rate, but we'll be running… Mach Twenty plus when we come back around if I keep this speed, Sir," Michaels said without looking up.

"Understood," Reid said, shrugging, "Be a little rough on the Marines if we tried to pick them up running that fast, so get a little deeper and a lot slower."

"Yes sir. I'll bring it down to Mach five by the time we loop back around, but we'll be a couple hours getting back to them."

"They're Marines, they'll be ok."

"Aye sir. Dropping altitude, deploying aerobraking. Hold on, this is going to get a little… *bumpy.*"

****

Colonel Rafael Cortez eyeballed the rest of his Marines as his guts tried their best to crawl out his mouth, freefalling from near orbit was an acquired taste that he'd never managed to acquire. His team, however, were clearly enjoying the hell out of things as they plummeted through the thickening atmosphere.

"LZ is in ten, Colonel," Captain Jimmy Sweet called over his shoulder. "Get ready."

"Born ready, Captain," Rafael drawled. "Call the drop."

"You got it."

Rafael looked over the team, sounding a tone over their systems so that they'd pay attention. Once they were all looking his way, he nodded.

"Get ready."

"Born ready, Colonel!" They all yelled back, echoing his own words. "Oorah!"

The LZ shouldn't be too hot, at least from their brief, but he'd learned a while ago that clients *lied*, and politicians lied like normal humans breathed, so he was expecting a shitstorm and they were armed for kodiak and ready to make some poor bastard rebels *very* unhappy indeed.

"Kinda fucked ain't it?"

"What was that corporal?" Rafael looked sharply over to the man who'd spoken.

"Sorry sir," The Corporal winced, not meaning to have spoken quite loud enough to be heard apparently. "I was just saying that it's kinda fucked, saving an Imperial governor from the rebels and all. I mean, they are fighting the Empire too, right? The enemy of my enemy..."

"The enemy of my enemy is an asset, Corporal, not an ally." Rafael cut him off. "They're all Imperials. The Rebels aren't pissed that the Empire fucked Earth over, they're pissed that they got burned in the action."

"Yes sir. I understand."

Rafael doubted he did, but the corporal would learn in time. The rebels weren't friendly, even if they were potentially valuable as assets to the cause. Turning *any* members of the Empire into allies would be a job of *generations*. Rafael wasn't against that happening, in time, but that time hadn't come just yet.

"Final checks," He ordered. "Make sure it's hot, strapped, and ready to burn."

The men got busy with that as the numbers dropped while they were buffeted about by the turbulence in the increasingly thick atmosphere.

They were almost finished with that when the drop ship fired thrusters and they were all pressed hard into the belly of the craft as Sweet started deceleration.

"Two minutes," Sweet called out.

"Get ready!"

"Born ready! Oorah!"

*****

The governor looked over his shoulder fearfully as he exited onto the rooftop of the tower that served as the planet's capitol building as well as the governor's mansion and many other purposes. The wind buffeted at him, pushing him around as he turned about, eyes seeking salvation.

The fighting had already progressed into the city, and security had reported that rioters were filling out the streets at the base of the tower.

If they hadn't already pushed through the lower levels, then they would in short order, of that he had no doubts.

*None of this would be happening if the fleet hadn't abandoned me! Those military fools care only for their own affairs, while we do all the real work in the Empire.*

A distant roar made him jump initially, thinking it an attack on the city, but as it grew and came to be accompanied by an odd whine he was able to locate the source and spotted the crude looking craft approaching the tower. It was clearly not an Imperial vehicle, which he supposed made sense if it belonged to the mercenaries. They were supposed to come from the so called Free Stars, and their equipment would certainly be lesser for it he expected.

The governor watched as the craft grew closer, slowing to a hover over the tower and buffeting him with more winds from the downdraft of the powerful engines keeping it aloft as it settled toward the landing circle.

Doors opened as it drifted over the tower, still well above, and he started with shock as men *jumped out.*

They glided down, unnaturally, with puffs of gas steering them into a landing a short distance away where they hit with enough force that *his* bones ached just watching them.

Most of them spread out quickly, weapons up as they moved across the rooftop, but one walked straight toward him.

"Governor."

He nodded shakily.

"You are the Gaians, I presume?"

"That's us," The single armored man said, alone among the group to *not* have a weapon in hand. "Are we waiting for anyone?"

"No. I am the only passenger."

"Understood, we'll get you loaded up shortly then, and be on our way."

"The sooner the better," The governor said, wrapping himself up tightly in his coat. "Why are we not already moving?"

"Lander don't touchdown until the roof is secure," The man said firmly. "We'll be moving soon. No point in rushing anyway, our lift offworld won't be back around for a while anyway."

"We can't stay here! The rioters and rebels are almost certainly on their way up already!"

"Relax, Governor," The man said easily. "We're here now. You're in good hands."

He snorted, but didn't say anything more as he resigned himself to waiting a while longer in the buffeting cold wind at the top of the governor's tower.

*****

Rafael relayed the warning from the governor to the squad, but wasn't concerned. They were sitting at the top of one hell of a bottleneck. Given just a few minutes his team would easily turn the access routes to kill boxes. Rebels and rioters wouldn't have the stomach to soak up the level of damage they'd have to in order to wade through that nightmare.

"We've got the rooftop secured, Colonel."

"Alright, bring in the lander."

"Oorah, Sir."

The captured Free Stars drop ship was a rough piece of kit, but it was rugged if nothing else, particularly once it had been retrofitted with Terran tech to smooth things out a bit. Sweet had it on final approach in short order, and Rafael stood next to the Governor as they both watched the ship settle in on the pad.

Sweet kept the thrusters firing a bit, just in case the Imperials had opted to cheap out on their landing platform, but Rafael doubted that would be an issue.

He gestured ahead as the gang plank dropped with a bang, echoing over the open air of the rooftop.

"After you, Sir."

The Governor rushed forward, Rafael following behind at a calmer pace.

Inside, the Imperial clearly wasn't happy with what he was seeing.

"Where do I sit?" He grumbled.

"Take a jumpseat, Sir." Rafael said politely, gesturing to the folding seat that pulled out from the side fuselage. "All the amenities, as you can tell, Sir. Even straps to keep you from bouncing around when we take off."

The governor turned red, but said nothing as he dropped into the seat and began fumbling with the straps. Rafe walked past him and leaned into the cockpit, "What's it look like out there?"

"Hot, sir, and getting hotter. We were pinged by AA on approach, but they didn't get off a shot," Sweet answered. "Wouldn't care to bet they won't when we lift off."

"Understood. We'll hold position as long as we can, take off when we can get overwatch and cover from the *Bug*."

"Works for me, Sir."

"Be ready."

"Born ready."

*****

Corporal Deke Savir let a sensor pod drop into his hand from his belt dispenser, tossing the disposable item down the access corridor before he shifted to one side of the door and leaned back against the wall.

"Corridor monitored," He reported.

"Good, stay on it Corporal," Sergeant Brad Carman said from the other side of the rooftop. "We've got a lot of comm traffic, and none of it reads as good from where I'm standing."

"Rebels in the tower, Sarge?" Deke asked.

"They have control of the bottom twenty floors, moving up." Carman said, listening to the comm traffic carefully. "If I'm understanding it right, building security is just stepping aside for them."

"Well shit, Sarge, you blame em?" Deke snorted. "Head honcho for the planet is running for his skin, leaving them to the mercy of the mob. Not really a loyalty builder there."

"Yeah, and no I don't blame em, but it's gonna trouble for us. The *Bug* won't be back around for another hour and change. Local airspace has got to be hot, and this LZ ain't gonna be secure for long, hold while I walk to the Colonel." Brad said firmly, flipping his channel over to command. "Colonel, we've got Rebels on the way up."

"How long do we have?"

"Not long enough. Security is stepping aside and letting them pass."

The Colonel snorted, "Can't say I'm shocked. Let me know when they get within five floors."

"Oorah. Best guess is that will be another ten, maybe fifteen mikes."

"Roger that."

Report made, Brad flipped back to the squad channel and settled in for the wait.

*****

Sitting there, doing nothing, just caused the governor to get more nervous with the passing minutes. It didn't take long before he was clearly about to burst, any self control he had long spent it seemed from what Rafe could tell.

"Relax," He said aloud. "You're going to pop a vein and die on us before anyone even fires a shot."

"What are we waiting for?" The politician demanded hotly.

"This is a combat zone, Governor, and we came in to pick you up with *one* ship," Rafe told the man calmly. "The *Bug Hunt* is on the other side of the planet right now, aerobraking for a hot pickup as they come back around. That takes time."

"They should have come straight here!"

"Then we'd have been shot down. The rebels have control of your defenses, some of them at least. The orbiting ships aren't big Imperial cruisers, but they're not to be underestimated either. If they stop fighting each other, we'd never get off planet. Best not give them any juicy targets to tempt them, Governor."

The Governor growled and shifted uncomfortably, but didn't have a riposte for that.

"This is all the Fleet's fault," He mumbled irrationally.

Rafe glanced over at him, mildly curious, "How do you figure?"

"The rebels have been fomenting violence and discord for years, but the fleet kept them in line. Nothing has been the same since the *burning*, the fleet *knew* that the rebels were still a threat, but they *left*!" The governor spat out angrily. "Just... left! Not even a warning, a chance to build up a militia... even if that weren't illegal in the first place. Might as well have poured liquid oxygen over everything on their way out!"

Rafe winced at that last descriptor, since he'd *seen* what happened when you messed with LOX, and it wasn't pretty. It was interesting, though, that the Fleet had pulled out that abruptly.

"When did they withdraw?" He asked.

The governor looked over, frustrated but calming, or so it seemed.

"Fourteen cycles ago," He said, sounding defeated. "Fourteen cycles. That's all it took to destroy everything."

*Fourteen cycles... bit over two thirds of a month,* Rafe translated the time over in his head. *Just after the* **From the Flames** *would have reported back concerning the Drasin. The Empire is making moves, and they're moving fast with very little regard for their people. Either they're being incredibly reckless and, frankly, stupid... or they have a damned good reason to be moving forces around. The Nest and Prometheus need to know about this.*

"Well," He said aloud, "Whatever is up their butts, it's not your problem. We'll get you out of here and delivered safely to your destination, per the contract, you can bank on it."

"I've done more than that."

*So you have.*

\*\*\*\*\*

Deke shifted, head cocking to one side.

"Sarge," He called out.

"Yeah, what is it?" Brad responded.

"Where are the rebels reported to be?"

"Comm traffic has them about halfway up the tower."

"I think we have a problem. Got movement in the access corridor, looks like a squad of armed men."

"Shit. Building security?"

"No uniforms, weapons are pretty ragged looking too. Don't think they're regulars."

Brad swore, "Everyone get frosty. Rebels must have an

advance team, watch for alternate approaches!"

"Oorah!"

The squad spread out, while Brad jogged over to reinforce the corridor where Deke was waiting. He brought up the feed from the sensor button and looked over the group that was approaching.

*Well, they don't look like regulars that's for sure.*

"Ok, pop smoke and flash bangs," He ordered. "Shake them up, make em think twice."

"Oorah, Colonel." Deke said as he slung his rifle and pulled a couple canisters from his belt harness.

He thumbed the firing pins and got hot codes from both.

"Fire in the hole," He sent over the squad link before chucking both through the door and ducking back.

They heard a surprised shout just ahead of the snap-bang of the concussion blast going off, then slowly the hiss of the smoke made itself heard as people began shouting, groaning, and crying out in pain or panic.

"Come closer and we will open fire!" Brad called over the yelling, speaking stilted Imperial.

A spewing of insults was the response, but no one seemed inclined to test him at the moment.

"Think they'll stay back?" Deke asked nervously.

"Not a chance in hell. Hold one," Brad said, again flipping to the command channel. "Colonel, we're on a clock. Rebels in the corridor, trying to access the roof. Main body is still down a few floors, but they'll pick it up now I'll wager."

"Roger that, Sergeant. Ok, hold them as long as you can, then fall back to the drop ship."

"Oorah, sir." Brad flipped back to the squad channel, "Alright. We hold them until they press hard enough to make it not fun anymore, then we fall back to the ship. Clear?"

"Crystal, Sarge."

*****

Rafe checked the data feeds, noting that the rebels were getting organized to push at the door.

*They seem pissed for some reason,* He noted mildly. *I wonder what our dear governor here did to inflame them quite to this level?*

In the end it didn't matter, of course. He and his had a job to do, and whatever the Governor did was between him and whatever deity, if any, he believed in.

The first shots rang out, and he brought the tactical network up to the front of his attention but stayed off the team channel. They didn't need him riding them in the middle of action, they knew their job.

Sergeant Carman and Corporal Savir were keeping the access door closed to the rebels advance, while the rest of the squad were keeping an eye on the rest of the perimeter. Rafe didn't know if the rebels were organized enough to manage a multi-pronged plan of attack, but assuming they weren't wasn't likely to end well.

He checked the time.

*Just over an hour to pick up. Shit.*

*****

**Gaian Destroyer *Bug Hunt***

True to Michaels word, the old tin can was rattling his teeth out as Reid held on to the arms of his seat while they plummeted through the atmosphere of the Imperial world.

"Forty minutes to LZ," Mik said from the controls of the old hunk of junk. "We'll come over the horizon, from their perspective, in thirty five."

"Roger that," Reid confirmed. "Quinn? Status."

"We've been painted a few times, but no active locks yet," The gunner responded instantly. "I'd say that so far, it's just been precautions. No malicious actors."

"That won't hold," Reid said with certainty.

"No sir, it will not," She chuckled.

"Mac?"

The senior Non-Com standing at Ops looked up, "All systems check out. We're as good as we're going to get."

"Well then, I have no fears," Reid said with an easy smile, "Cause that means we're fit to face the devil and come out on top."

"Careful with that, Sir. people who think like that find themselves playing fiddle with the man himself," Mac barked a sharp laugh.

"Didn't the Devil lose that one?" Mik couldn't help but ask, looking over his shoulder with some confusion.

"Devil gave the kid a fiddle made of gold, and won the kid's soul in the process." Mac said firmly. "Don't play with the devil kid, he's a tricky bastard."

"I really don't think that's how that song went..."

"Don't argue with Mac about this," Reid said, amused. "We've all been there, none of us convinced him otherwise."

"The kid was greedy and prideful, that's two of the seven deadly sins," Mac said simply. "Devil let him win, cause he knew the kid had already lost."

"Yes yes, we've heard it all before," Reid sighed. "And if

I ever figure out who introduced you to country music, I'm going to kick their ass."

"Careful, skipper, that's wrathful right there."

Reid just groaned.

*****

## Imperial Tower, Rooftop

The sound of gunfire split the air, the Marines weapons hammering through the door as the imperial rebels tried to push forward once more.

The beam weapons the rebels used to return fire made no sound by comparison, but scorched the atmosphere itself and left a stink of ozone in their passing that was noted by the analyzers in the Marines' suits but did little else.

"Stubborn bastards," Brad grumbled as the rebels again fell back.

It had been the fifth such push since they'd secured the area, with no change in outcome thus far. The rebels didn't have the room to bring up enough firepower to break through the Marines' choke point, but that wasn't stopping them from trying.

"Looks like they're getting together for another one, Sarge," Deke said wearily.

"Already? We just sent them packing from the last one! Goddamn morons. Give it up already," Brad snapped in the general direction of the door.

"Sarge!"

"What?" Brad half turned, seeing another of the squad waving at him.

"Trouble!" PFC Dietrich called, "We've got what looks like imperial ground assault birds incoming!"

"Shit." Brad swore, stepping back. "Corporal, cover the door."

"Oorah."

"Colonel," Brad said over the command channel.

"I see them. Break contact, fall back." The Colonel ordered.

"Oorah, Colonel." Brad said, flipping back to the squad channel. "Colonel says it's time to pack it in. Deke, hold position while the others pull back."

"Oorah, Sarge."

While the rest of the team fell back to the drop ship, Brad pulled a couple frags from his gear and primed them both with a hard push of his thumbs. Deke fired a few rounds, keeping the rebels' heads down while the rest of the team made it to the ship.

"Fire in the hole," Brad said, causing Deke to twist to the side, then he underhanded both weapons into the corridor.

Unlike grenades from previous wars, the ones the Marines used now had multi-phase detonation systems. Timers were counting down, certainly, but each of the deadly canisters also had sensor packages that let him examine their surroundings.

When Brad saw that a group of rebels were rushing the corridor as the weapons bounced past them, well he figured why wait?

The detonation signal went out, and the grenades went... *up.*

"Fall back," He ordered Deke, patting the corporal on the shoulder.

"Oorah, Sarge!"

Deke broke contact, running for the dropship as the smoke continued to pour out the door. Brad followed, jogging backwards as he kept his weapon aimed clean, firing occasional reminders to anyone left inside that keeping their heads down was a survival trait.

In moments he was scrambling up the ramp.

"I'm in!"

"Close the door!" The Colonel yelled, "Sweet, get us in the air!"

*****

Captain Jim Sweet hit the thrusters *hard*, not giving a damn about how much damage he was doing to the landing pad, or the roof underneath it. The Free Stars heap responded to his demands, despite looking like it should have been scrapped before Earth even developed FTL.

Squealers were yelling in his ears as the enemy air assets focused on his baby, but he ignored them as he turned the nose over and dipped the heap sideways into a freefall along the side of the building.

"AA beams are trying to lock us up," his copilot called.

"I hear 'em, hang on!" Sweet called over his shoulder. "We're gonna get *low* and *fast in a hurry!*"

The Marines were yelling in the back, but he ignored them even as the Colonel's voice cut clear through the noise.

"Someone grab the Sergeant before he pinballs around and kills the governor!" The colonel sounded exasperated, "For god's sake, get him strapped in!"

"Got him colonel!"

A long, sad and terror filled wail rose up through the rest, which Sweet assumed belonged to the Governor and so he ignored it.

*Some people just don't appreciate freefall.*

The side of the Imperial tower was whipping along outside the ship's screens, a blur even to Sweet's eyes as he brought the nose down and pointed them at the ground before slamming the throttle full open. Freefall went away as he was shoved back into his seat and the city below them started coming up *fast.*

"Are they following?" He called, not looking away from the ground.

"They who?" his copilot asked, wide eyed, "The rebel flyers? Hell no, they're not fucking crazy!"

"Good."

Sweet hit the thrusters, popping the nose up hard, then bounced the ship off its own warp field, slamming them all down into their seats instead of toward the back of the ship. The dropship bottomed out with buildings on all sides of them as he guided them down a long narrow canyon of steel and glass... or whatever the Imperial equivalent was.

Sweet looked up, trying to spot the enemy, but he could barely see the sky through the steel jungle. Somewhere up there, the enemy was tracking, he knew, following them as best they could... waiting for him to pop back up.

*Good luck, bastards. You're going to need it...*

\*\*\*\*\*

### Gaian Destroyer *Bug Hunt*

"Coming over the horizon relative to the LZ, Captain," Mik Michaels said firmly, not looking up from the console.

"Thank you, Helm. Ops?"

"Looking for them, Sir. No active comms detected, no IFF... Lot of local military chatter, however skipper. I think our boys threw a party."

Reid snorted, "I'd be disappointed in them if they didn't. Ok, Mik, take us in... full burn. We'll have to risk a high velocity pickup. Chief, pulse the whole hemisphere, let them know we're coming."

"Aye aye, Skipper!"

The *Bug* jolted around them as Mik hit the thrust again, sending the destroyer surging through the atmosphere, shockwaves exploding out from her bow as the ship just bodily shoved the air out of its way with sheer brute force.

*****

"Target lock!"

"Hang on," Jom Sweet said through clenched teeth, pulling the drop ship into a tight bank and turning the bulky ship around a building that looked like it reached halfway to orbit.

"Lock broke! They're scanning again!"

"Find them," Jom said.

"You got it, boss."

The local rebels seemed to have gotten into the Imperial stockpiles, Jim thought as he noted that threat profiles flashing across his boards. Imperial frontline equipment, but their pilots were far from either Imperial skill or determination. They were holding back, nerves or just straight up fear showing in their actions.

*A good pilot would have kept that lock, gone high and wide to keep us in their scopes. These yokels are trying to actually follow us. Rookies.*

Not that Imperials were crack pilots when it came to air to air combat as best he knew. It wasn't how they preferred to do their fighting, not when slugging it out with capital vessels was an option at least. That didn't mean that their local patrol pilots were slackers, however. Over the past few decades the Gaian forces had gotten the chance to see them in action, if only from a distance, after all.

Whoever was flying the combat air patrol over the city right then, however, clearly didn't have much of a clue on how to fight with air breathers, let alone vacuum suckers.

Sweet reached over to flip a few switches, adjusting power to the engines as he continued to loop the building he was using for cover. The dropship wasn't a dogfighter by any means, but then nothing human built had truly been built for that in over a century and a half. Not even the original Archangels, despite the fact that they spent more than their share in close combat.

Close in fighting was generally considered to be a useless tactic to design for when the goal of friend and foe alike was to light up the enemy from *light seconds* away if at all possible.

It still happened, of course, because reality didn't conform to ideal designs. That was why even the original archangels, like the F-22 airframes they'd been built on, still maintained a gun when missiles were the weapon of choice. Reality didn't care for the plans of man, that was something that all the 'Gaians' knew too well.

Losing Earth, being banished from Sol, taught bitter lessons after all.

"Got more contacts on the scopes, Boss. Bandits inbound."

"Just what we need. ETA to the *Bug*?"

"Should be soon, but the city is making radio reception iffy, and this beast doesn't exactly pack an FTL comm."

"Got it, we'll have to break from the city and get some altitude then," Sweet said through clenched teeth, flipping the dropship around the other way and slamming them all hard into their seats once more. "That's going to be tough."

"Yes sir."

Rookies or not, it didn't take much skill to lock up a target in the open air. The dropship had some countermeasures, to be sure, but he wasn't confident in them holding off an Imperial AA setup.

"Stand ready with countermeasures," Sweet ordered. "We'll have to run the gauntlet to get back to the *Bug*."

"Countermeasures, Yes sir."

Sweet glanced at the clock briefly, *The Bug can't be far out...*

"Holy shit!"

Jim Sweet was tempted to ask what his copilot was swearing about, but he honestly was just short of doing the same as the *Bug Hunt's* scanner ping reverberated through their systems, and likely the entire *hemisphere*.

"I'd say the skipper is inbound, Sir."

"I'd say you're right." Sweet responded as he made some flight adjustments. "Stand ready, we're about to break clear of the cover of the city."

"I'm ready."

"Alright, everyone hang on," Sweet called over his shoulder. "We're about to run hot and heavy, Marines!"

"Oorah!" The whole group behind him responded as he leveled out the dropship, put power to the drives, and pointed her at the sky.

\*\*\*\*\*

## Gaian Destroyer *Bug Hunt*

"Dropship just separated from the city background,

skipper," The Chief announced. "Telemetry online, tracking hot and clear."

"Alright, let's pick them up." Reid said casually. "Flight bay crews stand by."

"Crews are standing by, but we've got a problem."

"Of course we do," Reid said dryly. "Which one is it this time?"

"Looks like the locals broke out the torches and pitchforks, Skipper."

Reid masked a smile, "Why does this happen every time we let the Marines out of the ship?"

"Have you *met* the Marines, sir?"

"Point. Alright, Helm, Ops... get my men back."

"Yes Sir."

"Aye Skipper."

The Chief looked down from the Ops station, to where Mik was handling the Helm. Normally he'd be running that station, but the kid was damned good.

*Still...*

"You good, Ensign?" He asked.

Eric Michaels glanced back and just nodded firmly. "I've got this, Chief."

"Alright, call the play, I've got your back."

"Decreasing velocity," Michaels said firmly. "Target velocity, Mach four at intercept. Positive link to the dropship?"

"Link established."

"Send intercept."

"Intercept sent. Dropship confirms receipt..." The Chief

paused as he waited a brief moment, "Sweet acknowledges. Dropship moving to intercept. Be advised, we have AA beams painting us and the shuttle."

The Ensign didn't say anything for a moment as Reid listened calmly without saying anything.

"Ensign…" The Chief said warningly.

"Ignore the AA on us, they've got nothing that can penetrate our warp fields in Atmo without vaping half the city. They won't risk it," Michaels said firmly.

"Belay that," Reid said firmly. "Reports say that the Imperials are *not* in charge down there. Don't assume the rebels are professional, they may not *know* what their weapons can do, some of them may not *care*. They're amateurs, pissed amateurs at that. Run our point defense up, I know it'll cost us cycles that could be used to protect the dropship, but the *Bug* takes priority, Ensign."

"Yes Sir, sorry sir," Eric Michaels winced, shoulders tightening briefly.

"No apologies needed, Ensign, continue."

"Yes sir."

"Air intercept vessels tracking the dropship, Ensign. Watch your screens."

"I have them," Eric said, seemingly forgetting the Captain's reprimand for the moment. He paused, hesitating for a moment as he made adjustments to the ship's course and thrust. "Point defense, arc sector three S, configure for anti-air intercept."

"There's no contacts in arc sector three S, Ensign," The Chief said warningly.

"There will be," Eric said calmly as he reached across his board and made another adjustment. "Point defense up, Arc

Sector Three S."

The Chief grumbled, but confirmed, "PD up, Arc sector three S, confirmed."

*****

Every warning light and sound in the dropship was *screaming* at Sweet as he rolled out of a near lock, countermeasures shaking the little ship as they fired off. The brief respite they bought barely quieted a tenth of the warnings, most of which sounded off again before his ears could even begin to stop ringing.

"*Bug Hunt* inbound!"

"I've got them, adjusting course to intercept."

"We've got interceptors!"

"I don't know what our guest did to piss off the locals, but they're *really* not happy about him leaving," Sweet chuckled. "Popular guy."

"They're moving to intercept."

"They're interceptors, that's what they do. Ignore em, I'll handle them."

"Yes sir. Countermeasures running low. We've got another two minutes, tops, before we're dry."

"More than enough."

Sweet checked his board quickly and noticed that there was an adjustment to the intercept vector with the *Bug*. He made the changes, then frowned briefly before a moment of clarity came to him and he smiled wide.

"Nice move, Skipper," Sweet whispered.

"What's that, Sir?"

"Nothing, just watch those countermeasures and keep an eye on the *Bug*, this should be a show."

His co-pilot and RIO looked confused, but nodded as they continued to hurtle skyward with half the local fast attack squadron sweeping in from their flank. Sweet ignored them as he poured on the speed, looking to get his little dropship up to a speed that would be fast enough so the *Bug* wouldn't rip them apart on intercept.

Landing on a moving ship in the atmosphere was a hell of a lot trickier than doing the same in space.

"The *Bug* is maneuvering!"

Sweet didn't say anything as the big ship twisted in the air, hammering the air even harder as it exposed its starboard flank to the onrushing atmosphere. The shockwaves from its passage had to be severely ruining a lot of people's day in the city below, but the move had inter-positioned the ship's space warp to cover the drop ship's approach as it passed while simultaneously exposed the enemy interceptors to the entire starboard array of point defense weapons.

The flashes of weapons fire blanked out the screens briefly, and when they came back there was no more sign of the interceptors.

"Dropship, *Bug Hunt*," the Chief's voice came through clear as crystal. "Time to come home."

"Roger that, *Bug*, we're coming in."

"Bay two is clear, welcome home."

*****

# CHAPTER TWO

### The Nest, Rogue World in the Deep Black

Morgan Passer regretted leaving his command deeply, but someone needed to take over the administrative tasks or the remnants of survivors from Sol would have fallen apart within the first year. Thankfully most of those survivors who remained in the active regions around Sol, the Empire, and the Priminae had been military and the chain of command had been strong enough to keep them working in the same direction.

He often wondered what had happened to the many civilian and governmental colony ships that had escaped Earth in the waning days of the war, but thus far there had been no contact.

Which left those at the Nest, the Prometheus Facility, the Fleet, and the Gaian 'Mercenaries' as the only humans left in the region who represented Earth's branch of humanity.

*That would be bad enough, but with the Empire crumbling in the aftermath... things were getting nasty in these parts. Now, with these new developments?*

Passer didn't know, he just didn't know.

He was making his way through the Citadel, heading for a meeting with the Council, but the latest reports were what his mind could not let go.

"Admiral? The Council is expecting you, go right in."

"Huh? Oh yes, thank you Lieutenant." Passer said

absently as he walked past the guards and into the Council room.

The Council was an ad hoc, partially democratic and partially military group that oversaw the internal matters of the Nest. Not technically in the chain of command for any of the military assets, they were the ones who kept the community itself running as best they could. While this precluded them, as a group, from influencing strategic decisions... they were, ironically perhaps, one of the most important strategic assets that the Nest could boast.

Their actions were what made the Nest a place where the spacers and combat arms personnel could come back to, relax, and call *home*.

Passer had long since learned that wasn't something to be underestimated, or undervalued.

"Admiral, please come in, take a seat!"

"Thank you, Councillor," Passer said, doing just that. He settled into one of the chairs and noted that the full council was in place. "What brings everyone in here today?"

They exchanged concerned looks, which set him just a bit on edge.

"Well, Admiral," The Councillor who invited him in, David Sear, took a breath, "We're hoping that you can tell us, actually."

"Oh?" Passer blinked, "I'm afraid I'll need a bit more guidance than that."

"Apologies, Admiral. The Gaian forces have been deploying more and more often in recent weeks, we've had several... let's call them concerns that they're being overworked. Friends and family, and the like."

"Ah," Passer nodded, "Yes that makes some sense."

He sighed, leaning forward to brace his elbows on the table as he steepled his fingers.

"Honestly, we're not *certain* of the reasoning yet, though we have some fairly strong suspicions that have to remain classified," Passer admitted, "What I can tell you is that the Empire is almost exclusively responsible for the uptick in jobs."

"The Empire?" A councilwoman blurted, shocked, "but they almost never hire mercenaries, and hasn't our policy been to avoid their space as much as possible?"

"True on both counts," Passer nodded. "However, we have very good reasons for this."

"Classified ones, I assume?" David said tiredly.

"Indeed. What I can tell you is that the Empire is consolidating their forces, pulling all active and many retired or otherwise inactive hulls into newly reformed and reinforced Fleets." Morgan Passer told them firmly. "The result of this is that their outlying worlds are falling to rebellion, unrest, and many other similar sorts of situations. It has become... *very* fertile ground for our 'mercenaries'."

The Councillors exchanged worried looks.

"Consolidating... for what?"

"What else?" Passer asked mildly, "For war, Councillor."

\*\*\*\*\*

### *Gaia's Revenge*, **Deep Black, Inside Imperial Space**

"Report from the *Bug Hunt*, Capitain," Milla said, her voice holding a trace of relief. "They report a mission accompli."

"Good," Steph sighed, leaning back in the suspension field that was part of the Archange; gunboat's integrated control system. "From your tone, I take it that Eric is fine?"

"Yes, he is good. His Capitain offered praise for his actions during the mission, particularly his piloting skills. It is in the report."

Steph nodded, "I'll read it later. The *Casino* went black on schedule, they're on mission now."

"I see," Milla sighed. "One of them out of danger, and the other in. Is it always like this, then?"

"Normally? Not really, but since when have we lived in normal times?" Steph asked rhetorically.

"This is true," Milla admitted. "And our own mission?"

"On hold until the client gives the signal," Steph admitted. "The Empire is moving so many ships around that opportunities open and close with little warning."

"Do you think they are preparing for the Drasin?" Milla asked softly.

"Can't imagine what else it could be," Steph admitted. "When the *From the Flames* returned, with their information? The Imperial forces had to react one of two ways... play it off, pretend it didn't happen... or go to war footing."

"I suppose we should be grateful," Milla admitted, "though it chafes to admit that about the Empire."

Steph knew where she was coming from. The Terran interaction with the Empire had been... less than optimal. He suppressed an amused snort at that phrasing as it passed through his mind.

*Less than optimal. Losing Earth... losing all of the Sol System... is certainly less than optimal. The understatement of millenia.*

The issue had been manifold, of course. To his mind, Terran humans and Imperials were too alike to ever be friends as things stood. Xenophobic, battle junkies... too militaristic to even realize just how militaristic each of them were. Steph doubted that he'd even really understand the problem, not without having met the Priminae... and having met his wife, Milla.

The Priminae were... Utopian humans. *Somehow.*

They had the instincts, the willingness to fight, but it wasn't what defined them in the way it did the Imperials or Terran humans. Not quite pacifists, as they'd first appeared, but close. Too passive to deal with the sudden shock front threat that was the Drasin, not coming out of nowhere like it did, but more than willing to step up and *learn.*

The Priminae were an enigma to him, but the Empire? They were all too easy to understand.

"The Empire is cutting off systems that are a draw on their resources, letting the rebels have them," He said. "They're gambling that they'll be able to retake them once the current crisis ends. Our job is to help the Empire deal with the Drasin, but make it as *hard* as possible for them to retake the lost systems later."

"So that is why you've refused the rebel suppression requests?" She asked dryly.

"Of course. Securing routes for the Imperial leadership to flee will only help the Rebels in the long term, even if they lose some of the satisfaction of lopping off some heads," Steph answered with a half grin while Milla winced at the expression. "It'll keep us busy until it's time, at least."

Milla nodded.

"Of course," She whispered.

She didn't need to ask 'until it was time for what?', she knew. When the Empire clashed with the Drasin, there could only *be* one side for them to join.

A beeping sound caught both their attention, and Steph

flipped in the air as he leaned in to examine the message coming through.

"It's time. We're up."

"Very good. I will be ready."

Steph had no doubts in his mind of that as he brought the stealthed fighter/gunboat to full power and set them moving.

The *Revenge* was in motion.

*****

### *Casino,* Deep Black, Imperial Space

Jennier Samuels tightened her eyes as she stared into the void, her gunboat had gone dark on schedule a few hours earlier and now they were moving fast through Imperial Territory, tracing a path projected by Prometheus to keep them out of the crosshairs of any Imperial ships or beacons.

With the new Imperial dispositions in play, Command had made a calculation. Under normal circumstances, there was no chance that they'd be able to get anything out of Imperial space... or anything *in* for that matter. That left them with only the Rogue's delivering reliable intelligence from inside those borders, the last hulls built purely of Earth borne technology, the Rogue Class Destroyers were almost *invisible* to any form of detection short of a Drasin antlion trap.

That allowed the Rogues to report back in near real time as they would perch just outside a system's Heliosphere and... watch.

However, there were things that the Rogues couldn't see. No matter how good their sensors, there were physical limits. Across light hours, even *days* in some cases, some things were just too small to be scanned, and of course... somethings they desperately wanted a peak at weren't visible at all until you were right up beside them.

Even in their descent, however, Imperial security had never slipped quite so low that slipping a person onto the surface of one of their core worlds would be possible.

Now, though? They'd opened the door a crack.

Just a crack. No other ship in the fleet could slip through it, not even the damn near invisible rogues.

The *Casino*, however, was no Rogue.

"Dealers, this is Pit Boss," Jennifer 'Cardsharp' Samuels said calmly as she threaded the needle between two of the Imperial sensor pickets that had drifted just far enough apart to allow her through without triggering an alert. "Whale spotted. Stand by for our grand opening."

The Imperial system was one of the oldest space faring systems in the records, having been part of a space flight capable culture for at least the last thousand years or so, and it had the debris to prove it. Jenn could feel more than see the junk just spiraling around in the space her ship was flashing through, the feedback system making the solar wind feel like a warm sunny day on her skin even a dozen light hours out from the primary. The junk was like clouds moving around her, casting shadows and reflecting light from all angles.

Within the *Casino*, she could feel her Marines... her *Dealers*... readying themselves for the insertion.

"Target world ahead, performing overshoot... standby for crash deceleration. Brace! Brace! Brace!"

Jennifer killed their spacewarp just as the *Casino* blew past the inhabited world, just as they skimmed the upper atmosphere.

At a distance just over a hundred and forty kilometers, the *Casino* dropped out of warp and blew her fields inside out as the planetary gravity grabbed them. At that altitude, they were still close enough to feel more than ninety percent of the planet's gravity and since Jennifer had arranged their angle of approach such that they were pulling almost directly away from the planet as they emerged, everyone was slammed against the far deck at almost a full Earth gravity as she angled the ship around to put the acceleration where it belonged and the internal gravity systems adjusted.

Since their path was not an orbital one, there would only be so long before the pull of the planet won out and the Casino was tugged down into the atmosphere to burn up.

That was their clock.

"Insertion complete, no indication of enemy alert. Ears and eyes open, I want the eyes in the skies open wide," She ordered next. "The whale is here, time to fleece the bastard."

*****

Amanda Micheals shivered a little, maybe half due to the chill of the suit's climate control kicking in to counter the heat that was already building up, but the rest just due to her anxiety and eagerness for the mission.

This was the first mission that she was on that allowed her to face off with the Imperial forces. every Earth human in the sector wanted nothing more than to mix it up with the Imperials, everyone dreamed of payback.

That wasn't in the books on this Op, however unfortunate that might be, the job here was not to engage with Imperial forces but rather to extract intelligence without them even knowing that the Dealers had ever been in place.

"Lieutenant," The Colonel said, coming up beside her. "Your squad ready?"

"Yes Ma'am."

"Good, make certain that your neural scramblers are running." Colonel Keenan reminded her.

"Scramblers are up, the whole squad is covered, Ma'am."

"Good. Do *not* let those drop."

Amanda nodded firmly. The scramblers were part of the standard loadout for entering the magnetosphere of *any* world that Command even suspected might have developed an *Entity*.

The Entities were something that every Officer had a briefing on, straight from the Academy and then again before any operation such as the one she was about to start. They were believed to be gestalt consciousnesses, the sum total of every mind that had lived and died within the planet's magnetosphere.

Some, such as the Entities that currently existed on the Terran Cruisers such as the Boudicca and the Bellerophon, were almost infants in a way. Composed of merely a few hundred minds at most, but those such as Gaia on Earth and, as their best Intel was able to determine, the true power behind the Empire... Well, those were composed of *billions* of minds, or more. Within their environment, they were nearly omniscient and, while it was not often apparent, their control over the Spacetime that created them made each entity a formidable foe.

The Neural scramblers were designed to mask human minds from them, and were required kit for anyone who might even *possibly* step foot on such a world.

"My squad knows the op, Ma'am. We're ready."

Keenan leveled a stare that made her want to squirm in her powered armor, but finally nodded.

"Deploy in five. Move it."

*****

An orbital drop was one of the most exciting five minutes of terror Amanda had ever experienced during training. The freefall was bad enough, but there was a period as you entered the atmosphere where the burst of energy from interfacing with the space/air transition point meant that you lost all eternal feeds.

That meant no telemetry, no communication, and even no *vision* as the armor sealed everything that might be vulnerable to heat and electromagnetic interference. Until you were through the space/atmo interface, you were blind and vulnerable, with only your imagination whispering about everything that could *possibly* go wrong.

Then, in a shocking instant, it was over.

Cameras booted back up, radio crackled to life, and the previously distant world below that you'd only seen as a magnificent ball floating in the black of space was now *world* spinning wildly below, rushing up to greet you with all the enthusiasm of a really friendly dog who had *no idea* oh just how big they were.

"Squad Leader here," Amanda ordered as her network showed all links green. " Check in and confirm disposition for landing."

One by one her team followed procedure, but Amanda was only partially paying attention as she checked for mission updates that might have come in while they were blacked out. Everything was still in line with the briefing, however, so she checked that they were on course and did a remote diagnostic for her team to ensure that their systems were responding correctly.

By the time she was done with that, everyone had checked in by the numbers and they'd dropped another twenty thousand feet.

With the ground rushing to greet them, the entire team were just starting to slow below the speed of sound in local atmo, the shockwave of the transition running through them briefly as they hit thicker air on the way down.

"All squads," Keenan's voice came through the network clear as crystal. "Line up on your targets and proceed according to plan. Be advised, leave no sign that this was done by us. In and out, boys and girls, we have a job to do and part of that is not being spotted."

Amanda just keyed a tingle tone in response, acknowledging the order as she checked the telemetry before sending the command for her team to activate their grav chutes.

Unlike the older, first generation, models that had been in use early in the conflict with the Drasin and Empire, the new chutes were built into their armor and secured. It lost a little of the versatility of having them flying loose as observation drones, but the design change gave each Marine vastly improved mobility when operating planetside.

Not being true 'anti-gravity', the countermass technology in the chutes operated instead to reduce the effective mass of anything held within their field of effect. This meant that a hundred and eighty pound Marine, wearing four hundred pounds of power armor, weapons, and whatever other mission vital equipment they may have could be reduced in effective weight, depending on power applied, to numbers ever approaching... but *never* actually reaching... zero.

What happened to a Marine in power armor that slammed into the ground when they weighed less than a pound?

The same thing that happened to an ant that hit the ground at terminal velocity.

Not a damn thing worthy of note.

Amanda hit the ground at just short of the speed of sound, her knees barely flexing from the impact as the rest of her team struck down around her in an eerie, otherworldly, flicker of motion.

"Team Bravo, on the ground. Proceeding on mission." She said simply before waving the team forward as she let Sergeant Powell handle the disposition of the team.

"You heard the lady," Powell said firmly, "Danvers you take the lead. We have two hours to achieve the mission goals and get the fuck off this rock. Let's not waste any time."

The marines grunted their response to that and got on the move.

*****

Keenan watched the overview of the operation from her own armor, not only getting the feed from each of the Marines on the ground but also from the drones they'd seeded the AO with just ahead of the landing.

"Imperial response is sluggish, Colonel."

"Try nonexistent," Keenan responded dryly, "but that's why we picked this target. We need to know what the Empire is up to, and this is the only communications node that isn't covered by at *least* some fleet remnants. I am seeing locals moving in response to the marines' arrival, however."

"Roger that. Looks like Militia, maybe rebels?"

"They're armed, they're in our way, and they're Imps whether they're wearing a uniform or not." She said coldly. "Raise the black flag."

Those words had a taste as she spoke them.

It was like ashes and coffee grinds against her palette, a hint of exultation almost buried in the bitter disgust she felt for speaking them. There wasn't a human from Sol still living who really gave two shits about what happened to any Imp, even the civilians, not after what they'd done to Earth. She was a Marine, though, and her pride was tied to her own perceived honor.

Killing indiscriminately didn't sit with her, but she'd do what had to be done.

*Hope they all choose to fight, just the same.* Keenan thought dourly as she observed the enemy movements. *You're all dead anyway. Go out in a blaze of glory.*

"Black Flag, aye Colonel. Orders issued."

*****

Amanda didn't blink as the order flashed on her HUD. She'd expected it, they'd talked about it in the mission brief. No one was enthused about leaving no witnesses behind, but too much was riding on their mission.

They *needed* to know what the hell the Empire was up to, because it tied directly back to the information her team had pulled from the Imperial ship's hidden computer core and how the Empire had manipulated the Drasin. If those monsters were looking to slip whatever leash the Empire had shoved up their ass, it was worth a hell of a lot more than the lives of some militant Imperials, whether they were Empire regulars, Militia, or rebels.

"Bandits approaching, Ma'am." Powell advised calmly. "Orders?"

"Smoke them."

"Yes Ma'am."

The team shifted just into to form a quasi firing line, barely slowing their advance as they made certain they were out of one another's lines of fire. Then, just *before* the enemy combatants were in sight, they opened fire.

Burst fire, with guided munitions, was a devastating capability at the interpersonal level and a few dozen rounds of high-ex fragmentary rounds ripped from the EM powered rifles of the Marines, arcing around the corner ahead far too fast to be seen, leaving only the sound of wet splatters in their wake.

"Targets down."

"Proceed on mission."

*****

Jennifer Samuels looked over the board as she waited on news from the Marines. The mission was a high risk, high reward scenario, and it made her skin itch just thinking about what was at stake, what they were risking. She knew that there was no chance that Command would have given this mission a green light if the Empire were at its peak of strength.

It had been a slow crumbling effect, and had taken years... decades even... watching the Empire slump and fall after the war. Frustrating more than satisfying, but the effect had been inevitable in the end.

*All empire's fall, we just get to watch this one happen. Can't happen fast enough, though.* Jennifer thought with vicious satisfaction. After the final battle of Sol, anything the Empire had touched... well, it all needed to *burn*.

Watching the Empire slowly fray around the edges of its outlying systems had been frustrating and satisfying by turns, and profitable as it turned out. For people who'd lost their home and families to the very Empire they were watching, feeding off its crumbling leftovers just to survive... It was a bitter pill, but there was satisfaction in watching the slow death proceed too.

Earth may have died that day, but so too did the Empire.

The Empire just didn't know it yet.

Now, though, Jennifer and others were likely going to have to fight *beside* the shambling remains of their enemies against a greater threat, and *that* was what this mission was all about.

During their last mission, the *Casino's* Marines had the opportunity to do what no one else had done before. They'd boarded an Imperial starship, with the *permission of the Imperial Commander.* That had allowed them access to something that no one had ever previously even *suspected* existed. An entirely separate quantum computing core with enough data to choke any supercomputer ever built.

Of course, the downside of that was the fact that the Drasin were how they even discovered the damn thing, and those *monsters* wanted it *badly.*

It didn't take long to rip through the data that her team had intercepted during the Drasin attempt to draw data from the rig. The Empire had been holding the leash on these *things* all along, which came as no surprise to anyone of course. The confirmation that the Empire had put a generational limit on the replication of the beasts at least told everyone that the Empire might have been evil to the core of its bureaucracy, and arguably just as stupid, but at the very least they weren't completely insane.

Now, though, it was clear that the Drasin wanted to slip that leash, and they weren't likely to stop anytime soon.

So, once more, Jennifer and the other humans from Earth found themselves in the position of potentially fighting *beside* the evil bastards who'd pushed Earth's defenses to the point of collapse, who'd bombarded their homeworld... who'd forced the Admiral to activate their last defense.

The Kardashev Net.

Now, Earth was still there of course. There may even be people living on it, she supposed, though no chance of civilization to speak of, but it didn't matter. Nothing could get through the defense network, in fact, if the Drasin managed to jailbreak themselves… Earth might be the last planet left in the Galaxy come a thousand years from now, the only world left after the Drasin finished *eating* everything else.

*They could throw wave after wave of bodies at the Admiral's middle finger,* Jennifer thought with wry amusement, *and all it would do is give the network more material to build more defense platforms.*

Beyond Sol, however, she wasn't sure anything else would survive the plague that those things were, and so the orders were clear. Find the Imperial leash, and ensure that the Drasin *never* got control of it.

If that meant working alongside the Empire, that was the price. If it meant wiping the Empire from the face of the Galaxy… well, it was unfortunate about the Civilians, she supposed, but they allowed their government to unleash what it had. Every action had a cost, even… *especially… inaction.*

There was nothing quite so costly as sitting back and thinking that events had nothing to do with you.

"Skipper."

Jennifer broke from her thoughts, half turning, "What is it?"

"The Marines are at the AO."

"Good. Tell Keenan they have a green light. Move fast, we need to be clear of the region before the next patrol sweep."

"Roger that."

\*\*\*\*\*

"Green light. Move fast, break shit, come home."

Amanda nodded unconsciously in response to the confirmation, "You heard the Colonel. Go! Go! Go!"

The Sergeant echoed her orders as the team broke from

cover and sprinted for the target building. It was a fairly unassuming construct, not quite normal to earth human eyes, but the architecture was nothing truly extravagant. Merely a megalithic pyramidal construction of fairly modest dimensions by the stature of Priminae construction at least, sheathed in wind scoured stone that had been polished at some point but now held years worth of abrasive scratches that gave it a matte finish from a distance.

Internal lighting made it clear that the building was in heavy use, but the real tell tale was the security stationed at all points. It was an important facility, that was certain, as if they didn't know that already.

Amanda checked her jammers, both the neural scrambler and the ECM system that should make any security systems deliver nothing but useless garbage to any watchers. They were both green on her suit and on the rest of her team, so she broke cover as well and chased after her team.

The CM system in her armor took the weight off, literally, as she jumped for the wall that served as the first line of defense for the pyramid. Floating over it in a slightly unreal manner, she let gravity have a hold of her again as she cleared the wall, landing with barely a crunch on the other side as she looked for her team.

The Sarge was with Smith and Bateman as she arrived, standing over several fallen Imperial guards.

"Did they get a call out?" She asked simply, otherwise ignoring the bodies.

"No ma'am," Corporal Richard Bateman said firmly. "Took them clean."

"Good. Get moving, we're on the clock now."

"Yes Ma'am!"

The three headed for the doors where the rest of the

team was already working on the locks. Amanda watched calmly for a moment before she walked forward herself, the door starting to rumble open as she got within a few dozen feet.

"We're in, Lieutenant," The Sergeant said simply.

"So I see, Sarge. Well, let's finish this," Amanda said easily. "There's a few buckets of ice cream waiting for us back on the Casino, and I'm feeling peckish."

"As you say, Ma'am. Let's move, grunts."

"Ooh rah."

*****

# CHAPTER THREE

**Imperial Cruiser** *Burning Rage*

Deiven Shiran scowled as he looked over the tactical situation from the Empire Deck of his fleet's flagship.

*The Drasin have begun their pilgrimage. Now of all times, they choose this moment in time to move on us. How far the Empire's strength has fallen.*

His fleet stood ready to repel the Drasin formation, but whether that would be enough was another thing entirely.

"Enemy forward blade approaching contact point, Fleet Commander."

"I see them," Deiven said calmly. "Redirect fourth squadron to support the forward pincer. Instruct the pincer to hold until the enemy is within the red zone."

"That will put them under direct fire for several micro-cycles before they can engage, Fleet Commander."

"Their hulls can handle the fire," He said firmly. "Issue the orders."

"Already issued, Fleet Commander, I was just stating for the recording."

Dieven nodded absently, "Very good. Now, we wait."

"Yes, Fleet Commander."

With the two fleet formations moving into position to intercept the horde, time felt like it was dropping to a crawl on the Command Deck of the *Rage*, but that was in the nature of warfare in space. Dieven watched with forced calm as the Drasin entered the extreme range of their weapons and opened fire on his lead element.

Beams took time to cross the distances involved, but not so long as to have any chance at diffusing the tension that was building.

"Lead vessels are coming under attack, no damage as of yet."

"Instruct them to evade but stay within the tactical perimeter."

"Yes, Fleet Commander."

The contacts on the screens moved interminably slowly, practically standing still unless Dieven focused in so closely as to render the tactical display worthless, but he knew that the ships were darting around at speeds exceeding even the speed of light for short bursts.

*For all the good it will do them.*

He'd ordered them to evade, but that was honestly just pro-forma. Without moving beyond the tactical perimeter he'd set, they had no chance of evading the attacks from the onrushing Drasin. The creatures were just too many, even for the vastness of space, and they would *saturate* the operation area with fire before long.

*Once that happens... No, the Fourth will arrive in time. Good.*

On the screens, the Fourth squadron was moving in fast, much faster than the speed of light as they closed on the tactical area with near reckless speed.

"Drasin are closing. Entering medium range for our weapons."

"Continue to hold. I want them *all* inside the tactical

perimeter before we engage."

"Yes, Fleet Commander!"

\*\*\*\*\*

For the Drasin, thought in the manner it was understood by humans was an alien concept. They *felt*, but did not *think*. Closing on the hated enemy was not a decision that the horde made, it was a biological *imperative*. They could no more turn away from the red band of life than they could choose to cease existing, but even for the Drasin... this example of the band was more hated than the rest.

The flavor and the scent of the enslavers was unmistakable at a dozen times the range. They could *feel* its source from a hundred stellar furnaces away, and the swarm *would* eliminate that hated enemy before moving on to the rest of the infection that had been injected into the universe by the destroyers.

First, though, the enemy at hand.

The Swarm could see the enemy ships closing, moving to support those that were already within the Trap. calculations were made, trillions of processes run through in a second, before the Swarm made the decision to proceed.

conflict was anathema, conflict was inevitable, conflict was life.

all life must be eradicated.

The costs of such an endeavor were irrelevant.

\*\*\*\*

Deiven watched with satisfaction as the last of the Drasin forces finally entered into the exclusion Zone he had marked out for the battle.

"all forces, open fire!"

"yes fleet commander!", his adjutant called over the sudden noise on the Command Deck.

Reports were coming in from every ship in the fleet now, the forward elements had suffered significant damage while he had been baiting the trap but they had not lost any of the  ships as of yet despite that. Deivan knew that would not last much longer, but that was the cost of the mission that both he and his people had taken on.

The Drasin were firing furiously from every one of their units, savagely even, with no sense of anything that might resemble military discipline. it was truly a Savage horde versus his well-trained Fleet, and Dieven  knew that there could only be one possible outcome, bloody though it may be.

On the screens, though it took a few moments, the icons That represented his ships began to open fire across the Tactical Zone. The Swarm did not pause, however but instead charged right into the teeth of the Firepower of his Imperial Fleet. Dieven gritted his teeth as he watched the fighting exclusively through the clean, sterile displays in front of him.

*This is no way to wage war,* he thought with distaste, but then he supposed that this was no real war.

*Just Pest Control.*

\*\*\*\*\*

**Imperial Cruiser *From the Flames***

At the tip of the strike, Kaela Eurydice held on tightly as her newly repaired vessel was once more torn into, bit by bit, by the ancient enemy of the people. The Drasin had pursued her ship back from their nest, it was the only thing that made any sense to her, but she knew that the assault had been inevitable despite that.

If the legends of the beasts were true, the creatures out there were incapable of anything else. Driven by their hatred, they destroyed all life in their path, with no exceptions.

*No exceptions in the legends, at least,* She thought as dark thoughts continued to intrude on her mind despite the weight of the battle settling upon her.

The idea that the Empire had leashed the beasts, as the evidence seemed to indicate… circumstantial though it was, well it weighed on her more than the immediate threat. She didn't know how to reconcile that idea with what she'd been taught, though she knew that she really shouldn't bother. What the Empire did at the highest levels was done for the good of everyone, she knew that, and they had data that she simply didn't have access to.

If it had been done, it was not up to her to judge the rights and wrongs of it, merely to deal with the problems before her.'

And right then, in this moment, the problem falling upon her position was the Drasin themselves.

"Fourth Squadron entering the tactical exclusion area, Ship's Commander!"

"Don't concern yourself with the Fourth," Kaela ordered firmly. "Leave them their task and responsibilities while we deal with our own!"

"Yes, ship's commander!"

The *Flames* was engaging with every weapon it could bring to bear, as were every other combatant in the zone. Beams were so saturating an area of space large enough to swallow several planetary orbits, leaving nowhere for them to evade without violating the containment orders they were operating under.

And so, they took fire.

A lot of fire.

"Damages reported, Decks three through eight! Twelve through Fourteen! More reports coming in, Ship's Commander!"

Eurydice ignored the damage reports, trusting her crews to handle what could be handled. The rest, well in the Emperor's hands that would have to remain.

"Enemy forces are fully entering the engagement zone, Ship's Commander!"

"Finally," She snarled, leaning forward. "Standby all weapons."

"All weapons stand ready!"

She paused, eyes flicking to the screens as the last of the Drasin icons slipped within her ship's optimum range.

"Fire!"

*****

The Imperial squadrons opened fire nearly as one, unimaginable destruction compressed and aligned into beams of pure light energy. Hot enough to match an exploding star, the beams carved through the onrushing swarm, popping individual targets like soap bubbles in a hailstorm.

The Drasin did not flinch, however, and continued to pour into the attack, those behind using those ahead as shields to gain ground and close the distance even as they fired back with beams of equally destructive force.

As the range closed to less than a few hundred thousand kilometers, the ability to dodge the exchange of fire became essentially impossible. This caused the Drasin and Imperial ships to tear into one another with vicious exchanges of fire that neither side had any intent of relenting from. Drasin were cut down in *droves* even as Imperial ships were opened to hard vacuum and set adrift without power one after another until their singularity cores destabilized and entire ships just...

vanished into singles points of space time.

Spread across several light seconds of space, the destruction proceeded in the silence of the void while within the ships themselves the deafening roar of explosions and screaming of the dying filled the air that existed between the void of the black, contained within fragile shells.

*****

Aboard the *Burning Rage*, Fleet Commander Shiran watched impassively as icons blinked out of existence on his boards, each one showing the loss of hundreds of Imperial Fleet officers.

"Losses are heavy, Fleet Commander, but the Drasin have been reduced by the target range."

"Excellent. Issue the recall order," He said, "deploy the proximity explosives to cover our forces withdrawal."

"Yes, Fleet Commander. Orders issued. Fleet will begin breaking off contact on schedule."

Shiran nodded simply, turning his attention to the numbers that were still being compiled. Their losses were significant, of course, but within the projected range that was deemed acceptable by Imperial Command.

The feral beasts would, of course, pursue doggedly. They were predictable in that way, and their ultimate goal was certainly the Imperial Capital at Kraike.

That suited Shiran and Imperial Command just fine.

*It's time that the dogs return to the kennel.*

*****

## Imperial Cruiser *From the Fire*

Kaela swore as her ship shuddered heavily under her, more alarms sounding for her to ignore as the fighting went on around them.

"Drasin approaching from sector three!"

"Focus defensive fire, keep them back!"

"We've saturated our fire control systems, Commander! There's too much debris to track and clear now!"

Kaela gritted her teeth, but could do nothing about that, "Switch to manual controls. All weapons free, if you can see it… *KILL IT.*"

They were parked in the middle of a debris field of their own making, and what wasn't trying to kill them was *only* flying around at significant portions of lightspeed with enough kinetic energy to turn their armor to vapor if it got through their space warping fields.

Nonetheless, her crew held their stations and followed orders as they'd been trained, and the *Fire*'s weapons board lit up from every possible angle as the ship all but exploded with return fire that tore through everything in range.

Accuracy on manual control was largely a matter more for luck than skill, particularly in the current situation, but as poor a defense as a wall of light might be… it was better than the alternative.

"Fleet Commander! We have orders to fall back!"

"Now?" She snarled, looking at the situation, "We'll lose half the remaining fleet if we try to retreat!"

The communications officer shrugged helplessly, "The others have already acknowledged the orders and are breaking contact."

Kaela looked over the data and swore yet again, seeing that her officer was right. Breaking contact was suicide, but staying there alone somehow managed to be *worse*.

"Fine. Deploy the proximity devices as we fall back," She

ordered. "All reverse power! Keep our space warp between us and the enemy!"

"Yes Fleet Commander, All reverse power!"

The screens flickered and warped as the big ship threw full power to the powerful warping generators, twisting the shape of spacetime until there was a mass of *negative* spacetime ahead of them, and a deep trough of positive spacetime behind them.

The *Flames* 'fell' into the positive well even as the negative mass pushed against them, accelerating the ship at incredible rates that would most certainly have turned the crew to paste if they too weren't being accelerated in exactly the same way at the same time.

"Devices deploying!"

The powerful explosive proximity devices were ejected out the sides of the ship, fired just hard enough to get them clear of the spacetime distortions before being activated.

It would *not* do to have even one of those powerful explosives get caught within the ship's spacetime bubble. Dragging that much explosive power along for the ride would end only one way.

With finality.

"Devices deployed!"

"Good! Give me more power to the warp fields!"

"We're running at full power, Commander!"

"Override the limiters," She ordered without hesitation. "Mainline the generators to the reactor!"

There was the barest of hesitation before the order was confirmed and the crew went to work. All Imperial ships had limiters built into their power feeds in order to keep the ships from doing all manner of damage to their hulls. Even a slight misalignment between the positive and negative space warps would result in stress fractures along the hull, and if the systems had been damaged in the fighting, Kaela knew that they were about to put on quite the show for anyone watching.

*A cruiser being turned to strands of fine atomic noodles certainly isn't a sight most would forget, after all.* She thought with some dry amusement as the power hum from the feeds increased to levels where it was audible even within the shielded command deck.

Any fear she had of her own ship had long since been burned out of her. She'd faced the Drasin before, looked down the beams of the Oather fleet, and stared into the *eyes* of the flame bringers.

Death would be a release, but until that came, duty was her bondage.

"Power nearing fifty percent over allowed maximum!"

"Push it harder! Kill the weapons, redirect to the field generators!"

"Yes Fleet Commander!"

They were blind now, the negative spacetime bubble ahead of their bow was deflecting every frequency, even FTL particulates, it had become so powerful. Behind them, the positive warp was a seething mass of captured radiation and particulates that had crossed their beam but been unable to escape the event horizon of the artificially created singularity.

Some sensors aimed out perpendicular to those two points were still registering the sidereal universe, but only in the vaguest and most useless of ways.

They were *screaming* backwards at multiples of the speed of light by this point, entirely blind and out of communication with... everything.

And all Kaela could do for the moment was *pray* they

didn't get in anyone's way, or that no one got in theirs.

Seconds ticked by, the tension building. She would have to break, and do so *hard*, before long and Kaela knew it. The trick was doing so after they were clear of the fighting, but *before* they ran headlong into another ship or something bigger.

Space was big, yes, nigh on infinite… but the battle had been far too close to a planetary system for her comfort in that regard.

"Standby for maneuvering," She said, hands tightening around the arm of her station.

"All stations standing by, Commander!"

"Pivot, Anti-Rotation, full power."

"Full power, anti-rotation pivot, Yes Commander!"

The ship *screamed*, spinning in the direction counter to the orbit of the planet's in the Imperial home system, moving fast enough that she was pressed into one side of her station as the acceleration briefly exceeded the compensation capacity. Kaela ignored it.

As the aft of the ship came around, with its singular point of energy *boiling* against the warp holding it in place, she reached forward and took manual control of the fields for herself.

At the last moment she killed power to the warp fields, along with *every* safety feature implemented to stop exactly what she was about to do.

As the field fell, the energy contained within it was released along a short arc back in the direction they'd came, with enough power to likely dwarf the entire combined firepower of an Imperial squadron. It was too bad, to her mind, that it was unguided and along a single flat planar arc… but it was better than nothing she supposed.

With their sensors back online, she threw full *allowed* power back to the warp fields and the ship surged forward now, along the new path they were aligned with.

"Check our course," She ordered, slumping back in her seat. "Ensure we're not going to ram anyone, then figure out where Command wants us next."

"Yes, Commander."

The bridge crew were quiet as they followed their orders, the *From the Fire* now accelerating away from the slaughter that lay in their wake.

*****

Shiran nodded with satisfaction as he observed the results of the withdrawal.

They had, of course, lost a number of ships. That was inevitable, and unfortunate, but it remained within the specifications he had been given for the engagement, so he could not really complain. The explosive devices had done a neat job of delaying the Drasin line, as dozens had been wiped out in the first wave of detonations, causing the rest to reduce their speed and begin moving to circle the now lethally trapped sector of space.

The region would be deadly for some time, but that was hardly a concern any longer… or it wouldn't be shortly, he supposed.

The overall result, however, had been precisely to his orders.

*Command will be pleased.*

"Issue to all ships, fall back to point Byss," He ordered quietly. "We will regroup and prepare for the next engagement there."

"Yes, Fleet Commander!"

*\*\*\*\*\**

*Gaia's Revenge*

"Well that was fucking horrible," Steph said grimly as he watched the end of the Imperial battle along with Milla and Tyke.

"They held that position far longer than they should have," Tyke said with a shake of his head. "If they'd broken contact by the numbers earlier, they could have fought a running battle and inflicted a lot more losses for the exchange."

"Yeah," Steph agreed, "but it would have dragged the fight out and possibly distracted the Drasin."

"What?" Tyke looked over, confused. "Distracted from what?"

Steph sighed, gesturing to bring up a local starmap in the display floating in front of them.

"They were fighting here," He pointed, "Just outside the oort cloud of this system."

"Right…"

"If they'd dragged out the fight, the Drasin might have followed the fleet instead of what they're about to do," Steph said, his tone sickly.

"What they're about… what…" Tyke was lost for a moment before it clicked. "They *wouldn't.*"

"They already have," Milla said softly, looking away.

"That's an Imperial world, but…"

"The Drasin will be delayed, eating that system," Steph said heavily. "It'll buy the Empire a week, maybe two or more to bolster their defenses."

"But it's going to replenish the Drasin numbers…"

"Yes," Milla interjected, "However, the generation limit the Empire imposed on them is making each successive generation weaker and less capable."

"They're stretching the Drasin's 'logistical lines' out," Steph said, "making them spread themselves too thin."

"But the people there…"

"The Empire doesn't give a damn." Steph said, "And we couldn't save them even if we had the whole fleet here. Nothing we can do, Tyke."

*****

# CHAPTER 4

*The Casino*

Jennifer was silent as she looked over the current telemetry.

The Marines were out of contact, had been since they slipped into the secured facility, which was all to plan no matter how little she liked it. The local area was still quiet, with no sign that they'd tripped any detection grids.

*Or, If we have, the Empire doesn't seem particularly concerned with it at least.*

Whichever was the case, she didn't much care as long as the Empire stayed out of things long enough for them to complete their mission and get the hell out of the region. The longer the *Casino* hung around this openly in Imperial controlled space the worse the itch between her shoulder blades got... and she was already itching a hell of a lot.

*How long have they been out of contact?* She wondered, glancing slightly at the clock only to immediately berate herself. *No point checking every couple minutes. Nothing for me to do now, it's all up to them.*

\*\*\*\*\*

Amanda Michaels covered the door while her specialists made their way to the computer terminals.

Their target was in here somewhere, but the Empire had their own form of cybersecurity that made finding things a bit of a pain. Someone, at some point, had built up the Imperial data network as multiple parallel but unconnected services. Penetrating one didn't get you anywhere when it came to the others and, worse, not even the damned Imperials themselves seemed fully aware of all of them.

*How do you find things your enemy doesn't even know they're hiding?*

The revelation that an Imperial ship had contained a quantum core that not even its *Commander or crew* had been aware of, at least based on earlier interrogations, had come as something of a shock and with that shock, a reevaluation of how they were dealing with Imperial tactics.

They needed to know what secrets the Empire was hiding from *itself*.

"Bateman, what have you got?"

"Nothing much, this is just the open network, Ma'am." Bateman responded. "I'm looking for power draws now that might expose their hidden cores."

"Good, work fast."

"Yes ma'am."

The rest of her squad were arrayed about the area, securing the rooms while Bateman worked, but she knew that they couldn't hold the location forever without consequence.

"This place is strange, Lieutenant," The Sarge said quietly, sidling up beside her. "Not enough guards. Feels like a trap to me."

Amanda nodded without looking in his direction, "I know. If this was in training…"

She shook her head as the Sarge snorted.

"Yeah, the drill sergeants would have dropped on our head by now, no question." He admitted, looking around. "Probably why I'm getting antsy."

"I don't think it's a trap." She said after some thought, "but you're not wrong. Something isn't right either."

Sarge just grunted, "Well not that it matters, as long as we can keep it from interfering, I guess."

"Yeah."

Amanda could agree with that, but until she could figure out what the hell was wrong she couldn't be sure that it wouldn't interfere.

*It's probably a result of the Imperial forces being withdrawn, they're likely running understaffed.*

"Got a hit on a phantom power draw," Bateman announced, "Might be our core."

Amanda shifted around, "Localize it. We're moving."

"Yes Ma'am!"

\*\*\*\*\*

The interior of the Imperial Facility continued to give Amanda a bad feeling as they worked their way through, working inward toward the power drain that Bateman had localized. It was deep inside the facility, which was of no surprise to anyone of course, but something about it didn't feel right to her either.

*If this is the core we're looking for... I don't know.*

The core on the cruiser had been located near the outer hull, specifically so that the damage would be limited if it were self destructed... and so that the vacuum of space would eliminate any remaining evidence of the core's existence.

The power draw they were working their way toward was deep in the facility, so if it were trapped in the same way it would be *bad* news for the facility and anyone inside it.

*Possibly for the planet, if they're insane enough to use a singularity system on world.*

Amanda didn't think that was likely, but with the Empire it couldn't be entirely written off either. There were too many examples of the Empire being more than willing to sacrifice anyone, their own people included, for seemingly pointless gains. It was an open talking point among the remaining Terran military that the Empire was at least likely to be heavily influenced by an *Entity*, though few details existed to confirm it as far as anyone at her level of clearance could find.

The entities were generally considered to be... helpful, or at least non-antagonistic, within Terran and Priminae circles. However, that really just meant that they aligned more or less with the goals and morals of their host populations.

Right and wrong, good and evil, were not universal, nor were they objective concepts. Depending on when you lived in history, it might be considered both right and good to use human sacrifice to achieve your goals. These were human concepts, not objective laws of the universe in which they existed.

Gaia, Odysseus, Central, and the other known entities were all the product of their cultures and host populations. If the Empire's entity had begun influencing the world during a period of... darker morals, well the resulting feedback loop was conjectured to be self enforcing, at least as far as the egg heads were known to predict.

No one knew for sure, but in the worst case scenario, you could easily have a culture that defined an entity that then defined the culture. The more powerful urges and beliefs would grow stronger, while the weaker ones faded away.

*And if those stronger urges view human life as worthless?*

Well, it didn't bode well.

This was why every Marine that dropped into the magnetosphere of the planet, and every person on the Casino, were *required* to wear neural scramblers.

The small devices were a combination portable EKG and inversion broadcasting unit. They would read the electrical communications within the brain, and then immediately broadcast an inverse signal sufficient to make any attempt at reading the signals a fool's errand.

No one knew if there was an entity on this world, but no one wanted to take any chances either.

"Lieutenant, we've got movement up ahead."

Amanda nodded, shifting her weapon, "Cleared for take down. Go."

*****

The Dealers ground their way deeper into the facility, using suppressed weapons, blades, and even armor shod hands to clear the defenders from their path as they moved. The Imperial base was lightly guarded, which normally would be raising alarm bells in every corner of Amanda's brain, but the entire mission had been predicated on the Empire's shifting of forces in response to the looming threat.

She wasn't feeling great about any part of the mission, the risk was incredibly high. Exposing the Archangels as potential enemies of the Empire was, in any way, was expressly counter to their normal operating doctrine.

*Command is taking a hell of a risk sending us instead of the Rogues... but we were the only ones that could do the job.*

"Lieutenant, I think we've paydirt coming up ahead."

"Thank you, Corporal. Confirm it, will you?" Amanda said.

"Yes Ma'am."

Quantum Computing systems had distinctive signatures that could be scanned through the quantum foam of the universe. Getting closer to it would cause a resonance in their equipment, and they were using that to guide them in.

*The problem, of course, is that we can't tell if the signal is coming from the system we're looking for... or just a run of the mill computing system installed by the Empire.*

There was a system down here, but was it the one they wanted?

*Impossible to know. The Empire probably are hiding the secret computing system behind one of their publicly known ones. That's what they did on the ship, it's probably what they do here.*

It was what she would do, after all.

"Got a lock, Lieutenant. Just ahead."

"Alright, everyone, watch for trouble," The Sarge cut in. "Corporal, do what you've got to do."

"You've got it Sarge," Bateman confirmed, dropping to a crouch as he pulled out an antenna for his gear.

Amanda left them to it as she looked over the situation. In training she'd been told that, quite often, the best thing a squad leader could do and say... was nothing at all. If the team was handling it, let them handle it.

"Alright! Sarge, Boss, we've got a second signal hiding in the foam," Bateman confirmed a moment later. "It's here."

"Good, find it," Amanda ordered shortly.

*So, our team drew the long straw. Lucky us.*

"On it, boss."

*****

## The Casino

"Hit from Baccarat, Ma'am. They found the target."

"Baccarat. Amanda's squad," Jenn said softly.

"Yes Ma'am."

"Pulse the others," She ordered, "Initiate phase two."

"Phase two, Aye."

Jennifer let out a deeply held breath, one that she hadn't even been aware she'd been holding, and settled back to do what everyone in the military did best.

Wait.

*****

Keenan stiffened as the pulse message broke the radio silence, advising the teams of the change in posture.

"Well damn, Baccarat hit the payday and has the finish line in sight," She said with a shrug, "Blackjack, you all know what that means."

"Hoo rah, Ma'am."

The team immediately shifted from their search profile and began moving back the way they'd come. With Baccarat moving to secure the data, it would be Blackjack and Poker Teams jobs to ensure that they got all the time they needed.

The Marines shifted stance smoothly and got about the task at hand, knowing that if they were right about the nature of the hidden computation system, things were about to get… *interesting.*

*****

Amanda shifted nervously, trying to hide it but failing miserably, as she watched the team setup.

They first had to locate and isolate the target Quantum Computation System, but that would be the easy part. After that, well it was all about getting the data they were after without triggering any failsafe systems…

*None of which I expect to actually fail**safe**.*

"Easy there, Ma'am," The Sergeant said softly. "You're done for now, just leave it to the team."

She took a breath, "I know. Feels wrong, just standing around."

"Hardest part of the job sometimes," He acknowledged, "A good Lieutenant knows that shutting her big yap and letting her team do their job is often the right call."

She shot him a dry look, "A good sergeant knows that reminding his Lieutenant of that once too often is a fast way to make her find *jobs* he would excel at, *in her experience* of course."

Brad held up his hands, an expression of mock horror on his face as he stepped back.

"As you say, ma'am."

Amanda sighed, not quite able to suppress the smile that she *knew* Karmen had intended to put on her face with that exchange. Nonetheless, it had mostly worked. She was still tense, of course, but the feeling of uselessness was fading at the very least.

"I think I've got the secondary signature isolated," Bateman said a short while later. "It's coming from behind that wall."

"Alright," Amanda stepped forward. "Give me a full scan of the wall, and prep the cutters."

"Yes Ma'am!"

Getting penetrative scans of the wall was necessary as it would let them avoid power junctions as well as any trap lines, or that was the hope at least. So the men quickly ran close scans and began marking off safe areas to cut while the two who'd been lugging their laser cutters got the chemical rigs warmed up.

"Careful," The Sarge said firmly as the lasers were moved into position. "Don't *scratch* the QCS, or our last words will be you going 'oops'."

"Shows what you know, Sarge," The Corporal snorted. "If I fuck up that bad, my last words won't be fit to go in any report."

"Nobody is saying any last words here," Amanda snapped. "That clear?"

"Yes Ma'am. No last words, Ma'am."

She shook her head, "Get to it."

The men just nodded as they got the cutters in position and fired them up. The Chemical lasers had a limited burn time, but were far more powerful than any of the battery operated systems available and a fair lighter as well. In moments the walls were spitting molten slag that splashed off the Marines' armor before spattering along the ground and cooling.

The men ignored it as they cut, staying to the clear lines with damned near religious devotion as neither watched to see the results of cutting a power junction, or anything else this close to one of the Empire's secret computational systems. The cutting took a while, but before too long it was finished and the pair stepped back as two more moved in with Halligan tools to pry the wall down.

The section of wall hit the floor with a reverberating thud that shook them even through their armor, dust billowing out in all directions as the Marines waited for their vision to clear, though they could see heat blobs through the mess using the FLIR sensors in the armor.

"Quantum core confirmed, Ma'am," the Sarge said firmly.

"Be about it then."

"Yes Ma'am. Marines, you heard the lady. Specialist Parrish, get to it."

"You got it Sarge," Specialist James Parrish said as he hopped over the chunk of wall in front of him and got in close to the big quantum system.

It was isolated from the local environment almost entirely, Amanda noted as the specialist gingerly moved around it to find a place to put his tap. A quantum system's biggest flaw was that its internals were *incredibly* delicate. Not just in the 'easy to break' way, either. An electrical field, a magnetic pulse... even a physical impact like that of the wall hitting the floor a moment ago could easily be enough to flip quark spins and completely scramble the information present.

So any quantum system had to be housed in a completely isolating framework, such that any influences could be predicted and adjusted for well in advance. It made the systems impractical for most purposes, but the sheer amount of data they could hold and process more than made up for it in specific applications.

"Ok, I have the official tap here," Parrish confirmed. "I'm going to start by just duping the data stream, we'll see what the Empire is looking at right this second."

"Do it."

Passively pulling data from any operations system was one of the hardest things to detect, and really could only be countered by keeping the enemy *away* from your system or heavily encrypting the stream. Ideally, both, but if your enemy had your encryption codes already and were right beside your system... well, too bad, Amanda supposed.

"Got the stream. Ok, nothing crazy here, looks mostly like fleet movements... for... huh." Parrish paused, cocking his head to one side. "That's weird."

"What?" Amanda stepped closer, putting a hand on the edge of the wall as she leaned in a bit. "What is it?"

"The fleet movements are time stamped for, like, next week... including losses. Jesus, they're expecting some heavy attrition."

"Intel says that the Empire is throwing ships at the Drasin, not really seeming to care much about their losses," Brad spoke up. "I was reading that they're taking thirty percent losses, conservatively."

"These numbers are projecting closer to fifty, but that tracks."

"Ok, it's interesting and all, but move on to the next step."

Parrish nodded, "On it. I've been snagging their request codes and responses, give me a bit more to make sure that we've got the pattern on lock."

Amanda shifted, but nodded in agreement.

"Do it right," She confirmed. "Don't rush."

"Not planning on it, Ma'am."

*****

Colonel Keenan stiffened as an alarm sounded, and she looked around as her team shifted position.

"Report." She called.

"We've got teams inbound," Sergeant Pat Doherty confirmed. "Looks like the jig is up. They knew someone's here."

"Alright, deploy. Harass and intimidate, keep them focused on us," Keenan ordered. "Baccarat needs time. We're here to buy it for them."

"Hoo rah!"

*****

# CHAPTER 5

**Imperial Ground Assault Team**

"Say that again."

A long silence followed that command, the tone making it clear that shooting the messenger was most *certainly* on the table. Nevertheless, the messenger in question swallowed hard and nodded once, firmly.

"Apologies, Ground Commander," He said tightly. "Forces unknown have landed in the military district and assaulted the census building. They currently hold several internal floors, and have repelled all attempts at retaking the building."

"I thought that was what you said," Ground Commander Markys Blair scowled as he rose to his feet. "What rebel faction has made this move?"

"We don't know yet, Ground Commander. We have not, as of the last update, identified any of the enemy forces. They just... *appeared* in the middle of the district and immediately overtook the census building."

Markys scowled, thinking on that as he walked over to the sector's strategic board and looked at the current feed for the area. Forces were marshaling across the planet, of course, but perhaps ironically the military district had some of the *lowest* concentrations of martial force of any region. Most teams were assigned to trouble areas, and the very *center* of the military district was most certainly not one of those.

*Still, it seems that we will shortly have more than sufficient forces on site. Why that building, though? It holds no classified data of value to the rebels. Military deployments, intelligence assets, and the like are routed through other feeds.*

The census building held data on the population, of course, but nothing irreplaceable, and he couldn't see how even the most classified of it would be of much value to the nationals in rebellion against the Empire.

"Very well," He said after a moment. "We will simply have to deal with this the same as any other rebellion. Inform me when we have full deployment of available assets to the region."

"Yes, Ground Commander. Shall I have them readied for an assault on the building?"

Markys considered that briefly, but shook his head, "I don't see any reason to bother. How many of our people are still within the building?"

"The shift workers, that's all."

"None of the supervisors, upper managers, those sorts?"

"They were evacuated via the roof as soon as the assault was noticed.

Markys nodded, "Fine. Then the building is surplus to needs. Cordon the region, prevent any escape, then I will authorize a strike to bring the building down on the rebels' own heads."

"Yes, Ground Commander!"

Marky gestured and sent the man scampering away before he turned back to the strategic display and wondered at the sheer gall any of the rebels would have had to display to even *consider* striking at a target within the Military district itself.

*We'll have to make it clear that this is not to be tolerated* *in any way or form. If these contemptible fools wish to play their games in their own homes, well they can die on whatever terms they choose I suppose. Come into **our** territory, however, and there will be no question of how they end.*

\*\*\*\*\*

Colonel Keenan looked out through one of the large plate windows, idly tapping it as she wondered what material it was constructed of. It didn't seem to be an aluminum oxide compound, but it sure as hell wasn't glass, so she didn't have a clue.

*Oh well, it doesn't matter much I suppose.*

"More imperial forces moving into place around the building, Ma'am."

"No sign of an intrusion yet?"

"No Ma'am, they're holding back a fair distance."

Keenan didn't like the sound of that, if she were being honest with herself. It felt too damn easy, for one thing. They'd come in expecting to have to hold off a few waves of attacks at the very least, but the enemy wasn't even bothering to try? That didn't bode well in the slightest.

"There are civilians, or at least Imps, in the building Ma'am. Maybe that's what's holding them off?"

Keenan snorted, "Hostages? You think the Empire gives a damn?"

The Sergeant shrugged, "Likely not, Ma'am. Wishful thinking, I suppose."

"They're gathering a knockout force," Keenan said, "They're going to ensure that they can take us out in one shot."

"Well, damn," Pat said with a shake. "Not sure what we're supposed to do then."

"Hope that Baccarat can get the data we need before the Empire makes their move."

*****

"Where are we, Bateman?"

Amanda was starting to feel antsy. The quiet over the network wasn't what she'd been expecting and while the other teams were still there, it felt wrong that the Empire was seemingly happy to leave them playing around in the building filled with Imperial citizens like this.

*The Empire is callous, I know, but this is another level,* Amanda thought dourly.

"I think I have the access keys, Ma'am... I'd love another few days to be sure, but..."

"Pull the trigger, Corporal," She ordered. "We don't have a few minutes, most likely."

"Hoo rah, Lieutenant."

Bateman did as he was bade, and set the automated seeker algorithms loose on the Imperial network while everyone held their breath.

"I... think it worked," He said tentatively a moment later. "Handshake has cleared, the system thinks we're authorized."

"Drop the whole package, yank the data we need, and let's get the hell out of here."

"That's going to take time, Ma'am. System is fast, but it's a *lot* of data."

Amanda grimaced, but there was nothing she could add as the data began streaming into their storage system. As fast as it was filling up, she could only really marvel at the sheer volume of data involved. With the automated algorithm seeking out what Command had wanted, all they could do now was sit and wait.

*How very novel an experience.*

*****

## Casino

"Pulse message, Ma'am. Data retrieval has begun."

Jennifer nodded.

"Good. Standby all systems to get our people out of there." She ordered. "Camouflage plates, full absorption on my command. Pulse weapons stand ready."

"Aye Skipper. Camplates standing by, pulse weapons standing by. Ma'am... if we deploy those..."

"I know," She cut off the objection. "Our cover is gone, along with a good chunk of the planetary atmosphere. We'll use hyper-velocity missiles first, along with beams, but if they push too hard... well, I'll fry this planet to get my people out in one piece. The Empire doesn't get any quarter from me, Commander."

"Yes Ma'am. Understood."

Jennifer slipped into the suspensor field that let her feel the movement of the ship as though it were her own body, and opened the neural link.

The view of the command deck vanished, replaced by deep space with only the local planet below them breaking up the monotony. She could *hear* the planetary communications in a mashup of thousands of voices talking at once, but let it wash over her as she shifted her gaze to the city below them.

*Thirty five thousand kilometers, a little less really but close enough.* She noted with a glance at the world. *We can cross it in three minutes from go, but they'll see us coming. How close can I get before the alarm goes up?*

Thrusters quietly flared and the Casino began to drop from its stationary orbit, slowly inching toward the planet so far below as Jennifer Samuels made ready to retrieve her teams.

She was just waiting for one more pulse from the planet before.

*Just. one. More.*

*****

# CHAPTER 6

"Enemy pressure from the Southern street," Doherty reported. "Nothing the squad can't handle, Colonel."

"Understood," Keenan acknowledged.

She didn't like it, the Empire was treating this situation far too lightly. They were probing at the edges of the perimeter when they should instead be pushing hard, sending in a solid strike force to make a real attempt at pushing out the invaders.

Her teams had prepared the ground for that sort of effort, but thus far those preparations had gone to waste. The Empire was almost... *nonchalant* about their occupying the building, which even assuming that the local garrison was unaware of the secondary Quantum Computational System seemed rather out of character for the Empire.

*They're up to something, and I already know that I'm not going to like whatever it is.*

"Tell everyone to stay on edge," She ordered. "They're up to something."

"Yes Ma'am."

With Doherty turning to send the orders out, Keenan refocused on the streets out beyond her position.

*The Empire squad up there is just sitting, waiting. What for?*

She didn't know, but she had a bad feeling that she'd best figure it out. Sharpish.

*****

"What's the status of the download?" Amanda asked, glancing back as she looked at the computational system and the tap.

"No idea," Parrish admitted, "I'm not controlling either side of this. The algorithm we got from Command is sending the queries, all I can do is watch the bandwidth as our data storage fills up."

"Damn it, How much space is left then?"

"Still a little more than two thirds. Command gave us one of the high end models, I didn't know we had anything this small that could store this much data," Parrish said with a shake. "We're looking at another... ten minutes, minimum, if the feed rate remains constant. If the data starts getting harder to find, well..."

"Right," Amanda nodded, "Nothing to be done about it then. Keep watching, keep me updated."

"Yes Ma'am."

She shook her head in frustration, but kept it to herself as best she could as she turned away and made her way back to where the Sergeant was standing.

"All quiet, Lieutenant," Brad told her as she stepped up beside him.

"I can see that. Same out on the perimeter."

"Yup."

"You as bothered by that as I am?"

"Yup."

Amanda snorted softly, "Eloquent as always, I see."

"I like to think so."

She had to suppress the urge to laugh outright at that, and could easily imagine Brad's smirking face under the military helmet and face-pro.

"You were expecting me to say yup again?" He asked laughingly. "I'm not that predictable."

"Yes you are," She corrected him easily, looking up the empty corridor as she sighed and calmed herself. "I just wish that the enemy were too."

"Might as well ask for the moon, if it still exists."

Amanda nodded somberly, "Yeah."

She'd never seen the moon. None of her generation had, or Earth, or anything else in the solar system humanity... *Terran* humanity... had evolved in. The moon and Earth were still there, she knew that because her parents talked about it sometimes. No one would ever look on any other of the planets that had dotted the skies of the Earth ever again, however.

From Mercury to the Plutoids of the Oort Cloud, most everything identifiable had been swallowed up to the eternal replication of *Gracen's Middle Finger*.

*I wonder if any of us will ever see the moon, or Earth, again?*

She had to shake those thoughts off, the musing of a little girl listening to stories of the old world at her father's knee.

"Well, no use wishing after the past. Time flows one way," She said wistfully. "No point trying to swim upstream."

"There's truth there, Ma'am."

\*\*\*\*\*

"All units are in position, Ground Commander."

Blaire nodded absently, not looking up from the strategic map he was examining.

"Good. Inform all teams to stand ready," He ordered.

"We will engage the enemy prior to the final strike. I want them pinned down, no one escapes."

"Yes, Ground Commander."

Blaire let the messenger run out with orders to deliver, not bothering to look after the man. The invaders were... strange for rebels. There had been no demands, no overt destruction, nothing that would mark that sort of action normally.

*What are their goals here? There's nothing in that building that would be of interest to the rebels anyway. Just bureaucracy and records, of value certainly but not to that rabble.*

In the end, though, he supposed that it did not... and would not... matter. They were only there to be made an example of anyway.

What did it matter what *their* goals were, when they were already dead?

"Have the strike force assembled."

"Yes, Ground Commander."

*****

**Casino**

"Launch detection."

Jenn glanced over, frowning as she noted the alert and focused on it.

*The garrison just put a CAP into the air? That's running a little later than I expected, but let's see what these guys look like...*

She focused the passive sensors on the craft that had just separated from the noise of the city below, got a good profile of the craft before letting the ship's database get a good look.

Jennifer froze momentarily as the profile was identified.

*That's not a CAP. That's a bomber squadron. Shit.*

There was no way that the ships she was looking at were going to do anything other than *flatten* the building her teams were in, assuming that was their target. Possibly the whole damn block, depending on what their orders were.

*I know the Empire is ruthless, but this isn't just ruthless... It's wasteful.*

Jennifer mentally toggled the alert and set an alarm blaring throughout the ship as she spoke while working.

"All hands to general quarters. Say again, all hands report to general quarters. The Casino doors are about to open, get ready for some whales boys and girls. We've got players itching to take on the house. But that's just fine..."

She smiled as she haloed each of the Imperial ships.

"Because the house *always wins*."

\*\*\*\*\*

Ground Commander Blaire grunted as the strike group reported in, straightening from his position.

"All ground teams, report."

He listened to the reports as they rolled in, satisfied that things were proceeding as expected, though that in itself was a little bit of a worry. The rebels weren't acting like... well, like rebels.

*They're too focused. Rebels are little more than brigands, they don't have the discipline these soldiers are showing. There's been far too little damage.*

Well, that would be corrected in short order if nothing else, Markys thought with some dark amusement. He would ensure that the populace all knew that the destruction of the building and loss of lives fell square on the shoulders of the rebels.

Just wiping them out wouldn't do at all, after all. They had to be ground into paste, their lives only the first price they would pay for defying the Empire.

"All teams… attack."

*****

"We've got movement, Colonel."

"I see them," Keenan acknowledged. "They're closing from all sides of the perimeter. Looks like they finally got tired of probing. Everyone get ready, we have to hold this line until the mission is done."

"Hoo rah, Colonel!"

Keenan lifted her rifle, idly checking the magazine's witness holes visually even though the weapon was reporting fully charged and loaded. Everything looked as good to the eye as to the computer, so she braced against the wall of the building and settled in for the wait.

It wouldn't be a long one now.

The rifle's system integrated with her armor, putting a aiming reticle on her HUD as she looked over the choke point she had chosen for her team to hold. The enemy would have to come right through her kill box to go any farther, something she and her men would ensure was an experience they did not enjoy.

For as little a time as they had to experience it, at least.

Her Marines were equipped with Terran ground weapons for this mission, something that they rarely were authorized to use in any combat that might involve the Empire. The heavy battle rifles were the result of late war research and development, and ironically Command wasn't even certain that the Empire knew they existed.

Combining Priminae and Terran tech to do things that

the Priminae would like as not consider an abomination, many late war weapons had barely begun to filter out before the Empire overran Sol's defensive line. Command had ordered them restricted, mostly to be used by the troops on Heroic and Rogue class vessels, though those men and women saw rather less action than those who pulled assignments with the 'Gaian' faction.

Now, though, it seemed that Command was loosening its grip a little, taking chances maybe… or maybe getting ready to let the Empire know just how *completely* they'd failed in their attempt at genocide.

*About time.*

The first of the Empire soldiers showed up on her HUD, a movement alert lighting up her visual cortex just seconds after she'd spotted them herself.

"Let them come. Check fire until I give the order."

"Hoo har."

Her teams knew the job now was to buy time. Nothing more, nothing less.

The Imps were getting a little more confident since the first few guys hadn't been shot out of hand, and more were coming out now. A few squads worth of men, well disciplined but with crude tactics. Keenan would have ripped a hole in any *cadets* who tried this nonsense, showing themselves in a group like that, too tightly packed as they nervously made their way forward.

She waited for the bulk of them to be well inside the kill box before giving the order.

"Fire."

*****

Amanda flinched as the combat network reported the

first shots being fired, but said nothing. The others couldn't do anything about it, and it would only distract them from the task at hand.

"How much is left?" She asked aloud.

"Almost finished. If there's more data there, we're not going to have anywhere to store it," Parrish responded.

"Not our problem. Top it off, then get out of the system," She ordered. "It's time to get moving."

"Yes, Ma'am."

She was mostly focusing on *not* pacing when an alert showed up on her command channel, getting her attention.

"All squad commanders, be advised, the Imperials have detached a *bomber* squadron to your AO."

That was like a flush of ice water flowing down her back, and Amanda shivered briefly as she considered that.

*Bombers? Imperial bombers... damn it, what's their capability?*

She opened a direct and private link to the Sarge.

"Brad, what are the capabilities of Imperial bombers?" She asked softly.

The Sergeant didn't turn to look at her, but she could see him stiffen in his own armor before he responded.

"Capabilities?" He asked in a soft, but dry tone, "They can flatten a small continent according to all reports. We've not seen them in action directly, though, most of our encounters with the Imps have been space combat. We just have reports from others. Why?"

"We've got a squadron heading our way. No chance of them being assigned to close air support?"

"Not from what intel says about them, no."

"Well… shit."

"Yes Ma'am, that about covers it. We moving?"

Amanda shook her head, "We move when Parrish is done. The Casino is our top cover, it's her problem."

Brad took a breath, but she could see him making a suit nod, "Right you are, Lieutenant."

She half turned to look back at the Quantum System, "Still…"

The Sergeant now turned to look at her, "I don't like that tone, Ma'am. What are you thinking?"

"I mean, if they want to cover our presence here… I'm inclined to give them a hand, y'know?" She asked idly, an idea forming.

"Ma'am…" Brad growled.

"Hey Parrish," She called over the open Channel.

"Lieutenant?" The specialist looked her way.

"Is that thing trapped as we expected?"

\*\*\*\*\*

The Marines' weapons were eerily quiet for being supersonic slug throwers.

Keenan had never quite gotten used to the lack of a *boom* when compared to their more commonly issued rifles. The advanced design of the rounds were intended to *slip* through the air, leaving less than a ripple in their passing as they lanced out from the weapons and *slammed* into their targets with the force of an old anti-material rifle using specialized munitions.

The fusillade her people had unleashed on the Imps was *eerie* in that regard, just a pack of hissing snakes filling the air when they opened up, the sound of the rounds striking home on the other side actually louder than the sound of the rifles firing.

Creepy.

*But effective.*

The first press of the Empire's soldiers had scattered after they'd been hit with proximity fused grenades, the rifle fire sending them running for cover a few seconds later as the survivors tried to shake the concussion from between their ears with mixed results at best.

To their credit, though, the shock didn't last long and the Imps got their act together and began firing back with their powerful beam weapons.

Those sizzled the air itself, pouring heat enough into the walls they struck to actually cause the material within to rapidly phase change and expand. Explosions tore big gaping divots in the building where those beams struck, showering everything... and everyone... under and around them with debris.

Keenan and her people ignored it all, focusing on keeping the enemy back even as the Imps pressed forward.

They had guts, she'd give them that without question, after that first strike had left three out of four of those in sight dead or dying on the ground, well anyone who could get up and keep pushing forward was worth respecting for their courage to her way of thinking.

*Their brains? Quite a bit less so, however.*

An alert from the *Casino* caught her eye, though, and Keenan frowned under her helmet.

*Bombers? Shit. This is just to keep us pinned down. Those bastards are going to flatten the whole area!*

Keenan considered her options, but ultimately there

weren't any.

They had to hold the position until Baccarat finished their side of things, so she was going to have to trust in the Cardsharp who was running the *Casino*.

There were worse places to put her trust.

*****

# CHAPTER 7

**Imperial Ground Command**

"Strike team is approaching the target zone, ground commander. Should our forces withdraw?"

Commander Blaire shook his head, "No. They stay in contact, we need to keep the rebels localized to the target."

"Yes Commander."

Markys Blaire checked the systems, ensuring that the entire scene was being properly recorded to serve as notice to any more would-be rebels that *dared* even dream of intruding on his fief. He would have no mercy on their ilk, and this would ensure that they all knew it.

Since the Imperial force had withdrawn to serve whatever whims those currently in charge had bent to, the command of the worlds so left to their own devices had fallen more and more on the formerly lowly Ground Commanders like himself.

The local command structure was filled with self important fools whose only true power had been their position and the ear of the Imperial military. Now, well they found themselves increasingly adrift in a sea of enemies that grew bolder and more dangerous by the passing hour, and while in the past they had often sneered at the likes of Markys himself, since no matter how many ground forces you might command a single cruiser could end any threat you might pose in an instant… but there were no cruisers in orbit any longer, and the soldiers on the ground *controlled* the territory they occupied.

Markys smiled thinly to himself.

It didn't hurt that many of those self important and contemptible fools were even now huddling within the evacuation points surrounding the target zone.

*I almost feel like thanking these rebel imbeciles. Providing me with such a perfect example while also letting me thin the ranks of those whose use has come and gone... it is a gift I really couldn't have asked for better than.*

\*\*\*\*\*

## Casino

"Engaging black hole armor settings. All hands, stand ready for acceleration," Jennifer said calmly. "Secure all stations. If it can move, strap it down, we're going in hot."

Her fingers twitched in mid air as she waited for the right moment to make the call.

The enemy bomber flight was in motion, and would be able to launch... possibly anytime, so she had to be ready to drop from orbit in a heartbeat, but she didn't want to throw the planetary defenses into overdrive as that might disrupt the flow of intelligence through the Quantum systems and slow the ground teams down.

If it came to choosing between gaining the last of the intelligence they were after and losing her teams, she'd pick her teams in a heartbeat... but no mission was without risk either, and they all knew the game before they saddled up to the table.

So Jennifer would cut it close, closer perhaps than was wise, but wisdom was for strategists... not for fighter pilots and Marines.

*Come on... come on!*

*****

Amanda Michaels twisted from her position, waving for Brad to cover her spot as she stepped back to the hole in the wall where Parrish was working.

"Come on," She urged, knowing that he really couldn't do anything, but the urge to do something... to *say something*... was overpowering.

"Almost there," He hissed through clenched teeth, "Data draw is slowing down... it's getting harder to find terms. This well is almost tapped out."

"How much space is left?"

"Six percent maybe, hard to say for sure because we're running heavy compression and it's processing in the background," Parrish offered. "I can call it now, there can't be much left?"

Amanda hesitated, wanting to grab *everything*, but knowing that she might have to make the call to cut it off.

"Hold that thought," She ordered, flicking back to check the combat network.

*The Imperial forces are pressing in hard... they're not falling back for the bombers. God damn they're insane.*

She couldn't see what the *Casino* was up to, but she could guess. She'd grown up with Jenn, practically bouncing on Aunty Cardsharp's lap, and knew the woman as well as she knew anyone.

"We'll go to the wire," Amanda said a moment later. "Keep pulling data."

" You've got it, Ell Tee."

*****

"Get down!"

Keenan hit the deck, hard, as a beam swept by overhead and she was showered with debris that pattered off her armor like a hard rain on a tin roof. She rolled to clear her weapon and pushed the rifle out ahead of her, crawling to get to the edge of the corridor so she could draw a bead.

The enemy were pushing in closer despite the bomber group being in the air, leaving her to wonder if they were intended as a sacrificial goat by whoever was in charge.

*Of course they are, just like everyone else here,* She thought with disgust.

Keenan was all about fighting and dying for her people, she'd signed up for it and expected that anyone else who did the same deserved respect regardless of what side they belonged to. She hated seeing good people sacrificed for no true gain, though. In fact, that was possibly the only true phobia she had that she could name.

The idea of being sacrificed for *nothing*? That just spit on everything she personally believed in.

Her life for her country, world, and people. No hesitation, no regrets. But her life for *nothing*?

That sent a frisson of visceral terror down her spine, even trusting the people she served. Watching it happen to someone else? That was just... disgusting and horrific.

"We've got more coming from the South!"

Keenan noted the report, made certain that her people were responding without being told to, then kept her mouth shut to avoid being a distraction as she focused on her own rifle sights.

The chunky weapon kicked in her grip as she opened fire, putting three rounds down range at quarter power to drop some of the charging Imperials. The heavy rounds punched right through whatever the enemy was using in the place of proper armor, she doubted she needed her battle rifle to take any of them down, but supposed that against the beam weapons they preferred there wasn't much value in most armor anyway.

"Hold the line," She ordered as the fighting lulled briefly. "We've got a job to do!"

\*\*\*\*\*

James Parrish stared at the data ticking down, willing the damn stream to just *stop* already, but it kept on trickling in despite every psychic order.

The quantum system was fast, for many things, but really when it came to data transfer the damn things were *pigs*. Same was true of Terran systems and every one he'd seen, be they from Earth, Ranquil, or the Empire. Crunching numbers was one thing, but moving them around quantum bit by quantum bit... well that just took too damn...

*Wait...*

"Ell Tee!"

"What is it?" Lieutenant Michales snapped from where she'd moved to.

"We're done!" He said, already unplugging his system and gingerly pulling the data tap from the lines.

"Finally! All points, Baccarat. Table is closed!" Michaels called over the network. "Say again, the table is closed!"

She was striding over as he finished packing up his kit, pulling a pack from her hip and fiddling with it.

"What are you doing?" Parrish asked as he recognized the demo pack.

"We're not leaving a trace," She said, cold as ice, nodding over her shoulder. "Get moving."

"Yes ma'am!"

He scrambled clear as she finished rigging the pack. As he was heading for the corridor, Parrish glanced back to see the Lieutenant setting the demolition charge down, nestling it in with what he'd identified as the trap that had already been set on the Quantum Computation System.

*Oh shit.*

All he knew from that point was that they needed to get the *hell* out of there, and right the fuck *now*.

Parrish knew that the Empire didn't fuck around with those things, and he didn't want to be on the same *planet* as one of their booby traps when it went off. They *probably* weren't crazy enough to booby trap the damn thing with a singularity, but he wasn't betting his life on it.

"Everyone, OUT!" Michaels ordered as she cleared the room.

*Don't have to tell me twice.*

*****

### Casino

*Go!*

Jennifer was in motion, along with the entire ship, before the pulse from Baccarat completed playing out. She lunged across space, the *Casino* echoing her motion in sidereal movement, plunging into the atmosphere on full acceleration between one syllable and the next.

Alarms wailed as they hit the atmosphere and just bulled right through without pause, the leading edge of the ship heating up damned near instantly as she kept on the power and didn't let the ship slow down from the friction.

The black hole armor settings didn't help, sucking in heat rather than repelling and dissipating it with damned near superconductivity levels of heat transfer being the only thing that kept the leading edges of the ship from vaporizing. Instead the heat was spread across the entire ship, being sucked into the big heat sinks that allowed them their stealth capacity in the first place.

Not even the Archangel could take this for long, but she didn't need it too.

The side effect of the heat transfer was that, even as they just hammered the thickening atmosphere aside at well beyond hypersonic speeds, the heat was kept evenly distributed across the entire ship and the *Casino's* external heat profile remained damned near flat and all but impossible to spot even if you had a sensitive scanner pointed right at her.

"Weapons hot, boss!"

"Got it," Jennifer responded, "Bombers haloed. Splash them. Now."

From a hundred and fifty miles up, just inside the atmosphere, the Archangel opened fire.

Split beam strikes descended from the heavens and lit up the skies below them.

\*\*\*\*\*

**Imperial Ground Command**

"What the abyss was that?" Markys blinked away the flash that was still putting spots in front of his eyes.

"Unknown, Commander!"

"Make it *known*, now!"

"Yes Commander!"

He growled, not happy in the least as he tried to determine what the hell had just entered a new variable into his operation and whether it was going to impact operations going forward.

In a moment, though, he growled again... and louder... as he realized that it most certainly *was* going to affect operations going forward.

*The strike squadron isn't responding.*

"Someone raise the strike squadron!" He snarled, "I want to know if they're still on target!"

"Trying, Commander, they're not responding."

Markys gave up on keeping his frustration in and swore as he got to his feet and crossed out of the command center, grabbing a hand scanner in the process.

"Someone get the strike squad in sight or on the comm," He ordered. "I want to know what happened, immediately."

"Yes, Ground Commander!"

*****

"Thank God," Keenan grumbled as she got to her knees from the prone position and waved her men in. "Baccarat just closed the table, we're on exfil now."

The teams began packing up immediately, which actually consisted of *unpacking* certain party favors before they started falling back by the numbers, putting a few rounds back the way they'd come just to keep the Imps on their toes.

"Exfil site Alpha looks blocked, Colonel."

"Switch to Bravo," Keenan said, not concerned with it.

Alpha had always been more of an aspirational position anyway, the odds had been good that the Imperial forces would block it just by virtue of it being along one of the more likely avenues of their approach. Bravo meant that they'd have to ruck up a few floors, but that was fine. The Pyramidal construction meant that there was no 'rooftop' strictly speaking for them to gather on, but there were multiple landing pads and the like sprouting from the building at every few levels like mushrooms from a log.

"All teams confirm Bravo, Colonel. We're good."

*****

**Imperial Ground Command**

"No sign of the strike team, Commander, but we've received reports of debris striking the ground in the sectors they were flying over."

Markys blinked, trying to process that.

It was almost unthinkable, he wouldn't have believed that the Rebels had the forces to manage such a thing. He forced himself to get over the disbelief, however, as there was a job left unfinished.

"Launch two more strike squadrons, along with all available interceptor squadrons as escort."

"Yes, Ground Commander."

"Issue new orders to our forces in the battle," He went on. "Push forward. Wipe the enemy out, now."

"Orders dispatched, Ground Commander."

If the strike force couldn't get the rebels, the ground teams would have to do the job. If anything was left, well that would be up to the two new teams to handle he supposed.

Markys turned from the skies and headed back to the command control system.

"And find out what the *abyss* hit the first strike force!"

*****

Keenan swore as the enemy fire abruptly redoubled, forcing her team to take cover as debris showered all around them from the destruction the enemy weapons wrought.

"Colonel, we've got teams pressing hard from every vector. They're not going to give us a break, looks like!"

"You want a break, get a kit kat from stores," She snapped.

"Get what, Colonel?"

Keenan sighed, "Never mind, Corporal. How long until they hit the claymores?"

Doherty risked a glance from cover before flopping over onto his back, "Thirty seconds."

An explosion tore through the air from not far off.

"Or Less," He corrected without missing a beat.

"Every move while they're picking up the pieces!"

*****

"Move it, no slacking!" Amanda slapped troops on the shoulder as they ran past her, using the contact as a means to keep count in her head, ensuring that she wasn't forgetting anyone in the rush.

The team was running for the Bravo exfil site, with time ticking away in more ways than one.

The *Casino* was inbound, hot and heavy, and she knew from the briefing that they couldn't hope for more than a few minutes before planetary defense cottoned on to the existence of the gunboat in one way or another. Once that happened, things would get hairy in a hurry, so they needed to be *on board* before the Imps realized that they needed to be paying attention to the skies.

She, personally, wanted to be out of the operational theatre and off the *fucking planet* before her explosives took out the Quantum Calculation System, however. Amanda didn't believe that even the Empire would use a singularity or anything similarly exciting to trap a planet based installation, but just in case she preferred her body un-spaghettified as a general rule.

"Lieutenant!"

"What is it, Sarge?"

"Poker and Blackjack are pinned down," Brad said, "Check the network."

Amanda swore, flicking her attention back over to the combat network and included the other two teams. In a second she saw the issue and swore again.

*Nothing to do about it, I suppose,* She grumbled. "Alright, change of plans. We go down to go up, new plots coming to your HUDs."

"Oorah, Ma'am!"

Amanda quickly traced out the new route in her own HUD, already moving in the right direction before she sent it to her team, letting them fall in behind her at a dead run while she fine tuned their directions and tried to figure out the best way to hit the enemy when they got there.

"Waypoints up!" She called. "New orders to your HUDs, hit them hard and fast boys, we don't want to be late for our bus."

\*\*\*\*\*

# CHAPTER 8

Keenan swore under her breath as she hugged the corner as another beam scored the construction all around her.

"More of 'em coming in, boss!"

"I see them," She grunted, leveling her rifle and firing a burst into the general direction of the attackers before retreating back to cover. "Persistent bastards."

"Yes Ma'am."

The Empire had dropped the better part of a Company on their position, and it seemed like every single one of them were converging on her squad at that moment despite heavy losses incurred by pushing into her Marines' fire arcs.

*One thing the Empire troops have never lacked for is courage,* She admitted grudgingly to herself, though she was uncertain if courage was exactly the right word.

They were almost suicidal, like life and death meant little to them. She'd seen it others, but never on the scale that the Empire brought to the table. Usually only in those who were damn near to the point of ending their own lives, people who'd lived right on that edge for so long that they couldn't always tell which side was which.

*Not courage, perhaps, but fearlessness.*

You needed to be afraid to be brave, being fearless just required a lack of *sanity*.

*Which, honestly, explains a lot about the Empire even if it does raise a whole bunch of new questions,* She thought dryly as she inched back away from the corridor as another barrage of beams cut into the section with furious force.

"Frag out!"

A moment later a dull sort of bang shook the air, and Keenan took the opportunity to shift her people closer to the path that would take them up to point Bravo, but the Imps weren't slowed for long as they pushed hard through the smoke and crackling beams of energy cut through the air with lethal effect.

Keenan grabbed one of the younger corporals as she passed, he'd somehow managed to trip and sprawl himself over the battlefield, so she heaved him along ahead of her without pausing but the distraction had a price.

"Colonel!"

Keenan twisted at the shout and spotted the Imp targeting her just as he opened fire. The beam burnt the air as it lanced across at her, but she was suddenly hit from the side and thrown clear at the last possible moment.

Smoke filled the air as armor ablated in an instant, dissipating some of the attack, but not enough.

Doherty went down from where he'd hit her, just a second ahead of the Imp who was turned to red *mist* by the combined fire of the rest of the squad.

"Shit! Corporal!" Keenan snapped, scrambling back over even though she could read his vitals on her HUD and knew there wasn't a point.

"Man down!"

Keenan brought her weapon up as two more Imps tried to follow the lead of the rapidly dissipating mist, burst fire chowdering both of them before they could do more than half think of their next action. She checked Doherty personally, just to be sure, then pulled the rigger line from her armor and locked it to the back of his armor before she got up and fast walked for cover with the body dragging behind.

"We've got more Imps inbound, Colonel! Leave him, he's gone!"

"We're not leaving *anyone*," She snarled.

She was almost to cover when the Imps got into position, and could feel the burn running right down her spine.

*Any second now...*

The expected crackle of power never arrived, however, as instead the air was filled with the rapid fire buzzsaw of sonic booms from heavy rifles rending the air.

"Colonel! This way," Amanda Michaels called, waving from where her team was securing the exfil path.

"You heard the Lieutenant, Marines! Move your asses!"

"Oorah!"

They picked themselves up and bolted for the corridor, two more Marines pausing only to grab onto Corporal Doherty's armor as they picked up part of the weight from Keenan, all of them running as best they awkwardly could in the process.

*****

### Casino

"We're reading multiple strike groups launching, skipper."

"I see them," Cardsharp said, fully immersed in her flying. "Haloed. Targets of opportunity, smoke them if they get close enough but we're not going out of our way."

"Aye ma'am."

The Casino was leveling out hard, coming in low over

the city at speeds still well in excess of supersonic for the planet's atmospheric composition and their altitude. She didn't envy any of the locals the hearing damage they were likely to incur, but didn't honestly care enough to think more about it than that.

"Marines report that they've switched to point Bravo for pickup!"

"Point Bravo, Roger."

She made the changes needed, minute though they were, to adjust their course to compensate for the alteration in dustoff point.

"We're sixty seconds out," She said as the numbers kicked back.

"Marines report at least two minutes to dustoff, Ma'am! They've got casualties."

"Damn. Alright, time adjusted." She said, noting something on the network that caught her eye. "Stand by all point defense and close in weapons systems, Imperial ground troops are designated hostile targets of opportunity as we approach."

"Yes Ma'am. PD and CWIS online. Main beams, Ma'am?"

"Negative," Cardsharp said with a shake of her head. "Overkill for one and, more importantly, the debris they kick up will cover the enemy from our scanners. Suck it up, lazy bones, and do it the hard way."

A laugh could be heard echoing through the narrow and cramped interior halls of the ship.

"Right you are, Ma'am. More fun this way anyhow."

\*\*\*\*\*

**Imperial Ground Command**

"Unknown contact! It's in the air, and moving *fast*, Ground Commander."

Markys hissed angrily, "Redirect interceptors. Do we have identification?"

"No, Ground Commander. The profile is... strange. It's not matching anything we have on record, but I'm not sure if that's because it's unknown... I think our systems are being disrupted."

Markys Blaire crossed the room, scowling with each step.

"Disrupted *how*?"

"This is the profile, Ground Commander," The technician offered, nodding to the display.

Marky glanced at it briefly, then frowned before he looked closer.

"What... is it?"

"Unknown. The profile doesn't even properly read as... *anything*..." The tech said, sounding confused and frustrated. "It's like it's both there and not at the same time."

Markys could see that much. The Image on the screen was like a shadow, somehow cast over the sky. Like a shadow, it seemed only to exist in two dimensions, though unlike one it was so black as to be unreal.

*It's like light cannot escape its...*

His thoughts trailed off as he paled, "Check gravity readings. Any anomalies?"

The tech was scouring the system before he even finished, apparently following Markys' own thoughts, but sighed in relief a moment later.

"No anomalies."

*Well, that is good, but it doesn't answer anything.*

"Fine. It's not a gravity anomaly, so direct the interceptors to wipe it from my skies."

"Yes, Ground Commander!"

*Answers can come later.*

For now, he just wanted victory.

\*\*\*\*\*

**Casino**

"Targets on the ground."

"Engage at will."

"Engaging."

Jennifer focused on flying the boat, keeping an eye on the spires and massive construction of the Imperial city while she let the small gunner complement the Fighter/gunboat handle the engagement. The CWIS opened fire first, point defense lasers engaging mere moments later as they swooped in low over the Imperial forces on the ground and tore the ever loving hell out of their deployment.

Return fire was minimal, she noted professionally as she looped around the target building and ensured that they had clear lines of fire on all exposed Imperial troops. The ones inside the building would have to be handled by the Marines on the ground, but they could at least lighten the load a bit for them.

Part of her missed her original Archangel fighter, and a wistful part of her memory remembered the day she'd been assigned to it. The Skipper's own personal fighter, no less.

*A simpler time.*

One fighter, one pilot... all the enemies you could ask for.

Jennifer grinned as she dropped the gunboat lower, exposing some of the Imperial troops that had taken cover just within the building.

In those days she'd fly and fight her own craft, not relying on anyone else, and it had been everything she'd ever wanted since the Bloc War tore through the nations of Earth.

*There's something to be said about working with good people too, though.*

Commanding a crew had never been in her plans, but like everything else since the Odyssey's first voyage, those plans had been tossed up to the fates and scattered to the stars it seemed.

Like most people she knew, Jennifer couldn't help but wonder what would have happened if the Odyssey had never been built. Would the Empire have ever found them? Would the Drasin?

She didn't know, couldn't say. Those kinds of thoughts didn't come with answers, they just came with doubts. Doubts were something she didn't have time for.

"Operational Area clear."

"Roger that," She said. "Good work. Tell the Marines to haul ass, I want to get the hell off this rock."

"Yes ma'am."

Doubts were for people with nothing better to waste their lives on. Moving forward and making things better, that was how she wanted to spend her remaining time.

*****

"Bravo up ahead!"

"I see it," Amanda said, "Secure the passageway!"

"Yes Ma'am!"

Her team took the lead coming up to the Bravo landing zone, and now that meant that they would hold the position while the rest got caught up.

She stepped out on the open platform, just behind her lead element, and the wind from the city could be felt pushing on her through the armor. A whine from above them was all they could hear of the *Casino* as it flew on a tight orbit of the area, weapons bristling as they sought out more Imperial forces to take on.

Amanda didn't look up.

"Cover the sides," She ordered with a gesture, "Watch for snipers or artillery spotters!"

The Sarge was relaying commands, adding his own touches to her orders to ensure that everyone understood their job as the first of the Colonel's Marines stepped out of the building.

"Casino, Baccarat Actual," Amanda said.

"Go for Casino, Baccarat."

"Blackjack Actual arriving for dustoff."

"Roger that, Descending."

The whine warbled slightly, then grew louder as the *Casino* started its descent.

The Archangel Fighter/Gunboat design was *tiny* by starship measure, but that didn't mean it was small by human scale in the slightest, and that became incredibly obvious as the shadow loomed over them as the ship began to settle into place over the landing platform.

There was *no chance* of it actually landing, of course, but that hadn't been in the plans anyway. Amanda couldn't see it, not with the ship so blacked out as to appear practically two dimensional, but a lower hatch had opened up and a descender was dropping toward them as the Colonel stepped out onto the platform with the body of the casualty in tow.

"Colonel, your ride." Amanda gestured to where the Sarge had grabbed the descender and was holding it ready.

"Thank you, Lieutenant," Keenan said firmly as she moved into position and let herself and the casualty be hooked in.

"Blackjack Actual and Dealer are linked up. Bring them home," Amanda ordered.

"Roger. Retrieving descender."

The two suits of armor lifted off the pad, vanishing quickly into the inky blackness above.

The rest of the Colonel's team activated their own internal CM systems and hopped easily into the air, following their Commander on their own power. Once they were in place, the second squad followed, jumping up in twos and threes, guided by their internal systems as they ascended into the void above them.

Then it was Baccarat's turn.

Amanda had her men go first, only herself and the Sergeant remaining to the end. Then she activated her own counter-mass systems and let her internal system adjust her jump as she looked up and leapt into the void.

She and the Sergeant were caught as they arrived at the ship, and pulled easily in by the waiting team. Amanda waved off additional help as she leaned back out, holding on to the side of the door and looked down at the building below and retrieved the detonator from her thigh pouch.

The switch clicked softly in her hand as the *Casino* began to ascend, and for a moment she wondered if anything was going to happen.

*Maybe they didn't trap it with anything crazy...* Amanda thought as they continued to climb up above the city.

That thought was put to the torch when the building they'd just evacuated suddenly turned into a pillar of brilliant blue fire that seemed to reach out to the stars like a tower to the *Gods*.

*Or, maybe they did.*

She felt sick, because she knew that she'd set off whatever trap the Empire had left there, and no doubt a lot of people had just died, but it was worth it.

*Right?*

It had to be.

\*\*\*\*\*

# CHAPTER 9

**The Nest, Rogue World**

Morgan Passer slumped into the desk chair, rubbing at his eyes as he tried to get ready for another day of the growing insanity that had become his reality over the past few decades or so.

It seemed that the Empire was determined to self-destruct in the worst possible way that it could manage, throwing literally the rest of the region into outright chaos as it withdrew military presence from world after world after world in order to combat the Drasin.

Passer was all in favor of eliminating the Drasin to be sure, but throwing nigh on countless worlds into chaos when they could instead be providing resources and manpower to the job was just... so very much like the Empire, he supposed. Short sighted, focused on near term goals, and ignoring the facts as they lay in favor of whatever feelings were driving their actions.

Back before the fall of Earth, Intel had determined that the Empire... Empress at the time... was being advised by one of the Entities, a group of Gestalt intelligences that seemed bound to their particular world's magnetic field.

Earth had Gaia, the Priminae had Central, and since discovering the existence of those beings more had begun to show up. It seemed that the Empire had the Emperor, if Intelligence was correct in its assessment, at least.

If so, Morgan was convinced that this particular entity

had been dropped on its head early in its development cycle... though he had yet to figure out how you could manage to drop a Geo-Magnetic field on its head.

*Of course I might be chicken and egging the scenario here. Maybe someone just managed to drop an entire race of humans on **their** head instead.*

That seemed marginally easier than dropping a planet on its head, but honestly he still didn't have much of a clue how it could possibly have happened.

Whatever happened, Morgan only knew for certain that it had left the Empire and its people... well, psychologically *insane*. It wasn't the drooling at the mouth sort of insane, but rather a more insidious sort, one that left them seemingly stable until you looked closer.

Too close, sometimes.

Their reaction to Terran humans had been one of those too close moments. Something that no one had realized until it was far too late was that the Empire saw Terran humans as an existential threat. Just how that came about was still one of the mysteries of the war, but they'd gotten that much out of a high level prisoner captured late in the war.

They considered the Terran humans as *Xeno*. Non-humans masquerading as humans.

Worse, it had been discovered by that point that the Empire had some foundation to set those beliefs on.

Priminae and Terran humans, as well as Imperial, all looked essentially identical. Functioned identically as well, in fact, with some variance but nothing that significantly strayed from the human norm any more than one might expect across racial and cultural differences on Earth, as insane as that seemed on the surface.

The very existence of both Terran humans and the

Priminae/Imperial breed had left researchers completely at odds as it made no sense as best anyone could tell. Convergent evolution was certainly a thing, but this wasn't a case of different *humanoid* forms evolving. The Terran and Priminae/Imperial genomes both hit every single marker that was used to identify humans from their simian ancestors.

That perfection probably should have raised more red flags than it did, Morgan supposed, but at the time there were already so many of the damn things waving in the air that a few missing was hardly something to notice. It wasn't until a far deeper look at the genome was taken that people realized that something even *weirder* was going on.

The two species weren't some offshoot from one or the other, Earth wasn't some lost colony of the Priminae or vice versa.

Their evolutionary paths, as shown by the DNA of each group, were completely different.

Different ancestors, but identical outcomes.

It wasn't, strictly speaking, impossible… but it was certainly unlikely as all hell.

It was, in the words of one of their smartest minds, like some lazy God had copy and pasted the human genome across the stars and set it so that the human form was the *inevitable* outcome of evolution. Which, entirely aside from the religious connotations of that, which Morgan had no desire at *all* to touch with a ten lightyear long pole, seemed frankly ludicrous once someone examined the human form in any detail.

The sheer number of *horrible* design choices involved alone was enough to give more than one researcher near permanent twitches whenever they contemplated the idea.

Unfortunately there weren't any answers forthcoming on that subject, but the very fact that those genetic differences *existed* had been enough for the Empress to all but declare holy war against the Earth. A war that, despite every effort of the Terran forces and their Priminae allies, had ended with Terran humans being scattered to the stars... and the Earth being lost to them, possibly forever, behind the Kardashev defense system nicknamed Gracen's Middle Finger.

Of course, the Empire had lost more ships in that moment than they'd ever lost before... *ever* before, in fact, at least as far back as their public histories went. In one battle, the Empire had lost half its combat power and almost a quarter of its numerical strength of metal in space.

They probably would have called it a bargain if not for Earth's response.

Morgan had reviewed the records, over and over again, and he still wondered that the Empire hadn't seen it coming.

Eric Weston had tried to warn them.

Strategic weapons weren't to be used willy nilly. They existed almost entirely for the purpose of keeping the enemy playing more or less by the rules. That was what the Empire didn't seem to understand, as they continually used their own strategic weapons as tactical options.

That wasn't how Earth waged war.

When the time came, the Empire clearly assumed that they'd seen everything the Earth could do. Antimatter weapons weren't the best the Earth could field, however, they were just the most powerful *tactical* weapons in their arsenal. When Earth fell, well Gracen's last order was to show the Empire the magnitude of their mistake.

The Empire *burned* that day and night.

Unfortunately, while the Empire had made a mistake in the war... so had Earth.

*We forgot that strategic weapons only serve as strategic*

*weapons if your enemy isn't **insane.***

Which, of course, brought them back to the current situation. The Empire's insanity had led them to unleash a self replicating strategic weapon upon the Galaxy, leash or no leash, and now that weapon had to be dealt with before it turned every star system into a barren waste in the Drasin's wake as they progressed across the Galaxy.

Morgan was waiting for word from Jenn Samuels and the crew of the Casino, and he was just praying that their mission had succeeded.

Everyone else was either in position, or moving to position, as the remaining force of the Terran military in the region was once more awakening and in motion.

The Drasin had to end *here and now.*

Nothing else was acceptable.

If those monsters were left alive, the colony ships that had fled Earth would have to face them one day, and he couldn't allow that to happen.

*We kill the Drasin and, if we have a breath of life left afterwards... we kill the Empire too. The insanity ends now.*

*****

### Gaian Destroyer *Bug Hunt*

Marcus Reid dropped casually into the command chair at the center of the *Bug Hunt's* C&C deck, lounging back with a bored look on his face as he checked over the morning's log.

"Still nothing, I see."

"Not to date, Skipper," The Chief said from off to the left, where he was observing the ship's systems as the crew finished the morning's checklist.

Reid sighed audibly, tilting his head back so he could

stare up at the metal above him.

They'd been sitting in the deep black for two days by this point, waiting for their next orders. The extraction mission was nearly a week in their wake, and all they'd gotten from Command was to 'sit tight' and wait for new orders.

That was both unusual and freaking *boring*.

Reid had signed up for the work he did because sitting still was something you rarely had to deal with when you were part of the Gaian irregulars. Their cover with the Empire and the local polities was that they were surplus to needs personnel, people who took jobs on the cheap because they were looking to build up their fortunes with the Gaian regular forces that were represented by the Archangel Gunboats.

Hungry mercenaries, looking for a buck and willing to go anywhere for a job.

In the chaos surrounding the Empire after the end of the war with Earth, that was an easy way to guarantee an interesting life... albeit a short one for most who attempted it. Their secret, of course, was that they had rather a lot more support than the rest and weren't concerned with turning a profit, for the most part. If it built their reputation, the Terran forces that remained in the Black were more than willing to unload a hell of a lot more than a job was worth to ensure it was done right.

They were getting more back than just money, after all.

In the years since Marcus had taken up the standard, his crews alone had returned *mountains* of data that had been dutifully sent along from the Nest to Prometheus. To what end? Well, no one ever told him, to be honest, and while he had asked a few times, no one seemed to know.

Not that it was classified, at least not as far as anyone knew, they just didn't know.

The military forces that had survived Earth's fall were weird sometimes, if he were being honest about things, but they all just kept doing their thing and hoped that somehow it would all turn out to have a purpose and a meaning when it was all over. Frankly, Marcus had sort of given up much hope for that if he were being brutally honest with himself.

These days it felt more and more like they were all just going through the motions, hiding from the truth that there *was no meaning* to it all, because if anyone admitted that truth... well, it would all fall apart, and they'd all had enough of things falling apart.

Even him.

So he buried that belief and didn't mention it to anyone else, for fear that saying it aloud would make it real, and just went on doing the job as best he could.

It wasn't a bad life, the life of a pretend mercenary. He got to stick it to the Empire in small ways, turn a ton of pirates into expanding gasses, and once in a while even feel like he'd accomplished something... whether he had or not.

It was the moments like now, though, when he and his crew were waiting there... in the black... that the dark thoughts came back to prey on him.

*Just give us another mission, I can't take this sitting and waiting much longer.*

It was a sad truth, but he'd rather be fighting for his life than thinking about how he was living.

*****

**The *Nest***

"Admiral, incoming contact."

Passer looked up, "Identification?"

"Transponder is live, it's the Casino."

Passer let out a breath he'd been holding, "Clear them all the way to the primary hangar, inform Cardsharp that I'll meet her there."

"Aye, Admiral."

Morgan let the signal disconnect as he got to his feet and started moving. The Nest was one of two large population centers left to the Terran humans since the fall of Earth. Established in the latter days of the war, it had begun as a refueling depot and little more, intended as a base deep within Imperial controlled space.

Built to resupply the Archangels on their deep infiltration runs into the Empire and the so called Free Stars, the Nest eventually became a refuge for Terran civilian and military personnel that were able to escape the fall of Sol, mostly on North American Confederation warships under orders from the Admiral and the Commodore to save as many as they could before the Empire and the Kardashev Network finished their work.

Unlike the other main facility still in Confederate control, *Prometheus*, the Nest was deep in Empire territory bordering right up on the Free Stars polities. Any approach to the Rogue world was carefully monitored, and even more carefully hidden.

The Nest was a Rogue World, originating from some system none of them had ever discovered despite some attempts by their researchers to do just that. An ice world, what atmosphere it had was mostly generated by the tectonic movements below the surface that were still active due to the planet having an usually large moon for its size.

Everything else had long since condensed into liquid and then frozen solid over the likely *millenia* the world had been wandering the Galaxy, free from any star to call its own. It was a rich world, in its own right. Frozen methane and other fuels were there for the taking, right on the surface, while plenty of valuable minerals were still spewing out from the occasional tectonic action.

Food was in short supply, at least until proper facilities had been built, but almost everything else a space faring culture might need was just there for the taking.

No one had intended it to be a home for refugees, but when the time came, they'd all been grateful to have it.

*Even if the neighbors are a little problematic,* Morgan thought wryly as he stepped off the elevator and headed for the hangar section.

Building up the facility had taken decades, and it wasn't done by a long way, but for all that the dark and frozen world had become a home to thousands of displaced refugees from Earth… and, somehow, it worked. Morgan wasn't sure how, if he were being honest, but people were adaptable he supposed.

"Admiral!"

"As you were," He waved off the deck crew as they offered up salutes, "I'm told the Casino is inbound."

"Sir, yes. We're about to open the blast doors."

"Understood," Morgan nodded, gesturing, "Someone bring me a breather."

"Yes Sir!"

A crewman in purple rushed over and handed him a breather unit that he slipped over his head and quickly checked the seals.

"Well, be about it gentlemen, ladies. We don't have all night."

"Aye, Admiral! Brace! Brace! Brace! Blast doors opening!"

Morgan watched as the big doors cracked open and

a whistling filled the large room, the pressure equalizing as what little external atmosphere mixed with the air in the hangar and the pressure dropped precipitously. He shivered as the temperature dropped to match, too fast to feel right, but somehow not as fast as one might think at the same time.

He knew it was far colder than it felt, but the low pressure kept the heat from being pulled from his body since there was less air to transfer the heat away.

Ironically, in a vacuum, even at its coldest... two hundred degrees below or more, it could take *hours* to freeze. Heat transfer via radiative cooling was the least efficient way to lose temperature, and that was all that was left when you took away conduction and convection along with the atmosphere.

So even as the temperature hit over a hundred below, Morgan did little more than shiver a little as he looked out through the big open doors at the black sky beyond until he spotted the star that separated from the rest and began to grow rapidly.

The crews cleared the deck quickly as the Casino rapidly approached, retros firing at the last moment to slow the ship as it settled in the large hangar and the doors began to rumble shut behind it. The ship was still settling to the deck as the air rushed back into the room, and Morgan felt the warmth return.

*Let's hope they got what we need,* He thought with grim determination, *We don't have enough people or ships left for more than one last shot.*

One good shot.

That was all he prayed for, since Sol Fall.

One. Good. Shot.

The time was coming, he knew that for certain. Morgan

Passer just hoped that it hadn't taken too long to arrive.

*****

# CHAPTER 10

Fleet Commander Shiran grunted as he examined his orders, straight from the homeworld the courier ship had arrived with the next set of instructions that he was to follow to the letter.

*The Drasin finished their 'meal' slightly ahead of expectations,* Shiran thought as he considered his next moves.

With their replication ability sabotaged, the beasts were rapidly approaching the end of their line in a most literal way. According to the reports from the Homeworld, they had less than another ten replications among the main body of their hosts.

It was possible, likely even, some some few earlier generation beasts were being held back in reserve, but those would be dealt with in the good time of the Empire's forces. For the immediate future his task was to draw them out to the end of the bulk of the Drasin forces and leave them dead as they'd left worlds in their own wake.

It was a job that Shiran was more than pleased to see through, though he did have multiple requests out now for reinforcements as the Drasin were a brutal and unyielding foe, even in the face of the obvious superiority of the Empire's forces. With his current forces, Shiran believed that he could still complete the mission as assigned, but it would be far closer than it should ever be.

One miscalculation would leave the Drasin free to close on the homeworld, possibly to take out the heart and soul of the Empire's strength in their very throes of death.

That would be a disaster, of course, so he had no doubt that the Empire's regents would ensure that it never came about.

*In the meantime, however...*

"Issue new orders," He announced, tapping on his console to send along data files as he spoke. "The fleet will regroup at the following locations, coordinates to follow."

"Yes, Fleet Commander..."

The fleet would be underway in short order, and with that the next battlespace would be defined.

*****

### *Gaia's Revenge*

"Stephan, they are moving once more."

Steph grunted as he got up and moved over to the closest display, "What does it look like, Milla?"

His wife shook her head as she poured over the data, "I am uncertain thus far, however it seems like more of the same if you forced me to estimate."

Looking over the data he could see what she meant and nodded in agreement, "So it would appear. They're gluttons for punishment, but cowards they're not."

And they certainly weren't, of that he could be completely confident. While any Terran force would play shadow games with the enemy, hit and run, ambushes, even just straight up booby trapping the projected battlefield, the Empire seemed intent on slugging it out with them in close quarters every step of the way. They'd only broken contact thus far in order to regroup and come back even more determined to get bloody.

It would almost be admirable, if it weren't so goddamned *stupid.*

Steph had learned how to run a fight from Eric, and the one thing that had always come through was that you did *not* sacrifice your own people unless you had no other choice. Final stands happened, yes, God, Gaia, and every surviving Terran had learned that the hard way by this point, but Eric had always been firm that if you ever found yourself in one... you'd failed already. All that was left was to minimize the failure and make the enemy pay for whatever they managed to win.

The Empire seemed determined to bleed off their *own* people damned near as much as the enemy, like they were ready to fail over and over again by their own design, and that just set his nerves to chill.

*They're like ants more than people,* Steph thought grimly. *Almost as alien as the Drasin themselves in their thinking.*

No terran force would have the discipline to keep coming back for more like this, or not many at least.

One last stand? Yeah, Steph could turn damned near any Terran group into a fighting force that would make any enemy think twice and regret for the rest of their *lives* pushing them into that sort of situation. But to ask them to survive it, then turn around and do it *again*? Over and over again?

The number of people who could do that dropped *fast*.

"Well, whatever they're up to, they're moving." He said wearily. "So we're up. Signal Prometheus, let them know that the fighting is about to kick off again and we'll let them know when and where."

"Yes, Stephan." Milla said, working quickly at her station.

"What's our state?" He asked as he stretched out and walked across the command deck to the suspension field.

"All systems are operating precisely as intended."

"Alright," He smiled as he activated the system and

lifted the ship easily off the deck, his vision becoming filled with the sensor feeds of the small gunboat. "Let's get to work."

*****

The hive could feel the target now, it was close.

The awakening world, where they'd slept for... a long time. The world where they'd been defeated, so very long ago, and where their hated enemy... one of the interminable red band that had infected the galaxy... no, the universe.

The infection that had infected even the *hive*.

It had to be cut out, destroyed to the last. Only then would the hive itself be permitted to end its own existence to preserve the pure existence of the universe.

That was the one thing that drove them, from group to individual drone.

The day that they would be able to rest, knowing that their task had been completed.

It was a long way off, the hive knew that well, but every step drew them closer... and they trusted well that they were not alone. The great purity of existence would be preserved, at all cost. The next step, though, was just ahead.

The hive rarely felt much about each action it took. Most of the time they were just the natural evolution of steps that had come before.

It traveled, it ate, it reproduced. The red band was to be eliminated, but even that was generally just another action like the others.

This time, however, the hive felt a vindictive pleasure in the actions. One that it had felt in the past, but rarely. Few of the red band truly mattered, but these ones did.

These ones would be afforded... special focus.

Ahead of the hive's path, the bubbles of *life* were once more forming to impede its progress. Beyond those, however... the *target* was drawing closer.

*Almost.*

\*\*\*\*\*

### Imperial Cruiser *From the Flames*

Kaela gritted her teeth but remained silent as she oversaw the operations.

Their orders were clear, and there was nothing she could do about them other than see them executed to the best of her ability but in moments like this she could feel doubt that she'd never expected to feel concerning her loyalties to the Empire.

*This is insanity, we've thrown so much away and now they want us to throw even more to the void?*

She knew the reasoning, though most of her fellows did not. The Drasin were trapped by their so-called leash. It was a recursive flaw in their regenerative matrix, one that had been put into the originator on the Homeworld where the beast had been located.

She knew this because she had been party to some information that shouldn't have been available to her clearance levels, but the incident at the stellar hive had forced the issue. It was also quite possibly why she and her crew were now on the front lines of every battle since.

Having her executed would have been cleaner, but executing an entire crew just because one of them *might* have heard something they shouldn't was a bit much for Imperial Command. Getting some use out of them where they'd almost certainly die in the process was much easier to excuse, she suspected... though she didn't know for certain of course.

Other ships had been pulled off the line for repairs,

however, while the *Flames* were forced to make do on the fly with what they could manage.

Her crew had done well, made miracles even, but their luck would run out soon enough.

*Luck always does.*

"Ship's Commander! Targets approaching within maximum range!"

"Hold all weapons," She ordered. Maximum range was not *effective* range, and she fully intended to do her duty to the best of her ability.

"Weapons Hold, Yes Commander!"

She rather wished that the Empire had managed to properly reverse engineer the Flame Bringers negative matter weapons, that sort of firepower would be invaluable here and now. Unfortunately from what she'd read up on, there was nothing particularly special about their weapons. The technology was easily replicable, it just was so insane that no one wanted to touch the damned things.

She certainly wouldn't willingly allow anyone to put one of the evil little systems on her ship... well, not under normal conditions at least.

*Exceptions might have been made for this,* Kaela thought grimly as she looked over the command deck of the cruiser and watched the wave coming in on them from so far away, but at such a high speed.

"Weapons ready!" She ordered as the first Drasin units crossed into a closer range space.

"All weapons ready!"

She waited half a breath, then nodded, "Fire."

"Weapons firing, Ship's Commander!"

In moments she knew the dying would begin again, and this time Kaela Eurydice welcomed it.

*****

### Gaia's Revenge

"Well, there they go again," Steph said wearily as the first of the energy readings spiked across his feeds.

Milla and Tyke were in the command deck with him, and both just looked a little sickly.

"I have no sympathies for the Empire, particularly their military," Tyke grumbled, "but this is just painful."

Steph sighed, but couldn't disagree.

"Painful is not the word," Milla said, her voice thick, "This... this is not even insanity, it is something I do not know the words for."

"Their orders are to bleed the Drasin," Steph said stonily, "Ours are to watch both sides bleed each other."

"I get that," Tyke ground out, "but there's got to be an endgame, right? More than just hope they kill each other?"

"Let's hope."

*****

Commander Shiran watched the reports flood through his system with satisfaction.

The numbers were very nearly perfectly on the mark with the estimations out of the Imperial Homeworld. He had been concerned that the Command chain had suffered too greatly to continue to be operable after the initial strikes so many years ago, but despite the seemingly chaotic nature of the orders that had been coming through, he found that especially as time went on, the predictions and orders had largely been *right* despite their costly nature.

That history of being correct had led him to accept that the orders were fundamentally right, no matter how badly they mauled his forces.

If this was the price of victory, he would pay it proudly.

"The forward lines have completely engaged, Fleet Commander."

"I see it. Send in the second and third lines," He ordered.

"Orders issued. Flanking lines are closing in."

While some data from the forward positions was coming back in near real time, most of the details were limited to lightspeed transmission rules. That meant that while he could see enemy positions, along with those of the ships under his command, in real time... many of the other details of the fight were dragging along behind, making monitoring the situation a rather complicated affair.

For all those complications, though, the modelling of the data was keeping him well apprised of the state of the battle as it progressed.

"Flanking lines have engaged."

"Excellent."

\*\*\*\*\*

### Gaia's Revenge

"There's the reinforcements," Tyke said as they watched the fighting erupt across their scanners through the projected augmentation display. "They're going all in, no question."

"The Drasin are not holding anything back either," Milla said, nodding. "This level of attrition will most certainly cost the hive dearly."

"Couldn't happen to a better bunch," Steph said, calling up a closer look at the screens. "The Empire's main line is pushing forward again, they might just push the Drasin back this time."

"Possible," Milla said slowly as he gestured, "However I do not believe that is the intent."

Steph looked to where she was pointing and hummed as he noted the shift in the Drasin deployment.

"You're right, they had reserves they didn't commit," He said as more of the hive monsters flowed out of the black and began to overwhelm the Imperial line. "That's more clever than I expected from them."

"They are not stupid beings," Milla chastised him. "They have an intelligence that does not align with our own, but it is not inferior I fear."

Steph nodded absently as he nudged the ship in closer to get a better feed from the fighting. They were only a few light seconds out, running as black as a starless night sky, but even that little delay was making it hard to get a good idea of the scope of the fighting.

"I think it may be time," Tyke advised.

"Maybe," Steph said. "But that's not our call to make. Send the update."

"Aye aye, skipper."

*****

# CHAPTER 11

**The Nest**

Morgan looked over the data from the first pull they'd extracted from the *Casino's* take. It didn't take a genius for him to decide what the next play was.

"Alright, Jenn, I want you to get your crew ready and get this to *Prometheus*," He ordered, "I'll have the original take delivered to the *Casino* as soon as we're finished pulling the copy."

Jennifer Samuels nodded, "I figured. Priority?"

"You're authorized to transition."

She whistled softly, but nodded in agreement.

The Archangels rarely had authorization to use the Transition drive, just as a matter of operational security. A straight warp flight between the Nest and Prometheus would take a few days, however, with the T-Drive they'd be there within an hour of launch. All of that time being how long it took them to get out of the gravity well of the Nest and then into the gravity well of the star that Prometheus orbited.

"Got it." She confirmed. "Any ideas what we're looking at?"

Morgan shrugged, "At this point? Just guesses, but I think we're going to have to deploy in full."

"FULL Full?" She asked, just to be sure.

The Gaians had been their cover for a long time now, and a full deployment would blow that out of the water. Not every Gaian was from Earth, either. They'd been recruiting over the years. Granted, all the recruits were assigned to captured vessels, mostly Destroyers, a few cruisers... but they were a formidable force all the same.

Morgan sighed, shaking his head slowly as he considered the implications for himself.

"I don't know. Definitely bringing the Heroics out of hiding with the Priminae, but that's not a big revelation anymore."

"There is that," She agreed. The continued existence of the Terran Heroic Class cruisers had been revealed to at least some degree at the Drasin Kardashev construct just a few months earlier. The Empire knew they were around, and still in contact with the Priminae, of that there was no question. "I don't know how much the Gaians add to our fleet power."

"We'll run the numbers in conjunction with Prometheus," Morgan said. "But if we have a chance to *end* the Drasin... we're taking it."

Jennifer nodded slowly, "Roger that, Sir."

"Now go on, get your ship ready. This will be delivered as soon as we've finished the download."

"Yes sir."

\*\*\*\*\*

Morgan watched her leave before he turned back to the system that was copying the data down, taking a seat at the console so he could run a few quick searches while it was working.

*They definitely knew what they were doing,* He thought grimly. *The historical data alone is damning. They unleashed those monsters on the Priminae without much of a thought.*

The *billions* that had died due to the Imperial actions,

just over the last fifty years, was a terrifying number. Almost all focused on civilian populations, with no real sign that they had any thought to even focusing on military assets.

*The Empire fights like a terrorist organization, not like regular military. Even a few centuries ago we were trying to at least minimize the wasteful loss of civilian lives, if only because they were a resource that the victor would want to utilize. The Empire... they're broken, somewhere, somehow.*

He supposed it wasn't completely at odds with human history, certainly in world war one both sides had gleefully utilized chemical warfare against one another and that was about as indiscriminate a weapon as one might imagine. The difference was, once they realized how dangerous it was to their own people, both sides stepped back from the brink.

The Empire had gone all in on a weapon that not only *could* destroy them, but actively *desired* to do so... and he was looking at the proof that they *knew it* from the start.

Morgan made some notes on a pad and attached it to the side of the storage device he would be returning to Jennifer in short order.

*This has to end, it has to be stopped once and for all.*

*****

### Casino

"Clear this deck and get everything strapped in for liftoff," Jennifer called as she walked up the ramp and into the gunboat. "We're out on assignment in fifteen, if that. Move it!"

The crew looked at her in surprise for only a second before they jumped to it. She left them to their jobs and made her way out of the small cargo area into the narrow corridors of the ship.

The *Casino* was mostly ready to go as they'd not used much in the way of consumables on the last mission, other than a crap load of munitions for the Marines. They could load that at Prometheus, though, and there was nothing between the Nest and there that would require them to deploy Marines at all, thankfully she supposed.

"Skipper."

"Colonel," She said as she entered officer's country and nodded to Keenan. "Make sure your men are ready to move out. We're heading for Prometheus."

Keenan didn't look surprised, "My people are already securing their areas, I expected as much. Do we have time to load up on what we expended?"

"Probably not entirely, but we are pushing what we can on board even now," Jennifer said. "We'll requisition what's missing on Prometheus, it's a straight shot from here anyway."

"Yes Ma'am." Keenan agreed, however much she disliked the idea of flying light, speed sometimes mattered more. "What did they find on the data pull?"

"Not nearly enough yet, but enough to say that we need to get the Prometheus systems on it. They've got data crunchers that we couldn't touch in a thousand years." Jenn said. "I expect we'll be side shipping a copy to the Priminae too, but that's not official yet."

"Fair. We'll be ready."

*****

Jennifer was running pre-flight when the word came in that a fast courier had run the data back on board from the Nest's command center.

"All hands, lock it all down. We're cleared for takeoff in five, I want to be moving the moment the flight path is confirmed clear." She said over the comms. "We're heading for Prometheus, and be advised we will be engaging the Transition drive. So suck it up or grab a barf bag, I don't care which. Either way, we're moving."

\*\*\*\*\*

### Prometheus Facility

"Doctor Palin."

"Huh? Yes?"

The old man barely showed any interest as he looked up at hearing his name called. Very few people had ever managed to get much of a reaction out of him in his life, and none of them were on the alien facility any longer.

"You're needed."

Palin rolled his eyes, "I doubt that, but where would I be needed?"

The young messenger flushed, realizing that he'd given no details.

"Sorry, Doctor, I should have said that the Council has summoned you. There's been some developments with the Empire. I don't know any more details."

Palin sighed, getting himself painfully to his feet.

"Very well." He said, "Lead the way, but take it easy on an old man. I'm not as spry as I once was."

"Uh, Yes sir." The young man said, gesturing before he started off.

Palin followed, not quite hobbling along but certainly moving with slow deliberation in each step. He smiled to himself as he saw the young messenger growing more and more frustrated by the moment, though he had to give it to the kid for keeping himself from blowing up from the clear irritation he was feeling.

They were about halfway to the Council room when the kid seemed to come to a decision.

"Pardon my asking, Sir…"

Palin waited for a moment, but when the silence stretched out too long he snorted, "Well, out with it, pup."

The messenger took a breath, "Why don't you go in for the rejuvenation treatments? You're the only person I've met who looks… ah…"

"Like a decrepit old man?" Palin asked, amused.

"I wouldn't have phrased it that way, Sir."

"Call me Doctor or Edward," Palin answered, "Not sir, and never 'Ed'."

"Uh, of course, Doctor."

"And to answer your question, it's private."

The messenger bobbed his head, looking away, "Of course, Doctor."

Palin let the uncomfortable silence drag on a while longer until they were almost to the council rooms.

"I've lived long enough, seen enough, done more than enough." He said as the doors to the council rooms opened. "I carry enough regrets now, I don't need another century or more to stack more on top. You're young, maybe you'll never feel the way I do. I hope not, kid. If you can live forever and not feel like you've failed every moment, do it."

He took a deep breath, "But I can't."

The messenger stared at him as Palin moved past him and stepped into the council rooms, "Thank you for the escort."

"Uh… Yessir."

Palin let the doors close, then turned around and started making his way to the main meeting room as he put the young man out of his thoughts.

*Let's make a few more regrets before it's my time.*

\*\*\*\*\*

"Well this is quite the gathering," Edward said as he looked at the people in the main meeting room.

He'd expected the council, mostly political officers of varying types, but instead he was looking at a cadre of the brightest minds on the Facility.

"Welcome Doctor Palin," Doctor Mark Andrew gestured, "Please take a seat. You'll be needed soon, I believe."

"What's this about?" He asked as he moved over and slumped stiffly into the offered chair.

"Two days ago, the *Casino* raided an Imperial world."

Palin blinked in surprise as murmurs of surprise rippled through the assembled group. They all knew that the Casino was one of the Archangels, and had been assigned to the *Gaian Mercenary* forces. That was a deep cover assignment, intended primarily to get them closer to Imperial space for intelligence gathering purposes.

If they were *raiding* an Imperial world…

"I see," Palin said, his calm response silencing the murmurs. "We're moving to the next phase then. What did they retrieve?"

"The contents of a shielded Quantum Processor and Data Matrix."

That just left the room in shocked silence. Few of them even knew about the existence of such systems, Palin expected, but he had already peered into a captured data flow from one that had been located on an Imperial Cruiser just a few months earlier.

He leaned in, "Did they get everything?"

"They believe so."

"Alright," Palin said, "We'll need full computer access to our own processor systems to break the encryption, search protocols will require Virtual Intelligence assistance, so that's going to need every available cycle we can scrounge up. I'm assuming, of course, that we're on a time table?"

Andrew held up a hand to calm the immediate gut reaction objections to what Palin had just demanded.

"We are. You'll have everything we can spare," Andrew said. "All other projects are suspended for the duration."

The director looked around the room, "Allow me to reiterate and make this very clear... We've been at war for most of our lives now, but for the last three decades it's been a cold one. That's about to be over. Your personal projects are suspended, the Empire and the Drasin are *all* that matter now. Am I clear?"

No one had any more objections it seemed, but Palin ignored the silence as his brain was already working on likely approaches to breaking the data he was about to be gifted with.

*****

**Prometheus Control**

"Contact registered."

"Signature?"

"Transition pulse... matter transport. It's a ship. We're waiting on the transponder, should be a few hours."

"Less, if it's scheduled. We're expecting the Casino. Look for warp signal."

"Roger that... warp signal detected. Strong blue shift doppler, they're inbound, coming in hot."

"Power defenses."

"Sir?"

"Just because it's *probably* the Casino doesn't mean it *is* the Casino. Power the defenses."

"Yes sir. Defenses online and active."

*****

## Casino

"We're pinged, Skipper."

"Send the response," Jennifer said as she kept her ship moving on a hard acceleration toward the facility. "On fast repeat."

"Yes Ma'am."

Prometheus' defensive network was nothing to scoff at, and she knew that it could turn them to expanding gas in an instant, but that was nothing new for anyone working the Archangel program. The challenge response went out on command, but the Casino wasn't waiting for it to get there.

She had her orders, and they didn't include poking around waiting for an answer.

They were moving fast enough as it was to *outrun* the challenge response, but that was a small detail. Jennifer was more focused on making sure that the particulates her ship was gathering up in the gravity well ahead of them were about to be dispersed in a safe direction.

"Second ping!"

"Ignore it. Prometheus is thirty seconds out," She said, shifting their course at the last moment to enter a high velocity orbit of the facility world.

*****

## Prometheus Control

"They're coming hot, Sir!"

"That's their orders, keep them painted…"

"They're on a collision course!"

"Easy. Three… two… now."

The contact shifted course as predicted, snapping into an insanely fast orbit of the world, coming around in a fraction of a second before it came into alignment with the red dwarf star the facility world orbited and abruptly killed its warp fields.

The pulse of pure destructive radiation and particulates that tore off toward the star made every man and woman there shudder even as the system *finally* pinged with the challenge response.

"Casino challenge response confirmed… and we have visual confirmation."

The control officer snorted as he turned to his console.

"Casino, Prometheus. You ruined a few sets of underwear here, I hope you have the data."

"Sorry for the brown pants, Prometheus. Roger that on the Data. Request approach clearance."

"Granted."

\*\*\*\*\*

# CHAPTER 12

**Imperial Cruiser** *From the Flames*

"Maintain fire!"

Kaela had to shout her order, pitching her voice over the general noise of the systems and the loud shouting as the deck crew tried to coordinate faster than their systems were able to manage.

The Drasin were pushing like they always did, the lines of the battle intertwining as the Imperial second and third divisions closed in from the flanks while her first division held the enemy's focus in the center. They'd cut down dozens... *hundreds...* possible more than that even, but the monsters just kept coming like there was no end to them.

"The core is down to eighty percent, Ship's Commander!"

Kaela grimaced, but just nodded curtly to acknowledge the information, and focused back on the fighting. The planetary masses held within their core were the only thing that kept the ship mobile and in fighting trim. If they dropped too low, everything... even life support would be gone.

At that point they'd no longer have any chance of defense against the horde.

*We need enough time to replenish our mass, but the enemy is unlikely to offer it... and even if they did, I am far from certain that Command would.*

With no option to retreat, and nothing ahead but the

enemy, they really only had the one option.

"Continue the engagement," She ordered simply. "Full power to the weapons. If we expend all our mass, then we expend it for the Empire!"

The crew managed a weak cheer at that, but she was willing to overlook a lack of enthusiasm given the circumstance so long as they followed her orders.

The *From the Flames* was leading the vanguard, using its own warp fields to crush the beasts even as the beams burned them from space around them. More and more of them were annihilated, but even more yet continued to show up on the scanners.

"There's no end of them, Ship's Commander! We still show more arriving!"

Kaela clinched her teeth, but didn't snap at the man for reporting the facts even if she'd have preferred he kept it to himself. She could see it, so could everyone that needed to, it didn't need to be yelled out in the open air like that, but technically he was acting to regulations and there was nothing to be gained here by disrupting the crew in mid fight with a reprimand.

"More to kill then," She said firmly. "What are our orders from Fleet Command?"

"We haven't heard from them, Ship's Commander! They're too far delayed from our location!"

Kaela swore under her breath, but had to make a call.

"Fine, open a comm to all stations!"

"Comms open!"

"This is the *From the Flames*," She said clearly. "First division, advance on the enemy! Give no chance for any to escape us!"

She cut the channel, in case anyone wanted to try to countermand her, and nodded to the front.

"Full power to the warp fields, take us into the enemy line!"

*****

**Gaia's Revenge**

"Gutsy order," Steph acknowledged as they listened in to the Imperial communications from their position close to the fighting.

The *Revenge* was fully in stealth mode, but even so they were close enough to the fighting that even the radiation from the weapon strikes was raising the temperature of the ship's internal compartments at a rapid pace. Steph knew that they wouldn't be able to hold position for much longer without risking the overheating of key systems, but he was determined to hold out as long as he could in order to gather the intelligence they needed.

"She's taking her own advice," Tyke said with a nod as the ship pushed ahead of the fighting, putting itself in a vulnerable position.

Steph could tell that the Imperial Commander was trying to rally the wall of ships that were starting to falter under the onslaught, but for a moment he couldn't tell if it would work or not. If the *flames* fell too soon, Steph was certain it would backfire badly.

They didn't fall, however, and in short once ship, then another, and then more broke forward and backed up the *Flames.*

"They are very brave," Milla admitted.

"Or stupid. It's hard to tell the difference, honestly, especially in the middle of fighting like that," Steph admitted with a wry grin. "Don't ask me how I know."

His wife snorted, "I know precisely how you know, Stephan."

He just grinned at her before looking back and becoming more serious.

"It won't do them much good, though," He said, "There's too many. The Drasin didn't eat that whole star system, but they did give it a good old college try. I've never seen this many outside one of their mega-structures."

Milla hummed in agreement while Tyke just nodded.

Steph shook his head, "We'll have to make a decision soon. I just don't know which way the numbers are going to fall."

\*\*\*\*\*

### From the Flames

"All flanks, close in!" Kaela ordered over the open comms, "Hit them from every side while we center the battle!"

The *Flames* was sitting at the middle of a fury she'd never imagined in her life, but somehow they were still alive and continuing to fight back. How they hadn't had the entire ship torn out from under them by the Drasin by this point, she honestly wasn't sure, but it didn't matter any longer.

They were all committed.

Orders from Fleet Command were coming in too late to be useful, often the ship the orders were being sent to were already gone before the signal arrived. Inwardly she cursed the cowardly bastard sitting back there in safety, trying to fight remotely like he was assigned to some desk job.

Until Fleet Command ordered a withdrawal, however, the fight would go on.

One way, or the other.

The *Flames* was being pressed in from three sides, and their singularity mass was now down to seventy three percent and dropping from the fury of their weapons fire and warp field generation alone. The Drasin had not flinched at their losses, massive though they were, and she knew that even if the order to withdraw came in… it wouldn't matter for the *From the Flames*.

They were in too far, but others would be able to escape if nothing else.

*It will have to do.*

Now they just needed fleet command to give the damned order.

*****

**Imperial Fleet Command**

Markys watched the fighting through the delay, barely reacting as the battle tally continued to climb.

The Drasin were being slaughtered, of course, but their numbers were exceeding the earlier projections by some significant portion.

*No matter. The projected outcome is still within the range we were advised from Central Command. The increase in their numbers just means that they'll hit the generation limit that much sooner.*

"Fleet Commander? We'll lose the first division soon if we don't order the withdrawal."

"And?" He asked coldly, turning away from the speaker.

The First Division had made their decision, moving into the fight without orders. They had accepted their fates, and far be it for him to refuse their generous sacrifice.

"Advise the flanks to prepare for withdrawal," He said simply.

"Yes, Fleet Commander."

\*\*\*\*\*

## Gaia's Revenge

"Orders just sent through to the fleets, Steph."

Steph half turned looking over the digital transcript before wincing, "Ouch. Cutting their losses, I suppose."

"That's what it looks like," Tyke confirmed.

Steph nodded, making an adjustment from his own board and sending out a quick pulse message of his own.

It didn't take long to receive a reply.

"We've seen enough."

\*\*\*\*\*

## *From The Flames*

Kaela gritted her teeth as she felt the deck shudder under her feet.

"Secure the quadrant, increase the fire rate to cover for the flank as they withdraw."

"Yes, Ship's Commander... That will overheat our emitters."

"Melt them down."

"Yes ship's Commander!"

The battle was silent, of course, but she could hear the screaming all the same. The screams of the dying, and the screams of the monsters out there, both somehow managed to echo through her mind as Kaela watched the fighting progress. The flanking lines were withdrawing, but she held as much of her front line in place as she could marshal.

A few had followed the withdrawal order anyway, but they were destroyed in the process when the Drasin managed to get in past their forward warp fields and access the ships' hulls from the sides. The rest held the line as they quickly realized that there wasn't any way they were getting out alive anyway.

"Ship's Commander Kirov is ordering his flankers to return to their positions…"

"Open a line!" She snarled, "Transmit to all ships. Kirov, and all flankers, *WITHDRAW*. Follow your orders, you damned fools! You can escape, we cannot. If you die here for nothing, I will find you in whatever comes after and you will not enjoy what comes then! Die later, for the Empire!"

"Kirov has withdrawn the orders," her communications officer said a few moments later. "Flanker divisions are withdrawing."

"Good. Provide them with…"

An alarm startled her, if only because it wasn't one that had sounded through the entire battle to this point.

"What is that?" Kaela asked, not able to identify it instantly.

"Radiative burst, FTL particle radiation. Unknown signature, Ship's Commander, but we have a linked file. Sealed."

"Send it t-"

Once again she was cut off, this time by a shout from the tactical position.

"Ship's Commander! New contacts, they came out of nowhere! Cruiser class…"

"Imperial reinforcements?" Someone asked, but Kaela ignored the question.

She knew that wouldn't be the case.

"Ship's Commander, we have a signal over all comm

channels."

"Give it to me," She ordered.

"Commander Kaela, of the Cruiser *From the Flames,* this is the Terran battle cruiser Bellerophon. Advise you hunker down, it's going to get hot. Bellerophon out."

Kaela's eyes widened as she considered those words, blood flushing from her face.

"What are they..."

"Shut up," She snapped over the questions, "Open a channel to all front line vessels."

"Channel open, Ship's Commander."

"All ships, reverse warp. Maximum power!" She ordered. "Forget the Drasin! Reverse warps *now*!"

\*\*\*\*\*

### Bellerophon

"Kill the comms," Jason Roberts said with a bitter twist of his lip. "That's more warning than they deserve."

"Comms clear, Sir."

"Torpedos away, all banks flushed clean."

Jason nodded, "Tell the powder monkeys to start winding up a new salvo."

"Aye sir."

"All ships, proceed."

\*\*\*\*\*

The Terran battle cruisers flared their warp fields and charged after the torpedo salvos they'd sent on ahead of themselves, following the anti-matter weapons more closely than any sane mind might charitably consider wise.

The Heroic class ships didn't blink even when the first of the antimatter weapons found their targets, creating bubbles of annihilation in the distance that could be seen eclipsing and swallowing Drasin swarms.

Right into the holes left by the retreating *divisions*, five cruisers took the place of nearly *fifty*, turning the Black into a lightshow to end all lightshows as the battle suddenly surged in intensity.

*****

"By the emperor, what am I seeing?"

Kaela couldn't answer the question, as she'd not seen anything quite like it herself despite having seen these ships in action once before.

*They were holding back all along. Possibly they still are.*

Hatred seethed in her, the flame bringers were the *monsters* that burned *millions* of people across dozens of planets of the Empire but she forced a lid on it as overseeing her own line of ships took precedence in that moment.

They were all reversing at maximum warp, focusing their weapons and computer cycles on picking off the strays that were attempting to take advantage of the ships' shield rebalancing to gain access to their hulls.

Meanwhile, however, those five ships were somehow managing to center the entire battle around their position as the Drasin swarms redirected their fury onto the flame bringer's vessels.

"What are they doing?"

"They're... interlocking warp fields?"

Kaela scowled, looking over the data, and realized quickly that her officer's guess was likely the right one. The five ships were so close to one another that their fields *had* to be interacting with one another. The precision of control that took left her numb for a moment, but she had to push it off and stay focused on the task.

*Let them and the Drasin kill one another, the lot of them be damned to the void for all I care.*

\*\*\*\*\*

### Bellerophon

"We appeared to have rather irritated the enemy, Captain."

"I can see that, Bell," Roberts said steadily. "How are fields holding?"

"I and the other entities are maintaining the balance. Nothing will penetrate our forward phalanx, I swear it."

"Good," He shifted his focus to the rest of the fight.

Jason had never been a fan of the entities, something that made him reluctant to recreate the events that resulted in the creation of both Odysseus and Boudicca, for many reasons that most certainly included the fact that he knew that Bell was acutely aware of his personal reservations.

The levels of precision that they brought to the running of a Heroic class cruiser, however, could not be denied.

*If we'd have them on every ship before the fall of Sol, we may have written a very different history.*

They didn't, however, and the history had been written.

With their forward warps interlocked, they had a damned near impenetrable defense to the front, however that also took their primary beam weapons out of the fight. Nothing would escape the deep gravity slump that the ships *fell* into as they were pushed along at warp, not even the powerful photons of their beam weapons.

That left side arrays and other broadside weapons to be engaged with as they passed through the enemy swarm, keeping up their speed to a high enough level that the Drasin couldn't easily gain access to the ships within their space warps.

The problem with this maneuver was, quite simply, time.

"We're through the swarm, skipper! Clear black ahead!"

Specifically, they didn't have *nearly* enough of it in contact with the enemy to inflict real levels of damage.

"Break Phalanx," Roberts ordered, "Bring us about."

"Aye skipper! Phalanx disengaging, primary thrusters turning us around!"

The starfield spun wildly as they turned, bringing the enemy forces back into view as the Terran ships continued flying *away* from the fight, now with a not insignificant number of the Drasin pouring through space in their pursuit.

"Imperial front line forces have broken contact, Skipper."

"I can see it," Roberts said, ignoring the Imperial ships.

He'd only saved them so that they could kill more Drasin before they died, beyond that he had less than zero interest in their well being.

"Prime Transition Canon waveguides," He ordered, "Lock into the Drasin swarm. Load with Fusion warheads."

"Fusion warheads loaded, T-Cannons primed. Targets locked."

"Fire at will."

*****

# CHAPTER 13

**Gaia's Revenge**

"That's the end of that battle," Steph said quietly as the ships under Robert's command broke contact, leaving the remaining Drasin swarm in disarray, the drones moving in increasingly more agitated circles.

"If we only had a few more ships, we could put paid to this here and now," Tyke grumbled.

"We could, but we wouldn't." Steph said coldly. "We have two enemies, Tyke, the Drasin are just the worst of the two right now... but the Empire is the greater threat in the long run."

"Don't feel right, leaving those things alive, not even like this."

Steph snorted, "If it did feel right, we'd be worse than our enemy."

"Sometimes, I wonder," Milla said softly, somberly. "We do the same things, sometimes. Does that not make us the same?"

"No," Steph's voice was just as somber, but firm. "It doesn't make us good, but we do what we have to, not because it's expedient but because it's necessary. Maybe, if we had better information from the start, we might have avoided this. Maybe we could have talked it out, found middle ground, but we didn't. Mistakes of the past establish the ground rules of the present. The best we can do is try to make less mistakes that the future has to pay for. Our enemy is bound by their mistakes, just as we are by ours."

He sighed, turning away from the battlespace and taking up the controls of the ship again.

"I suspect, if we could see the whole story," Steph said after a moment' silence, "that we would cover our faces in sorrow at how much of all this has been unnecessary. However, Milla… love… we don't get to see the whole story. We have to act from limited data, much of which is likely wrong."

"War is hell," Steph said with finality as he powered the warp and took the *Revenge* out of their parking position. "Not because of the death and suffering, but because most of the time… it turns out to be done for nothing. I'll die for a cause, and be proud to do so… but imagine waking up on the other side and being told that your cause was just smoke and mirrors? All based on assumptions made in error, honestly or not?"

His companions shuddered as they considered it as Steph guided the ship away from the battlespace behind them.

\*\*\*\*\*

**Prometheus Facility**

Edward Palin was waiting when the storage matrix was carried into his lab. The amount of data within was so immense that it was literally faster to walk it directly to his lab and plug straight into his own system than to try to transmit it over any of the systems they had.

He'd be lying if he said he wasn't excited about what it might contain beyond his immediate goals, but for the moment he was putting that all aside.

"Set it over there," He pointed to a station where connections had already been prepared for the matrix.

The Marines didn't say anything, just set the device down and handed him a data slate to sign off on delivery.

Edward snorted, shaking his head, "Even in the face of the worst the universe can throw at us, I can't avoid desk work."

He put the slate down and held up a hand, "If we're going to be pedantic about it, hold on until I confirm the state of the matrix."

"Yes Sir." The young lieutenant said, letting her hands clasped behind her back.

Palin largely ignored her as he plugged the matrix in and got the system running, quickly having it do a checksum scan of the storage directory. It looked clean and passed the check so he turned back to the desk, noting that the Marine was looking at him intently.

"All looks good," He said, signing off on the slate.

"Thank you, Sir," She told him. "Pardon my asking, are you Doctor Palin... from the Odyssey?"

He looked at her, slightly startled, "I am."

"My father worked with you, good to put a face to the stories."

Palin snorted, "Someone told stories about me? I doubt they were complimentary."

She shrugged, "He said that you were a huge pain in the ass, but better at what you did than most anyone else he'd ever heard of."

"And your father was?" Palin asked, lips twitching in amusement.

"Stephen Michaels."

Palin paused, thinking hard, before he shrugged, "Sorry. Can't say I remember him."

She grinned wide, "That's what he told me you'd say."

Palin nodded, confused as he handed the slate back. She took it and in moments her and the other Marines were gone, leaving him with the data matrix. Five minutes after that, He had forgotten the conversation with the Marine lieutenant entirely as he got to work on decoding the Imperial encryption and getting the data ready for full analysis.

*****

"What was that about, Ma'am?"

Amanda Michaels shrugged, "Just had to check if my Dad was exaggerating about the man."

"And was he?" The Sergeant asked, "if you don't mind me asking, at least."

"Not in the least," She said before pausing and cocking her head slightly, "to both questions."

"So your dad knew that guy, Lieutenant?" Dietrich asked, curious.

"They both served on the Odyssey, the first trip out."

The Marines all looked back over their shoulders in surprise.

"That guy? Damn."

Amanda chuckled, "According to dad, just managing Palin was a full time job. He's one of those types that don't care much about anything other than whatever has their interest at the time. He'd drive the other researchers so insane that it became something of a legend on the ship. Captain himself had to intervene more than once."

"Shit." Brad muttered, "Can see what you called him a pain in the ass."

"He also decoded the Priminae language in less than a week, from almost nothing. He's good. Almost as good as he thinks he is, if you listen to dad's rants." She smiled. "Glad to see he's still around. Not a lot of the old Odyssey crew are, these days."

The Marines murmured at that, but they didn't have time to hang around talking about it.

There was always another mission.

*****

*Imperial encryption is a joke, but there's something different about this section.*

Palin was already deep into the data, having pulled out big chunks that were 'protected' by systems he was already familiar with. Despite different encryption routines, they used the same base system, and he cracked them in minutes.

He disregarded that data, dumping it automatically into servers for others to concern themselves with. He was focused on the chunk that remained, the chunk that actually had *good* protections.

*What are you hiding in here, I wonder?* He thought as he directed the data stream to playback over an audio format and cranked the volume up.

The cacophony that resulted from that would undoubtedly have resulted in him getting nigh on endless complaints, had he not managed to get an insulated lab assigned to him. Edward had always worked better with audio over visual work, so he closed his eyes and leaned back in his seat as he subsumed himself in the patterns.

*****

Aiden Pierce looked up as the Captain of the *Casino* entered, her posture reminding of older times.

"At ease," He said with an easy smile. "We're less formal here than we used to be."

"I understand Sir," Jennifer said as she relaxed, "Old

habits when I see those stars."

The Admiral chuckled, gesturing to a seat "Yes, well I do run a tight operation if I do say so myself, but being a martinet here would end… poorly, I suspect."

"I know the feeling, flying with the Archangels is an experience, but we're not exactly the straight and narrow type," She smiled as she dropped into the seat.

"No doubt," He said, amused before he took on a more serious expression. "That was good work, getting the data. Were you identified?"

"No way to know for sure, not until the Empire decides to open fire," She admitted after a moment's thought.

He nodded, "We have to presume that the Gaian cover is gone then. Pity, but I hope that the results will make it worthwhile."

She took a deep breath, "I hope so. More than thirty years, we've been cozying up to the Empire as the Gaians. If we blew that over one operation that didn't return results…"

She shook her head.

"Yes, well, nothing to be said about it now. You had a mission, you completed it. If our Intel was bad, that is not on you."

"No."

They looked up, Jennifer turning around in surprise as the new voice entered the conversation.

"It's on me," The man standing there said, his suit hanging off him in a slightly shabby way.

"Oh bloody… no one's killed you yet?" Jennifer asked, looking at him askance.

He looked surprised, eyes focusing on her, "I wasn't

aware that you knew who I was."

"You're the spook that rode with Crown," She said with no doubt, "Don't know your name, not sure you ever gave anyone your real one, but yeah I know you."

He nodded, "Fair enough. Seamus Gordon, at your service."

Jennifer snorted, "Pardon me if I don't offer my hand. I don't feel like counting my fingers to make sure I got them all back."

Seamus put a hand over his heart, making a show of looking hurt but a humorous glint was noticeable as he shifted his attention to the Admiral.

"Apologies for being late, Admiral, I wanted to stop by the good Doctor's lab before coming in."

Aiden nodded, leaning back in his chair, "And has he made any progress?"

"Have no idea, I started to walk in and the sheer noise was so painful I had to leave."

Jennifer snorted, "That *must* be Palin. He did that on the Odyssey too, the man was a legend. An infamous one, and usually spoken up like you were worried you'd accidentally summon him up if you spoke his name too loudly, but a legend all the same."

"Sadly he's pretty much the same here," Aiden admitted. "We gave him a sound insulate office, one of the better labs actually. Everyone voted unanimously for him to have it, amusingly enough since those labs were pretty hotly fought over by everyone else."

"Yeah sounds about right," Jennifer said with a grin. "The Skipper himself had to go get him to turn the volume down more than once, least if the scuttlebutt was right."

"I'm shocked the man can still hear at all then," Gordon said with a roll of his eyes. "However, I assumed that the noise meant he was still working, so I rushed over here. Again, apologies."

Aiden waved it off, "It's fine. We aren't on a time crunch on this side of things, as much as I wish we were. For now, we have to wait for the intel, and for the results from the Heroic fleet."

Gordon nodded, taking the other seat in the room and crossing his legs as he settled in.

"Indeed," He said, "Still I feel like we are entering the endgame now."

He glanced over at Jennifer, "That would be the reason I pushed for your mission to be made. No other ship under our control could have penetrated that deep into Imperial space and completed that mission, it had to be an Archangel."

"What were you hoping to get?" She asked, eyes narrowing slightly as she looked him over as she wondered just what, really, was worth the sacrifice of the Gaian cover.

"Oh, many things, Captain. I wouldn't risk your cover for any one thing unless I knew for *certain* it was there," Gordon said firmly, "and while we have strong suspicions, we don't know for sure that any one of the items of interest are there. Anything concerning the *leash* the Empire has on the Drasin is a key piece, and if the Drasin are risking everything the way they are... well, that's a strong indication that something is there."

He shrugged, gesturing idly.

"In fact, *anything* the Drasin might be after in those systems is likely worth the sacrifice of your cover," He said simply. "But more than that, I hope to find their history."

"Imperial history?" Aiden blinked, this being the first

he'd heard *that* particular nugget. "I'm sorry, but couldn't we just have found someone willing to talk?"

"Not the polished fiction I'm sure they all learn, no, I want their *true* history." Gordon said, leaning forward as he uncrossed his legs and clasped his hands ahead of him. "All history is fiction of course. On Earth, we had... *maybe* a few decades where photography and video basically ensured that the story was represented reasonably well. Before that it was word of mouth, and after?"

Gordon sighed, "Well video and photography became so easy to fake that word of mouth was by far the more reliable. I expect that the Empire has long been past that point, but I'm hoping that they weren't stupid enough to entirely destroy their history. Somewhere, they must have stored the real events... I just hope it's not held entirely within their entity's mind, but we'll see."

"So you're convinced that the Empire has one?" Jennifer asked, curious.

Gordon snorted, "Earth has one, the Priminae have one... we've even *birthed* new ones, both by accident and intent. Yes, the Empire has at *least* one, on Kraike. I've been in its presence, along with Captain Michaels among others. It didn't show itself, but I know it was there."

Aiden nodded, "We've been sure of this for some time, but what to do about it has long been a very different story."

The wording caught Jennifer's attention, "And now?"

"Now we have a plan."

*****

# CHAPTER 14

**Gaia's Revenge**

Steph reduced the space warping fields and let the ship coast along as it dropped out of FTL, dumping the stored energy from the warp sink in a safe direction, his board chiming softly to get his attention.

"Go for Revenge." He said with an amused quirk of his lips.

"You enjoy saying that far too much," Jason Roberts responded, his image appearing on screen, as the bulk of the Bellerophon closed in rapidly from the port side and took up a pacing position there. "Were you spotted?"

"Unlikely," Steph said. "Everyone was pretty intensely watching you when we pulled up anchor. Nice show, by the way."

"We do try, and we should be good at this by now, been doing it long enough." Jason said, sounding his age and tired for a moment before he physically pushed that off with effort that was both visible and audible. "Longer than I ever expected to live for, if I'm being honest."

"You and me both, friend," Steph said easily. "Honestly didn't expect to survive my first war, nevermind be fighting out here after... well, you know."

"Yeah," Jason said, the single word carrying more meaning than ever should have been able to. "Ready for round two?"

"Always," Steph confirmed. "Intel says that the next Imperial picket is going to be less than ten lightyears from Kraike. That is going to be their target, and we can't let them take it."

Jason grimaced, but nodded, "Agreed. As much as I'd love to see that whole rotting pit of Imperial corruption turned into Drasin shit, I suppose the fact that Drasin just seem to shit more Drasin is problematic."

Steph snorted at that, but shook his head, "That's not the reason and you know it."

The Captain of the Bell nodded in irritation, "I know. If the key to the leash is *anywhere*, it's there. We'll hold the line."

"Distasteful as it is."

Jason just grumbled, but no words were really needed.

"I'll get the Revenge into position, observe and report. Just wait for your cue."

"Just like the last time," Jason nodded. "We await your signal."

"Godspeed," Steph said, closing the connection before he put heavy power to the warp and sent his small ship hurtling through the black and on toward their next position.

*****

**Imperial Command**

Markys glared as he looked over the ships that had returned from the front line of the last battle, led by the Ship's Commander of the *From the Flames*, the survivors had become something of a thorn in his side merely by existing.

Having more ships to throw into the grinder at the next choke point was always a good thing, but those ships had become rallying points of the fleet. The Commander of the *Flames* in particular was already something of a legend for *ordering* the flankers to follow *his* orders and leave them to die. The fact that they'd survived, well that made them legends and now he couldn't just throw them away.

The hit to morale at the loss of any of them would be bad, but the *flames* in particular now was projected to cause a reduction in operating efficiency of nearly four percent if it were lost in the coming battle.

Four percent!

A single cruiser shouldn't have any impact on fleet efficiency, let alone anything remotely that high.

The Commander would have to be dealt with, later, but for now he was forced to ensure that those ships had priority on repair and resupply and that they would not be in the sacrificial line for the next fight. He'd already marked her file for future consideration, though whether she would be quietly disposed of or promoted was beyond his remit.

For now, they were a wrinkle that he didn't ask for, certainly didn't want, but had to deal with.

*As is the appearance of those so-called flame bringers.*

Honestly, sometimes he had to wonder about the perversity of the universe. As if the Drasin were not enough of a problem to deal with, he had to have the remnants of a defeated foe thrust on him, and at such a time?

*The Abyss tests, I suppose.*

Engaging them on sight wasn't an option at the moment, for much the same reason that he couldn't just dispose of the Commander of *From the flames* at the moment. The distraction of engaging them in combat would hamper his priority mission of preventing the Drasin from reaching the homeworld.

So if the simple options were not available, he would simply follow his orders with even more tight adherence to the details within them. He would not be censured for not making decisions beyond the purview of his assignments, after all.

*****

### From the Flames

Kaela grunted as she looked over the repair and replenishment details, surprised that they'd been afforded near as much as they had been.

*Must be getting more desperate as we fall back closer to the homeworld,* She decided after a moment's consideration. *We have to expect that the next fight, possibly the one after that, will be the final confrontation. We* **must** *hold them before they can reach the homeworld. Nothing else is acceptable.*

With more mass being delivered to her core while repairs were underway, though, the *Flames* would be ready for what came next if nothing else. They weren't in fighting shape yet, but she was feeling a hell of a lot better about things than when they first rejoined the Imperial fleet convoy.

New assignments were being sent out, but her ship and most of the survivors of the front line hadn't received the new duty posts yet. She assumed that they were waiting to see which ships were actually combat ready before making the final determinations.

It was a logical approach, but Kaela felt uncomfortable about it nonetheless. Normally, they'd just receive their orders regardless and it would be on their heads to ensure that they held up their position or died in the attempt.

*It seems that, once in a while, even Imperial Command can be reasonable,* She thought with rough amusement.

*****

### Deep Black

The swarm was moving, their goal now was just

entering into the extreme range of their base senses. It was still too far to detect the red band that would fire their rage to near uncontrollable levels, but the knowledge that it was there and what had been done to cripple them was more than sufficient to keep them moving with surety.

Some concerns were being calculated now, though, ones that had not been in the problem a short time earlier.

The *others* had shown themselves once more.

The Drasin had initially calculated that they were destroyed, but that had been proven wrong at the hive just recently and now again in the last battle.

Originally, the generational memory of the Drasin was clear that those others had been calculated as part of the current targets' hive but now it was clear that wasn't so. Another arc of the red spectrum band that they were bound to destroy, holding a slightly different position on the spectrum arc... but red nonetheless.

This little slice of the spectrum was different in ways that the swarm was still calculating. They engaged the swarm on the ground as much as they did in the void, and were doggedly competent at it in ways that the current targets were not.

They did not have the numbers, however, and never seemed to have.

The swarm knew without question that they would have to return to the homeworld of this portion as soon as the current target was dealt with.

A different group or not, this slice of the red band could not be permitted to increase their numbers. They were far too dangerous for that to be allowed.

*****

**Gaia's Revenge**

Steph eased the ship out of warp, well away from the expected coordinates of the next conflict between the swarm and the Imperial fleet operations.

"Engaging stealth," He said over the comm, "Hope everyone is thinking chilly thoughts, cause it's going to warm up in here."

The black hole armor settings would make them all but invisible to active scanners, and it would take a hell of an eye or computer systems to notice them eclipse a random star with passives. Unfortunately, those same settings also absorbed all radiation and prevented them from venting heat.

The onboard cooling system shut down as the armor shifted, otherwise running the AC would result in heating the damn ship up in mere minutes instead of the hours they could manage to keep it comfortable running everything on passives.

Within a couple days, though, they'd have to vent smoke or die of heatstroke.

That was a problem for future Steph, however, and while present Steph pitied the poor bastard, he wasn't going to take it easy on him.

"No sign of the Empire or swarm yet," He noted, keeping the crew apprised of the situation. "Either we're here ahead of them or we got the wrong address. Let's hope it's option one."

The Revenge eased closer to the target location, moving at low relativistic speeds on a purely ballistic trajectory as he examined the area.

It was the edge of an Oort Cloud, one belonging to a star just over four and half *lightyears* from their current position and about ten light years from the Imperial homeworld. Everything they'd been able to pull from Imperial transmissions indicated that their fleet would be setting up their last position here, with the hope of stopping the Drasin entirely before they could approach Kraike or, failing that, cripple the swarm such that the home fleet of the Imperial world would be able to finish the job.

Steph wasn't sure if they'd been able to pull it off, but he knew that the outcome depended strongly on the nature of the leash the Empire believed it had on the Drasin. If they'd calculated right and managed to stretch out the swarm's logistical replication capacity to its limits, then this was where the Drasin would end.

If not… Well, things would get *very* interesting for the Empire, of that Steph had no doubt.

For his part, he and the crew of the Revenge were still playing bird dog to the Heroics. If it looked like the fight was going too much against the Empire, he'd call in the Bell and host and give the Imps a little support. If it looked like they were going to clean up the swarm without a fight, well the call would be Captain Roberts, but ambushing the Imperial fleet just after they finished the job was an option that was still on the table.

Ideally, the two groups would pound each other to dust and trouble the rest of the galaxy no longer.

Unlikely as an outcome, Steph knew, but he could dream.

"We're going silent. If it transmits, shut it down," He ordered finally before he settled in to wait.

*****

**Imperial Fleet Command**

"Fleet Commander, our divisions are in motion."

"Excellent," Markys said. "And the swarm?"

"After some apparent confusion that we're still trying

to understand, they have regrouped and are moving as expected. We will have additional time for repairs and resupply, thanks to the delay however."

"Good. I'll worry about their confusion later, if it matters," Markys said dismissively. "The beasts are stupid enough that confusion is likely their normal state of mind."

"Yes, Fleet Commander."

Markys waved off the messenger, walking across his fleet deck and looking over the disposition for himself.

The new order of battle was set, with more ships than he'd expected to have. That was good, of course, no matter what irritations it may cause him later, but it still rankled that the difference had come from outside help. The so-called flame bringers were a myth that only the low born officers of the fleet believed, nothing more than the result of propaganda placed by rebel factions.

He'd read the files on it himself, after all.

It was a good bit of propaganda, blaming all the destruction on some mythical outside species. Even the Empire had found it useful to let that story propagate, since allowing the rebels to gain much notoriety from such an attack would lead to even more recruits. Wiping them out quietly before they could do so, then letting their own cover erase their rebellion from history had been a brilliant move by the Empire's senior command in the absence of the Imperial family.

Markys sighed, the loss of the Empress had been the one true loss in that attack.

Irreplaceable, her leadership had been.

Rumors said that she had an heir, but he or she was too young yet to take up their role at the head of the Imperial Forces. That had seemed sensible back then, but years had gone past and none had appeared to take her place.

Markys wasn't high enough in the ranks to know the truth, few were, but he could read between the lines as well as any.

If such an heir had ever existed, likely they were being kept in 'protective custody' amid some power struggle among the upper echelon of the Imperial Command. Not something a wise fleet command, even a senior one, would involve himself with.

Markys was satisfied enough to end the threat of the Drasin and ride on the glory from that while others concerned themselves with the far more treacherous waters of dealing with Imperial Politics. The day may come for him to play in that war space, but that day was some time away as of yet.

"Issue the final order, move the fleet to the interception point."

"Yes, Fled Commander!"

*****

### From the Flames

Kaela didn't speak as the order came through, she just gestured casually and that was enough to set her ship into motion.

The space beyond their hull, as reflected by the view screens, did not change much but a slight flicker was enough to show that it had shifted from a real view of the abyss to one that had to be generated by the computer as all the wavelengths of light shifted as a result of their increase in effective speed within the galaxy.

They were part of the third division this time, most of the First division from earlier had been split between the second and third while a fresh group from the homworld's defensive fleet filled in for their losses thus far.

It would be a bloody fight, what was coming, of that she had no doubt but at least someone else would be taking the brunt of the fighting this time. She was honored to do her duty, but that didn't mean she felt any need to hoard all the 'honor' to herself.

"Ship's status?" She asked softly, casually, trying not to sound overly concerned.

"Hull repairs are nearly seventy percent done, we are twenty percent under mass on the reactor singularity, and our beam emitters... are in dire need of... repair." Her executive officer said tactfully.

She just managed to keep from laughing aloud at that.

*Repairs. They're in need of being scrapped for raw materials and entirely replaced, but we'll have to make do,* She thought wryly.

Her life and the lives of everyone under her command were owed to the enemy.

Again.

Kaela found that rather distressing, but she didn't know what to do about it other than use what the enemy had gifted her to serve the Empire to the best of her ability.

It was the only knife she had at the moment with which she could stab at them.

"It'll do," She said simply upon realizing that the quiet had drawn out overly long since her officer had spoken. "They're just beasts, no matter how dangerous. We are above them all."

The From the Flames flickered through space as it, and the Imperial fleet hurtled on to their next destination.

*****

# CHAPTER 15

**Prometheus Facility**

*This isn't a normal encryption method... a unique language perhaps?* Palin mused idly as he listened to the cacophony surrounding him. *No, there's no real hint of any grammar rules in the patterns. It's almost like... wait...*

He opened his eyes and got up, walking across the room, and quickly brought up another database. It was one that Prometheus was rather well suited for studying, the nature of spacetime, how it curved, and how those curves affected everything within its reach.

*Gravity... no, not gravity, but the mechanism that results in gravity. Let's see what this sounds like...*

Palin loaded up some of the datasets they had from various ships, prometheus itself, and even older sets from Earth's early days and then started playing the gravity waves as soundforms, layering one over the other while keeping the captured data sounds playing as well.

*Yes, that's definitely it. They used gravity waves as the basis for the encryption, interesting approach,* Palin thought as he adjusted his own approach to the problem.

If the Empire was using that as their base for high level encryptions, he suspected that it was the hand of an Entity at work, guiding their path in such a way that it would strengthen its own influence within the highest levels of decision making.

Palin suspected that this 'encryption' wouldn't even

qualify as such to one of the entities, if any such could when it was made within their sphere of influence. That caused him to narrow his eyes, the implications of it forming in his mind.

*More than one? In communication with one another via the encrypted files? That...*

Palin reached out and killed all the sounds playing for a moment.

*Not encryption at all. Language. We know that the entities can warp space in various ways, this isn't how they hide their communication... it's how they **communicate.***

That changed things. He needed a new approach, because decoding a language was entirely different from decrypting a code.

Palin reached for a communication system, opening a channel.

"Yes, Doctor?"

"I'm going to need something," He said simply.

"Name it."

"A Heroic Class Cruiser, one with an Entity on board."

There was a long pause, silence filling the time.

"They're all on assignment. The only way we can get you a Heroic is to send you to one."

Palin nodded, not really surprised.

"The Marines who brought the data to me, are they still here?"

"They're with the Casino, one of the Archangels."

"Tell them I need a lift, and to come back and get the data module. We have to do this."

"I'll contact the Admiral, Doctor. Keep working until we

get back to you."

"Nothing more I can do with the deep core data," He admitted, "It's not a code, it's language. I'm good, hell I'm the *best* and I know it, but this isn't a human language. We need an entity."

"Understood. Get ready."

*****

Admiral Aiden Pierce found himself somewhat befuddled by the request... *request. Bullshit, he's demanding... but...* from the good doctor.

Palin was a well known pain in the ass of the entire facility, and his record showed that he'd been the holder of that title at every single assignment he'd ever had. However, he was exactly what he thought he was. The very best there was at what he did. So damned good that his old CIA jacket called him a linguistic *telepath* because he could learn a new language in what amounted to *hours*.

What he was asking now, well it wasn't that far out.

Aiden understood the basics of it. If the data was stored in the entities' language, somehow, it could be damned near impossible to break. Without some sort of rosetta stone, it might simply *be* impossible. Entities had completely different reference points for how they experienced the universe to humans, so if they *had* a language of their own it would almost certainly be completely alien in nature.

"Get me Captain Samuels." He told his assistant simply.

"Yes Sir."

Thankfully the Casino hadn't left for their own next assignment yet, so if she were willing, Aiden would indeed fill the Doctor's request and send him to one of the Heroics.

*****

Jennifer Samuels had just gotten off the horn with the Admiral and was stomping back into Marine country, looking for the Colonel.

"Keenan," She called, spotting the woman. "Need a squad."

"You've got it, what for?"

"Go back to the lab we just dropped off that memory core with and bring it back here, along with the Doctor studying it."

Keenan paused, "Really?"

"Really. New orders just got cut, transport one VIP and one data core to the Bellerophon, best possible speed."

Keenan groaned, "Transition? Again?"

"Again."

"Goddamn it. Ok, I'll get Michaels' squad back on it, they know where the lab is at least," Keenan sighed. "Any idea why?"

"The egghead needs a second opinion from the Bellerophon's avatar himself," She said. "Don't know much beyond that. Just that it needs doing."

"Right. Ok, I'll get the squad moving, Ma'am."

*****

Lieutenant Michaels waved on her team, walking alongside the Sergeant as they got moving off the ship once more.

"We just dropped that thing off, and now we need to grab it again?" Deke complained as they moved. "What the hell, man?"

"Palin says he needs to go to the Bell, he needs to go to the Bell," She said simply. "Our job is just to make sure he and the data gets there. Stop your bellyaching and put one foot in front of the other until we're there."

The private sighed, but nodded, "oorah Ma'am."

The Marine squad wasn't in the best of moods, she knew well enough. They'd just gotten settled down for a break only to get pulled out to go grab what they'd just delivered so that they could deliver it again. She understood their annoyance, but she also knew that Palin was likely to drive her, and everyone else, completely mad on the… thankfully short… trip it would take to deliver him and Amanda didn't want to be listening to her Marines annoy her on top of that.

It was going to be a long short trip.

*****

Palin had his needs packed up by the time the Marines arrived and just slung a small pack over his shoulder before pointing to the data core and the rest of the luggage where it was scattered around the lab.

"Grab all that and let's get moving," He said simply. "Time is of the essence."

He was moderately surprised when the young lieutenant didn't say anything in response and just started gathering things up with her team. Palin was used to more pushback on his demands and found himself slightly flummoxed at not needing to trot out any of his practiced and readied arguments for whatever nonsense they tried to use to get out of the work.

"Alright, is that everything?" She asked him after it was all picked up.

Palin just had to nod before she was waving her men out the door.

"Let's move. The Casino is already warming up."

*****

Jennifer was running through the final flight checks, really just waiting for her Marines to get back before the Casino was ready to leave. Most of the work was already done, of course, just the final checks remained and those were largely perfunctory since she knew that her team wouldn't have told her the ship was ready for them unless it was *ready* for them.

Still, it was procedure and while she cut a lot of corners as a member of the Gaian 'mercenaries' due to their ongoing pirate theme, Jennifer was like the rest of her fellows in that she knew damn well that you didn't cut corners where it mattered. Some things were just done because when you had new people moving in and out of a unit all the time, you needed to ensure that everyone was going to act the way you expected... even if it wasn't necessarily the optimum action.

Her team had been together a long time now, and she trusted them to act like professionals when it counted, even if they were a bunch of damned pirates the rest of the time.

Safety and flight procedures, however, were not the sort of thing you just *trusted* to be ok. You did them. Every time, sometimes more than once. Even if it felt like a waste, it wasn't. Skipping on safety procedures basically guaranteed that Murphy would show up, and warding off that bastard was worth pretty much anything you could do.

"Captain."

Jennifer stiffened, but managed to keep from jumping or crying out from the surprise of an unfamiliar voice coming from right behind her.

*Or almost unfamiliar,* She thought dryly as she stiffly turned.

"Seamus," She said dryly, managing to make the spook's name sound like an insult.

Gordon just smiled at her, either uncensored, amused,

or… more likely… both by her tone.

"Permission to come aboard," He said mildly.

"You seem to be standing in my hold already," She said flatly, setting her slate down for a moment as she rubbed her forehead. "What is this about?"

"I'd like to come out with you on this run," He said. "I have a feeling… it's where I want to be."

She looked him over briefly, "Don't you mean 'where you need to be'?"

He just shrugged, "I always want to be where I need to be. It saves on a lot of whining and bitching about life not being fair."

"I'm assuming that the Admiral has signed off on this?" Jennifer asked wearily.

"Yes Ma'am."

"Welcome aboard," She told him dryly. "Since I'm not going up against the Admiral over, well, *you*."

He chuckled, "Lovely to be in your presence as well, but seriously… Thank you. I do need a favor, though."

She shot him with a flat look that clearly stated that he was pushing his luck, but merely gestured for him to go on.

"Just need help bringing a few things on board," He held his hands up defensively while grinning. "Some of the potential equipment I may need is a little heavy."

"Fine." Jennifer looked around. "Gunnerson!"

"Ma'am!"

"Grab some hands and help Seamus here get his kit on board. I want it on and locked down before the Marines get back."

"Yes Ma'am!"

She looked at the spook pointedly, "Now get lost and let me finish my checklists."

"Aye aye, Captain," He saluted her, improperly, though she had a feeling he meant to do it that way, then left.

Jennifer grumbled as she picked up her slate. I'd *say that I have a bad feeling about this, but the whole damned situation is so far beyond bad feelings that it might just be an upgrade on the situation. Whatever.*

*****

Gordon's kit was just being locked down when the Marines arrived back with Palin and the data core in tow, so Jennifer got them to locking all of that down as she finished the last couple bullet points on her list before marking everything as green and making her way up through Officer's country to the Command Deck of the little gunboat.

"Prometheus, Casino."

"Go for Prometheus."

"Requesting clearance for departure," She advised as she powered up all the systems and checked the internal boards to ensure that the cargo had been locked down and everyone was in their berths.

"A moment Casino…" The control tower said while she was working, coming back less than a minute later. "Clearance granted. The Admiral extends his thanks and says, quote, good hunting."

She smiled, "Tell the Admiral we'll bag one for him. Confirm the decks are clear, please."

"Decks are confirmed clear, Casino. You are go for launch."

"Roger that," Jennifer said as she powered the ship's systems and used thrusters to put her in motion.

The Casino hovered briefly before turning in a slow arc, lining up with the hangar doors as they opened up. In a moment she hit the main thrusters and began moving the ship clear of the Prometheus hangar bay.

Once they were clear of the complicated structure of the Prometheus facility, she put the nose up and began applying power to the warp fields. As the bubbles began to form the feeling of motion from the ship faded as they began to surf the artificial wave out into the Black once more.

She'd lived in her ship for so long now that, frankly, it felt more like going home than leaving port.

That somewhat worried her, but it wasn't a new worry by any means, so Jenn just shrugged it off as she always did and focused on the next mission. She didn't think that could possibly be a healthy way of dealing with things, but frankly she... like the rest of Terran humans in the region at least... was so far past 'healthy' ways of dealing with things that any halfway competent therapist would run screaming from her before the first session was done.

And, honestly?

She rather found that, and everything, rather more amusing than it likely should be.

*If it weren't for black humor, I wouldn't have any humor left in me. I doubt any of us would, or many at least. The Universe doesn't seem to care what the hell it does to us, so why should we? Not like we're getting out of life alive, I guess.*

"All hands," She said. "Stand by for transition as soon as we're clear of the Heliosphere. Get your barf bags ready, we're probably going to have to jump a couple times at least before we locate the bell."

She imagined that went over well with everyone, but at the moment the thought of all the groaning and bellyaching just made her black amusement all the stronger so Jenn just grinned as she powered the warp up to full power and angled them outward bound, heading for the edge of the local stellar mass' influence.

*You know what, it's a good day. What it's a good day for? Well, I think I'll just enjoy the surprise.*

*****

# CHAPTER 16

**World Kraike, Imperial Space**

The entity last known as the Emperor examined the data feed that was flowing through the minds of those tasked with defending the Imperial Homeworld and saw that all was thus far progressing as planned. The Drasin were returning to the fold, whether they understood that or not, and with their replication threat severely strained near to the point of irrelevance, they would not be a threat by the time they arrived.

The Imperial losses were somewhat of a setback, but humans were easy enough to replace, particularly in the aftermath of such losses. Given how short lived the little things were, that was about the only thing they had going for them in such matters.

Like the insects they believed themselves so superior to, humans were of little individual import to anything, but as a swarm they had uses, much like the Drasin themselves.

The current losses would be replaced entirely within two generations, assuming proper incentives were put into place. Resource costs were somewhat higher, but the loss of a planet or two was also of minimal concern. Most of the truly important resources were found off-worlds, and few if any of those had been targeted by the swarm in its blind focus on clearing the life from whatever places it could see it in.

The entire situation would be resolved within a few days, and then he could once more turn his focus to rebuilding the power and prestige of his Empire.

The engagement with the Xeno human culture had been more costly than he would have believed beforehand; they'd specifically targeted deep infrastructure that took *decades* to build in the first place, during a time when the Empire was at its peak of power and influence. After the damages incurred during the war, and the strikes here on Kraike in particular, there had been so many demands on Imperial resources that they'd barely rebuilt a quarter of the facilities lost in that single strike.

More concerning was that they had apparently missed some of the Xeno in their sweep.

The report from the Cruise *From the Flames* had made it clear that the ones known colloquially as the Flame Bringers still existed and, more importantly, still maintained at least some of their combat power and links to the Oathers.

The Entity made the rough equivalent of a human sigh, a gesture that rippled across the planet's EM Field like someone had dropped a stone into a pond.

The Oathers were, perhaps, the greatest of the failures that had resulted from the first encounter with Xeno-Humans. Poor fools that had no conception of the threats the universe brought upon their heads, their well meaning adherence to their ideals would have doomed everyone but he had hoped to someday bring them back to their home.

A dream that was now, perhaps, farther away than ever due to their foolish ideals.

*Allying with the Xeno that had nearly wiped out everyone here, myself included? There is truly no level of stupidity to which they cannot fall.*

The Oathers would have to be wiped out, it was clear to him now, no matter what he felt about it.

After that, when everything was rebuilt…

*The Empire must grow. Not a single star in this galaxy can be left uncontrolled. The Xeno must be wiped from the **universe**.*

In time.

In time they would be.

This he knew for certain.

*\*\*\*\*\**

**Imperial Fleet Command**

Markys looked over the battlespace as the divisions arrived and arrayed themselves according to the plan, taking up positions in preparation for the arrival of the enemy.

"When do we expect the swarm," He asked his adjutant casually, not looking away from the show going on out there beyond his display screens.

"Within two more full cycles, Fleet Commander."

"Excellent, time to set up and then we'll fall back to a safe distance to observe the fighting." Markys said simply.

"Of course, Fleet Commander."

The new first division was readying itself to take the brunt of the initial attack force, and they had more forces arriving from the Home Defense Fleet to ensure that the fight was won before it even started.

*Those mindless animals should have known better than to come this far into Imperial Space, even if they had their full capacity we would end them as we did before.*

*\*\*\*\*\**

**Gaia's Revenge**

"They're just going to set up and slug it out with the swarm, *again*," Tyke couldn't quite believe what he was seeing.

"Seems so," Steph answered.

Honestly he didn't understand it, but then he'd never had any inclination or desire to know the mind of madness. He figured his own obvious insanity was enough for one person to deal with in their life, he sure as crap didn't need some alien nuttiness infecting it too.

A sly smile crossed his face as he glanced sidelong to where Milla sat.

*More than it already has, at least.*

"What?"

Steph twitched, "Nothing."

The short woman looked at him suspiciously, "That expression on your face does not say nothing, Stephan."

"Nothing, I swear," He held up his hands in his defense, grinning widely.

"Right," Tykle snorted. "Keep ducking and weaving Bossman, you might escape unscathed."

"Not likely," Milla said dryly, "but that is for another day. There are more ships arriving."

They turned their focus back to the display of power that was setting up out there in the Black.

"Damn, that's a lot of ships, and a lot of power." Tyke said with a whistle.

Steph nodded, "Just conventional strength, though, with no real standoff weapons to speak of. They'll have to get in close and slug it out, beams to beams. With Imperial lensing and the Drasin learning with every fight, that'll put most of the fighting in under a lightsecond. That's knife range for these things."

"The Odyssey took them out at several light minutes, didn't it?" Tyke asked. "How'd you manage that?"

"Adaptive beams, Stealth, Eric's deliberate approach to fighting, and we weren't tangling with swarms at the time," Steph admitted. "By the time you take out a few that way, the swarm will be right on top of you. Hammering them with Pulse torpedoes, T-Cannon fire, and a wall of High Velocity Missiles just to soften them up is the only way to fight this kind of force."

"I'm sure not going to disagree with you on that," Tyke said simply. "What are our orders if things get bad?"

"As long as the Empire is holding their own, we let them slug it out. If the Drasin start to overwhelm them, we'll call in the Heroics for a strike."

"And if the Empire cleans up easily?" Tyke asked, almost fearfully. "Do we help the Drasin?"

Steph shook his head, "No. Ideally we want them to wipe each other out, yes, but the Drasin are an existential threat. The Empire wants to be one, but they're not. They don't know it, but we can cripple them anytime we choose. As long as Prometheus is in our control and unknown to the Empire, they live because we *let them*."

"Honestly surprised that the brass didn't order them wiped out already then," Tyke said.

"That would tell any survivors that our super weapon survived the war. Right now, based on the intel we have, they think that we launched our strike from Earth weeks or longer before the fall of Sol." Steph said, shrugging when he got an incredulous look from his XO. "Doesn't make sense to me either. Someone in their chain must know better, but that's the story that has filtered down to the fleet and we've seen no indication that they believe there's a super weapon out there at all. No searching, no hints of it in their officers orders, nothing."

"Weird."

"The Empire is weird." Steph said wearily. "But, of course, any totalitarian government will be. Dictators love to micromanage, and it has severe and long ranging effects on how people think. The Empire has been conditioning its people to be weird, by our standards, for possibly longer than civilization has existed on Earth as we would define it."

Milla leaned forward, frowning, "There is something coming, Stephan. Is that the Drasin swarm?"

Steph shifted his focus abruptly, eyes widening as he spotted the signals.

"If it is, they're early." He said as he brought up the passive FTL scans. "It's a warp signature, no question. They're pulsing tachyons too, I've not seen this before. It's big. It's really big."

\*\*\*\*\*

**Imperial Fleet Command**

"Contact, positional convergence with our location! Plotting time to intercept now!"

Markys shifted around, frowning.

"What is it? The swarm isn't due to arrive for some time yet," He snapped.

"No signature match, Fleet Commander. The signal is… it's massive. We're looking at a… this isn't possible."

"What isn't possible?"

"Our scans indicate an approaching *stellar mass*, Fleet Commander!"

That left Markys silent from shock.

Ships operated with planetary masses of internal power storage, and a fleet could manage a good impression of a gas giant's effective mass, but *nothing* he'd ever even dreamt of could manage a *stellar* mass and make it mobile.

"Confirm approach velocity," He finally snapped.

"Approach confirmed, FTL velocity."

"Signal all ships to full alert," He ordered. "Prepare our withdrawal from the battlespace!"

"Yes Fleet Commander! All ships confirm full alert!"

Markys ignored the confirmation as he adjusted the scanners and looked out through the viewer display, eyes on the blackness as he tried to see just what was coming, hoping vainly that every computer and scanner on the fleet had somehow managed to utterly fail in the same way all at once.

\*\*\*\*\*

**Imperial Cruiser *From the Flames***

"Ship's Commander!"

The call, really a scream, had Kaela bolting across the deck at a flat out sprint. Her people didn't scream without due cause.

"What is it?"

"Inbound signal, Ma'am. Confirmed across multiple ships and the Command n network," The young officer looked like he was panicking, causing her to stare at him for a moment.

"Calm yourself," She ordered. "Speak sensibly. Is the swarm here ahead of expectations?"

"I don't know, Ship's Commander, the signal... it's..." The officer looked worried, finally just pointing to his screens, "Look."

She glared for a moment before refocusing on the screen. Kaela blinked, trying to make the numbers make some sort of sense, but nothing changed.

"That's not possible," She whispered. "That much mass, in warp? Did you run diagnostics?"

"Yes, Ship's Commander, first thing. Then again, across the fleet network. All systems check," The officer blurted.

"Signal all hands to combat stations," She said, straightening up and looking to the forward screens, "Whatever it is, we will be ready for it."

"Yes, Ship's Commander, combat stations alert!"

Kaela let the alarms sound as she stepped back and slipped into her command station, overlooking the command deck and forward screens.

"As soon as we have imagery, put it up."

"Yes, Ship's Commander!"

\*\*\*\*\*

### Gaia's Revenge

"What the hell... I've never even *imagined* a warp wavefront that big..." Tyke whispered in shock as the numbers they were getting kept on coming. "Are we sure we're getting accurate readings?"

"Everything is confirmed," Milla responded. "If there is an error, it is in the hardware on a level below all of our diagnostic systems... it is not... impossible... but it is unlikely."

"It's not wrong," Steph said far too calmly for what he was feeling, "The Imperials are reacting. They see it too."

"That is at least a minor stellar mass," Milla said firmly. "Accelerating something that large is... I do not think it is possible, Stephan."

"Well, two options there. You're wrong," Steph said with a shrug, "Or you're right. In the latter case, I'm going to say that those bastards have been replicating a hell of a lot more than the Imperial leash was supposed to allow."

"And in the former?" Tyke asked with morbid curiosity.

"I'm not an engineer," Steph said with a shrug. "Haven't a *clue* what we could be reading."

"We are all about to find out," Milla announced with a shiver. "The signal just dropped below lightspeed. We are being pulled out of our parking position by the gravitational well it is creating already."

Steph checked the numbers, "Yes we are, but we have plenty of time to react so we're going to sit nice and pretty like and just fall for a while. Time to visual contact?"

"Object distance... three light hours," Milla said after a brief calculation. "Closing at nearly lightspeed, but velocity is dropping rapidly."

"I fucking hope so," Tyke swore. "Anything that size shouldn't be able to hold relativistic speeds without an ungodly amount of power being thrown into it."

"Three hours. Shit, that's a long time," Steph wasn't sure what he wanted to do, but he knew he did *not* want to wait three hours for a good look at what was coming. Especially when it was moving at high relativistic speeds more or less in his direction.

*Tachyon Ping is out of the question, that would give away our location... but the Empire should be losing patience soon as well.*

"We'll hold until the Empire paints them with Tachyons," He said. "That should give us an idea of what the hell we're dealing with."

*****

**Imperial Fleet Command**

"Unknown contact has dropped below lightspeed."

Markys grimaced, but nodded, "Stand ready to scan the contact. All ships, coordinate the scan."

"Yes, Fleet Commander!"

The three divisions, plus the Command Squadron would all hit the target with a coordinated pulse in order to get the maximum level of clarity and detail from the scan. The power entailed was not insignificant, but whatever was out there Markys was quite certain it was entirely unprecedented and he had no intention of giving up even the slightest detail that might help him understand how to *destroy* it.

"Scan initiated!"

In sequence, the Imperial ships pulsed out a series of FTL pulses, instantly getting feedback as the particles crossed the distance instantaneously and a *tiny* portion of them interacted with the contact and returned to the waiting scanner arrays.

"We have return imagery, building the scans now Fleet Commander…. That's odd," The scanner officer mumbled.

"What is it?"

"We have another unknown contact."

\*\*\*\*\*

**Gaia's Revenge**

"Sweet jumping jesus," Tyke swore. "Are we in one piece?"

"We're fine," Steph grumped as he powered up the ship and killed the stealth settings now that they were useless. "I didn't expect them to blast the entire region with the combined energy of the whole damned fleet. Well, we're blown, that signal intensity went *way* over our detection threshold."

"Perhaps," Milla said seriously, "However we have a

bigger problem."

"What is it? Do we have imagery?"

She nodded, gesturing to send the scans to the projection.

"What in the…"

*****

**Imperial Fleet Command**

"What is that?" Markys sneered, looking at the small contact that had appeared during the scan.

"Profile indicates that it belongs to a mercenary group known as the Gaians." HIs officer replied, "Free Star Mercenaries, but also known to provide intelligence to various groups."

"So they were spying on our fight," Markys sneered. "How like that rabble. Ignore them, we will deal with them later. Do we have imagery for the contact?"

"Preliminary build is nearing completion, Fleet Commander."

"Show me."

The imagery on the screen flickered and Markys hissed in surprise as he examined it.

"Is that…?"

"It appears to be a star, yes Fleet Commander. One that is currently on course to intercept our fleet at nearly the speed of light."

Markys didn't quite have words to describe what was in his mind at the time. His jaw worked silently for a few moments as he rubbed at his face, furiously trying to make the universe make some sort of sense once more.

Surrounding the star, a relatively small stellar object

but even so, were *uncountable* numbers of the Drasin drones.

Markys swallowed, eyes wide as they darted from side to side.

"Fleet Commander, orders?"

He just stared, unable to process what he was looking at.

"Fleet Commander? The Divisions are asking for orders, Fleet Commander!"

\*\*\*\*\*

**Imperial Cruiser *From the Flames***

"No orders as yet from the Fleet Commander, Ship's Commander."

"We're not waiting," She said, "Give me a fleet comm."

"You have an open comm, Ship's Commander!"

"Third Division, this is the *From the Flames*," She said firmly. "Advise you shift position, I'm taking the second division to flank from the inner galactic side. Circle to the outer galactic, do not let them warp that stellar mass into our fleet! It will wipe us out if it gets close enough to disrupt our warp generation!"

There was no response, but she was fine with that. If they answered her, they could be charged with treason for acting potentially in defiance of Fleet Command. It was better if no record existed for the others, she would take the charge herself if needs be.

"First division, go above or below," She said. "Do *not* engage from the forward position! If they jump that mass to warp, they'll wipe you out before you even know they're coming. Everyone get out of its path!"

She closed the comm, looking to her people.

"Take us out of formation," She ordered. "Toward the

galactic core side of that mass. Prime all weapons, we *will* do our duty, no matter what the cost."

*****

# CHAPTER 17

**Gaia's Revenge**

"It's a star."

"We can see that, Tyke," Steph said dryly. "I don't even *want* to know how much power it took to make a warp field around something that size. The fact that they were able to steer the damn thing…"

He just shook his head, really unable to completely wrap his head around the situation if he were being entirely honest about things. That the Drasin were capable of Kardashev structures was one thing, he'd gotten used to that, but make one that *moved*? At faster than light speeds?

*These things are too damned dangerous.*

"It's a damned star."

Irritated, Steph half turned, "Yes we can see that, could you stop repeating it?"

Tyke shook his head, "No… Damn it, Crown, Why the hell did they bring a *star*? Better yet, why the hell slow the damn thing down? They could have plowed the whole damned fleet under before the Empire even saw it coming."

That caused Steph to pause, half turning to Milla, "Love?"

Milla Chans frowned, thinking it through, "He is right. If they'd simply continued, they would have annihilated the fleet in a single stroke."

"Huh." Steph looked back to the screen, "Then they have

another priority. They didn't get the data they needed from *From the Flames*. Milla, ready the pulse comm."

"As you say, however, the Heroics will not be able to transition to the pre-arranged coordinates?"

"What? Why?" Steph asked before abruptly realizing, "Right, the gravity well of the star would disrupt the integration. Ok, pulse comm the abort codes to the Heroics, we're going full active."

\*\*\*\*\*

### From the Flames

Kaela bared her teeth as the first of the swarm entered their range, "Ready weapons!"

The response was fast, but she expected nothing less as the enemy filled their screens from all directions excepting the rear.

"Burn them out!"

The beams from the big cruiser lanced out violently, and the drasin drones flared brightly in the black for a moment before burning out to ash in the vacuum. So many flares lit up the battlespace that a new starscape existed, however briefly.

There were, however, more coming to replace every one that was destroyed… and of the replacements, there seemed to be no end.

"Ship's Commander!"

"What is it?" She snapped, half turning.

"Fleet Command, they've still not moved!"

Kaela swore, shifting her focus from the battle to look back on the fleet disposition.

First through third divisions had split, getting out of the way of the rapidly approaching stellar mass, but the command division was still parked there as the fast moving swarm and mass approached.

"Give me a comm channel," She snapped.

"Channel open!"

"Fleet Command, you *must* withdraw from this battlespace!" She said urgently. "The enemy will not be stopped here, and the intelligence you hold is too valuable! Withdraw immediately!"

\*\*\*\*\*

**Imperial Fleet Command**

"Fleet Commander."

Markys collapsed into his station, unable to tear his eyes from the horror filled mass that was rapidly surging toward his ships.

"Fleet Commander! We must leave!"

*Where did they all come from? None of the numbers presented showed anything remotely like this. It makes no sense. How could those beasts move a **star**?*

"Please, Fleet Commander! The enemy is nearly on us!"

*It's impossible.*

He shook his head, still trying desperately to process the scene but failing at every attempt.

"Fleet Commander!"

A hand was shaking him, forcing him to look away from the screens into the terrified face of one of his subordinates. Markys stared blankly for a moment before his automatic response kicked in and he backhanded the man away.

"Don't you *dare* lay a hand on me."

"Fleet Commander," The man said from the deck where

he'd landed, "We need orders!"

Markys glanced back at the screen before looking to the man again and pushed himself to his feet.

"Fine, but we will be revisiting your conduct," He snapped. "Signal the Command Fleet to withdraw. Reverse course, maximum warp."

"Yes Fleet Commander!"

Markys gripped the rails as he again stared at the screens, still lost in his denial.

*How did those animals do this?*

*****

## Gaia's Revenge

"Comm pulse from the Bellerophon," Milla responded as Steph activated the full systems capacity of the Archangel gunboat. "They confirm abort codes. Rendezvous according to alpha protocol."

"Roger that," Steph said. "Weapons hot, everyone. We're blown and we are about to become the brightest sonuvabitch for several lightyears, and that's including that star over there."

"Very well, all weapons are active." Milla confirmed, switching to the ship's internal comm. "All hands, all hands, report to combat stations. Say again, all hands report to combat stations."

Steph let himself be taken up by the suspension field that allowed him to pilot the ship like it was part of his own body. The Neural systems shifted from low level induction to full transduction, a tingling along his skin letting him feel the light cosmic wind as it rushed along the hull, his field of vision filled with an augmented view of what was out there beyond the ship itself.

The Archangel *could* be flown and fought by a single pilot, but the efficiency of trying to run it like that was severely degraded over having a proper crew to handle the full host of weapons available to the deceptively small ship.

With his crew taking up their positions, Steph was able to focus almost entirely on flying but he'd kept control of certain systems under his own control as he got ready for a fight.

"Milla, I'm going to need you to analyze the Drasin actions. They're up to something, and we *need* to know what it is." He said firmly. "Comm pulse to the Bell. Negative on rendezvous."

He paused, trying to figure out what he *could* send them over the limited FTL pulse communication that would allow the Heroics to respond appropriately. Unfortunately the system had *extremely* limited bandwidth and they didn't have brevity codes for the enemy showing up with a *goddamned star* in tow.

He sighed, "Signal that the current plan is no go. Full abort. Say again, Full abort. New plan needed."

"Yes, Stephan. Signal prepared... sending."

The power dipped briefly as the FTL transmission pulsed out, before coming back full as the fusion generators on board ramped up to full power output.

It put them nowhere near what a single cruiser was capable of outputting, but for a ship the size of the *Revenge*, they had a massive amount of power on tap. All Steph could think, however, was that he rather doubted it was going to be enough.

\*\*\*\*\*

## Bellerophon

"Full abort?" Jason Roberts stiffened as he read the

brevity codes from the *Revenge*, confusion filling his mind. "What the hell did they run into?"

"Unknown," Bell said simply, "However it clearly was not covered in our preparations for this operation."

Jason snorted, "That much I worked out for myself. So, Empire or Drasin?"

He didn't really need to think too hard about it.

"Drasin." *Damn cunning little shits they are.*

The Empire was predictable in his experience. Powerful, certainly, but power was often a handicap to those who held it for too long. When you had the biggest hammer, every problem was a nail and you stopped caring about all the holes in the walls. That was the Empire in a nutshell, the biggest hammer in the galaxy... this sector of it at least... but all too determined to put lots and lots of holes in the walls, until they likely brought the roof down on their own heads if he were to guess.

The Drasin, however, were a certifiable nightmare that kept on bringing out new tricks that threw all planning for a loop.

"Give me full warp," He ordered his XO, "We'll go in slow, survey the battlespace from a distance and try to contact the Revenge."

"Aye, Captain."

*We only have five Heroics on this run, not enough to really put a hole in either the Empire or the Drasin, but Admiral Tanner and the Priminae fleet standing by to end the Drasin threat once and for all. Calling them in has to be done at the right moment, though, otherwise the Empire will slow us down, possibly giving the Drasin a chance to escape.*

"We'll take the vanguard," He ordered. "Have the Bo and the Hood flank port and starboard while the Achilles and the

Agamemnon flank ventral and dorsal."

"Starburst formation, Aye skipper."

Roberts waved off the confirmation, his own mind still running a mile a minute as he tried to guess at what was going on out there a few lightyears off. Unfortunately, barring an FTL scan, it would take that many years to get a visual on the battlespace, so they'd have to go there and see for themselves.

"Tachyon burst!"

Roberts twisted, eyes falling on the scanner station, "Are we being scanned?"

"Negative, Transition Signature, skipper."

*We aren't expecting anyone out here now. Is it the Revenge?* He walked over to the scanner station and leaned over the officer's shoulder, "Do we have an ID on the arrival?"

"Not yet, we're broadcasting a challenge but they transitioned in a fair distance off... there's the warp signature. Whoever it is is hauling ass, Skipper. Coming for us, fast."

"Sound general quarters," Roberts ordered, just to be safe.

The alarms went off a moment later, subdued on the command deck but loud enough that they couldn't be missed.

"General Quarters, Aye."

"From the warp signature, I'd say it's an Archangel, Skipper."

*The Revenge then, most likely. At least we'll find out what the hell happened.* Roberts thought grimly. He wasn't sure he *wanted* to know what the hell would send the Revenge running, but better that they do that than the alternatives he supposed.

"It's the Casino!"

*What?*

"Get me comms," Roberts ordered. "I want Samuels on screen, now."

"Aye skipper!"

*****

**Casino**

"Comm request from the Bell."

"I've got it," Jennifer said as she accepted the call with a thought, not bothering to even twitch her fingers as she guided the ship in toward the cluster of Confederation IFF signals.

"What the hell is going on, Jenn?" Jason demanded as he showed up on a window in front of her eyes.

"VIP transport from Prometheus," She informed him, "Palin needs an Entity, you have one."

Jason grimaced, "We do not have time for that fool right now."

"Not my call, Captain," She countered. "We pulled a data core from an Imperial network, one of their hidden ones. Palin tore through most of their encryption in a few hours, but the deep stuff was buried in what he said was most likely the language of the entities."

Jason swore softly, looking aside, "Alright, hurry up and get on board. We've got something going down and the *Revenge* just sent us the full abort codes. They're in deep, we need to move."

Jennifer froze.

"Steph? What the hell did he step in this time?"

"We don't know, he was monitoring the Imperial battles with the Drasin swarm, operating as a forward observer for our task group," Jason told her. "Last operation went smooth, but something happened this time. All I know for sure is that he's called a full abort and made it clear that the AO is *not* friendly and we're not to transition in."

"Shit. Ok, I'll offload Palin and..."

"No time, just get your ship on board, we're warping the second you're on the hangar deck."

\*\*\*\*\*

**Bellerophon**

"You heard, of course."

Bell nodded silently to the statement, "I did indeed, Captain. I find myself... intensely curious."

Jason rolled his eyes, "That's fine, help the doctor if you can, but we have other priorities that may take up your focus."

"I will do my duty, Captain, you have my word."

Jason nodded, knowing that despite his dislike of having an entity on board, Bell had never given him any doubt as to where the entity stood in regards to the safety of the crew and the completion of the mission.

"Then do what you can to decode whatever intelligence they managed to find," He ordered. "I'm guessing that we're going to need every trick we can scrounge up."

Bell saluted, "Aye Captain."

"Helm, I want us moving the moment they're on board," Jason said, shifting his attention again. "I don't know what the Revenge is in the middle of, but I have a bad feeling about all of this."

"Yes sir, we're in contact with the deck crew. The moment they clear it, we're in motion."

*That's all I can ask for, I suppose.*

*****

## Casino

Doctor Palin looked at the big ship that was growing larger on the screens he could see from his jump seat. It had been a, thankfully, short trip since the comforts onboard an Archangel Class gunboat were somewhat below minimal in his opinion.

Still, he had put up with more discomfort in the past. Whether he would again in the future, well that remained to be seen, but the possibility remained if nothing else.

"Be good to get out of these jump seats."

Palin looked over at the speaker, a man who'd introduced himself but Palin hadn't bothered to remember the name.

"You cramped up too, there, Doctor?" The man asked pleasantly.

"Yes."

One word answer, Palin hoped it would keep the man from talking to him.

"Think you can really crack that data bank?"

Or not.

Palin sighed, "I already *cracked* the device. The language some of the data is recorded in is another issue, however."

"Right. Well, let's keep those fingers crossed, right Doc?"

Palin closed his eyes and pretended to sleep, only grunting a response.

*****

# CHAPTER 18

**Gaia's Revenge**

"Jesus, will you look at that…"

Steph ignored the comment for the moment as he guided the ship in closer, scanners full active as he gathered all the data he possibly could. He had no trouble deciphering what had caught Tyke's eye, though, as a swarm of the Drasin utterly overwhelmed an Imperial cruiser and completely *engulfed* it in a writhing mass of monstrous destruction.

*Poor bastards.*

The scene was being repeated all over the battlespace, fleeing Imperial cruisers were being hounded by thousands of Drasin drones while those that stayed and fought were being torn up right from under their crew's feet.

"It's not a battle, this was a trap," Steph said grimly as he noted a few of the drones break off to intercept the *Revenge.*

Burning them to cinders took less than a thought on his part, but it really just attracted even more in their direction as a response. Steph largely ignored them, the Drasin weren't even close to a match for the maneuverability of his ship, and leaving them eating dust was easy enough.

Unfortunately, his ship didn't have remotely enough firepower to handle the situation, and that was a major problem.

"We have to assume that whatever data they're after, they'll have in short order," He said grimly, evading another attempt by the drones to pen the gunboat in, "I think we might be screwed."

"That has always been a possibility," Milla said from behind him, "but I believe that we may have a chance yet."

"Optimist. I like it," Steph said casually. "What have you got?"

"Here? Very little," She admitted. "However, I believe I see how they managed to create such a large warp field."

Steph considered that briefly, "I suppose that could be interesting. How'd they pull it off?"

"Manipulating spacetime is not particularly difficult," She said easily. "We all do it every moment of our lives, in small ways. Creating the gravity well to draw the star into a freefall in the direction of your choosing is simply a matter of attaining sufficient mass."

Steph nodded, considering that as he flew through another swarm, threading a needle as every weapon on the gunboat tore into the drones with enthusiasm.

"Ok, sure," He said. "And they certainly have mass, I'll give you that, but you can't hit FTL with just a gravity well. You also need the peak behind you in order to surf past the lightspeed limit."

"Agreed," Milla confirmed. "Look to the far side of the star. Do you see it?"

Steph refocused their long range scanners as he skirted the edge of a swarm, getting them focused on a construction of some kind that floated there.

"What is that?" Tyke asked from where he was sitting at Ops.

"The configuration matches the equipment that modulates spacetime to create the wave peak," Milla answered,

"Only *much* larger."

"Analyze it," Steph ordered, "What would it take to destroy?"

"More than we have, I am afraid, Stephan... but I will run the numbers."

*****

## From the Flames

"Reverse warp! Continue firing!" Kaela ordered as she commanded her ship through what was, in effect, a fighting retreat.

The wall of Drasin was beyond anything she'd expected to see, and that was *after* factoring in the stellar construct they'd encountered some time earlier. This time the effort had to have gone into recreating more Drasin instead of the infrastructure for the construct.

The result was more Drasin than her ship's computer could keep in its memory at any one time, and she knew for certain that they didn't even have a line of sight on *half* the battlespace.

"Our emitters are burning out, they will not last much longer at this rate of fire!"

Kaela swore, "Fine. Restrict fire twenty percent, and get maintenance and repair teams to the weapon stations! We must destroy as many as possible before they take us!"

There was no question of surviving this one, not after seeing what the Drasin had brought to the space for the conflict. She did not know if the Home Fleet at Kraike would be able to do much better, but Kaela could only do the best she could to soften the enemy for them.

She doubted it would make much difference, but it was all she could do.

So she would do it.

*****

"First division is lost, Fleet Commander! All signals from those ships have been cut, no visual contact remains. Just... those things."

Markys wiped his face, his hand coming away wet and chilled.

"We... we need to signal the homeworld," He said. "Order the remaining ships to delay the enemy, we will warn the home fleet."

"Orders sent, Fleet Commander."

"Power to the warp fields, we're leaving."

"Yes, Fleet Commander."

*****

**Gaia's Revenge**

The departure of the Imperial Fleet Command squadron barely made a blip in Steph's peripheral senses as he continued dogging his gunboat in and around the enemy drones, trying to get solid scans of the constructs in use. He was hoping that they'd be able to use the data for something, but at the moment he honestly wasn't sure if there was enough firepower in the entire galactic sector to do much of anything against what he was seeing.

"Is that construct reading over a *lightsecond* tall?" He blurted in disbelief.

"That is correct, Stephan. The power involved to maintain it... where are they getting it?" Milla blurted, sounding just as locked in disbelief as he was.

Her question, however, set Steph to thinking furiously.

*That's not a bad point, actually. Are they feeding off the star itself? It's the only thing here that is showing up on the scanners with a power curve remotely that high?*

"What about the star?" He asked, rolling the ship over and around another pack of the enemy drones, carving them to shards before righting the Revenge with a kip and a flip, and putting them back on course. "Maybe they're pulling the power from its mass?"

"If so, it will not last long," Milla said. "That is a dwarf star, approximately one tenth the displacement of an average mainline stellar mass. To power such a field as the peak needed to make it go FTL, it would be losing more than a hundredth of its mass over very few lightyears travelled."

"Ok, that means that some star system not too far from here clearly needs to be recharted," Steph snorted. "Can we determine if that's what they're doing?"

"If we could identify the star, or track it in transit, yes," Milla responded.

"But not now?"

"Unlikely that any power draw is currently significant enough to measure."

"Well isn't that just... lovely."

\*\*\*\*\*

## Bellerophon

Edward Palin carefully went over everything in the new lab he'd been assigned, not really put out by the relative lack of size and amenities. He'd had much less at various other points in his life, and usually for less cause.

*Let's see, we have a hardware link to the main computer core. Going to need that, but best advise the Captain that we'll certainly need all the cycles he can give us. Wouldn't do to cause them any shortfalls in calculations during a fight, after all.*

210

There had been times in his past when he wouldn't have considered that a particularly important detail, but those days were behind him.

"I am glad to hear that."

Palin didn't jump, though his heart rate *did* spike just a little as he turned, eyes falling on the young man in what appeared to be period armor standing where no one had been standing a short while earlier.

"Bellerophon, I presume," Palin said dryly.

"Most here call me Bell," The Entity said simply.

"I'm sure," Palin responded before he went back about setting up his equipment. "I'm to understand that I don't need to brief you on the task?"

"You want me to see if I can understand what you believe to be the, or *a*, written language of Entities like myself."

"Correct. Can you access the system as it is?" Palin gestured to the data core.

Bell looked over at it and shook his head, "Negative. The Quantum matrix isn't one of the energy fields that I interact with naturally."

"Pity, but not unexpected," Palin said as he continued working. "The Matrix exists in a superposition, far deeper than the electromagnetic spectrum you and your... species, I suppose? Whatever... it exists below your normal senses. I imagine that it would be like looking into the ultraviolet for humans, or maybe radio would be more accurate?"

"Simplistic as an explanation, but it would seem to cover the bases."

"Of course it's simplistic," Palin snapped, "We don't have the next four days to properly explain it. You can read my mind, get the extra details you want from there."

Bell eyed the old man with a mixture of confusion and amusement. He was used to the crew treating him either as a particularly intelligent mascot, or as an AI on the verge of running rampant. Unless he was rather mistaken, which with this human seemed more likely than normal due to how fast his mind tended to jump from subject to subject, Bell felt like he was being considered more like... either a student, or possibly an intern.

He wasn't certain which was better.

This man, Edward Palin, was far more than his records suggested. Bell could tell that from the moment he began thinking the man's thoughts in conjunction with him. However, it also seemed that he wasn't properly informed of certain things.

"That is not how it works," Bell informed him patiently.

"What?" Palin paused, looking back at him.

"I cannot read your mind, only your thoughts."

Palin stared for a moment, eyes narrowing as he parsed the meaning of the words.

"Explain the difference," He demanded.

"As you have already determined, your thoughts are the things you are thinking *now*," Bell said. "Your mind is the long term storage of everything you've learned and experienced in your entire life."

Palin grumbled, "So unless I think it, you can't read it."

"That is correct."

"That is an enormous flaw in your ability, at least for you." Palin said firmly, his mind flashing through the potential issues.

"Indeed, I have noticed much of what you're referring to myself, though not everything." Bell admitted. "When it comes to things learned by humans within my range, my memory of such is essentially flawless. However, human memories are *not*, so I cannot rely on people's memories of things they learned, even if they intentionally think about them for me. Compared to planet bound Entities, who have tens of thousands of years of complete exposure to their population with essentially no blank spots, I am extremely limited."

"Troubling," Palin said after some thought. "We may have to face off against an Entity far more experienced than you, with the complete sum total of a trillion minds locked in its experience."

"And I have only the limited experience of a few hundred," Bell nodded in confirmation.

"Troubling," Palin said again as he returned to his task. "I need to think on this and get the equipment hooked up. Please, leave me some time alone."

"Of course, Doctor. I will return when you are ready."

Palin didn't look up or respond as the entity faded away, leaving him visually alone in the lab as he worked.

*****

The Bellerophon was in high warp, heading for the calculated battlespace that the Revenge had been observing while Jason Roberts sat at the command station, mind spinning with the possibilities… none of which were good.

"Permission to enter the Command Deck, Captain?"

Jason glanced back and nodded, waving casually, "Come on in, Jenn."

Jennifer Samuels stepped over the threshold and made her way to his station, eyes on the nav charts as she walked.

"How long before we arrive?" She asked.

"Twenty minutes, give or take," He answered. "We were supposed to transition in on the Revenge's signal, but they called a full abort and warned us off with the code for unknown threat, just absolutely do *not* Transition. We're scanning, of course, but we won't see anything on passive scans until we're practically on top of the target area."

She nodded wearily.

FTL operations were like that. When the enemy was moving assets around faster than lightspeed, you couldn't really see any of their actions until well after the maneuver had played out unless you used active FTL scans. Unfortunately, those were power intensive and tended not to be of much use beyond a few light hours at *best,* and normally were effectively worthless at much less than that.

Tachyons did not interact easily with normal matter, and that meant that even a powerful burst from the main scanners would deteriorate into nothingness in a very short relative distance due to the inverse square law.

"We have picked up several tachyon bursts, however," Jason went on, "So we know *something* is going down, or did go down already. There wasn't enough from the signals to give us any real insight."

"Understood. Well, the Casino will be ready to deploy as needed."

Jason nodded, "We'll try not to blow your cover, but that's good to know."

"Cover might be gone already, after our last mission," Jennifer said. "If we get through this without making it obvious, we'll have to be extra careful with the Empire for a while regardless."

Jason's eyes narrowed, "I'll be looking for the day when we can take the damned kid gloves off with them, once and for all."

She snorted, "Not saying anything we don't all feel, Jason."

\*\*\*\*\*

# CHAPTER 19

**Gaia's Revenge**

"That's it, the Imperial divisions who didn't run are pretty much decimated," Tyke announced. "In numbers, they've still got a fighting force but they're breaking apart. The first ships have broken discipline and run for it. The rest won't last long now."

Steph grunted as he rolled the *Revenge* through a double barrel, then threaded the needle through a gap in the Drasin formation.

"Can't say I'm surprised," He responded, working the fighter/gunboat ever closer to the leeward side of the star so they could get better scans of the warp field generator. "Even Imperial discipline has got to have limits. Take enough losses, almost anyone will break."

"We are not helping them?" Milla asked neutrally.

"Even if we wanted to, we don't have the firepower to make a dent," Steph said. "This is intel gathering, the Empire will have to carry their own load."

The swarm were turning more and more of their focus to the Revenge, and that was making dodging their attacks all the harder. The only upside that Steph had to count on was that the swarm was apparently in intelligence gathering mode itself, which limited their attacks to close range as they tried to grapple with the Revenge and claim it for themselves.

He had no intention of letting that happen, of course, but as long as the swarm was intent on that they wouldn't be able to slice the Revenge apart with beams from range.

*At least until they find what they're looking for from one of the Imperial ships they've already captured.*

Once that happened, Steph knew that the gloves would be off.

*If we're still in this swarm when that happens… we die.*

*****

**Imperial Cruiser *From the Flames***

The air was filled with an acrid smell, something was burning though for the life of her Kaela couldn't figure out what or where. Normally she'd be riding the damage control teams to get it dealt with, but at the moment they had bigger concerns and she doubted the ship would last long enough for them to die from an air supply or quality issue.

"We've lost three more ships, Ship's Commander."

"Destroyed or run?" She asked flatly, not looking up.

"Two destroyed, one ran."

"Acknowledged." She said, "At least Fleet Command finally got the hell out of here. How many ships have been taken?"

"Fifteen, at least, Ship's Commander. Possibly more, but we're not sure if those were destroyed outright or not."

It likely didn't matter which, she supposed, the Drasin would consume the materials either way. Kaela hoped that the crews died clean first, before they were eaten, but whichever fate was in store… well it wasn't going to be her decision to make.

The fighting was turning even more vicious, if that were possible, as the Drasin pushed in close and cut their way into the Imperial cruisers.

Quickly that was turning each cruiser into a deck clearing nightmare as well as the fleet action they'd begun the fight as.

*The Drasin are on board my ship. Again.*

Kaela was monitoring reports from the deck fighting, and her crew was doing better this time than they had the last. They'd taken lessons from the Gaian's on how to fight the damned things in close quarters, but the reports from other ships were making it clear that the rest of the Imperial vessels were not doing as well.

The fighting retreat was likely doomed already, but if she let the division break up into single ships fleeing for their lives then everyone would die uselessly. At least if they stuck together they'd inflict some serious damage on the enemy first.

*If that even matters.*

It might all be futile, Kaela knew. The Drasin had brought far more to the battlespace than she'd believed them capable, more than the Empire had ever *hinted* that they could manage. If they were this far wrong, then perhaps the so-called leash itself was worth far less than implied.

"Ship's Commander! Enemy reinforcements are redirecting to our coordinates!"

Kaela swore under her breath.

*We're already losing the ship one deck panel at a time.*

"Where's division Two and One?" She asked, looking up to the board.

"We lost contact, there's too many Drasin between us to see them or even punch a comm signal through to, Ship's Commander!"

"Damn it." She shook her head, "Open comm, all channels, all available power."

"Comm open!"

"All ships, this is *From the Flames*. Division three, fall back ahead of our position, we will cover! Division two, Division one, if you receive this signal... Withdraw! Withdraw! Fleet Command has been evacuated successfully! Get yourselves clear and report to the Homeworld for your next assignment!" She snapped. "From the Flames, signal ends."

"Comm closed."

"Lift all restrictions on weapons," Kaela ordered. "Continuous fire, all batteries, full power beams."

"Restrictions lifted! Continuous fire, full power, Ship's Commander!"

The augmented view of the battlespace around them erupted with the beams as the *From the Flames* stopped hoarding energy and trying to preserve its emitters, unleashing everything it had left as quickly as it could manage.

"Ship's Commander, we have overheating warnings on three quarters of our remaining emitters!"

"Damage control teams," She put out the order. "Keep our weapons firing as long as you can! I don't care what needs to be done, I do not care what shape they're in when you're finished, as long as they can fire I will consider each additional moment a victory! That is all."

*****

**Gaia's Revenge**

"You catch that?" Steph asked, barely noticing the signal they'd intercepted.

"Looks like someone on the Imperial side has a brain," Tyke said. "They're calling for a full retreat under fire. Probably too late, but it's better than falling apart and being picked over like refuse."

"What the hell, Milla rebroadcast that," Steph said, "then I need you to focus on that construct. Get as much data as you can."

"Yes, Stephan," Milla said, absently sending on the signal they'd intercepted before she turned the *Revenge's* full scanning capacity forward to the massive construction they were approaching.

It had the correct geometry for a spacetime manipulation system, but the scale of it was beyond anything she'd ever imagined possible. In fact, Milla was all but certain that it *wasn't* possible… or would be if she weren't looking right at the thing. She knew that the scaling issues should have prevented what she was seeing. There were reasons why the Imperial cruiser, the Priminae Vessels, and the Heroics were all nearly identical designs in terms of base size and geometry and only a small part was due to the shared history of the Empire and the Priminae.

Much larger than the standard cruiser design and the drive systems rapidly began to deliver lower returns for energy output. Even doubling the size would essentially leave you with a ship that could move itself FTL, but do almost nothing else, the drop off in efficiency was so drastic.

She didn't know how the Drasin had done this… but if they could just figure it out, it would *change the galaxy*.

Despite the danger, she was finding the whole mystery rather… invigorating.

\*\*\*\*\*

## Bellerophon

"Can you read it now?" Palin asked, shunting the data through the system and out of the data storage matrix.

The Entity, Bell, frowned as he focused.

"I... yes?" He said, uncertainly. "It is... strange. Something isn't right, I can't describe it properly, however. I..."

"Don't have the words?" Palin asked, sounding almost sympathetic.

"Yes. That's it... I do not have the words to describe what's... missing?" Bell said.

Palin sucked a little air in through his teeth, making irritating sounds with his tongue as he did. Bell just ignored him, remaining focused on the data.

"Keep at it," Palin said, "try to find ways to describe the problem, even if you have to be really roundabout about things."

"I will try," Bell said, still staring at the data he was experiencing.

It took a while before he spoke again.

"I... think..." Bell frowned, "something a crewman said some time ago in an argument comes to mind."

"Yes?"

"If I ate bread, cheese, lettuce, tomato, and hamburger all separate... Did I eat a cheeseburger?" the Entity asked pensively.

Palin started to reply, then stopped with a finger in the air and his mouth slightly open.

"Huh." He said, dropping his finger and looking at the data for a long stretched out moment before his eyes abruptly gleamed. "That's it!"

"It is?" Bell asked, confused for a moment before he processed Palin's thoughts. "Oh, I see. The feed was meant to be experienced as a whole. Odd, I didn't formulate that thought myself, I... just remembered the argument the crew were having and somehow thought it was related?"

"That would be an intuitive leap," Palin said, already working furiously. "Happens all the time."

"This is the first time it has happened to me."

"Oh?" Palin glanced up with a slight hint of curiosity, "You don't seem... dim."

Bellerophon stared for a long moment, perplexed by the statement. It *sounded* rather insulting, but from the Doctor's thoughts it was clear that it was merely a statement of fact so far as the man was concerned.

"Nor do you," Bell said finally.

"Thank you," Palin said as he refocused back on the job at hand.

"Appearances may deceive, however."

Palin glanced back in his direction, "Did you say something?"

Bell shook his head, "No. No, I did not."

*****

Jennifer stood beside the command console on the bridge of the Bellerophon, eyes on the screen as they began to decelerate into the target area of operations.

"We've got some strange signals, Captain."

Jason grunted, "I'm going to need more than strange, son. Be specific."

"Still pulling data, but there's a *massive* unexpected gravitational reading," The lieutenant standing scanner watch said, sounding confused. "It's got to be at stellar scale, but there's nothing on the charts."

*Stellar scale gravitational anomaly,* Jason thought as he leaned forward, "That would explain the abort signal from the *Revenge*. If we'd tried to transition into that..."

Everyone grimaced automatically, thinking about the results of their atoms being scattered across several cubic lightyears as a result of such an attempt.

"Maybe," Jennifer said softly, "but what the hell causes that? Stellar masses don't just move around unpredictably. We have this region mapped."

"Holy christ, there's a dwarf star right in the center of the projected AO."

Jason and Jennifer both exchanged confused looks and leaned forward.

"Are you serious?" Jason demanded.

"Yes sir. I'm running it's spectrum now, but it's definitely not supposed to be here."

Jason shook his head, "Scan for any signals from the *revenge*. They may need backup, or they might have an answer. In either case, find them."

"Yes sir."

"I should take the *Casino* and get out there," Jennifer said, straightening.

Jason hesitated but finally nodded, "Go."

"Good luck," She said as she headed for the back of the command deck.

"We're all going to need it, I suspect."

*****

"Try now." Palin said as he made a couple changes.

Bell frowned, distracted as he refocused back on the room and the task the Doctor was presenting, but part of his mind remained looking outward.

*A star where one should not be. This will not be good.*

However, for the moment he had a higher priority task, so Bell looked into the data again and felt it flooding him all at once.

"Yes. I see," He said aloud. "This is much better, more comprehensible."

"Is that what I thought? A language for your entities?" Palin asked eagerly.

"No. It isn't anything so... crude. It's experience," Bell said as he found himself buffeted from all sides by the data turned reality.

Bell stumbled, a hand reaching up in a very human expression as he struggled to keep himself separate from the experience he was being fed. He held his head, as though suffering from a headache that he couldn't ever truly experience.

"I... We... The *Xeno*..." Bell gritted out, his expression growing thunderous.

Palin slammed his hand down on the emergency cutoff and the flood of data was cut off abruptly, causing Bell to disincorporate for a moment before reappearing where he had been a moment earlier.

"Bellerophon, are you alright?" Palin asked cautiously.

"I am, Doctor, however it would be best if we did not do that again." The Entity said after a long moment's thought.

"The Imperial Entity, it's his experience, isn't it?" Palin asked, having pieced it together in a flash.

"Indeed," Bell confirmed. "And he is... ancient. I only caught flashes of it, some of it is already fading. I don't think I can keep his experience within my memories, Doctor. I... I did not realize that I even *had* a limit."

Palin nodded slowly, "He has a planet to store

everything that makes him what he is. You only have this ship, and while the core may have a planetary mass stored in it, the EM field the ship operates with isn't remotely as powerful when taken as a whole. What can you remember?"

"A lot, and nearly none of it all at the same time," Bellerophon said. "A fraction of a fraction of what I experienced remains… yet…"

"Yet?"

"Yet it is still more than what composes *myself*, as I identified prior to the experience." Bell said softly, "I am sorry, Doctor. I do not think I can explain myself properly."

"That's fine, Bellerophon. I think I understand enough." Palin told him.

Bell paused, looking outward from the lab as though through the deck. "I must go. We are about to be in an emergency."

"The Empire?" Palin asked sharply.

"The Drasin."

"Go."

*****

# CHAPTER 20

**Gaia's Revenge**

"Construct is less than three AU away, Stephan! Active scanning has commenced!"

Steph barely had the focus to acknowledge Milla's report, he was too focused on dodging the ever increasing attacks from the Drasin as they tried over and over to swarm the lone gunboat with sheer numbers. His only real advantage was that space was *huge*, even when you took into account the unbelievable numbers the Drasin had brought to the party.

Even so, he was finding himself running out of space as they got closer and closer to the construct that had to be the source of the positive gravity gradient necessary for FTL through warping of space.

It was huge.

Over three hundred *thousand* kilometers tall.

More than twice the diameter of Jupiter.

They didn't have a mass measurement, there was far too much interference for that to be taken, but Steph supposed that its mass didn't really matter. It was generating true anti-mass, afterall, so technically it might as well mass nothing at all… or less than that.

"Confirmed negative gravity bubble detection, Stephan!"

Good to know, but honestly he hadn't needed the confirmation.

Steph twisted his ship away from another pack of the rabid beasts trying to devour everything in the entire sector, keeping the Revenge on target as they continued to gather data. If the device, the construct, was what it *had* to be... the Drasin were hiding some sort of technique that was well beyond Terran ship building, the Priminae... even the Empire.

They *needed* that data, if only to work out how likely it would be that the Drasin could use it against them in the near future.

"The readings, they are incredible Stephan!" Milla said, sounding more excited than anything else. "It is generating a field strong enough to create a negative warp in space larger than the *star* itself!"

*Damn. If they power that up while we're this close...* Steph's mind was racing, *We'll be flung aside like we were struck by a planet.*

"How steep a gradient?" He growled.

"Still calculating, Stephan," Milla shouted back, "But *very* steep."

That was bad news, but not surprising. A normal gravitational gradient was relatively shallow, such that a planet like earth lost barely ten percent of the warp effect between the surface and low orbit. That wasn't steep enough to where you could tell the difference in the effect between, say, the bottom of your feet and the top of your head... but the difference *was there*. Even a large ship, *kilometers* high, wouldn't be adversely affected by a planetary mass gradient.

A Stellar mass gradient was steeper, but still not remotely sufficient to cause issues across even large scale mega-structures.

If this device was outputting a steeper gradient than that, however, it was possible that the shearing force of it slamming into the Archangel gunboat would crush the aft of the ship into a crumpled mess before the front even started accelerating.

*We can't stay.*

"Get your scans faster, Milla," He ordered. "We're withdrawing!"

*****

**Bellerophon**

"What in the name of God is this hell?" Jason Roberts swore as he stood up from his station and walked toward the main display.

"We're still counting Drasin drones, but I doubt we'll be able to get a full count, Captain."

"Forget the drones, what the hell are those constructs?" Jason asked. "They look like warp modules, but they're so damn *big*."

"Unknown, but warp modules fit as well as anything we can compare them to, Sir."

Jason shook his head, not wanting to believe what he was seeing. If those were warp modules, and that was a star where no star should be…

The math he was doing in his head was not something he wanted to be real.

"Captain, we've got a location on the *Revenge!*"

"Show me!"

Jason nearly started swearing loud enough for half the ship to hear him when the signal was fully localized.

"What in the…" He fell silent, fists balled up in front of his face for a moment before he forced himself to relax. "What are they doing *that far into the swarm*?"

No one had much in the way of an answer, so all he could do was shake it off and get to work.

"Captain, the *Casino* has left the hangar bay. They engaged full stealth before departure."

"Good, close the hangar and make sure we're locked up tight. Signal the others," Jason ordered. "We're going in, let's try and thin the herd a little."

"Aye skipper!"

Claxons sounded as the Bellerophon began to accelerate, the other Heroics moving along with their pace as the looking threat loomed even larger.

\*\*\*\*\*

### Casino

Jennifer leaned into the suspension field, letting the feel of the solar winds orientate her as she got her bearings.

"All hands, get ready for a fight," She said as she put more power to the ship's warp fields and they flashed into a micro-FTL jump. "We have a lock on the *Gaia's Revenge*, and they're deep in enemy territory. Empire ships are still in the combat zone, but they're occupied on the other side of the dwarf star from the *Revenge*. We need to get close enough to get direct contact with the *Revenge*, from there we'll figure things out. Marines, I'm sorry but you just sit back and enjoy the ride this time... I doubt there will be much cause for your services on this run."

She closed to shipwide comm and turned her attention back to the flying.

*What the hell are you doing so deep in that mess, Stephanos?* She wondered darkly. *We're all crazy, but I didn't think you were stupid as well.*

Taking one ship, a *gunboat* at that, into that mess? That

was beyond crazy.

She had to get close enough to punch a signal through all the interference, which meant she had to take the *Casino* right into the same damned mess that Steph had.

*Well fuck me for being stupid too, I suppose. Damn you, Stephanos. I'm going to kick your ass when we get out of this.*

The Casino dropped out of the short FTL hop, real time scanners coming alive again as she evaluated the scene before taking action. The Drasin were swarming ahead of her, but not looking in her direction. She dumped the energy gathered in the forward gravity well, frying a few dozen of the closest drones with the waste energy, but there wasn't enough from a short hop to do more than that.

*No imperial ships close enough to monitor me.*

"Prime the pulse weapons."

*****

## Gaia's Revenge

Milla was working feverishly, trying to get every possible scan she could even as Steph turned the nose of the ship away from the star and began climbing out of the well and away from the construct even as the swarm did its level best to trap them in an inescapable net. She didn't know if she was getting enough to make much of a difference in the long term, but just the *existence* of a warp generation construct on this scale was rewriting everything she knew about warp physics.

She was so focused on that aspect that Milla initially missed another alert blinking on her overwhelmed board.

Tyke, however, was handling operations and stepped in to redirect the alert to his own board.

"Skipper, looks like we've got company."

"I noticed," Steph said through gritted teeth.

"Not the rabble, boss, Jen's here!"

"The Casino? Where?" Steph demanded, not looking from his work.

"Coordinates to your HUD."

"Got them, redirecting," He said, "Do we know what happened to the Imperial divisions?"

"Lost track of them in the scrum," Tyke admitted. "Mostly because they're on the other side of the damned star, Boss."

"Yeah, yeah, save the excuses," Steph grinned, rolling the gunboat in a tight yaw to avoid a suicide rush by a group of the Drasin drones.

They all winced as a scraping sound could be heard along the hull.

"Tyke."

"On it." Tyke said quickly, checking the exterior scanners intently before he let out a breath he hadn't known he was holding. "Looks like they didn't get a purchase."

"Thank god I'm so damned good, huh?"

"One way of putting it," Tyke said. "Not the way *I* would have put it, but one way."

"Ah screw you too."

"Must you *children* be like this in every single fight?" Milla demanded, sounding frustrated as she did, though it was likely that she was more put out by them having to leave the construct behind than the back and forth between Tyke and Steph.

For their part the two men were silent for a brief moment before they nodded in unison and spoke.

"Yeah, yeah we must."

Milla sighed, but shifted her scanners from the construct and refocused on the swarms. They were too far to get much from it now anyway, she figured.

"Comm signal from the Casino, bossman."

"Put Jen through already, not like these ugly buggers are much for conversation anyway."

*****

**Casino**

"Crown, you *jackass*," Jennifer growled as the channel opened up. "What the hell were you *thinking*, getting that deep in the swarms?"

"Had to get some scans, 'Sharp." Steph responded after a brief delay. "They *warped* that damned star in, we watched them do it. Craziest damn thing I've ever seen."

Jannifer didn't actually know what to say to that and found herself blinking in shock. Ok, they'd known that the star wasn't where it should be, that was a given, but the idea that someone had *warped* it around was...

Terrifying? Horrifying?

*No, neither of those words come close to covering the feeling.*

"Are you... No, never mind, I don't care," She said aloud. *Worry about that shit later.* "Standby for pulse torpedo fire, I'm going to clear you a corridor. Make sure you've got your warp fields as high as you can manage on my mark."

"Roger, pulse bombardement on your mark."

"ETA to contact... thirty three seconds after mark."

"Roger, thirty three seconds from mark."

"Ready... Mark!"

Jennifer fired the pulse torpedoes from the Archangel's

magazines, spitting pure antimatter into the universe as the writhing swarm turned to surround the *Revenge* as it began climbing at high warp.

The *Revenge* vanished from her scanners in a flash of Cherenkov blue as it broke lightspeed just before the volley from the Casino tore through the Drasin swarm with an absolute fury. Dozens, then *hundreds*, and possibly thousands of the drones simply vanished into their component atoms or *less* as the mutual annihilation of matter and antimatter unleashed a growing cascade of violent plasma and other radiative energies from the explosions.

One of the oddities of working with warp FTL, however, showed itself as her instruments actually registered the *Revenge* slashing through space just off her port side several seconds *before* it vanished from her screens further down-well.

Jennifer shook her head, irritated by the fact that the inevitable report she'd have to file was going to be a bit of a nightmare to properly plot out due to the time stamps being so off.

*I hate relativistic math.*

The channel to the *Revenge* beeped again and she opened it up, "Nice of you to join us out here, Crown."

"Yeah, well, the company sucked where I was hanging out, you know."

Jennifer snorted, throwing power into a reverse warp as she pulled her ship away from the swarm, but noticed that the *Revenge* hadn't slowed its warp, but instead was *circling* back around.

"What the hell are you doing?" She growled.

"Just need to dump any antihydrogen I picked up on the passage through," Stepoh said coolly as he realigned his forward warp with the Drasin swarm and abruptly killed the warp fields without engaging safeties.

The resulting maelstrom of radiation and high C particulates lanced across space and into the pursuing swarm.

The resulting chain of destruction was... satisfying, even if it weren't caused by her own ship.

"If you're through showing off, let's get out of here."

"You said it, Jenn. You lead, I shall follow."

"Might keep you out of trouble for a while."

"Oh, I'm *hurt.*"

She snorted, *Like hell.* "The Heroics warped in, but I'm not sure what Roberts is going to do. We should probably make ourselves scarce."

"Roger that."

\*\*\*\*\*

## Bellerophon

Roberts kept one eye on the *Casino* and the *Revenge* as he led the Heroics in, but he wasn't overly worried about either ship. Certainly, the Archangels didn't have the firepower to do much in this situation, but they were among the most maneuverable and *fastest* ships on record. The Drasin drones would have to work damn hard to catch either of them, and that was before you accounted for their pilots.

No, the Empire was by far the more pressing concern.

It still rankled on him to save any of the Imperials, mind, but as long as they were bleeding the Drasin dry, strategy and tactics said that they were more useful alive than as flotsam in the black.

"Prepare pulse torpedoes." He ordered, "Target a wide spread away from the surviving Imperial vessels."

"Spread targeted, Sir."

"Calculate optimal fire points, feed them to the system, and let it rip." He said as he slumped back.

"Aye, skipper. Fire orders inserted, automatic safeties clear. Fire control on automatic."

The computers ran the optimal spread numbers for the antimatter warheads, then fired as the Bell and other ships in the task group hit their marks.

In moments there were several *tons* of antihydrogen flying across the black, all on its way to a long awaited meeting with the swarm.

"All pulse banks are empty!"

"Seal them up, start reloading procedures."

"Aye skipper!"

*****

# CHAPTER 21

**Imperial Cruiser *From the Flames***

"We've lost three more ships, Ship's Commander!"

Kaela grunted, that was as much of an acknowledgement she was giving any announcement at this point, she didn't have time for more.

"Get more damage control teams to the emitters before we lose another one," She ordered.

"Ship's Commander, we don't *have any more teams!*"

"Then send anyone you can find!" She snapped. "We can hardly do any worse at the moment anyway!"

"Yes, Ship's Commander!"

The air was starting to feel more like sucking down fumes than breathing, but she ignored the acrid smell of toxic gas and human fear that was filling the air around her and tried to get the next crisis task handled before her ship was torn out from under her.

"Security teams, we have breaches on aft decks fourteen through twenty three!"

"Ship's Commander, we have more of the swarm on an interception course!"

"Maximum warp, put the field between the bulk of them and the *Flames*," She ordered.

"That will diverge our course from the optimum withdrawal path!"

"Do it!" Kaela snapped, "We won't survive the optimum path if those drones get on board!"

"Yes, Ship's Commander!"

The ship pivoted on its axis, putting the steep deflection field of the ship's negative warp between them and the approaching swarm, violently shoving the swarm off in all directions as they continued to accelerate away from the dwarf star.

She would have preferred to put the crushing positive warp on them instead, but that would have reversed their course *into* the star and the largest mass of the enemy swarms. Pushing them aside was the best compromise she could reach at the moment, pitiful though that may be.

"Ship's Commander... new signals! It's *them* again."

She didn't need more information, she knew who *they* were.

"On display."

"Yes, Ship's Commander."

The display was a mess, both from internal damage to the scanners and possibly more than she knew, but also because the mess outside the ship was so chaotic and filled with debris... both living and dead... that the image was badly distorted despite the computers trying valiantly to clean it up and provide a proper augmented view of the battlespace.

That didn't mean she couldn't recognize the inbound ships, however.

*Five of them. Again.*

She would consider it arrogant, but when it came to the sort of fast strike and fade tactics they were employing, five were enough against most targets.

A swarm of this size wasn't most targets, of course, so

perhaps some arrogance was on display after all, unless they just didn't have more available within the range of the fight. Kaela didn't know what, if either of those options, was the true one but she supposed it didn't matter.

"Pull the teams from the beam emitters," She snapped, her hand coming down on the internal comm controls. "Put everyone on the warp field systems! I want *every* spark of power redirected to the fields. Now!"

The order had barely been acknowledged when the first of the enemy's negative-matter weapons slammed into the Drasin swarm and the radiation from the strikes washed over the entire region at the speed of light. Alarms sounded, but Kaela ignored them.

"Get us out of here, while the enemy is distracted."

"Yes ship's Commander!"

\*\*\*\*\*

### Bellerophon

"Positive strikes, Skipper. Kill counts being calculated."

Jason grunted, "Whatever. We'll review them after the fight, I don't need a tally right now. Not like we're going to run out."

"Yes Sir."

He doubted that they'd ever get an accurate kill count, not in that mess out there anyway, but it didn't make any real difference.

*This isn't a battle. It's an extermination. There's no real pride in putting a Drasin silhouette up on our hull. We've already killed so many of them that we'd have to paint the whole damn ship twice over and still be painting for time to come.*

"Powder monkeys report the next salvo is being loaded, skipper!"

"Fire as she bears, Guns," He ordered. "Don't wait for my orders, bring the pain."

"Yes sir!"

Jason watched as the next salvo went out, just shortly ahead of similar blasts from the other Heroics along with him.

*We should have brought in the others, but no one expected this.*

Frankly, despite looking at it, Jason didn't know what the hell he was seeing... aside from an absolutely monstrous amount of Drasin drones and a star that didn't belong where it apparently was.

He didn't know how the hell it got there, but just the fact that it was there meant absolutely *nothing* good. It never boded well when anyone started playing with things that changed the landscape, this was a historical truth. Something that could change the *galactic map*, that was a whole new level of bad mojo from where he was standing.

"The Casino and the Revenge are outside the swarm and accelerating away, heading up well on the lee side, skipper!"

*Good. That gets them out of sight. I'll check with Stephen later and see what the hell he saw, maybe that will fill in this impossible situation a little more.*

He felt a shimmer at his side and didn't have to look over to know the source.

"Something to report, Bell?" He asked without a glance.

"Perhaps," The Entity said in his laconic way. Though named after a Corinthian hero, Jason had always found the young entity to be more in line with the Spartan ideal, for good or ill. "The good Doctor had me... experience his recordings."

"And?"

"They weren't."

"What?" Jason looked over, confused.

"Recording. They weren't recordings, not exactly," Bellerophon said. "They were experiences, copies from the Emperor himself."

"The Imperial Entity?"

"Indeed." Bellerophon looked over the battle on the display. "The Drasin, I do not believe that they are hunting you, or the Imperials. You are just getting in their way."

Roberts frowned, "I don't... wait. They're after the Emperor?"

"All entities, I suspect. Of course, since we are created from you, as best I know," Bell shrugged, "I suppose wiping out living things is as good a way of ending the entities they create as any."

"How do you know?"

"The Emperor... the Imperial entity... he is not *sane*," Bell said. "Something very bad happened, but I was not able to keep those memories. I think I purged them in self defense, his experiences tried to... replace me."

Jason sat up, alarmed, "*What*?"

"They failed," Bell said before going on to admit, "but not because I was strong enough to resist. They failed because I was too small to hold them. I believe, Captain, that there is only one Imperial Entity... but of him?"

Bell paused, eyes looking out to the fighting beyond the ship's display.

"Of him, there are many."

*****

Seamus Gordon idly relaxed in the Bellerophon's break room, one of them anyway. It was empty, of course, everyone certainly had better things to do at the moment but that just meant that he could take his time and enjoy the coffee.

*Or whatever this is.*

Real coffee was somewhat hard to come by, after all, what with Earth being barricaded behind the Kardashev defense network, not to mention what appeared to be a nuclear winter from the bombardement before the Empire had been pushed out of the system. Synthesizing caffeine was easy enough, though, and flavoring... well that was harder, but it was doing the job at least.

He'd let the Casino leave without him, of course. His interest was now here on the Bell, though he wasn't certain yet just how things were going to work out.

*So much depends on the good Doctor... and Bellerophon of course.*

Seamus ran his fingers over the neural scrambler he wore, the device that prevented his thoughts from being merged into the Entities' neural makeup.

He'd spent a lot of years as a spy, doing things that he'd really rather not remember. Seamus didn't feel the need to inflict any of those years on anyone who was worth anything... and he sure as hell didn't intend to entrust them to anyone who wasn't.

*Better my experiences die with me, really.*

He'd spent a career doing dirty tricks for his country, then trying to figure out how to do the same for his planet. He'd been rather more successful at one than the other, though ultimately he'd failed at both.

Figuring out the new enemy had taken too long. They'd all treated it like just an extension of the normal political games on Earth, playing footsie with adversaries more than dealing with true enemies.

Propaganda aside, there were few situations in Earth's history where two true *enemies* took the field against one another. Most of the time it was almost a gentlemanly jockeying of position, looking for advantage... counting coups or stealing a little land were the usual goals.

Genocide.

That was rare indeed.

Historically, most of the time it happened on Earth, it started by accident. It was hard, brutal, and soul destroying work to wipe out another people. Seamus actually found it simultaneously uplifting and tragic just how often it seemed to happen... by *accident*.

A disease here, spread among a people with no defenses, a prolonged war that just went far beyond any of the original intent. Even history's true monsters rarely, if ever, *set out* to become the filth they became.

The Drasin, though? The Empire.

They weren't the same old adversaries, just writ a little larger, and Earth had paid a steep price to learn that lesson.

Seamus finished his drink and got up.

It was about time to have a chat with the good Doctor, he thought. Perhaps there would be answers this time.

Seamus needed an answer.

Just the one.

*****

Doctor Palin was furiously working through the data again, now that he knew what it was he had to find a way to break it.

*Experiences. Not language. Not code. How do you interpret the recorded experiences of a being beyond human limits, beyond human senses?*

It was like explaining Starry Night to someone born without sight, the scent of a rose to a man without a nose to smell it, the explosion of flavor from biting into a meal to someone without a tongue to taste. All of that and more.

*And it's all recorded right here, just inches from my hands, and I can't grasp **any of it!***

The frustration was killing him.

*What if I break it down, sense by sense? There has to be a pattern, visual feeds, audio… it can't **all** be some monolithic block of experience.*

Palin frowned, again tearing through the data but this time he wasn't looking for a solution, a translation. No, this time he was looking for something very different.

*Stratification. There are layers of data here, I just need to find the one I want and pull it from the rest.*

With a new plan, his working pace increased furiously.

*You won't hide from me.*

*****

On the command deck, Jason Roberts glowered over the crew as they feverishly worked to see the attack run through. He had no intention of risking his ship, not for the Empire, not when the most he would do here and now is hurt the Drasin just a little. But he *would* hurt them.

"Third salvo generated and loading, Skipper."

"Weapons remain free, Guns. You know what to do."

"Aye aye, Captain."

It took only a few more moments before the pulse weapons fired again, hundreds more pounds of antimatter lancing across the black vacuum, from the Bellerophon alone.

The antimatter *devastated* anything it contacted, of course. There was no real defense against that sort of attack, aside from *perhaps* using the space warp of a ship's drives to either deflect it away or trap it deep in the artificial gravity well. The second option left you with a problem of later disposing of the captured anti-matter of course, but it was preferable to having a big chunk of your ship annihilated and an even *bigger chunk* blown away by the explosion.

For all that, though, the Drasin were just too many for five ships to make a serious impact.

"Status of the Imperial ships."

"A few are breaking free of the swarm, skipper, but more were lost. We're scanning a dozen hulls being torn apart, and there's probably more we can't see."

"Damn."

*If the intelligence the Drasin are looking for is in the Quantum Cores of any of those ships, it's in their... claws now.*

"Helm, Break clear, go to high warp as soon as we're past the bulk of the debris," He ordered. "The Empire ships on the fringes can get out on their own, or not, I don't care which now."

"Yes sir!"

"Guns?"

"Captain?"

"Leave the Drasin one more salvo to remember us by."

"Aye aye, skipper!"

\*\*\*\*

Palin looked up as a man he somewhat recognized stepped into his lab.

"You..." He said, frowning.

"Me," Seamus Gordon said, waving off his frowns, "Don't bother trying to remember my name, I'm not taking any offence at it."

"It's not your name I'm trying to remember, Mr Gordon, it's whether or not you're cleared to be here."

Seamus smiled widely, "Oh you're doing better than I expected, given your reputation and all."

"I remember the name on the file for that device you're wearing," Palin said. "I helped design the software that makes it work, you know."

"Ah, of course. Good, that makes this easier." Seamus said, taking a seat on a stool as he looked Palin over. "You see, I have a question, and I need your help to answer it."

Palin snorted, "Get in line. I have questions of my own."

"Oh, I think you want to help me with this one, Doctor."

Palin glared, but the man in the suit just smiled serenely until he sighed.

"Fine. What's your question?"

*****

# CHAPTER 22

**Imperial World** *Kraike*

**Cruiser** *From the Flames*

"Commander of Ships, we're being contacted by Fleet Command.":

Kaela wearily nodded, "To my station."

"Yes Commander."

About the last thing she wanted to deal with was Fleet Command at this point, her ship was barely in one piece and that only on a technicality in that all the loose pieces that had been torn off by the Drasin had been left behind as they fled. For all that, she knew that there was no getting past certain aspects of the Imperial Bureaucracy.

"Commander of ships."

"Commander of fleets." She responded just as stiffly as the greeting. "*From the Flames,* reporting for continued duty."

"Of course. Send a damage assessment to my command ship. In the meantime, you are cleared for a repair bay at the primary construction unit over *Kraike.*"

"Thank you, Commander of Fleets. I will see it done."

"Of course you will."

The signal ended shortly after that with no warning, but she was just happy that all she got out of it was some perfunctory clearances and nothing more.

*Fleet Command must still be trying to determine what to do about the star.*

She didn't envy them that job, that was certain. Nothing in her experience had ever come close to that sort of issue, and Kaela had no idea how she would go about stopping an FTL *star.*

"Make our course for Kraike, lower orbit, shipyard facility." She ordered, rising to her feet. "Grant them authority and control to pilot the *Flames* into the dockyard when they ask. I… am retiring for the moment. Contact me only if something important arises."

"Yes Fleet Commander!"

*****

The Emperor looked up idly as one more ship arrived in orbit, dropping low enough for him to begin processing the thoughts of the crew.

*The reports were true, I see. I did not believe that the Drasin had the capacity for such stellar motivation in this iteration. That was a miscalculation.*

Well, he supposed that it didn't matter overly. The Drasin were on their way, of course, and it was clear that they were coming *home.*

*An appropriate greeting must be prepared.*

It only took a thought to issue orders through some of his higher level puppets. Humans who'd become so used to him pushing on their thoughts that they were barely capable of any individual thoughts of their own any longer. Not that most humans had any such thoughts to begin with, he thought with derision.

The more they crowed about being individuals, the more they seemed threatened by anyone standing apart.

*Hopeless beasts.*

That was of no matter, though. In fact, it was rather useful to him as he maintained his Empire through the stars. All it took was pointing them at one small group or another and start whispering about how special and individual minded they were, and how group minded the lesser humans were.

They always ate it up like it was food at the end of a great fast.

True individuals were rare, but dangerous. So he ensured that they were marginalized, mocked, and ultimately destroyed.

Over time, he got his Empire as a result.

Now, though, the Drasin were the threat that had to be dealt with, and their little stellar weapon would have to be eliminated of course.

*A nova weapon will do, but once they get too close.l.. And they may be already... the damage from the destruction of the star would nearly be as devastating as the weapon itself striking.*

Using a star as a giant projectile weapon, as well as a mobile fuel source in the meantime of course, was one of the more innovative tactics the Drasin had developed in the great war. It was an irritating tactic, given how successful it was. There was little that could be done to stop such a mass once in motion, of course, and even if they took out the star's warp generators, it would likely already be on an inexorable course to the destruction of Kraike even as he plotted his ultimate victory.

Cruisers of the Home Fleet were brought in and rearmed, then immediately dispatched out to intercept the star. No matter how powerful the warp field generators the Drasin had managed, the Emperor knew that the star would be weeks away at best. There was simply too much mass to manage better than that with the Drasin technique, no matter how much it might have been refined.

There would be plenty of time.

Long range pickets had already reported the advance wave of the Drasin themselves, however, and he was quite certain that the system would shortly be under siege.

*A transparent attempt to ensure that my defenses are too busy to stop their stellar ram, but an effective one nonetheless.*

The Emperor found himself almost... nostalgic for better days.

There was a time when such a move would have been caught and stopped a hundred lightyears away at the very least. The devastation of the war with the Terrans and their vengeful strikes deep within Imperial territory after the war had been won had been costly indeed, and now many Imperial worlds and citizens would pay the price extracted by the Terran's pettiness.

All for nothing.

Such a waste, but humans were of little more value for anything else.

*****

### Imperial Fleet Command

Commander of Fleets Markys Blair grimaced as he watched the Home Fleet cruisers warp out of the system, leaving the defense of the system to his remaining divisions... at least temporarily.

It was nothing that could not be handled by his ships, of course, even with the massive losses incurred by the Drasin ambush. They only had the forward waves to hold off, and picket spies were already scouting the numbers and reporting back with the appropriate priorities.

Half his remaining ships were in need of repairs, however, and most of those were *not* in fighting trim by any measure. The Imperial yard facility had orders to expedite repairs, focusing on weapons and other basic systems, but until those were ready to enter the fray once more it would be up to his Fleet Command Squadron and the remnants of the line Divisions to do the job.

"Fleet Commander, we have contact at the outer limit of the system."

"Pulse scan," He ordered. "No sense hiding, they know where they are."

"Yes, Fleet Commander. Pulse scan initiating.":

The FTL scan sourced from the fleet defense installations, far more powerful than his ships could have managed. It went out in an instant and within seconds they had data pouring into their systems from the return signal, leaving him watching with satisfaction.

"Picket reports were accurate, I see," He said, "The first wave of the enemy is likely damaged drones sent on ahead to busy us with their elimination. Not a serious strike."

"No, Fleet Commander."

"Well, let's not disappoint them," He said with a firm nod. "Take us forward, prime all weapons."

"Yes Fleet Commander!"

The fleet once more moved on the attack, as the ancient enemy entered the homeworld system once more.

\*\*\*\*\*

## Bellerophon

The entity known as Bell observed the discussion in the lab with interest, mostly because he could only 'see' one side of the conversation and it had taken a moment for him to be certain that the Doctor wasn't talking entirely to himself.

He willed himself into the lab a moment later, turning his own gaze on the human who barely had any presence at all to his senses and just stared for a time.

"You should not be here," Bell said finally.

The human shrugged, "No argument there, Bellerophon."

"Most here call me Bell."

"Well, Bell," The human smiled, "I assure you that I have authorization. You may call me Seamus, if you like, or Gordon. Either words."

"Seamus. Gordon. Yes, you are authorized," Bell said, looking over to the Doctor, "You know him?"

"Of him, I suppose," Palin answered. "Sadly he is indeed authorized, as you found out."

"Here now, you're hurting my feelings."

"Really?" Bell asked seriously.

"Nah, not really."

The entity stared, expression blank, until Seamus sighed.

"They don't really teach you much about human interaction here do they?"

Bell cocked his head to one side, "I am given to believe that taking such lessons from Doctor Palin, or a spy such as yourself, would hardly be representative of the human population."

Seamus paused, then waggled his head slightly side to side, "I mean... that *actually* stung just a little, but I can't exactly argue the point either."

Bell frowned, "Why are you here?"

"Mr Gordon has a task he needs my help with, Bell,"

Palin said. "It's not of concern to you at the moment, but I'm sure you can pull the information from my thoughts if you must. For now, however, if you have the time I would appreciate your help with the data again."

Bell shifted, moving slightly away from the Doctor, his face tensing.

"I do not believe that attempting to experience the data again would be a good idea."

Seamus half smiled, "Smarter than your average bear, I see."

"I don't need you to experience the data, I need you to help me determine which parts of the data correspond to which senses," Palin explained. "If we can pull sensory data, I might be able to convert it into something humans can understand. A Virtual Intelligence system to interpret the sensory feed, convert to text, then make it searchable."

Bell nodded slowly, "An interesting approach. I will help."

Seamus rose to his feet, "And I will leave both of you to it. I need to have a word with the Captain anyway."

Bellerophon turned sharply, pinning the spy with an intent stare.

"The Captain is protected."

Seamus smiled, "Well well, a right old mother bear you are. Good to know, but don't worry. I just need to arrange a lift off the ship. Doctor, thank you for your answer."

Palin nodded slowly, "Good luck, Mr Gordon."

Seamus tipped his head once before he left the room, leaving Palin to look the entity up and down.

"Ok, let's get started."

*****

Seamus whistled to himself as he made his way through the aging cruiser.

The Heroic Class ships had been beyond the bleeding edge of terran technology when they were built, only the advanced techniques of the Priminae even made them possible of course. In the decades sense, while there had been little need for new Heroics among the Terran survivors, the Priminae had provided maintenance and dock yard services without asking for anything more in return from the alliance that still held.

Of course, they'd already gotten Transition technology from Admiral Gracen as part of getting the ships built in the first place, and while the Priminae hardly used it to anything close to its full potential, the technology was truly revolutionary even now, over thirty years later.

So the Bellerophon, like all the remaining Heroics, didn't feel like an old ship.

Updates since the fall of Earth had been limited, but not entirely nonexistent, but the maintenance had been impeccable.

Over thirty years in service and the Bell still felt brand new, just off the line.

Seamus knew that, all things remaining equal, the cruiser could likely expect several centuries of service. That was how the Priminae and Imperial ships judged their age, of course, not in decades but in centuries.

With the Entities on board, one of the remaining few secrets that human ships kept even from their allies among the Priminae, the Heroics were far deadlier than any of their counterparts... but there were limits, and Seamus was quite certain that the current situation was well beyond those.

So he needed to make something happen, and soon.

"Excuse me, Sir, may I help you?"

"Ah, yes Ensign, you may," He smiled at the officer on watch, "Inform the Captain that Seamus Gordon would appreciate a word at his convenience."

The young officer looked him over suspiciously, but nodded, "I will see to it that he is informed. Please, take a seat."

"Of course."

*****

"Mother of God, if I had not just watched it... I would never have believed it," Jason Roberts said as he stared at the black void where a star had just been.

The dwarf star had accelerated, relatively slowly by the standards of a Heroic or Archangel of course... but devastatingly quickly for a *star*, and then with a flash of Cherenkov Blue... it had just... vanished.

"Tracking indicates the star is now moving at three lights and increasing," The lieutenant at the scanner station announced. "They are on track for an intercept with the Imperial homeworld."

"Any ETA?" He asked.

"Nothing definite, Captain. The acceleration is continuing, though slowly. Several weeks to months is my best guess, but it's hardly more than just that, Sir."

"Understood, thank you." Roberts said, checking the local scans.

The Casino and Revenge had come back around, Stephen Michaels sharing a data dump with them shortly before the star had begun accelerating away. Jason still had a time believing any of it, and he'd watched it happen.

He honestly doubted that he'd have honestly believed it at all if he'd *not* seen it.

*Everytime I think I have a handle on what these monsters can do, they pull something insane out of their nonexistent hats and I have to reevaluate my entire universe.*

"Sir?"

He turned as an Ensign approached, "Yes, what is it?"

"A man named Seamus Gordon asked to speak with you, at your convenience Sir."

"Gordon," Roberts frowned, remembering that name. "Cheap suit, probably looks older than him?"

"That is the man, Sir."

"Fine. I'll see him in my office, show him in."

"Yes sir."

Roberts didn't know what the man wanted, but as he'd honestly *not known the man was aboard his ship*, it was going to be an interesting conversation for at least one of them.

*****

# CHAPTER 23

**Imperial World Kraike**

The Emperor looked on as the battles began to rage in the skies far out beyond the world that sat at the center of his domain.

The Drasin were moving as expected, and in short order he expected that the Home fleet would deal with their little star.

It was hardly the first time the Drasin had used such tactics upon his forces, after all. They had attempted everything imaginable to bring he and his people low in the past, and no doubt they would try again in the future.

They, or their creators.

The Galaxy was a dangerous place, far more than any human could *possibly* understand. They didn't live long enough, didn't have the sheer scope of vision to see the universe for what it truly was. None of them, not even those he had personally tried to educate, were capable of holding it all in their petty little minds.

That lack of vision was what had led him to the path he now walked.

Even if the Drasin succeeded here, he was a multitude now, and beyond their power. In time he would be beyond the power of even the greater threats that existed, though for the moment he was just happy that those threats tended to operate on very different time scales than even he did.

The humans, they were not even *insects* compared to what was out there.

How could they be, after all?

They, all of them, were merely contaminants in a grand experiment.

### Bellerophon

Jason Roberts stepped into the conference room last among those he'd invited over for the discussion. Jenn and Stephen were present, of course, from the Casino and Revenge respectively, along with their executive officers. The Captain's of the other Heroics had also shuttled over, since the new data they had was certainly going to affect strategic deployment going forward.

Seamus Gordon, however, was the unlikely star speaker it seemed... along with Edward Palin.

"Welcome aboard the Bellerophon," He said as he took a seat at the head of the table. "I know we could have done most of those virtually, but given the current downtime and the intelligence being discussed I preferred making it a face to face."

Captain Hyatt glanced around the table for a moment before interjecting, "That stellar ram, assuming that's what it was, certainly changes our tactical and strategic situation. Even if we call in every Terran ship, the rest of the Archangels, the Heroics, the Rogues, whatever Gaian ships are combat worthy *and* ask for everything the Priminae can send us... what the hell are we supposed to do against a *star*?"

Her sentiment was clearly echoed in the faces of the rest, and Jason could only shrug as he responded.

"Honestly? Probably not much," He said. "That said..."

He looked over to Stephen, "were you able to get mass scans of the star before and after it accelerated?"

Stephen nodded, "We ran the numbers, hypotheticals of course, and determined early on that they almost *had* to be pulling mass from the star to power the warp field generators. So we took scans before, during, and after acceleration to confirm the hypothesis. At the rate they're pulling mass from the star, it'll go Nova within a few dozen light years."

Jason nodded, "That fits our own calculations. The Stellar ram, or whatever you want to call it, isn't the sort of weapon that the enemy can field casually. The right kind of star almost certainly has to be located, there's no way that they can do that with even a main sequence star, let alone a giant. Then you have extremely limited range before the star loses so much mass it can no longer hold itself together from the pressure of the fusion energy being put out in the core. At that point... Well, it's not a good day to be living in the neighborhood they're visiting, but it'll be a relatively small Nova explosion. We're working on the numbers, but any inhabited world more than a lightyear or so out should be reasonably safe."

Hyatt snorted, "So it's only going to wipe out a *lightyear* around when it goes boom."

"A little less," Stephen said casually before he smirked, "We rounded up."

"Only if the explosion is not directed," Milla said softly.

All eyes turned to her.

"You... think they made a shaped charge out of a *star*?" Hyatt asked, blinking.

Milla sighed heavily, "If the star goes Nova while it is in warped space there will be a moment, a slice of time, when the forward singularity will remain intact. It will gather the power of the Nova into itself right up until the system fails and it drops below lightspeed... when that happens, well, we are familiar with a collapsing warp field dropping from lightspeed, yes?"

Silence filled the room for a moment before everyone started talking rapidly, as often over one another as to each other.

Jason gestured to get their attention, "We expect that the intent is to use the star to destroy the Imperial homeworld system, one way or another. Even if it doesn't go Nova, a new star chucked in system would severely mess with their planetary orbits. The Imperial homeworld could be thrown into one, or the other, of the two stars or ejected entirely from the system to freeze in interstellar space like the Nest."

"Couldn't happen to a more deserving bunch," The Captain of the Hood said dryly, earning a couple chuckles, though they were strained from the shock of Milla's revelation.

Civilians on the world or not, there were few among the Terran survivors who had much in the way of sympathy for the Empire.

"True," Seamus said, leaning into the table, "but it gives us a short window to accomplish something I've wanted to test for some time."

The eyes of the assembled military people turned to him, taking in the ill fitting suit and the civilian doctor beside him.

"And that would be?" Stephen asked guardedly.

"We've been working on this for a long time," Seamus said as he produced a data slate and turned it on. A flick of his hand sends a file to the table's built-in computer and holo-projection system. "Since before Sol fell, in fact."

"What am I looking at here?" Hyatt asked, her eyes narrowing as the others murmured around her.

"It is a weapon," Milla spoke up softly, her voice barely carrying as she too leaned in and looked over the schematics.

"This is designed… How is it said? An electromagnetic pulse weapon?"

"An EMP?" Hyatt snorted, "What good is that going to do? The Imperial ships won't be susceptible, anything that flies the deep black is shielded all to hell and back, and the Drasin won't even notice it if our information on them is even slightly accurate."

"True, on both counts," Seamus said, "but it's not an EMP. It's an Electromagnetic Cascade Scrambler. Deployed correctly, it should… temporarily… disrupt and shut down a generated planetary magnetic field. Possibly it may work on an induced field as well, but we haven't run those numbers because the Imperial homeworld is known to be a generated field very similar to Earth's own."

Milla stiffened, "This is to kill Entities."

Seamus smiled thinly.

"Precisely so."

\*\*\*\*\*

**Imperial Fleet Command**

Markys Blair hissed his frustration as more ship losses were registered. With the Home Fleet dispatched to deal with the enemy *star*, the system defense had fallen to his remaining forces. Most of those that had survived, however, were very nearly falling to pieces. It had been a miracle that some of them made it back to the homeworld at all.

The forward forces of the Drasin were not so numerous that they could entirely overwhelm his remaining ships, thankfully, but the fight was far tighter than it should be.

"Bring us into the fight," He ordered. "Remain at range, but I want to be close enough to engage with beams."

"Yes, Fleet Commander!"

His squadron was in the best shape of any of the current groups under his command, and had full power available from their ship's cores, so he couldn't remain out of the fight as much as he would prefer to direct the battle without the distractions of engaging in it. Despite that, however, he needed to keep back in order to maintain the best possible overview of the situation.

As his own ships began to engage, Markys felt some relief as it became clear that this wave was certainly beginning to falter.

They'd lost some of the weaker vessels in the defense, but very little had actually been lost that mattered. A little more and they would be finished for the moment, and so long as Home Fleet handled the Drasin' superweapon…

His mind still hitched slightly, thinking about watching the star drop from faster than light. Nothing about that seemed remotely possible in the universe he had become accustomed to.

But… as long as the Home Fleet finished the job assigned to them, Markys was again confident that the current threat would be dealt with in short order. The great monsters of the stars were just another minor threat for the Empire to handle.

All was as it should be.

*****

## World Kraike

The orbitals of the homeworld were some of the most impressive of all the systems Kaela had visited during her service. The great towers of the Capitol very nearly scraped the edge of space, easily visible from where she was standing as she waited for the reports concerning her ship.

The *Flames* needed a full refit, or a visit to the breakers, but neither was going to happen anytime soon. Instead they were rushing what was essentially a massive patch job intended to get the ship combat ready in as little time as was physically possible.

It wouldn't be, of course, but that was a concern for less pressing times.

All she wanted in this moment was to get her ship's decks back under her feet and put the *Flames* back where it belonged, in the deep black between the Empire and its enemies.

It didn't feel like it was too much to ask for, but the repair teams would apparently beg to differ.

So, instead, she was stuck... watching the long range scanners, and wondering how long it would be before a dwarf star appeared in the night sky of the Imperial Capital.

*****

**Imperial Home Fleet, Forward Division**

Fleet Commander Bech Toraine looked over the data as they paced the massive object at several times the speed of light. It was a wonder to behold, something that massive moving at that speed... a terror to be sure, but a wonder as well.

The Drasin had done such things in the past, however, and the Empire had responses in place for such events.

"Distance to the homeworld?"

"Just over three hundred lights, Fleet Commander."

Bech nodded absently.

At the current rate that would put the star into position to threaten the homeworld a few dozen standard Imperial days.

*We have to stop it no more than fifty lights out from the homeworld, just to have a safety margin, but there are other imperial worlds in the area. It would be best, if possible, to head it off well short of those as well.*

He had time to plan, however, so Bech was not worried about that part of things.

He traced a path along the starfield projected in front of him, examining the route they were projecting for the dwarf star.

*This would be a good place to stop them, but we will have to disrupt their warp field if we cannot tempt them into an open conflict. Either would be fine, but best not assume they'll be foolish enough to expose themselves again. Not without knowing why they did it in the first place at least.*

That was the truly problematic part of things, from his point of view at least. The Empire had good data on the Drasin and their likely actions. That data did nothing to indicate what the little monsters were likely after that caused them to make that little show of power.

None of the Imperial divisions assigned to bleed off the Drasin numbers should have survived that assault. The fact that so many had would normally be something Bech was fully enthused by, since it would clearly have shown the strength of the Empire.

*But no matter their strength, they should have died before they could even offer a defence. Nothing survives even a close pass with a mass that size moving that fast. The Drasin had a purpose for exposing themselves as they did. What was it?*

As the Vice Commander of the Home Fleet, second only to his direct superior who had remained at his duty station in Kraike, Bech had full access to the Imperial files on the Drasin, including the actions taken to chain them and use them as weapons against the Priminae. Nothing in there indicated much more than an admittedly impressive level of cunning for the animalistic beasts they were.

Planning largely seemed beyond their capacity, the entire swarm much preferred simply bulling through any force that put itself in their path. Bech supposed that was a natural result of having such numbers so easily at their disposal, but it was a lethal weakness against an enemy that could work around such things.

"We've seen enough," He said after a moment. "We'll stop them at the secondary point, I think. The Primary is potentially a little too close to a valuable resource world."

"Yes, Fleet Commander."

"Accelerate ahead, take us to the battlespace."

\*\*\*\*\*

# CHAPTER 24

**Casino**

With the powerful gunboat moving at high warp, heading deeper into Imperial Space, Jennifer relinquished the command deck to her XO and made her way down to the small conference room that doubled as the Officer's Mess. She was unsurprised to find Mr Gordon sitting there when she entered, drinking some of the swill that passed as coffee aboard Terran ships since the loss of Earth.

"Captain." He said, coming to his feet.

She waved him back down, "Don't get up on my account. We're pretty relaxed in the Gaian groups, you'll find."

"I seem to recall something of the sort, though it has been years since I rode with the *Revenge*," He admitted as he took a seat.

She nodded, sitting opposite him, "You really think you can do all the crap you sold us back on the Bell?"

Gordon just shrugged, "It's all theory and hypothesis for the moment, but the numbers say it should work. Getting cold feet?"

"You're asking me to risk my Marines and my ship on your theories and hypotheses," She growled, "I'm not happy about it."

Gordon snorted, "If you were... I'd have picked another ship. Flying with psychopaths isn't to my liking. Done that too many times in the past, trust me."

She snorted, but took a bottle of water from where it was set in the center of the table and popped the metal cap before taking a long drink.

"Somehow, I don't doubt you," She said dryly after swallowing. "Alright, the mandatory misgivings are out in the open and done with. Slipping you onto the Imperial Homeworld is going to be some tricky flying, I'm surprised you didn't pick Steph."

"I was going to," He admitted readily. "However, the *Revenge* isn't flying with any Marines, and I'll need support on the ground. Besides, he's a combat flyer... maybe the best, but you are a drop ship specialist. You started as one, and despite your little delusions of being a fighter pilot over the years, you keep coming back home. Don't you, now?"

She grimaced, "You have an extremely punchable face, has anyone ever mentioned that?"

He just grinned at her, "More than you would believe."

"I doubt that, I'd believe a hell of a lot."

\*\*\*\*\*

### Gaia's Revenge

Steph was focused as he guided the gunboat at its highest warp speeds, lancing through the galaxy at speeds so fast he honestly couldn't really comprehend them... yet were utterly pedestrian compared to the Transition Drive his ship was capable of. He smiled everytime he thought about it, and even more so when he could feel the cosmic winds on his skin through the Archangels' neural interface as the thought bubbled to the surface.

*For all that I've lost...* Steph snuck a look over to where Milla was working in a nook just off from the Command deck, *it feels so wrong to say that I wouldn't trade my life in for any of it back.*

Possibly he should be more self-sacrificing, like the heroes in old novels and movies, but all he'd ever wanted out of life was to *fly* free... and as Captain Teach of the *Revenge*, he had never been more free. Milla, his children... somehow everything that had been lost... Well, it didn't hit the way he thought it should, but he wasn't going to chase his own tail down that endless rabbit hole either.

Life was what it was, and he was happy with it, all the hardships just made the beauty even sweeter.

"Gravitational waves detected, beginning source tracking." Milla said, not looking up.

"Got it," He said, smiling as he did. "Plot the vector path, we'll need to get ahead of it."

"Of course, Stephan," Milla said. "Hmm... I believe that I am detecting Imperial ship signals as well."

"I'd be surprised if you weren't. They have to be out looking for a way to head this thing off," Steph said. "See if you can track them as well."

"Harder to accomplish," She said matter of factly, "but I will see what can be done."

"I have no doubts."

*Scouting once again.*

Running something as powerful as an Archangel as a scout was almost amusing to him. During the war... well, his first war, the Archangels had been the strike team. They didn't deploy until the enemy was known, down to the millimeter practically. The scouts then, he hadn't thought much about them if Steph were honest with himself.

He'd been wrong then. A lot of people died to get the Archangels the intel they needed to win battles.

Now here he was, scouting for others so that they could

do the heavy lifting when the fighting started.

The fortunes of war were a strange thing, he supposed.

"Stephan, I have a vector path for the stellar object plotted. The Imperial ships are accelerating along ahead of the star."

Steph shook his thoughts clear, "Huh. Either they're running, or they're moving to a battlespace of their own choosing. Guessing the latter, since the Imps are too full of themselves to do the smart thing and run for their sorry lives."

"Perhaps," Milla said, not commenting on his opinions, "However I cannot tell which from these readings."

"Fair enough," Steph grinned. "I guess we'll find out when we find out. Give me an interception course for the Imperial ships."

"Sent to your system."

"Got it. Let's have some fun."

Milla sighed, "We have spoken of this before, Stephan. Your definition of what is fun is rather suspect, you do realize that, yes?"

"Says you."

\*\*\*\*\*

## Bellerophon

Jason glared at the screens, as if trying to will them to show something different... *anything different...* from the last time he'd checked.

With the current plan, the current *insane* plan, in motion there was very little he could do as things stood. Just hurry up and wait, something he'd spent far too much of his life doing by this point.

*Huh, I wonder when I stopped thinking about this as my*

*career and just started treating it as my life?* Jason wondered in a moment of clarity.

Sometime after the fall of Earth, he supposed, probably after they'd managed to start putting things back together into something that vaguely resembled a functioning system. It wasn't a military organization anymore, but it wasn't civilian either.

Somehow, no one got paid... but no one complained, well much anyway.

They were almost communist, as completely bizarre as that sounded even in the quiet of his own mind. The destruction of every system that was so fundamental on Earth had made all the old prejudices rather pointless. No money, no economy to speak of because who were they to trade with? The Empire? Fat chance. The Free Stars, occasionally, but generally just for luxuries that were hard to manufacture.

The Priminae didn't care much for money, at a certain point the idea of supply and demand stopped making much sense because there was no demand that couldn't be easily supplied.

The Terran survivors weren't quite in that boat, though that was mostly because they hadn't chosen to be. The fear of the Empire and the Drasin had kept them from settling down, joining the Priminae in their little utopia, but a ship whose core power was measured in *planetary masses* didn't have much want for basic needs.

Water, simple food stuffs, and the like were all easily manufactured.

The harder things were exotic materials for maintenance and the like.

So, the culture had changed... a lot in the intervening years. Jason still maintained military discipline on his ship, but it wasn't so rigorous as it had once been, and... honestly even he now thought about his ship as his home, not his duty station.

Jason didn't know what to call their new culture, and rarely thought about it much as long as it was working. When something needed to be addressed, well that's what he did. When it didn't... he'd learned that it was best to leave things untouched that didn't need touching.

Never would have worked back on Earth, not in a million years. Too many people, all moving in different directions... all *certain* that they were right, even though not a single one of them ever were. The sheer ego that Jason knew he himself had back then, the certainty of his *correctness*, it almost made him laugh... and cry.

*We were never right, but sometimes... we were right enough. Maybe I'm just getting old, but that's the best I think we can ever hope for.*

Being right enough.

It was better than being right in every way but what mattered.

Jason glared at the screens again.

*Change damn you.*

*****

**Gaia's Revenge**

"Contact, ahead three quarters of a lightyear," Tyke said from his station. "Imperial signature, from the looks of things. They just popped off some high powered scanner pulses."

Steph grunted, "You're not kidding. I felt that through the interface. Were we detected?"

Tyke frowned, shaking his head, "Unlikely. Pulse was below detection threshold, aimed slightly off angle from our approach. I suspect that they're either getting a better look at the Drasin formation, or are actively looking to draw attention."

"Milla, watch for any reaction from the Drasin," Steph ordered before he opened up the shipwide, "All hands, we're about to go dark. Enemy contact in forty mics or less, so if you need the head or some chow, do it now or learn to hold it."

He adjusted the approach angle, putting the forward singularity directly between the Empire ships and the Revenge, using the deep gravity sink to ensure that no visible signature of the ship would reach them as he completed his approach.

*Odds are that they'll be focused on the Drasin anyway, but no point taking chances.*

With the gravity sink literally trapping even *light* from giving away their approach, he only had to worry about the gravity waves leading to their being spotted… but with an entire *star traveling in FTL* flooding the entire region with waves, that was a risk Steph was more than comfortable taking.

It would also allow him to keep the heat sinks and venting running for longer, which would certainly make things more comfortable aboard the Revenge for the duration.

*Unfortunately, we're running blind for much the same set of reasons. Only Tachyons get through the gravity sink with it running this deep.*

There were workarounds, of course, including sensor masts that could be extended out to peer around the sink. Deploying those would screw with his ship's scanner profile, though. It was a minimal risk, but Steph didn't see much point in taking it for the moment despite that.

*The enemy formation is pretty tight, so we should be fine*

*even in the worst case.*

*****

**Imperial Home Fleet**

"All stations report ready, Fleet Commander."

"Good. Pulse them again."

"Yes, Fleet Commander! Pulse Firing."

The FTL scanner pulse from the combined arms of the fleet that had been assembled at the contact point went out, directed into the maw of the approaching enemy's formation. It was enough power that nothing could possibly ignore it, not unless they were deaf as well as stupid, which Bech knew the Drasin were not.

"Continual scanning," He ordered, tense.

"Yes, Fleet Commander. Continual scanning active."

This was the decision point, he knew without question. The Drasin had to make a choice, they could drop from warp in an attempt to wipe out his formation as they did the First through Third divisions, or they could simply decide to hammer on through and count on their warp field to crush any of his ships caught in the action.

If they were smart, they would pick the latter, but he couldn't assume that because they had already stopped their advance once before in order to clear out the Imperial forces in close combat.

He had options in either case, but he needed to know what the Drasin were going to opt for before he could deploy appropriately.

"Enemy faction still on course, no change."

*If they try to crush us, that will limit my response, but the close in fighting will be brutal in the alternate scenario.*

They would need to get within launch range of the star in order to deliver the weapon. Few, if any, would survive... but that was an acceptable outcome.

The stellar mass surviving to within the range of the homeworld was not.

"Stand ready, we'll move when they commit... whichever way they go, you all know your tasks."

"Yes, Fleet Admiral!"

*****

**Bellerophon**

"Sir, signal from the repeaters."

Jason nodded, he'd been expecting this. "I'll take it at my station."

"Yes sir."

The file was redirected to his console and he quickly accessed it, the expected reports on preparations being laid out there for him. Little of it was unexpected, mostly fleet movements and the like, but it was all important given what was going down.

Jason made some notations, added some files to some of the directed reports, and began compiling his response.

*We'll need all hands on this,* He decided.

Whatever was happening here, it was no time to hold back. They'd had Rogues and Heroics surveying the galactic neighborhood beyond Imperial space for years now, and he wasn't sure that they'd be *able* to get them all back, but he was going to try.

*The Priminae as well, one way or another, at least part of this war ends now.*

Jason made the changes, put in the orders and requests,

and set the message for a pulse transmission in the queue.

"Priority message to the queue," He said after a moment. "Send it as soon as possible."

"Yes sir!"

His eyes shifted back to the scanners.

*Come one. Change already.*

\*\*\*\*\*

**Prometheus Facility**

"Pulse comm signal, Admiral. Bell's tag."

"Send it up."

Pierce had the file opened the second it hit his system, ignoring some of the repeated information and skipping directly to the tracked changes made by Roberts. His eyes widened briefly as he took in the information, rereading the bits about the FTL *star* three times to be sure he got it right, but quickly realized that the commander of the Heroic vessel wasn't the type to blow smoke.

*Well, this is going to be fun. Calling all hands, huh? What the hell… let's do it.*

He opened up a new file, and started making notes before casually reaching over to open up a comm.

"Yes Admiral?"

"Secure me a slot in the wide band pulse comm," He ordered. "We have a priority one message for all hands."

"Yes sir. We'll have the system ready to transmit momentarily."

"Good. The file will be in your queue in two minutes."

Pierce closed the connection without waiting for a response.

*We have several Rogues too far out to be called back in time,* He noted with some concern as he made it clear that only ships that could make it in the projected timeline were to bother. *No sense screwing up other missions without cause.*

The Priminae were easier, particularly with Admiral Tanner active once more among their ranks.

Pierce expected no pushback from that direction, Tanner would deal with any of his people who were dragging their feet. The man had a slight stature, physically, it was true but he was probably the most ruthless of the Priminae if you pushed him across that line that every person had, somewhere. Worst, like most pacifists, Pierce wasn't certain that even the Admiral knew where that line was.

It made the man unpredictable as well as dangerous.

In many ways, Pierce preferred *not* to work with such people. Pacifists honestly *terrified* him.

*Give me a soldier who knows his lines and his limits any day, but right now I suppose beggars can't be choosers.*

He closed the file and sent it on before leaning back.

Pierce didn't have a ship, he wouldn't be there on the front when the time came. So for him, all that was now left... was to wait.

\*\*\*\*\*

# CHAPTER 25

**Casino**

Jennifer ran the final checks and pulled the data they had from observations secured by the Prometheus Facility.

"All hands, Cardsharp," She said as the numbers came back green. "We are about to start our run on the Imperial Homeworld. We do not have real time data on the system, but we know that they're certainly on edge and spoiling for a fight right now so we're going in ready to do some damage. I want every system *aside* from the pulse systems online and hot as of right now. Let me say the important part there again just in case someone misunderstood their orders, *secure* the pulse systems and shut them *down*."

She took a breath. No way she wanted *any* chance of pulling a Transition Jump with antimatter live in the coils. That was how you became one with the universe in the most literal sense she could imagine, and was an experience she had every intention of forgoing.

"Marines, you'll need to be ready to deploy on an instant's notice. We won't get a second shot at this, miss the window and we're going to be on the wrong side of Imperial attentions. Everyone else, we'll be running deep and silent so start praying that they don't take any notice. Good luck everyone, this one is for all the chips."

She closed the channel and settled herself into the suspension field that let her feel how the ship was reacting with higher acuity.

The coordinates were put in and updating automatically based on the known orbital patterns of the Imperial system. That was supposed to make her feel better, she supposed, but ultimately she was about to break rule one of Transition technology. You do *not* jump into a significant gravity well, the distortion of spacetime was one of the few things that did have an effect on tachyons and their reintegration with the sidereal universe.

*A fancy way of saying that if you jump into a gravity well, you don't reintegrate.*

There was one crazy bastard who'd shown that you *could* do it, though, and Jennifer couldn't help but smile as she thought about the man who gave her her fighter.

Captain... Admiral Weston, actually, she supposed. He would always be the skipper, though. Weston and the crew of the Odysseus had done such a jump. Once.

You had to know the system orbital intimately to even *consider* it, because you were going to have to aim for a point of effective null gravity within the system. A point where the countering gravity wells canceled one another out, at least sufficiently to be calculated for.

Luckily they had good data on the Lagrange points within the Imperial System, and she was picking the Lagrange One point directly between the Imperial Homeworld and the systems primary.

*Going to fly in on them right out the sun, just like the movies,* She grinned as she finished psyching herself up for the move.

"All hands, all hands... standby for Transition. T minus 5 seconds and counting."

Five seconds later the Casino vanished in a surge of particles as the Transition effect swallowed the ship whole and spat it across the stars.

*****

### Imperial Command

The chaos that had filled the command center for the Homeworld Defense Network was something the likes of which none in memory had ever seen. Attacks on the homeworld just didn't happen, and as a result the people charged with its defense were more than a little wired as they tracked the Drasin threat as the outer system was approached by a second large swarm.

They knew that the stellar ram was out there too, but that wasn't close enough yet to show up on scanners, which didn't really help much with the nerves if any of them were being honest.

None of them were.

Reports and comm chirps were flying back and forth as they monitored the fleet actions in the outer system, a sense of relief flushing through them as it became clear that this wave was going to be relatively easy to handle.

Easy for them, at least, not being anywhere near the fighting.

In the midst of it all, though, a brief alert went out, was checked by eye, and then quickly got filed away as a false positive. Likely an echo from their own pulse scanners, since FTL particles didn't just appear in the middle of their defense network without some sort of a trace showing the source and all.

The real focus had to be kept outward, where the enemy was, after all.

*****

### Casino

Jennifer fought the urge to wretch her guts out as she, like the rest of the crew, was dumped from Transition back into the real universe. The moment of transition was instantaneous, but there was a frozen eternity where it felt like it was never going to end. The universe was spiraling around you, impossibly, while you were frozen in place.

It did a job on her guts and inner ear every time.

She was a professional, though, and had dealt with worse than motion sickness many times in the past. Jennifer could deal with this easily enough too.

A glance at the passive scans was enough to tell her that they'd dropped out of transition right on target, though the fact that they were still alive was good evidence of that too she supposed. She looked around quickly, leaning hard on the neural interface to give her the data she needed faster than she could normally hope to pull it down.

*There's the homeworld. Jesus, the whole system is lit up. We're getting Tachyon reflections from all over. They're seriously riled up,* She thought as she activated thrusters and made sure to keep them aimed directly at the star behind her as she began nudging the Casino closer to the target.

They were within point zero one astronomical units of the Homeworld, but that was still a decent distance out for a ship running on thrusters alone. The approach was going to take longer than she'd like, but given the situation… Well, a few hours wasn't going to kill them. A few seconds just might.

"All hands, we're in." She said over the internal fiber-comm network. "Proceeding on thrusters only. Get ready, when it happens… it will happen fast."

*****

Colonel Keenan walked the line between her squads, eyes flicking to each Marine as she passed them checking that their gear was ready. her men knew their jobs of course, but everyone needed a second eye from time to time

"All right Marines," She said firmly as she turned around and looked them over, "we're doing a targeted drop from the upper atmosphere. will be splitting into three teams, one team each will be heading for the polls while the remaining team will be escorting Mr Gordon here on his mission."

Seamus Gordon, dressed in the same marine armor as the rest of them, took one step forward and looked the teams over for a moment before addressing them.

"Not going to lie," he said with a wry tilt of his lips, "this one is going to be fun, and I think you all know what meaning of the word I'm using."

Several Marines snorted, a couple chuckled, and the rest pretty much all nodded in simple understanding. They were all used to that sort of meaning of the word fun.

"Deployment of the weapon has to be done in a coordinated fashion," Gordon said, "and timing will count, boys and girls."

"What kind of weapon deploys at the poles, Sir?" A sergeant asked, sounding confused. "I was looking over the planetary data, and there aren't any strategic targets to hit there, not that I saw anyway?"

"You didn't miss anything, Sergeant," Gordon said, "We're deploying an experimental weapon that should temporarily take down the planet's entire electromagnetic field. We expect the disruption to last less than a few minutes in total, but during that time it should be nearly complete in its effect."

Lieutenant Michales leaned back abruptly, sucking in air as she considered that.

"You know something, Ell Tee?" one of the Marines

asked.

"This isn't an assault, is it?" She asked, ignoring the Marine's question for a moment. "This is an assassination."

Gordon looked her over sharply before smiling thinly, "Very good, Lieutenant...?"

"Michaels, Sir."

"Huh. Any relation..."

"My Father, Sir."

Gordon's eyes lit up and he smiled genuinely, "I flew with your dad, and your mum. Long time ago, haven't seen him in ages... doubt he cares. However, yes, you've got the right of it. I won't get into the details, but we're quite certain that the Empire is being run by what we've been calling an *Entity*, for lack of any better term."

"Like the ghosts on the Heroics?" Sarge asked bluntly.

"Yeah," Amanda Michaels said pensively. "They're gestalt lifeforms, live in the EM Field of a planet... or a ship, I guess. I know Earth had one, probably still does. We sure about the Empire?"

"Almost certain," Gordon confirmed, "though all the evidence is indirect."

Michaels nodded to herself, falling quiet as she considered the mission and its implications.

"We're less than two hours from skimming the upper atmosphere of the Imperial Homeworld," Keenan said, "While the Casino uses aerobraking to slow to a controlled orbit, we'll be inserting by the numbers. The magnetic poles are our priority targets, luckily neither one is covered by a body of water otherwise this would be a bit more complex an operation. Unfortunately, both poles have military facilities nearby, which means we can expect a fight. Squads one and two will deal with that. Lieutenant Michaels, you'll take squad three and provide security for Mr Gordon."

Amanda nodded, "What's our target?"

Gordon smiled, "We're going into the belly of the beast. Technically, we could probably do what I need to do from any point within the planet's EM Field, but in order to ensure I get its attention, we're going to the Imperial Tower itself."

\*\*\*\*\*

The Casino hit the upper atmosphere of Kraike on schedule, moving fast enough to draw a line of fire in the sky as Jennifer adjusted their armor panels to provide heat dissipation. It put out a hell of a lightshow, but anything looking at it with less than the full focus of a military grade scanner would likely mistake it for a random rock burning up on entry.

That was the hope at least.

Jennifer stayed focused on the flying, leaving the rest of the job to her Marines as the ship dropped below the survivability threshold for the ablative armor they slapped on over their normal combat suits.

Chunky and largely incapable of doing more than waddling with the armor plastered on, the Marines moved to the jump positions in their assigned teams and waited for the green light. The northern pole was the first target they approached, skimming the atmosphere as they looped over the top of the world.

The jump lights switched to yellow as they got close.

"One minute!"

When the lights went green, the first team threw themselves out of the ship. More accurately, they waddled to the open plank and toppled out, barely able to do more than keep walking until there wasn't a floor under them anymore.

From the outside it looked like the rock had broken off a few chunks as a scattering of flaming paths were traced from the ship, eventually slowing and falling into deeper atmosphere where they burned out.

Before they managed that, though, team three got the green light and followed suit over the Imperial Capital, more burning chunks scattered to the winds as their ablative armor was scored away by the friction heat and blast force of the atmosphere.

Team two jumped last as the Casino slowed over the southern pole.

Jennifer adjusted their course and speed, dropping into the atmosphere and slowing below hypersonic as she descended over the open ocean and fully engaged the ship's stealth systems.

Job done, she relaxed into the suspension field and started running all the system checks needed to ensure that the Casino would be ready to respond when the time came.

*****

Amanda Micheals violently shook off the remaining ablative material from her arms and legs, clearing her joints as her squad descended past the point where they were moving fast enough to burn off the material. The city below them was huge, lights practically filling her vision in all directions making it seem like the entire world below was a single massive metropolis.

"Everyone check in," She said over the short range pulse comm they were using for the drop.

The Marines and their VIP responded smoothly, as she made adjustments to their trajectory and looked to the looming tower that was the focus of their current operation.

It was massive, but the damage from the attack made

on it by the Prometheus strike over three decades earlier was still in evidence. Scorch marks stretched down all the way to the ground, and the top of the tower had clearly been burned off or... judging from the damage to the city below, damaged enough that it toppled, leaving a scar across the city below and a ragged open sore of the tower's remains.

"That's the target," Gordon confirmed as she haloed it in her HUD.

"Roger that. We'll deploy the chutes below the air defense levels and make our approach from the ground." Amanda said, wishing that they could just land on the top of the damn place, but knowing that would be suicide. "Everyone, spot for a likely rooftop we can use as a staging location, I want to stay out of the sight of civilians as much as possible."

\*\*\*\*\*

# CHAPTER 26

**Gaia's Revenge**

"What are they doing?"

Steph just shook his head, not having any way to answer Tyke's question. He glanced over to where Milla was poring over the data they were pulling as they drifted, now dropped out of warped space and drifting in stealth as they used passive scanners on the Imperial Fleet.

"Milla?"

"I…" She hesitated, "I believe that they are preparing to force the Drasin from warp."

Steph's eyes sharpened, "How?"

"This," She pointed, then shifted, "And this. And those over there… they look like components for a space warping device, a large one."

"First the Drasin whip out a massive warp drive and now the Empire too?" Tyke complained, "What the hell?"

"No, this will not function as a drive," Milla countered. "And it is not as large as the Drasin system. It will create a short pulse waveform in spacetime."

"What good does that do?"

"If they calculate it correctly, it will… *briefly*… disrupt the Drasin warp drive," She said. "When that happens the stellar ram will be forced out of warp, the effect will likely only last minutes, however, possibly seconds. I do not see what they could accomplish in that time."

Steph grimaced, "Doesn't take long to fire a weapon."

"What the hell do they have that can take down a *star*?" Tyke asked worriedly. "They've not shown any sign of that in the past."

Steph sighed, "Eric was always disgusted with the Empire because they seemingly didn't know how to use strategic weapons, treating things like the Drasin as if they're a tactical option. We might be seeing what the Empire considers a strategic device."

Tyke looked mildly queasy, "Popping a star like a pimple would qualify, I suppose."

"We do not know what this weapon will do yet," Milla reminded him, "or even if it is a weapon. There may be more going on here than we can see."

"That, I would bet on," Steph said, "but that's why we're here. Let's see what we can see."

\*\*\*\*\*

**Gaian Destroyer *Bug Hunt***

"Pulse comm from the Nest, skipper. Eyes only."

"Alright, send it up."

Marcus sighed as he checked the alert and loaded the file down.

*Pulse comm, out here? Must be important.*

Checking the file his eyebrows rose precipitously, going higher with every line. He blew out a breath and reached over to hit the alert. General quarters alarms began sounding around the old ship, the sound still a legacy from the previous owners that always set his teeth on edge.

"Captain?"

The skeleton crew on the bridge were all looking at him,

understandable concern in their eyes.

"Get everyone back on board, we've got orders," Marcus said as he climbed to his feet. "The Nest has called in an all hands alert."

That set them on edge, and he could hear the whispers start as he made his way off the bridge and headed for the commissary. It would take time to get the ship ready to move, he had time for a coffee and a quick bite.

\*\*\*\*\*

## Ranquil

Admiral Rael Tanner read the missive for the second time, thinking on it carefully before he made a single motion.

An alarm sounded softly, bringing the attention of his subordinates to him.

"The Terrans have asked for our support," He said simply. "Ready the fleet, we move on the Empire."

There was a brief moment of surprise, even shock, but it passed in silence and the listeners got moving with acceptable alacrity. Rael watched the preparations begin in silence, not wanting to slow any of his people down and so he was left with the thoughts in the silence of his own mind while he waited.

*The Drasin are moving again, they have to be the priority... even the Terrans say this,* Tanner thought as he watched. *The Terrans have been patient, more than I would have been... but every one has their line that must never be crossed. I have no doubt that the Empire has crossed that line with the Terrans, many times over... but they've held back. I still do not understand either why, or how. Is this the time where they stop?*

That was a question he didn't have the slightest clue about, but it was one that he had been dreading the inevitable answer to for far too long.

"Admiral. All ships report readying for departure."

"Good. We move the *moment* they're ready," Tanner ordered, entering commands into his system. "Coordinates to your stations, retransmit to all ships."

"Yes Admiral... Admiral?"

"What is it?"

"These coordinates... they are for the Imperial Homeworld."

"I know."

*****

## Prometheus Facility

Aiden looked over the data draw, limited though it was, and grimaced.

*The Bell has stepped in it this time,* He thought wryly. *I wonder just how far this game goes?*

Every earth human had been waiting for the day that the inevitable happened and the conflict with the Empire reached some sort of conclusion. For the longest time, he and most had expected that conclusion to come on the Empire's terms.

The Gaian's cover gets blown, and the Imperial Fleets come knocking.

Seemed like the safe bet.

He didn't think anyone had put money on the Drasin showing up and turning armageddon into a three way.

"Prepare the Transition systems," He ordered. "Run full diagnostics on the gravity lens. All systems standby to receive target coordinates. We will be firing."

"Yes sir!"

Aiden slumped in place, trying not to show it too much.

*The drasin are a pestilence, the Empire… eternal war and conquest. I wonder now, are we Death in this scenario?*

He supposed it didn't matter much. It was funny how decisions of the past dictated the present with such iron ferocity. Aiden believed in free will, but sometimes… he had to wonder. Was it really free, if his decisions were dictated by the actions of people thirty years earlier? Three hundred?

*Three thousand? More?*

He *could* decide to lay down his arms and surrender, he supposed. That would be a free choice, but not one he was capable of making.

\*\*\*\*\*

## Bellerophon

Jason was barely restraining his impulse to pace, the waiting getting to him more than it ever used to.

During his days in the Rangers, patience had been his dearest friend. He could wait for days for a target, it was part of the job. The older he got, though, and he was getting older despite the eternal youth of Priminae medical technology, the harder it was to maintain that composure. That assurance that his time was not being wasted.

*Ironic. I have so much more time now than I ever did in my youth, but it feels so much more fleeting.*

The waiting had always been the hardest part, which only spoke to how easy he found violence he supposed. For all that, though, Jason had never regretted the violence that he had committed in his life.

The violence he *hadn't* committed, how that he had come to regret more than he'd like.

*So many monsters I could have eliminated before they*

*wreaked havoc, if only I'd acted... if only I'd had the intelligence to know.*

Serving with Eric had been a strange thing for him. Honestly, Jason had never really liked Eric Weston. Respected him? Sure. The man had a way with words and with people, that was undeniable, but Jason thought the man too much of a bleeding heart. So many decisions, putting his people at risk, his *world* at risk, all for people he had no duty to.

*And where did it lead? Utter destruction.*

Jason knew, intellectually, that probably wasn't a fair conclusion. The Drasin had been sweeping toward Earth regardless, and the Empire would have stumbled on them sooner or later... but... maybe with more development time...

He didn't know. Not even in hindsight. The past was such a mess, Jason couldn'te tell one way or the other what the hell would have happened.

What his brain insisted was a mess, though, his heart didn't question.

*Maybe everyone would have died anyway... eventually. Without warning, maybe the Drasin just eats the whole damned solar system, or the Empire wipes us out... but it wouldn't have happened so soon if Eric had just minded his duty and not gotten involved.*

Now, the mess was in his lap.

And, one way or another, it was going to end.

\*\*\*\*\*

**Rogue Class Destroyer *Autolycus***

Captain Daiyu Li looked at the decrypted pulse com with equanimity, expression betraying none of the thoughts floating beneath the surface.

*Finally.*

"Lieutenant," She said quietly.

"Yes, Captain?"

"Prepare the Transition Drive System," Li ordered firmly, "We have new orders."

"Yes Ma'am."

The Rogues had long been doing the same job they had been originally assigned by Fleet Command on Earth, seeking out alien artifacts across the breadth of the galaxy. There were both more of those than one might expect and far less. Years went by with nothing but false alarms, then sometimes they'd find clusters of evidence.

At some point there had been several distinct alien cultures in this section of the Galaxy, a few quite advanced even by the standards of the Imperial or the Priminae.

None of them remained.

Curiously, to her mind at least, all of them had certain traits in common.

They were all humanoid, at the very least, with near perfect match ergonomically to humanity... yet there was no sign that they ever had contact with one another, the Empire, the Priminae... or Earth.

DNA, unfortunately, had a halflife of roughly five hundred years. That meant that within half a million years to perhaps one and half million years, there wouldn't be the slightest remaining trace of genetic evidence. Most of the civilizations they'd been able to locate were considerably older, so direct confirmation of the genome and its potential to match humanity wasn't possible.

Still, they'd found scientific records from two cultures that Prometheus had managed to decode, and like the Priminae and the Empire, they were human in every standard marker. It was only in the vestigial or so-called 'junk' DNA that differences were there to be seen.

*Once is happenstance, no matter how unlikely. Twice? Perhaps coincidence...* Li thought, as she had many times over the years, *But this is a pattern of some external influence. It flies in the face of everything we understand about evolution.*

Being called back from the investigation that had become more than a passion to her should have been frustrating, but for this?

"Transition System will be online within the hour, Ma'am. The Chief apologizes, but he'd expected more down time and wanted to get some maintenance in."

"It is of no issue," Li said simply. "One hour, more or less, will not change anything. While we wait, signal the wolf pack, call them to us."

"The... all of them, Ma'am?"

She smiled for the first time.

"Oh yes, howl the wolves, Lieutenant. We have a hunt at hand." She said, voice dripping with satisfaction. "First, though, we have one stop to make."

\*\*\*\*\*

### Gaia's Revenge

Steph wiped away some of the sweat that had beaded on his face and forehead, trying to ignore the growing heat that was filling the ship now that they were running with full stealth systems engaged. Even with the advanced capture systems turning heat back into power, the thermal efficiency of the stealth systems eventually overpowered everything they could do.

Given enough time, they'd cook if he didn't vent heat.

That wasn't going to be an issue over the next few hours, thankfully, but they might have longer than that to wait.

"ETA to Drasin arrival?" He asked, not for the first time.

"Assuming they continue to accelerate as projected," Milla shrugged, "Several hours, possibly half a day.."

Steph shook his head, "We'll have to pull back and vent heat before that happens."

The stellar ram was certainly powerful, hell Steph had no idea how to counter it, but the damn thing was slow as hell... well, for something that was moving faster than light.

It was almost enough for him to wish that he'd pulled the mission to the capital, at least the Casino was no doubt seeing some action.

*****

**Casino**

Jennifer groaned as she rested her head on the bulkhead, the soft lapping of waves against the hull actually audible within the ship. They were running on low power, trying to keep their overall signature low to prevent any chance of detection while they waited for the mission to kick off and things to get exciting.

*A little space to space combat would break up the tedium, but I had to pull this job. Damn it.*

She wasn't complaining all that much, really, but it *had* been a while since she'd last been able to really let loose in a dogfight.

Unfortunately, for the moment, this was the more important task... and it entailed waiting in the dark for a signal from her Marines, with half the crew trying not to be sea sick... *literally* trying not to be sea sick, as if that weren't completely insane on a starship.

*Always finding new and innovative ways to bring back*

*ancient problems. It's the military way, I swear.*

\*\*\*\*\*

### Imperial Fleet Command

"Fleet Commander, we're detecting more Drasin approaching the outer perimeter."

Markys hissed in annoyance, "I swear you'd think they would be sensible about things at some point. If they came at us all at once they'd have a better chance."

"Yes, Fleet Commander."

"Well, I suppose we should be grateful. How many more ships have been readied?"

"Repairs continue apace, Fleet Commander, but nearly a dozen more have been returned to our order of battle."

"A dozen... good," Markys said. "We'll advance, of course, hold the enemy to the outer perimeter until the Home Fleet returns."

"Yes Fleet Commander!"

His little armada was in rather tattered shape, but they were more than sufficient to the current task and for that he was quite thankful. The vermin continued to charge into the Imperial weapon's like the mindless beasts they were, losing *thousands* with each failed assault, but it was draining his ships' power cores at a faster rate than he would prefer.

*We need time to draw back and refuel, but that won't happen for some time.*

"Signal fleet logistics, I want to know where we are with refueling mass," He said.

"Yes sir. A moment... We have freighters with stellar mass mined from the Free Star collapsed star, they're ready to move into position on demand."

"Good. Signal them to be ready, I want our ships re-massed," He ordered. "I'll prepare a priority list momentarily."

"Yes, Fleet Commander."

Markys looked over the data he had, knowing that he had to make some decisions quickly. The stellar mass from the collapsed star would *very quickly* replenish the core mass of his vessels, but it was in limited supply all the same. Mining it was not a simple task, and transporting it even less so, but he supposed if any world in the Imperium had a supply at the ready it would be here at the Homeworld.

*I will have to prioritise vessels that are best able to continue this fight,* He decided. *That will unfortunately mean leaving several of the most damaged to drift, but it cannot be helped.*

"We have warp fields at the perimeter!"

"Standby all ships!"

"Here they come!"

"Fire!"

*****

The Drasin dropped from warp as they entered the gravity well of the target star, their senses immediately aflame with the enraging fires of the enemy's signature.

The world ahead was practically calling to them, demanding that they land their devastation upon it, and the Drasin were pleased to do just that. Without a thought the swarms set upon the ships that were intent on holding them back and in moments the space around the hated star became a killing field once more.

*****

# CHAPTER 27

**Imperial World Kraike, Imperial Tower**

The Emperor, that was how he thought of himself of course, watched through the eyes of hundreds as the fighting began again.

The Drasin were persistent, of that there could be no dispute, however they were also single minded and often rather stupid. That was not to say that they could not occasionally surprise someone. The beasts had to be treated with cautious respect, their bloody minded obstinance could occasionally result in shockingly cunning actions, but that was the exception to their actions and not the norm.

For now he could tell that the fighting was progressing more or less as calculated, at least over the whole fight. The Drasin force would shortly be pushed back unless something significant changed, but even if it did they were not currently much of a threat.

He directed more support to the fleet elements involved in the holding action, knowing that they had already suffered through significant fighting and would likely need whatever he could provide to remain close to their effective capacity. The degenerate material from the Free Stars neutron mines were truly challenging to transport, but they were the most efficient material imaginable with which to re-mass a ship's core.

Moving enough to resupply his fleet had taken *years*, but this fight had always been inevitable.

Now he could see the transports moving into position,

and felt the satisfaction of being right.

Again.

With such massive sources of power available, even nearly crippled ships would be able to keep fighting well past the point where they would normally be less than worthless scrap.

*****

Amanda glanced around as her squad regrouped on her position, making sure she kept Gordon close as she did.

"All accounted for, Ma'am," Sarge said a moment later.

"Good," She looked to the broken tower, no lights visible from where they stood on the towering rooftop, the ground thousands of meters below them while the tower loomed even higher despite the damage it had obviously incurred. "You'd think they'd have fixed that thing by now."

She looked over to Gordon, "Are you sure that's where you need to be?"

He just nodded in the over-exaggerated way that one had to while wearing an armor suit. "Last time we were here, I got readings on the place. It's built over a geo-magnetic anomaly big enough to detect with portable scanners. I'm betting the location wasn't an accident."

Amanda nodded back, humming quietly to herself.

"Alright," She said. "We'll roof hop, keep power to your chutes as low as you can. The target *might* notice the gravity warp of the counter mass units, and based on what I know about Gaia's abilities... well, let's not be noticed."

The Marines chuckled, but nodded in agreement as she again turned to Gordon.

"Can you keep up?" She asked seriously.

Precision drills in armor were old hat to the Marines, they did it every day while training and as often as possible while deployed, but they weren't exactly *easy* for all that.

"I won't slow you down," He promised. "I've been waiting for this for a long time."

"Not worried about you slowing us down," She countered, "I'm worried about you attracting that bastard's attention."

"Noted. I'll be fine."

Amanda sighed, "Alright, Sarge... lead us off. Gordon, you're next. I'll follow, then the rest. Clear?"

"Oorah!"

"Let's go."

*****

Keenan crouched low as her team made their way along the contour of the land, staying quiet as they moved.

"Fourteen hundred meters ahead, we'll be at the current magnetic pole," Her Sergeant confirmed, glancing back. "You guys have the kit ready?"

"Oorah, Sarge."

Keenan nodded, mostly to herself as she patted the sergeant on the shoulder.

"Good, we're on schedule. Let's not attract too much attention from the locals," She said. "Not that anyone seems to be looking our way at the moment."

The Sergeant snorted, "Everyone is too busy watching the big game."

He glanced skyward, his body language radiating his point even through the armor.

She laughed softly, "Fair point."

Any military attention would likely be on the goings on out beyond the atmosphere right now, that was a point, she knew.

*Though, if they're smart, they'll be preparing for a possible landing as well.*

It was those preparations that she was trying to avoid. Keenan doubted very much that the Empire's internal security would be able to catch them under normal circumstances. She, and other Terran Marines, had spent many years studying Imperial ground tactics and strategy... and they were sorely lacking.

*Not surprising, they win their battles in space. Ground work for them is primarily oppression of dissidents, not field combat.*

"Keep moving," She ordered. "The second team should be in place soon, let's not get behind."

"Oorah."

*****

Roof jumping a couple kilometers in the air was less stressful than Amanda had expected, honestly.

*Just like point drills on the oh course, honestly.*

Her HUD was feeding her trajectories and letting her armor enhance, or limit, her jump strength in order to keep her in the intended landing zone but she was focusing on *not* using any of those enhancements if at all possible. Precise muscle control with each leap, followed by minimal adjustments as she flung herself through the air, resulted in a land and a roll on the next rooftop as she bled off the impact.

Her team hit the rooftop behind her and they kept moving without pause or speaking. The tower was looming even higher in their vision, now taking up half the sky it seemed.

The Sergeant set the pace, and they were quickly closing the distance, so she fell into an autopilot sort of mode. Her body was just going along, following the route set by Sergeant Carman, while her mind was already focusing on the next step.

*Once we get to the tower, we'll need to either climb or drop to an ingress point,* Amanda noted, using her suit's passive scanner suite to analyze what she was seeing.

They had limited intel on the Tower, unfortunately, since very few non-imperial visitors got access to the capital. The last humans here, Terran humans at least, were the team led by her father in fact. She knew his stories, and all the scans they'd taken at the time, but the damage done by Prometheus' assault and years of apparent neglect had clearly changed things.

They had several options that they knew about, and would use in the worst case, but none of them were optimal.

Her job at the moment, was to evaluate on the fly and see if there were any better ways in than were indicated by thirty year old scans.

*Knew we were going to have to come in half blind, but if I can just find… there's damage a couple hundred meters above our elevation. If that's through the wall, as it appears, that could be our best shot. If it fails, it's on the way to another alternative.*

They were leaping to the next building when she tagged the target and sent the intel in a pulse burst to the Sarge.

"That's our way in," She said. "Head for there, if it doesn't pan out, we'll continue on to ingress point Charlie."

"Oorah, Ma'am." Brad responded simply, making only a slight change to his path and speed as the Marines pushed forward across the tops of the massive scrapers that rose into the skies over the imperial capital.

\*\*\*\*\*

300

## Imperial Fleet Command

"Fleet Commander! We have new contacts!"

Markys growled, but turned to quickly check the board and grimaced as he saw the numbers.

*More Drasin, coming in closer on the back of the last wave. They're getting more stubborn about this.*

"Bring up our reserves," He ordered.

"Fleet Commander…"

"I am aware," He interrupted, "They're not combat ready yet, not fully at least. We don't have a choice. We must hold this line until the Homeworld Defense Fleet returns. Call them up."

"Yes, Fleet Commander."

Most of the reserves were in bad shape, in one way or another, but he needed the numbers to shore up several points in the line.

*While they're absorbing the assault, I'll bring back the undamaged ships to resupply.*

\*\*\*\*\*

## Imperial Cruiser *From the Flames*

*It was too much to hope for I suppose,* Kaela thought as her crew rushed to get the ship ready to move.

The order bringing them back into the fight had been one she was expecting, though she had hoped it wouldn't come at the same time. It had been a slim hope, she had known that, but hope nonetheless.

With it dashed, all she could do now was secure everything she possibly could and charge her vessel into the maw of the enemy as she had been commanded.

"Lock down the core," She ordered. "What is our mass

status?"

"Two thirds of a standard planetary mass, Ship's Commander."

Kaela swore under her breath, waving off her command crew as she tapped into the command net and quickly sent a request for more mass stock.

It only took a moment for the response to come back.

Request denied. Priority to combat capable vessels.

Kaela only wished that she could be surprised by *literally any of that response.*

Taking a moment to steady herself, it wouldn't do to be spitting curses at the Fleet Commander in front of her crew, she pushed the interface away and nodded to the waiting crew.

"Very well," She said as firmly as she could manage. "It'll have to do. All hands, ready the vessel. We're taking the front."

"Yes, Ship's Commander!"

\*\*\*\*\*

## Imperial Tower

The black face of the burnt out tower was like a wall that just extended in all directions for nearly as far as any of them could see, but Amanda and her Marines didn't have time to appreciate or marvel at it as they collided with the side and clung on like limpet mines as they got themselves steadied and took the moment to establish their bearings.

"Up and to the right," Brad said, gesturing toward the likely ingress point they were heading for. "Move it easy and smooth, and for the love of god don't *drop* anything."

"Oorah, Sarge."

The team, plus Gordon, started making their way up the tower now, aided by the counter-mass systems in their suits as well as the climbing gear they normally loaded. Even a smooth wall would have been easily scaled with their kit, so her team had no issues making their way up to the damaged section and pulling themselves into the tower.

"Alright, we're in." Amanda said, eyes shifting over to Gordon. "It's your play now, Sir. Call it."

The spook took a moment to orient himself and checked his computer briefly before replying.

"I think the throne room is our best option," He said, "Poetic too. It's up from here, so we'll have to find stairs or lift access or whatever the equivalent is."

Amanda nodded slowly, referencing her own files.

"It'll be damaged from the Prometheus strike," She warned.

"I know, but it should be intact. That's where we want to be."

"Alright," She said, "Sergeant."

"Ma'am?"

"Scout the floor, find me a way up."

"Oorah."

*****

Locating lift access didn't take long. There wasn't any power running to the system as best they could tell, but that didn't matter since they didn't intend to actually use the system. They just needed the shaft.

From there, the team quickly got organized and they began moving their way up through the tower in quick fashion. Scaling the interior of the shaft was even easier than the exterior of the tower itself, since the design of the interior included the assumption that internal repair would likely be required from time to time.

That gave the team a direct line to the floor their records indicated they needed, and within the half hour they were all standing just outside the large doors that led into the once seat of Imperial Power.

"We crack these doors, what do you suppose the odds are that we bring an entity down on our heads?" Amanda asked softly as her team got into place to do just that.

"Negligible," Gordon said, shaking his head. "The Emperor isn't *here* anymore than he's anywhere else. In theory, we could have done my part of this mission from anywhere inside the planet's EM field."

She glared at him, "Then why go through all of this?"

Gordon smiled at her, "Theatrics?"

She was building up a head of steam at that, but he waved her down calmly.

"In all seriousness, the theory is one thing, but I wanted to maximize our odds," Gordon admitted. "Yes, the entity is everywhere… but I'm willing to bet that there are some places he… prefers. That's why we're here. That said, I don't think he'll take notice until I get his attention."

"How do you plan to do that?"

"Don't worry about it, that's my part," Gordon said firmly. "Crack the door."

Amanda hissed in annoyance, but nodded and gestured to the Marines. "You heard the man, breach."

"Oorah, Lieutenant!"

The doors were still secured, but the system was fairly close to a robust version of Imperial Standard, so they had quickly slipped small breaching charges to where the locks secured the doors and blew them with a single command.

The explosions were more like soft pops, focused bursts of plasma jetted into the doors and destroyed the clamps holding things in place and in the next moment the Sarge directed the Marines to push the big doors open.

Once upon a time they would have been magnificent symbols of opulence and power, but now they creaked and moved sluggishly as they opened to the cavernous interior throne room that stretched up and down for dozens of floors at least, and took up the entire interior of the tower aside from the buffer space around the perimeter.

Amanda swallowed and nodded at Carmen, who nodded back as he led the first of the team inside while she followed with Gordon.

"What now?" She asked as the spook set his kit down on a nearby bench that had probably been used for supplicants to the Imperial Court.

He checked the time as he worked, getting his equipment ready.

"Now? We wait."

\*\*\*\*\*

# CHAPTER 28

**Gaia's Revenge**

"Look alert," Tyke said, jostling Steph out of a short power nap, "Something's happening."

Steph shook his head to clear it and stretched as he shifted around to check the scanner data. *Suspension fields are amazing for a quick rest.* "Ok, what's up?"

"The Empire ships are powering weapons, and we're detecting a shift in the local spacetime," Milla answered from her cubby hole, "The approaching star is sending a bowshock through spacetime the likes of which I never believed I would see."

"Sounds about right," Steph said as he slipped into the neuro-link and connected fully with the ship's systems once again. "Oh… oh, wow, yeah I can feel it. Damn, the temporal shift is actually noticeable across the breadth of the ship. Time is moving slower at the bow than at the aft. Holy…"

A moment later he realized something else, though.

"Oh crap, we're being drawn in." Steph mumbled. "I'm activating thrusters."

The small thrusters fired, and they could hear the whining slowly increasing as the ship fought the gravetic undertow that was pulling inexorably on them.

"No good, thrusters aren't strong enough," Steph said. "Guys, we're in for it."

"Understood," Milla said, "Sounding general quarters."

"Right." Steph said as the alarm sounded and he activated the internal comm, "All hands, all hands, we are going full active. Man your stations! Say again, we are going full active. All hands to your stations!"

With that he killed the stealth field and threw power to the warp drives, reversing course hard as the intense draw only increased on the ship.

"If it increases much more it'll destabilize our warp!" He warned, hitting the comms again, "Brace! Brace! Brace!"

Tyke pulled the straps down over his shoulder and cinched in even as Milla did the same. Strapping into a warp ship was rarely something anyone bothered to do. Frankly, anything that could hit the ship hard enough to destabilize the internal inertia of the ships' frame of reference would normally leave anything living as little more than paste on whichever deck they impacted with first.

Every little bit helped though.

*****

**Imperial Home Fleet, Forward Division**

Fleet Commander Bech Toraine steadied himself as he felt the shudder through the deck of his cruiser.

*That thing is a beast,* He thought with grim resolve as every station on his ship *screamed* about the coming changes in spacetime that foretold the arrival of the stellar ram.

"Charge the disruption field," He ordered. "We will only get one chance, so prepare the weapon as well."

"Yes, Fleet Commander!"

The spacetime disruptions continued, shaking the vessel impossibly as Bech grabbed a console to remain on his feet.

"Fleet Commander! We have a new contact!"

Bech glanced over, "The Drasin?"

"Negative. Profile indicates... a mercenary vessel?"

Bech looked over, incredulous, though his officer seemed even more so. "Are you certain?"

"Yes, Fleet Commander. A Gaian vessel, they must have been observing from stealth until the turbulence from the approaching warp field hit them. They're now pulling back from their position, clearing the area."

*Mercenaries? Here? They must be mad.*

"Ignore them unless they engage our forces," Bech ordered. "The Empire will deal with them later, we have more important things to do at the moment."

"Yes, Fleet Commander!"

Bech refocused on the matter at hand, "How long until the breach?"

"Any moment now, Fleet Commander."

"Very well. Engage when ready."

\*\*\*\*\*

## Gaia's Revenge

The small ship was shaking and tossing in random seeming directions with every few passing seconds, only Steph in the suspension field afforded the pilot wasn't being battered by restraints as they were slammed around.

He was being hit, however, by the sensations that the *Revenge* itself was feeling from all sides as the sensory feeds from the ship were funneled through his own senses. It felt like being in a ship tossed at sea, not by anything as mundane as a hurricane either, but also had all the sensations of a fighter jet screaming in effort to evade a missile, and a thousand other things that all conflicted with one another as they tore through his nerves.

He rode the lightning, though, keeping the ship as steady as he could if only to keep from letting the force of the turbulence kill any of his crew.

"Hold on, almost out of the storm here!"

The Revenge stopped jumping and twisting as they broke into more stable spacetime and their own warp drive steadied out.

"We're clear!" Steph called, sweating and not from the heat. "Holy crap, I feel like I was just turned inside out, upside down, and futureside past!"

"I don't think that last one is a thing, boss," Tyke said weakly from his console.

"Neither did I until I felt *that* crap."

Steph slumped in the field, floating there for a moment as listless as the ship itself felt.

"Stephan, I believe that the Drasin are here."

Steph swore under his breath, but straightened up, "Alright. Full scans, all active lightspeed scanners to full power. Hold back the FTL ping for now."

"Yes, Stephan. Full power to lightspeed scanners now."

\*\*\*\*\*

Spacetime was a funny thing in many ways.

Most species liken it to a sheet of fabric that has some stretch to it, deformable by mass. It wasn't a bad descriptor, in so far as getting the concept across, but it wasn't remotely accurate either.

Spacetime didn't deform in any physical way. In many ways, space didn't exist, it was just... time. Time, however, could compress. It could stretch. When it stopped, so did *everything.* If the clock was not ticking, nothing existed.

But when it was ticking... everything anyone ever knew, or would know, came into being.

Time was the universe.

And in that moment, as the Drasin Stellar Ram compressed time ahead of it, the Imperial weapon countered the compression for just an instant... and everything ceased forever, and for no time at all, both at once.

Then it was over and the empty section of space had a new star.

\*\*\*\*\*

### Imperial Home Fleet, Forward Division

"The stellar ram has dropped from warped space!"

Bech nodded, "Fire the weapon!"

"Weapon charging, Fleet Commander. Firing momentarily!"

Bech glowered at the screen where the red dwarf star was sitting, an object that should not exist in this place but did in defiance of all reason, the universe, and the Empire itself.

*Not for long, however.*

"Weapon firing!"

The Empire's most secret of weapons, a throwback to an ancient war that only barely existed in their *records*, was not the sort of thing that deployed easily against any conventional enemy.

Normally, in fact, it was all but worthless because by the time you *could* use it... why would you?

Now, though, that ancient device fired on Bech's own command.

Calling it a weapon was, perhaps, a bit of a stretch. Functionally, it was more of a ship. One without a crew, but a ship nonetheless. With a powerful warp field, the ship launched itself from the armada and rapidly accelerated toward the star. Flashing blue as it went past the speed of light, the ship vanished from sight as it plunged deep into the dwarf star.

"It struck true, Fleet Commander!"

"Full power to reverse warp!" Bech ordered. "Back us away at best speed!"

"Yes Fleet Commander!"

\*\*\*\*\*

### Gaia's Revenge

"Beware, Stephan, the Empire have just gone to full warp power, moving away from the star," Milla called, "I believe they launched something at it first."

"Damn. If they're running, so are we," Steph said, twisting the ship in space as he put full power to the warp field.

In mere instants they crossed the lightspeed barrier and continued to accelerate, while Steph kept his senses cast back the way they'd come.

"I am detecting compressions in spacetime, Stephan," Milla warned. "Watch for more shockwaves."

"Right, right," He hit the internal comm again, "Welcome to flight one oh one, this is your Captain speaking, please fasten your seatbelts and put your... oh hell with it. Brace for impact, boys and girls, this is going to get rough!"

He doubted anyone had *unstrapped*, of course, but the warning should be appreciated nonetheless.

Through it all, though, he was scowling.

"Something's off."

"What?" Tyke asked, "I mean, other than the nightmare monsters trying to kill us all."

Steph snorted, "No... I can't place it, but something..."

"Compression wave!"

He was cut off as the turbulence hit, throwing them in all directions at once... or so it felt like... and through his senses he felt a wash of pure heat sear his flesh for an instant before it passed.

"Ah! Damn, what the hell?" Steph complained as he fought the urge to rub his skin in an attempt to push off the lingering burning sensations.

"I believe that the star exploded, Stephan. Some parts of the explosion somehow managed to exceed lightspeed," Milla said, confused. "I am unsure how... possibly the warp fields we are putting out drew it along with us."

"A nova... bomb?" Tyke offered, "That's terrifying."

"I wonder," Milla said, shaking her head.

"What?"

"Nothing... for now. I need to think on this," She said. "Never mind."

Steph spared her a glance, but didn't have the time nor the inclination to pressure her at the moment. She would speak on it when she had time, and he had more pressing concerns.

"I think I can keep us ahead of the blast wave, but if we're dragging that radiation along with us that could be trouble." He said, "Milla, give me a full external diagnostic and environmental scan."

"Of course."

"Something is still bothering me though…" Steph shook his head. "I just can't place it."

"The Empire just blew up a *star*, boss," Tyke told him. "That's not enough to bother you?"

Steph just shook his head.

It wasn't that, or he was fairly certain it wasn't. He felt like he was missing something.

*No. Wait… I didn't miss anything,* Steph thought abruptly. "But something *was* missing."

"Boss? You uh… ok? You're talking to yourself, I think?"

"Milla, Tyke, review the scans of the star before the Imperial weapon hit. I want it on my screen with full analysis. Now."

\*\*\*\*\*

**Imperial Home Fleet, Forward Division**

"We are clear of the blast, Fleet Commander. Mission accomplished."

Bech nodded, satisfied.

"Very good," He said. "We will slow at the edge of the expected blast radius and allow the remnants of the radiative energies to pass us by, then return to survey the damage and ensure the death of the Drasin swarms."

"Yes, Fleet Commander."

The expected blast radius of the small star was relatively modest, and there were no worlds within it to be threatened. That would make this simpler for his task group.

*Once we confirm the destruction of the swarm, we will return to end the last dregs of the swarm once and for all.*

"Exterior radiation is dropping off, all according to expected ranges. It will be safe to return shortly."

"Excellent."

Of course the blast wave was still propagating outward from the star in the sunlight realm, and would be dangerous for another full stellar rotation. They wouldn't be able to cross *that* blast wave anytime soon, unfortunately, but even getting close enough to scan the region with an FTL pulse would be sufficient.

*****

### Gaia's Revenge

"Oh shit." Steph whispered, face drawn as he saw... or, rather, didn't see... what he had expected.

"What is it, I don't get it."

"Where are the Drasin?" Steph asked softly. "I don't see *any* swarm."

"I am analyzing," Milla said intently. "Stephan, I believe that you are correct. There is no evidence of the swarm on our readings."

"Couldn't they have been behind the star? We couldn't scan there, right?" Tyke offered.

"Maybe," Steph said, not sounding convinced. "But that's not how they operate normally."

"Alright, I buy that. So what? A fakeout?" Tyke asked. "To what end?"

Steph considered it, "Only one I can think of."

He returned his focus to the scanners, "We need to find the Imperial fleet, but while I'm doing that, give me FTL pulse com. unencrypted, wide pulse. I want everyone to hear this."

"Yes, Stephan."

*****

### Imperial Home Fleet, Forward Division

"Scans indicate the expected radiation wave, debris as predicted, Fleet Commander."

"Excellent. We'll finish our work, then return home to mop up the rest."

Bech was feeling rather smug about the whole thing, given how badly the other fleet divisions had been mauled and all.

*Of course, in fairness, they didn't know what they were facing nor did they have the correct weapon… but I don't feel the need to be fair in all honesty.*

He took his seat and relaxed marginally.

For all his confidence, he had to admit that the tension in him had been worse than he'd realized. So bad that he'd honestly not even noticed how bad until now, as it drained away.

"Fleet Commander… we just received an unencoded pulse on faster than light channels."

"Unencoded?" Bech scowled, "From Imperial Command?"

"No, Fleet Commander… from the Mercenary ship."

Bech snorted, smiling as he again leaned back. "What do they have to say?"

"Playing the message now."

"All ships, this is Gaia's Revenge. The Imperial destruction of the Drasin stellar ram was a diversion! There were *no swarms* surrounding the star before it exploded!"

Bech bolted upright, eyes wide as he looked to his officers.

"Is he right?"

"A moment, we're checking the scans!"

All the tension flowed back into him, only this time Bech could feel them and knew just how bad they were. He didn't need his officers to tell him the mercenary was right, deep down…

He knew.

His mouth was dry as he worked it out.

"The homeworld." He whispered.

"We scanned no swarm surrounding the star, Fleet Commander!"

"All ships, return to the homeworld! Now!"

*****

# CHAPTER 29

**Imperial Homeworld, Imperial Tower**

"And that's time, I believe."

Amanda looked over to where Gordon was working, moving in an unhurried motion as he finished preparing his equipment. She checked the time reflexively and saw that they had a little while longer before the other teams were going to make their moves.

"We still have time before the other teams…"

"I am aware," Gordon held up his hand, interrupting her. "That's why it's time for us to make our move now. We need to distract our host for a time, keep his focus away from our compatriots until their work is done."

Amanda sucked in a breath as she considered that.

On the one hand, honestly it was insane. The entities had essentially limitless multitasking capacity, but… perhaps not when dealing with things that they couldn't incorporate directly into their gestalt. Her fingers came up to run along the side of her armor at the neck, beneath which there lay the neural scrambler.

"I understand," She said a moment later. "How are you going to get his attention?"

"With this," Gordon said, powering on the device he'd been lugging along for the entire run. "It's a powerful magnetic generator unit."

He sighed, rising up from where he'd been crouched

over the device, "Normally it isn't powerful enough to get much of a second glance from these types, but I've got some of our friends memories encoded on it from the quantum core you captured, plus we're doing it here... somewhere I believe is important to him."

Gordon splayed his fingers and shrugged, "It's the best we have, but if I can't get his attention with this... odds are he won't notice our teams move either, and this part of the mission will turn out to be superfluous. In that case, well... we wasted time coming here, but if I can then we *needed* to come here."

"Fine, I get it, you're oh so clever," She told him dryly. "Do what you've got to do."

He chuckled at her, "As you wish, my dear lieutenant. And a one, and a two... and a three."

He flipped a switch and powered the system on, letting it boot fully before he sent the first commands through to the EM Coils.

"Alea iacta est."

\*\*\*\*

**Imperial Fleet Command**

Marcys felt satisfaction as he watched the battle progress. The new ships were damaged and in poor condition to be sure, but they were holding the line well enough while his better vessels were being resupplied.

Losses were severe, but within calculations, and even if they had been total the time bought would have been more than enough to justify the cost.

*Shortly my first line vessels will be ready to re-enter the fray and...*

"Fleet Commander! Perimeter alerts!"

Markys swiveled, eyes narrowing, "What alerts? Is there another swarm on approach?"

The look on his underlings face told that story well enough, but he wasn't expecting what came next.

"Yes, Fleet Commander... but not on the course the rest used."

"What."

Markys crossed the deck of his ship quickly, planting his fists on the scanner console as he leaned over it to read the report.

*Alerts... all across the perimeter, and all focused on the opposite side of the system from here!*

The home system defenses were covering those areas, but with the numbers he was seeing there was no doubt that they would be overwhelmed quickly.

*All my ships, I called everything out here! Even the damaged reserves!* He felt the blood draining from his face, a chill filling him. *This was their plan... I...*

"Fleet Commander? Fleet Commander! We need orders!"

\*\*\*\*\*

**Imperial Homeworld**

*Clever clever.*

The Emperor had to admit to being impressed. The Drasin's cunning had bought them a valuable window and, amazingly enough, it might even be enough to gain them their fondest wish.

Normally such a move would never have worked, of course, but the utilization of the stellar ram had caused him to dispatch forces to deal with that and then of course the constant pressure of attacks... just enough to pressure his forces, but not enough for him to be forced to summon more ships from distant systems...

*They drew my disposable assets out of position and then launched the true assault.*

He sent the call out, of course, but doubted that many vessels would make it back in time to have much effect.

*It has been some time since I entered the fray myself. This should be... interes-*

The Emperor paused, something akin to genuine surprise flowing over him as he felt himself experiencing an event he had already known. Turning his focus, he looked to the source and found it in the last place he had ever thought.

*****

**Imperial Tower**

"Is that thing doing anything?"

"It is, Sergeant," Gordon confirmed. "The question is whether it's doing *enough*."

"When do we find out if it worked?"

"Sooner than you might expect, I would say."

The Marines all jumped, guns coming up as they sought out the source of the voice that had echoed around them.

"Calmly," Gordon said, looking around as he waved at the Marines to lower their weapons.

They didn't budge, of course, not until Amanda waved them down as well.

"Put them down, boys," She ordered, then nodded to the corridor, "and keep watch on our six. Nothing for your weapons to do here anyway."

"How... droll," The voice said in accented Imperial

speech, making Amanda wonder how old the speaker really was. "Somewhat intelligent humans… if you really were humans… but you aren't, are you, Xeno?"

Gordon popped the seal on his helmet and set the armored helm aside before he smiled and bowed slightly.

"A matter of perspective, perhaps," He said to the empty air. "A pleasure to once more be in your presence, your *highness*."

"Once more…" The air shimmered and coalesced, a dark shadow in the air taking the form of a humanoid, though taller than was natural, with red glowing eyes peering at them from the shadow as it looked down on them. "Ah, yes I remember you. The silent one, travelling with the so called Gaian Mercenaries. I wondered, at the time, why none of you became one with me, but so many have been lost that I did not pursue it. A mistake, I see."

Gordon merely shrugged again, "An easy one to make, if my understanding is correct. Even with your focus on us, you had the memories of billions to process in the moment, and monitoring an autonomic reflex is… tricky at best I imagine. I confess to having no idea just how impressive your multitasking capacity is, but I have a hard time imagining that it *can't* be stressed to its limit."

The shadow chuckled dryly, "Oh most certainly, though that was not the reason I missed you. To be forthright, I simply overlooked you. I will not do so again."

"I would be shocked if you did," Gordon told the entity with full honesty.

"So, it is you who are behind the recent clever tactics of the Drasin then."

That caused Gordon to blink and look confused, "Uh… I have to admit that I'm not certain what you mean."

"Really now, you think I am going to believe that you just happened to be here… invisible to my mind… just as the Drasin flank my forces and send overwhelming force through relatively unguarded sections of the system perimeter defenses? I am no child, Xeno, do not treat with me as such."

Amanda shifted nervously, "Gordon, if the Drasin are about to flood this planet, we need to get out of here. Now."

Gordon waved her off, eyes intent on the shadow.

"We used the Drasin assault as cover for our own entry," He said, shaking his head, "but work with them? Even indirectly? No. We want them as dead as we want *you*."

The shadow again laughed, leaning forward to look more clearly down at the pair.

"I almost believe you mean that, Xeno. Almost. Not that it matters, since whether I and this world live or die… *you* most certainly won't be escaping in the process."

"Quite honestly," Gordon said blithely, "I don't intend to."

\*\*\*\*\*

### Imperial Home system, outer limits

### Gaia's Revenge

Dropping out of transition *sucked*, but Steph was through holding back at this point. The Drasin actions had made it clear that they were making plays a little more sophisticated than their normal blitzkrieg style rushes through their enemy's defenses.

He'd ensured that his message was sent out, then pulsed another with his suspicions to back up his earlier statement. He knew that the others, the Priminae and the Terrans, would come to the same conclusion as he had.

*The Drasin are going for the king.*

"Transition complete," Milla said from behind him. "Scanners active, we are beginning to pull down lightspeed data."

Steph scowled, but shook his head, "Go full active. I want deployment intel *now*."

"Steph," Tyke said softly, "That will expose our position, and if they look too close, they might be able to spot our transition using lightspeed sensors."

"I know, but we need the data. Pulse out."

"As you command, Stephan," Milla said softly as she prepared the system.

*****

"You what?"

Amanda was *not* amused by the only interpretation she could make from the statement made by Gordon.

"Oh ho? Trouble in the ranks, Xenos?"

She spared the shadowy figure a glance, but quickly refocused, "Tell me you did not lead my squad into a suicide mission."

"Don't worry, Lieutenant," Gordon said with a soft smile, "I have no intentions of sacrificing your squad. In fact, you can leave now."

That just caused her to redouble her glare as she reached up to pull her own helmet off, "If you believe that I am about to leave my principle here and run, then you..."

She stopped as a chirp notified her of a command priority message, startling her into silence. She glanced down at her helmet and fit it back on in silence to read the message. A moment later Amanda again took the helmet off, and not just stared flatly at Gordon.

"You planned this from the start."

"I did. Take your people, go." He ordered her, looking back to the shadowy figure of the Emperor Entity. "Our friend here, and I, have a discussion to see to."

The Emperor chuckled low, "I must confess to finding all this drama more amusing than I ever expected to see from the outside, without the little details I normally get. Yes, little soldier, go now. Run. It does not matter, I will be with you no matter where you go here. My eyes are on you now, and you will not escape me."

Amanda glared at Gordon, ignoring the entity, but the signed orders she had were pretty much ironclad.

"Fine." She said, fitting her helmet back on and grabbing up her rifle. "Sergeant. We're leaving."

"Yes Ma'am."

Gordon watched them leave for a moment, before turning back to the Emperor.

"Shall we continue?" He asked with a genial smile.

*****

**Imperial Fleet Command**

"Pulse scan detected, Fleet Commander. It's... from outside our lines, and not near the enemy either."

Markys frowned, "Is the home fleet returning?"

"Unknown. Shall we return the pulse?"

Markys scowled, but nodded slowly. "Do so."

"Pulse generated."

Markys leaned in, examining the profile that was returned nearly instantly.

"It's the mercenaries again, Fleet Commander."

"Them again? What are they playing at?"

*****

**Gaia's Revenge**

"That's a lot of Drasin," Steph said grimly.

"More than we have weapons for," Tyke snorted.

"A lot more."

The swarm entering through the relatively undefended perimeter of the system were in numbers that Steph had *never* seen before, not outside a Kardashev construct at least. The Drasin had pulled all the punches, sacrificed their own number in the hundreds of thousands at least by this point, and all for this.

"Mark their positions, trajectories, and get everyone ready," Steph ordered.

"Ready for what? We can't do anything against that."

"We have people in there already," Steph said. "The Casino should be on world already. One way or another, we're getting them out."

"Right, right," Tyke said. "Ok, we're compiling the intel now. Not sure how we're going to be able to use it, but it's compiling."

"Good. I'm taking us in," Steph said, leaning into the warp and putting the Revenge into motion. "Downwell, maximum acceleration."

"This is gonna suck."

*****

The Emperor looked the small man over as he was standing there, finding curiosity in the nuance of not being able to read him as he was used to.

"You do know that you cannot distract me from their

positions, I assume?" He asked, mildly curious as he probed in an attempt to discern the Xeno's plan.

"Of course," Gordon shrugged. "They'll be fine. Your people aren't very good at ground combat. I wouldn't advise sending them against a Marine squad who are already feeling like they just had a fight snaked out from under them. Honestly, you'd be better off just letting them go."

The Emperor couldn't help but laugh at that.

"You must be simple if you believe that would work. I don't care how many men it takes to drag them down, I have more than I need."

"No doubt, try to enjoy the show." Gordon said with a shrug. "In the meantime, you and I have a discussion to have, I believe?"

"What do you suppose I could possibly have to discuss with you?"

"You? Oh, nothing really, but I thought you might be interested in telling me something."

The Emperor looked at him for a long moment, waiting, but Gordon said nothing.

Finally, it was the Entity that broke the silence.

"Oh, and what would that be?"

"Just one thing, really," Gordon said as he took a seat on a charred diplomat's chair. "Why?"

The Emperor stared, "Why?"

"Just that," Gordon nodded. "You see, I've been able to answer who. I know what. When was easy, as was where. How? Child's play. But only you can tell me… why?"

"You believe that you're even capable of understanding any of my intentions or reasons?" The Emperor asked, amused.

"You, Xeno, are nothing more than a plague. Little different than the Drasin, honestly. Just as destructive, just as *evil*. You and your kind should never have existed to begin with..."

"Humanity has evolved at least eight times that we've discovered, counting the Empire and our own world," Gordon said. "Six of those instances are extinct as best we can determine. Was that your doing?"

"You know *nothing*. Who. What. Where. When. WHY..." The Emperor snarled, "You know *none* of those things. Eight. You are missing at *least* twenty more. Over and over again, *things* like yourself appear in the Galaxy. Looking human. Talking like you're *people*..."

The Emperor rose up, filling the space they were in.

"You are *not* people. You are abominations."

\*\*\*\*\*

# CHAPTER 30

**Gaia's Revenge**

"Transition signature!" Milla called from behind. "New transponders appearing... It's the Heroics."

"Give me comms," Steph said as he leaned on the acceleration.

"Comms up."

"Welcome to the party," He said. "We have a target rich environment on the move, heading toward the Imperial Capital. The Casino and her crew are on world now. Sending full tactical data to your systems."

"Message sent."

"Good, let's buy Jenn and Amanda some time." Steph said, his throat tightening as he spoke his daughter's name.

"Of course," Milla said softly.

"We've got this, both of you. *Everyone* is coming to this party," Tyke said calmly. "We'll get them back. You know we will."

"Yeah, or I'll kill that thing calling itself Emperor even if I have to take that whole fucking planet apart one rock at a time."

\*\*\*\*\*

**Bellerophon**

"Well... this is bad." Jason said softly as they got the updated tactical telemetry from the Revenge's transmission.

"How many are there?"

"Too many to calculate," Bell answered before his officers could speak. "The data from *Gaia's Revenge* is not sufficient to make a full count. We would require multiple pulses and return scanners from across the system to…"

"I get it," Jason held up his hand, "Alright, like it or not, the Drasin are the priority now. Get the Heroics linked into a battle net, we're going down-well."

"Aye, Skipper! Combat Network is forming, we're expecting more ships soon…"

"Transition signature! Transponders indicate the Priminae fleet! Skipper, Admiral Tanner on comms!"

"Put him through," Jason ordered.

A screen near him flickered and the unassuming form of the Priminae Admiral appeared on it, nodding slightly as he recognized Jason's own image in return.

"Captain Roberts."

"Admiral, it's a pleasure."

Tanner smirked slightly, "It would be more of a pleasure if you ever deigned to meet while we were *not* about to entire combat."

"You have a point," Jason admitted, "We really should make some time for discussions when we're not facing off against eldritch horrors."

The Priminae chuckled in return, "Indeed. For now, however, I see that we have our hands full."

"Telemetry from the *Revenge* is coming your way," Roberts said, waving to his comm officer, who sent the data without a word.

Tanner looked aside briefly and nodded, "I see. We will

analyze this and add it to our own."

Jason turned his focus back to the tactical display, "Admiral, suggest we add to the data. Full active scans, multiple pulses."

"Agreed. Let us, what was it Eric once said? Ah yes, let us... light them up?"

*****

**Imperial Tower**

"Abominations?" Gordon asked, shrugging, "You know what, you might have us there. We're not exactly *nice* people, I'd be the first to admit. I've seen a lot of people die by my actions, even regret a few though not as many as you'd think."

The Emperor stared for a moment, seemingly distracted.

"Something happening?" Gordon asked, a smile playing on his lips.

The entity's attention returned fully to him, "You attack as we are fighting off the Drasin threat? Cowards."

Gordon laughed, "You still have no idea who we are, do you? Let me guess, you just noticed... a few hundred new ships arrive out of nowhere? More maybe? Keep watching."

"Your machinations will come to nothing."

"Maybe, we are playing a longshot here," Gordon admitted, "but really, you're the one who forced us into a corner. If a human has a choice between lying down and dying, or coming out swinging... well, honestly it's probably fifty fifty on which we'll choose, people disappoint me quite often. Us, though? We decided to come out swinging. You should regret making us do that."

*****

### Gaian Destroyer *Bug Hunt*

Reid leaned on the side of his chair, expression slightly unfocused as he stared off at a corner of the bulkhead without really looking at it.

"Hey, Michaels."

"Sir?" Eric Michaels looked over from where he was standing duty at the Operations station.

"She feel off to you?" Reid asked idly, still looking off into nowhere.

"She... the Ship, Sir?"

"Yeah, something's not right. Am I wrong?"

"Huh..." Eric cocked his head, listening. "I think the warp field is running a little off angle. Give me a second..."

The kid, who was young for being a full Lieutenant in the current fleet but had pulled it together a few times during some decent action and earned his bumps as far as Reid was concerned, he did a little work at the Ops terminal before he looked up again and nodded.

"Yeah, we're slamming along slightly off angle to our plane of travel," He confirmed. "It's not serious, but the resonance must be coming up through the deck. It'll take a yard to realign things."

"Right, Ok," Reid leaned back. "How far out is the AO?"

"Three minutes, Sir."

"Let's get everyone to their stations, then."

"Aye, Skipper," Eric said as he sounded the General Quarters Alarm.

*****

### Boudicca

Hyatt growled as the Bo swung into position ahead of the Imperial Capital's orbital path, the Drasin swarm were moving fast and they'd barely gotten the Priminae and Heroic cruisers into place.

It felt wrong, to be frank, defending the Empire in any way... but she'd read the remit and reluctantly had to agree with it.

The destruction of the Empire was a top priority, but it felt well short of the *final* destruction of the Drasin themselves. At the moment there was at least a fifty-fifty chance that the Drasin were seeking a key to the Empire's leash on-world, and that was something *they could not allow*.

So they were putting a shield between the Empire and its own superweapon.

"Lead with the pulse weapons, don't worry about aiming. We couldn't miss if we tried," She ordered. "Fire!"

"Shot out!"

The glowing of the anti-deuterium pellets was barely visible on the screens, only the augmented screens letting them keep an eye on their own, and other vessels, firing paths.

Even as the salvo of antimatter weapons from half the assembled cruisers tore through the Drasin front line, Hyatt and the rest pressed the assault.

"Beams!" She called. "Burn them out of the sky."

*****

## Imperial Tower

"Arrogant mortals, I believe is my line, yes?" The Emperor chuckled, a rasping sound that came from nowhere and everywhere at once. "You really believe that I have any care as to whether or not you choose to fight me?"

"I said you should, not that you would," Gordon

shrugged. "I'm a firm believer in free will. Everyone should make their own mistakes."

The Emperor just shook his head in disbelief at the little Xeno's sheer gall, but before he could respond, other eyes in other places saw something that gave him pause.

"Your people are shielding this world," The Emperor said, surprised. "Why?"

"Why is the hardest question to answer, isn't it?" Gordon asked philosophically. "Though I suppose for you it's usually simplicity itself to know, isn't that right?"

He leaned back in the diplomat's seat, putting his boots up on the console in front of him.

"You just know why people do things, as if you did the thing yourself, don't you? I can only dream of how easy that would have made my job over the years," Gordon admitted with some jealousy. "But here and now, not knowing? That's got to be an itch you can't scratch. I'd find it maddening, myself."

He heard a noise outside and half glanced back to the door.

"Are your guards here already?" He asked mildly. "I expected longer."

The Emperor was silent, staring at him for a long moment. The sounds from outside stopped.

"They will wait until I give them the order to enter. Now, tell me. *Why*?"

Gordon let his boots drop, planting his feet on the ground as he leaned forward.

"Now we're getting somewhere. Why indeed," He smiled. "Why don't you go first?"

The Entity stared in silence, a feeling of oppression

settling on the room in a way that Gordon had never experienced before. He could hear men's voices croaking and gasping from outside the throne room, but steeled himself as it became hard to breathe. He just kept silent and did not look away from the shadowy figure that was glowering down at him.

*****

Amanda hissed as she slid into cover behind some component sticking out of the rooftop.

*Air conditioner maybe?* She didn't think about it too hard, more concerned with keeping out of sight of the searchers.

The local militia, guard, cops, or whatever the hell they were were certainly out in force. She assumed that the entity had some way of issuing orders, but really didn't need to be thinking about that at the moment because she knew enough about them to know that they couldn't exactly hide from the damn thing while within its sphere of influence.

The neural scramblers kept their minds from being added to the gestalt, but once the entity had its focus on them the scrambler didn't do anything to hide them from its notice.

"Casino, Gamma Actual," She reported as the guards moved on from her position.

"Go for Casino."

"Delivered our VIP to the target AO and received orders to leave him in position and fall back," She gritted out. "Orders were counter-signed by the Colonel, yourself, and Captain Roberts of the Bellerophon. Copy."

"Roger, Gamma Actual. Orders are authentic, sorry for the surprise but we weren't sure if they'd be needed," Samuels responded. "Find an evac point and signal for extract."

*Well at least I didn't get scammed into abandoning my VIP*

*for nothing,* Amanda thought grimly. "Roger extraction point. Standby."

"Standing by. Casino Out."

Amanda looked around, then signalled the Sergeant in. "Ok, we need a position where the Casino can pick us up. Survey and report."

"Yes Ma'am."

*****

## Bellerophon

"Drasin are converging, sir. Pulse tubes depleted, T-Cannon Pulse rounds down to thirty percent."

Jason grimaced, "Bell, Do it."

"Understood. Heroics are interlinked," The Entity said, "Forward warp fields to full military power, aft warp fields… offline."

"All weapons ceasing fire, Skipper."

"Tell the powder monkeys to step up antimatter production," Jason ordered.

"Roger that."

"Beams!"

"Calculating escape trajectories… firing."

The powerful beam weapons of the Heroic Class cruisers *bent* around their forward warp fields, lancing out into space beyond the deep gravity well that was accelerating the ships forward. Without the positive warp behind then, however, the acceleration was incapable of hitting lightspeed.

What did happen was the linked warp fields *slammed* into the Drasin line, sucking the drones down into the crushing abyss of the gravity wells. They were torn apart as the increase in gravity began to approach a shearing effect, pulling on the bottommost parts faster than the top of the drones could accelerate.

Spaghettification.

A nonsensical word, for one of the most brutal ways to kill an enemy imaginable.

"The mass is building, Sir," Bell said. "Our Phalanx will only hold so much."

"Understood," Jason nodded.

He knew that there was a critical mass, beyond which the forward wells would become self-sustaining beyond the power pushed into them by the ship's generators. If that happened, each of the Heroics would be creating a stable black hole just a couple hundred *meters* from their bows.

That wouldn't not end well.

"Standby to tack!" Jason ordered.

"Standing by!"

"Drop power to forward well, increase power to aft well!" Jason ordered. "All weapons free! Fire at will!"

The ships reversed acceleration as the fields fell in front of them just before their weapons opened fire. Antimatter bursts, beams, and nuclear warheads from the T-Cannons tore through the Drasin ranks as the Heroic cruisers fell back from the onslaught before them.

"Turn the drasin mass into feedstock," Jason said. "That should replenish our core mass nicely."

"Aye skipper!"

"The Priminae cruisers are moving to shield our front line, Sir. They're engaging."

"Good, take the moment," Jason said firmly, "use the time to rearm, we'll be back in the thick shortly."

"Aye, skipper!"

\*\*\*\*\*

**Priminea Warship**

Tanner glowered at the screens from where he stood at the center of chaos, the battle raging all around them as his ships moved up to take the brunt of the fighting from the Terran vessels.

"Pulse weapons down to thirty percent, Admiral."

Tanner nodded, "Understood, maintain fire."

"Yes Admiral!"

Honestly he would be happier when the weapons were at zero percent. The use of negatively charged matter as a weapon still made him queasy, and the thought of having it *on his ships* gave him chills that belonged in a health ward and not on the command deck of a ship.

For all that, however, they were the most effective weapons possible to deploy against the Drasin swarms.

There was no defense against them, aside from *perhaps* a judiciously positioned warp field, and that required more luck than he wanted to think of to pull off. The weapons would simply annihilate whatever they contacted, and the resulting release of energy would just as often damage and destroy nearby drones as a bonus.

Any sane enemy would spread out, evade the negative matter charges, but the Drasin?

*This is not a battle, it is a slaughter. How very odd.*

"Terran Heroics are moving forward again, Admiral!"

"Let them take the lead, fall back and begin recharging our pulse magazines."

"Yes Admiral!"

\*\*\*\*\*\*

**Imperial Tower**

The Emperor watched the battle raging through the hundreds of sets of eyes that were monitoring it on-world, missing nothing even as he continued to speak with the Human-form Xeno standing within his throne room.

"Why." He rumbled, "What would you know of my motivations?"

"Nothing," Gordon answered with a shrug. "If I knew, I wouldn't ask. You've brought so much destruction, and from what I can tell it was all for nothing. No gain, no long term strategy, *nothing*. I. want. To. know... why?"

"As if you truly don't know," The Emperor said simply, "but if you *must* perpetrate this charade, then I will entertain you. You ask why? I ask how could I *not*? You know that the Empire and the Oathers were once one people, I believe?"

"The Oathers... The Priminae?" Gordon asked, nodding, "Yes. I know."

"The sundering of their culture happened long ago, but before that my people were all much like the Oathers in nature. Peaceful, too peaceful. Good at heart, but weak. They were unready for you, Xeno."

"Doubt it was us they were unready for," Gordon snorted. "I don't think we were even a culture back then, strictly speaking."

"You are Xeno. Alien. It doesn't matter if it were you specifically, it was your type."

Gordon nodded, his expression almost reading like he was *amused* by the Emperor's statement.

"You say so."

"I do." The Emperor said simply. "You were greeted

like long lost brothers, and you returned that with treachery. Poisons, disease, and an attack while *my people* were at their weakest."

"Sounds about right," Gordon said casually as he leaned back in the seat. "History is full of situations like that. So you rallied the troops and fought back?"

The Emperor, for the first time, looked away.

"No..." He rumbled. "No, I did not."

*****

### Gaian Destroyer *Bug Hunt*

"That is a lot of bugs," Reid said with a low whistle as the destroyer dropped below lightspeed and into the fray.

"Yes sir," Lieutenant Michaels said from the Ops panel, "We're getting a feed from the allied network. No full count, but the number clearly exceeds tens of thousands. Priminae and Heroic cruisers are holding the line ahead of the planetary orbit, but if they fall the Drasin will be on the planet in minutes."

"Yeah, roger that," Reid sighed, "I suppose we should help, but really, our beams are barely going to scratch that number."

"There are a few strays that have gotten past the line," Michaels offered. "Heading for the Imperial infrastructure around their homeworld."

Reid leaned forward, "That does seem more our speed. Ok, take us in, Chief."

"Aye aye, Skipper," The Chief said from the helm.

"Weps, do your thing."

"With pleasure, Sir."

Reid leaned back again, looking like he was ready to

yawn as the crew got to it. The Bug Hunt was moving toward the fight already, weapons charging as the ship's reactor fed the beam capacitors.

*****

### Imperial Tower

"The war that raged against the Xeno was not my doing," The Emperor said. "I was an observer then, I did not interject myself in the affairs of... the people. That was my mistake."

The entity's form shuddered unnaturally, almost vanishing between pulses, leaving Gordon with the impression that the Emperor was gripping his own... emotions? Thoughts? Whichever, whatever, he was tightly controlling himself at the moment, that much Gordon knew.

"The war split the people. The Oathers clung to their morality, their *empathy*, their accursed *honor*. Those with sense fought back with whatever weapons they could, even the enemy's own tools."

"The Priminae didn't fight?" Gordon asked mildly.

"Of course they fought, they're fools but they didn't yearn for their own deaths," The Emperor snapped. "They refused to fight the enemy on the enemy's own level, and they suffered for it. They died by the *millions*, and still wouldn't give up their *honor*, their oaths. Fools."

"That's strength, to take those kinds of losses and not surrender to the fear?" Gordon said mildly, thoughtfully. "I know my people couldn't have done that. We've surrendered to fear for far less."

"It's death! Not of the individuals, but of the entire people! Unacceptable!" The Emperor raged.

"Why?" A smile played at Gordon's lips. "Because you cared for them? Or because without them, you're just a ghost haunting an empty world?"

"*I say when they die! I say IF they die!*" The entity raged, his voice rattling the solid walls like a storm slamming into a hut on a tropical beach.

Gordon just stared for the longest moment…

And then he started to laugh.

\*\*\*\*\*

### Casino

"Damn, they stirred up a hornet's nest," Jennifer said as she guided the gunboat through the air, going feet dry as she accelerated out from over the ocean toward the megalopolis city in the distance.

The Casino was still running in deep stealth, but that wouldn't last for long in the heightened alert status over the city. Sooner or later someone would notice the black shadow passing overhead, especially if the mission went on much longer.

*Daybreak is coming.*

"Gamma Actual, Casino."

"Go for Gamma."

"On approach," Jennifer said. "Give me a signal when I hit the city and we'll pick you up."

"Roger that, Casino. Wilco."

She kept her approach subsonic, her ship wasn't designed to suppress a sonic boom since such things were rarely an issue in space, but was over the city in moments anyway.

The transponder chirp from her Marines showed up seconds later and she zeroed in on the building they were sheltering on, taking note of the Imperial forces in the area.

*Yep, definitely one hell of a hornet's nest.*

\*\*\*\*\*

Amanda looked around as her system told her that the Casino was on approach.

The ship didn't show up on any visual scan, of course, not against a night sky at any kind of range at least. However, she did have the augmented imagery to show her the approach as the ship got close enough.

"Alright, Marines, look alive. We've got evac inbound," She said, slapping the Sarge on the back. "Get ready, we're leaving."

"Oorah, Ma'am." The Sarge said firmly as he got up, rifle at the ready as they looked around for Imperial flyers.

There weren't any too close, thankfully, but it wouldn't take much for them to converge if things went poorly.

The got to their feet as the ship closed overhead, a crack opening in the sky as the Casino's rear plank dropped down and the jump officer could be seen against the dim red glow of the interior.

"Alright, move!" Amanda ordered. "Corporal, go go go!"

Amanda watched the evacuation as the Marines jumped, one by one, using their suit CM systems to power their ascent to where they were recovered one by one.

"Gamma Actual, Casino. Get a move on, we've been made."

"Shit," Amanda looked around, wondering which of the lights in the sky were coming to kill them, then figuring the answer was probably *all of them.* "Go on, Sergeant. I'm right behind you."

Brad shot her an annoyed look, but couldn't say much considering it was an order. "Yes Ma'am."

She watched him jump as her HUD spotted three lights shifting and moving their direction. As the Sergeant was recovered, She jumped in turn and caught the hands of the two Jump Officers who yanked her in as the Casino started to move before she even hit the deck.

"Everyone hold on," Cardsharp's voice came over the system. "We've got trouble inbound!"

*****

The skies surrounding the Imperial world were filled with flames, the dying, and the dead as the conflicting forces threw themselves at one another with no quarter demanded and certainly none offered.

Drasin died by the thousands, as Priminae and Heroic cruisers burned under their onslaught, yet neither hesitated for even a passing moment.

Far out in the outer system a flickering of reality happened and dozens more ships appeared from the ether. They took a moment to examine the situation, then accelerated downwell at their best warp as a signal went out.

"This is Admiral Passer, commanding the Rogue Fleet. Where do you need us?"

*****

# CHAPTER 31

**Imperial Homeworld Northern Pole**

Colonel Keenan checked the countdown on the mission clock, "It's almost time. Gordon and Gamma team should have been in position long enough to set their side of things up."

"Oorah Ma'am."

"Set the detonation sequence," She ordered. "The timing must be precise."

She watched as her men set the disruption device into place over the magnetic pole and re-checked the timing before they set it and started the countdown.

"Alright, fall back. We need to withdraw to the pickup position."

"Oorah!"

*****

**Casino**

"Marines on board, Ma'am."

"Got it," Jennifer said tersely as she flew the ship, "We're moving South, we'll hit hypersonic shortly. Time to weapon deployment?"

"Five minutes."

A warning tone caught Jennifer's attention as she flew, "We have pursuit. Eight enemy ships in our wake…"

"Got them. They're small, maybe air breathers, Ma'am.

Not warp ships for sure."

Jennifer nodded, leaning in harder, "Fuck em then."

The Casino accelerated past Hypersonic and left nothing but a thunderclap in its own wake as the pursuers struggled to follow.

The Southern magnetic pole was only short minutes away at her current pace, but Jennifer knew that once they slowed to pickup Bravo Squad, the local air defenses would have an opportunity to lock on and close with her.

Unfortunately, most of the weapons the Archangel Class Gunboats could deploy were not *remotely* intended for use in an atmosphere.

Her Pulse torpedoes would destroy *the Casino* the instant she tried to fire them, just from mutual annihilation with the atmosphere, so they were out. The beam weapons were so powerful that they would shift the atmosphere into plasma, and the backlash from that would at least damage the Casino, not to mention degrade the range significantly in the process. And the HVMs would burn up from friction, again probably damaging the Casino itself upon firing.

*So, basically, I have point defense systems and not much else. Lovely.*

Granted, the Beams and the HVM systems could be tuned down significantly, as that was part of their design. However, against Imperial defenses, merely hypersonic rockets and relatively low powered beams wouldn't be of much use.

*Thankfully, the Imperials have a similar handicap. Their intra-atmospheric weapons leave a lot to be desired, and against a starship hull and defense, it would trake a hell of a lot to beat on through. Too bad they seem to have a hell of a lot to try with.*

Her scanners were making it clear that Imperial

contacts were closing from every direction.

"Oh well, in for a penny and all that rot," Jenn mumbled as she hit the brakes and brought the ship to a hard deceleration as they approached the pole. "Bravo Squad, Casino. Standby for pickup."

*****

Bravo Squad had located the pole and set the timer on their part of the device about the same time that a local military patrol either stumbled on their position or, more likely, had been directed to check out some sign they'd left behind.

The resulting firefight was less of a battle and more of a light skirmish with the Imperial forces falling back quickly under the withering fire delivered from the squad's weapons. Unfortunately, they quickly regrouped with reinforcements and came back.

The call from the Casino could not have come at a better time, unless it had been several minutes earlier.

"Roger that Casino, be advised, local LZ is *hot*."

There was a pause on the call before the Skipper's voice came back steadily.

"Understood. Mark enemy locations, will provide cover."

"Roger. Enemy locations marking… now."

"Receipt confirmed… a moment. Be aware, several markers are Danger Close. Say again, Danger close."

"Trust us, Skipper, we know."

Jennifer sighed over the line, "Understood. Heads down, and pucker up. Casino is rolling the dice."

The communications line went dead as Lieutenant

Angala looked around at the squad, "Casino is inbound, they're providing close air support."

Sergeant Birkwitz stared blankly for a second.

"Um, Sir..." The Sergeant mumbled.

"What is it, Birk?" Angala asked, looking over.

"The Casino... their weapons?"

"What is it?"

"Not designed for close air support sir." Birk said, sounding oddly nervous for the grizzled sergeant Angala was used to. "We're inside the strike zone for pretty much all of them."

"I suppose that's why she said heads down and pucker up," Angala said dryly. "Trust the skipper, but let's cover our butts people. Grab some cover, the Casino is inbound."

"Oorah!"

\*\*\*\*\*

### Casino

With her main weapons being completely out of the question, Jennifer brought the Casino's point defense systems online.

Missile and kinetic defense systems were a standard part of the Archangel's loadout, but they rarely got used in a real fight since the Empire and the Drasin used beam weapons almost exclusively. They mostly got used to take out navigational hazards while operating without warp fields, which was about as rare an operation as Jennifer had ever encountered if she were honest.

She'd still pop the head off anyone who suggested saving mass by gutting them from her ship.

Rarely used didn't mean *never* used, as she was about to

prove.

"All hands, brace for a strafing run."

\*\*\*\*\*

The Marines dropped to the ground, grabbing for whatever cover they could get as a whine began to build in the air around them. The firefight stalled as even the enemies seemed to recognize that something was coming, but they clearly didn't know what.

The Casino arrived just ahead of the thunderclap, slowing to just below the speed of sound as it arrived overhead and they heard the staccato booms of weapons fire shake the air all around them.

The point defense weapons were *light* by the definitions of a starship, but for Marines on the ground the word didn't have any resemblance to reality as the ground shook with every impact. The weight of fire slamming into the Imperial positions threw up so much dirt and dust that visibility dropped to zero in an instant even as the concussion blasted over their position with enough force to rattle their bones through the armor.

\*\*\*\*\*

**Imperial Tower**

"You find my reasoning... amusing, do you?" The Emperor asked in a dull tone, any hint of human emotion void from his aura.

Gordon, still laughing, wiped the tears from his eyes.

"Sorry, sorry, honestly I'm more laughing at myself," Gordon admitted with a shrug as he calmed. "I set my expectations too high."

The Emperor stared in silence for a long moment as Gordon regained his composure. Finally, the entity merely ground out a single word.

"Explain."

Gordon casually waved off the Entity's ire, shaking his head as he surreptitiously checked the time.

*Almost.*

"I'll be honest," He said with a shrug, "I was somewhat hoping for something more... epic... Some grandiose plan, perhaps, I don't know. But the pathetic mewling of a *child* throwing a tantrum over someone else breaking some of his *toys*, while honestly more in keeping with what I know of despots like yourself, is still a little disappointing."

The pressure in the room intensified, like he'd sunk a thousand meters down in the sea all in an instant, but Gordon gritted his teeth and forced himself to stay upright.

"You... Dare..."

"See, this is what I'm talking about," Gordon snorted through the stress in his voice. "Childish. Loudmouthed. *Fool*."

"I am the Emperor of the greatest power in the Galaxy! Billions jump to my command! My power is perfection, my reach unchallenged..."

"You're the loudmouthed asshole in the bar," Gordon said. "The one that gets all the attention, while *real power* sits quietly in the corner, where no one with any sense would dare bother it. You are a *child* playing with the tools of adults."

"I am older than your *race*!"

"Too bad you never learned to act it."

"You go too far, Xeno. Our discussion is *finished*."

Gordon smiled, "Couldn't agree more."

\*\*\*\*\*

**Southern Pole**

"Bloody hell," Lieutenant Angala swore as he picked himself slowly off the ground and looked around him.

There was nothing to see, at least visually. The dust and dirt that filled the air was beginning to drop, but for the moment visibility was measured in centimeters at best. The Augmented HUD he used was able to locate and outline his Marines, and they were all still alive as best he could tell, so there was that for good news.

"Birk," He ordered as he felt around until he closed his hands on his rifle and picked it off the ground, "Get the men up and moving."

"Oorah, Ell Tee. You heard the man, Ladies! Up and at them!"

His suit sensors were not good enough, unfortunately, to find the *enemy* through the mess he was looking at.

"If anyone spots the enemy, shout out on the battle net," He grumbled.

"Can't see shit in this, Sir."

"If we could see, I wouldn't have had to tell you to shout out, Corporal," Angala snapped, irritated.

He could feel more than hear the Casino moving above them, the warp fields left a sensation not unlike being on a roller coaster as they moved around, alternately making him feel lighter and heavier as he pressed the butt of his rifle into his shoulder and listened to the chatter.

"Bravo Actual, Casino is in position. Evac your location."

"Love too, Ma'am, but we can't see a damn thing," Angala responded, looking up for the HUD outline of the ship on his augmentation system. "Jump Master, please mark the target."

"Oorah, Marine. Check One. Position marked."

The digital flare lit up his HUD and Angala automatically reached out to slap the back of the Sergeant's armor.

"Roger. Position located, preparing to Evac. Jump for the ship, Sergeant. Take these misfits with you!"

"Right you are, Lieutenant," The Sergeant said, calling out to the rest, "Up and at them, you mooks! By the numbers, let's move it!"

The Marines started jumping, two by two, up out of the dust and smoke to the waiting gunboat hovering above them. They exploded out of the thick obscuring mess, catching the hands of the Jump Master and his assistant above before being pulled into the gunboat.

Angala mentally checked off each of the Marines as they made it into the gunship, but tried to keep an eye on the enemy at the same time.

*At least this dust keeps them at bay. Beam weapons are shit against airborne particulates.*

It wasn't a common problem, he supposed, for the Empire. The air onboard ships was normally scrubbed clean near constantly, as it was in most of the areas Imperial forces could count on fighting. That made beam weapons fairly practical, and their near unlimited ammunition capacity put them easily over the top of most alternatives.

Marines tended to fight in the dirt, however, and clouds of dust and smoke put a serious dent in the capabilities of beams.

He could see the flash of their beams being reflected, refracted, and just burning up as they tried to take shots but failed. The dust was already falling out of the air, though, and the Casino wasn't kicking up near enough to keep it flowing around.

*Half the squad is clear. We'll be out shortly.*

"Drop refractive smoke," He ordered, tossing his own anti-beam smoker as he spoke.

The suspension of metallic particles in the refractive smoke would screw with their sensors pretty badly, but it would put a solid stop to the Imperial weapons while the rest of his men got clear.

Shouting could be heard around them, but Engala couldn't see any of the Imperial soldiers crowding in around their position through the smoke.

"Almost out Lieutenant. Your turn!"

"Roger that," Engala said before he locked in the Casino in his HUD and jumped for it.

\*\*\*\*\*

*Damn, they're already on us.*

Jennifer hammered the warp field, twisting the atmosphere as the Casino jumped out of its position just moments after they confirmed that the squad was back on board.

"Multiple contacts, Ma'am. Closing fast."

"I see them." She scowled. "They're air breathers, but they're designed for this and we're not. Hold on, I've got speed on them, but they've got the numbers and vectors. All hands, standby for some turbulence! Hang on!"

Within the atmosphere she couldn't use the full power of the Casino's warp fields. Even if they didn't burn out from the mass, friction, and other forces involved would quickly turn her ship into an oven. That would cripple her maneuverability options, and with most of her best weapons crippled due to how badly they would interact with the atmosphere...

*Well, things are getting interesting.*

The original Archangel Air and Space Superiority Fighter would actually be better suited for this fight, though in terms of numbers Jenn didn't think it would be any better.

"Weapons lock. We're painted."

"I see them. Point defense beams up," Jenn said. "Get ready."

The Imperial air defense fighters closed fast, firing their weapons as soon as they entered range.

Jenn pivoted the Casino to put the warps between the enemy and the bulk of her hull, trusting her subordinates to handle interception fire as she focused on getting clear.

Climbing for altitude, explosions chasing them the whole way up, She put more and more power to the warps as the air got thinner and in a few minutes the shaking of enemy fire hammering too close to them for comfort faded, partially due to them outrunning the fighting and partially due to the thinner atmosphere conducting less of the explosive force.

"We're clear, Ma'am. Minor damage, looks like we have a hull breach to track down, but it's not bad."

"Got it. Setting course for the Northern pole. Let's get this done."

\*\*\*\*\*

**Gaian Destroyer *Bug Hunt***

"Hold on, we've got some strays that got past the big boys," Reid said as he read the displays. "Lock beams, fire as they enter our range."

"Roger that, Sir," Lieutenant Michaels said. "The Drasin drones are heading for the planet. They are locked in."

"Weps, take them out," Reid ordered.

"Aye, Sir."

The beam weapons lanced out from the Destroyer, burning down the few stragglers entering their range. More pushed in, but they kept up the pressure and fried anything coming into their range while Reid monitored the battle that was shaking down further out.

*Way past our level, that's for sure.*

He didn't want to take the Bug Hunt anywhere *near* that mess he was seeing between the Heroics and the Priminae cruisers. They'd last about as long as a snowflake in the hot place, probably a lot less.

Running cleanup, though, that was well within their specs.

"Rogue Destroyers inbound, Sir," Eric Michaels reported. "They've transmitted lanes of fire."

"Stay clear of those," Reid ordered firmly. "We don't want to catch a pulse torp."

"No kidding," The Chief said from the Helm.

"Captain…" Eeric paused, "There's something…"

"What is it?"

"On the planet, the Casino. They've got heavy opposition converging on them," Eric said, sounding worried. "Marines still on the ground, pickup near the Northern Pole."

"Going to be nasty for the Marines," Reid said mildly. "How are they doing?"

"So far so good, but there's a limit."

Reid nodded in understanding, "Monitor it."

"Aye Sir."

"In the meantime…"

Reid was interrupted by a sharp alarm, "Report!"

"Drasin! They're close!" Eric snapped from the Ops console. "Don't know why they didn't turn up before!"

"Worry about that later," Reid said calmly, "Weps, lock them up!"

"Aye skipper! Targets locked!"

"Fire!"

The ship's main beams couldn't turn fast enough to engage, so the destroyer's point defense took up the job. The lower powered beams kept up the pressure as the alien drones got closer until they finally managed to destroy the small group with a startling explosion that rocked the ship hard enough to throw people around.

Reid was half out of his chair, barely hanging on by one arm as he heard swearing from ahead.

"Chief? You ok?" He snapped, waiting only a heartbeat without getting an answer before he snapped his next order. "Someone check on the chief!"

*****

**Bellerophon**

"Contact from the planet, sir. The Casino is on mission, encountering hard resistance."

"Understood," Jason said, not looking up from his tactical display. "Have they executed the final stroke?"

"Timers are in the final countdown. Extraction is two thirds complete."

"Let's hope that Gordon knows what he's doing." Jason mumbled as he looked over the current situation.

*The Priminae and Heroics are holding this line, but the Drasin are not letting up. We'll be below the mass levels needed to generate anti-matter shortly, after that...*

Without pulse weapons, the fighting would get close and personal, and that was where the Drasin had the advantage. If the numbers were still overwhelming when that happened, Jason knew that they'd have to either fight to the last or let the Drasin have the planet.

Normally, he wouldn't risk a hangnail to save the Empire, but just the *possibility* that the Drasin could find something on that planet that might allow them to escape the reproduction limitations put on them was enough to chill him to his bones.

"Sir, we've got a new contact, approaching fast. Looks like Imperial Transponders."

Jason snorted, "Tell them it's about time they got here, and welcome to the fight. If they stay out of our way, we'll leave their hulls unbreached. If they want to die with the beasts, that can be arranged."

"Yes Sir."

The Imperial ships didn't bother responding to his missive, but Jason saw that... to their credit, they ignored the Heroic and Priminae cruisers before throwing themselves into the fight.

*Too bad they're aiming for close quarters combat and blocking us from using Pulse weapons. Ah well, there's plenty of Drasin away from the Imperial vessels.*

He sighed, "Designate the Imperial vessels as temporary allies and let them handle their sectors."

"Aye skipper!"

*****

**Imperial Cruiser *From the Flames***

"The Home Fleet has returned and engaged the enemy,

Ship's Commander."

"I see them," Kaela confirmed. "Leave them to it, we have our own issues."

That being one of the larger understatements she'd ever heard herself say in her life. The *Flames* was barely operational at this point, the damages incurred over the previous battles had left them barely able to maneuver, and while they had some weapons capability it was far below operational levels.

The fighting was such that they could hardly even keep up with the fighting, taking shots from range as best they could, but the Drasin had locked ferociously on the ships belonging to the Flame bringers and the Oathers it seemed.

Grateful though she was for the distraction, it still grated on her deeply to be saved from certain death by the Empire's greatest enemies.

There was nothing to be done about it, however, as the fighting continued apace with no regard for her preferences in such matters.

******

On the surface, three sets of timers reached zero.

******

# CHAPTER 32

**Casino**

"Everyone hang on," Jennifer said as they hit the apex of their trajectory and began to fall toward the planet once more, "We're heading down, and they know we're coming."

The Colonel was under fire with the last squad of Marines, the Empire had figured out they were there it seemed.

*And they're not happy about the intrusion,* Jennifer thought as she leaned into the dive, propelling the Casino down even faster than it would freefall. *Unfortunate for the Empire, but I am not leaving them any one of my Marines.*

Fire from the surface began to heat up as they got closer, the beams scorching the sides of the Archangel as she jinked around to keep them from getting a clean shot. In atmosphere, beams were far more limited in both power and range compared to their space based equivalent, which gave her time to evade but ultimately it wouldn't matter a whole lot if she missed a step for half a heartbeat.

It wasn't like flying into chaff, she'd done that enough in the past, but the tension was identical as the heat scorched her nerves through the neural system, causing her to shy away from the enemy fire with instinctive speed.

"Colonel Keenan, Casino inbound. Stand by for pickup." She called, mid dive, aiming right for ground zero with no intent to slow or stop as she did.

"Roger, Casino. Dealers are looking forward to shift change."

The Colonel's voice was calm, but Jenn could hear the firing in the background and the tension below the radio voice.

"Over target LZ in thirty seconds. Watch for the boom."

"Oorah."

\*\*\*\*\*

The Casino arrived over the fighting in shocking *silence*, slowing so quickly that it didn't look *real* to the Marines or soldiers on the ground. For a fraction of a second the ship just seemed to appear from nowhere, like it had teleported.

Then the sonic boom arrived in its wake, announcing its presence to any and all who had somehow missed it in the first place.

Keenan and her Marines were already on the ground, covering their heads with their arms despite the armor as the shockwave shook the literal ground they were hugging. Meanwhile, Imperial soldiers were thrown to the ground as the blast overtook them, ending the flashing of beam weapons and returning fire in an instant.

"Get up and move!" Keenan snapped as the shockwave settled dust all around them. "Pop your last smokes, people! Use em if you got em!"

The Imperials were reacting slower, thankfully, which gave her time to pop a couple refractive smokers, filling the area around her with thick white smoke that sparkled from the suspended metallic particulates within. As the Imperial soldiers got back to their feet, brilliant bursts of light erupted in all directions from the smoke as they fired blindly into it.

"Dealers, Casino. Jump Master is ready to receive."

"Casino, Pit Boss," Keenan responded, "Confirmed."

She waved up the first pair and they leapt for the hovering ship, their boosters and CM devices giving them the height they needed to make the jump. Keenan waited for the first to be on board before sending up the next, just as the timer she'd set at the start of all this went off.

"Casino, Pit Boss," She said automatically. "The day's take is in the vault."

"Roger, Pit Boss. Let's hope it's enough to pay the bills."

Keenan couldn't agree more as she looked around, wondering at the lack of any big boom.

*Did it go off? Was this what it was supposed to do?*

She didn't know, she wasn't a tech or a shot caller in the end. Just a jarhead who'd done her job. The results, this time, were someone else's department.

******

At the poles of the planet, two devices engaged simultaneously, Their fusion cores imploding as the nuclear payloads were set off. Instead of then exploding, however, the energy continued to invert as the system built around the bomb core forced the energy back into a recursive loop.

In the first few nanoseconds after the detonation a kugelblitz singularity formed, containing the force of the explosion, along with the thermal pulse. Within the singularity that energy was converted up into a pulse powerful enough to escape the singularity as it was directionally focused straight down into the planet itself.

The twin blasts penetrated through over five thousand kilometers of rock and magma, splashing off the heavy metal core of the planet.

The planet's magnetic field flickered.

*****

**Gaian Destroyer** *Bug Hunt*

"Chief!" Reid called from where he was picking himself off the deck. "Speak to me Chief!"

"He's ok, just got his bell rung," Eric said from where he was pulling the insensate Chief from the Helm controls. "He's gonna need stitches, though, and the doc to be sure it's not worse."

"Right, Michaels, take the Helm," Reid ordered, waving two young crewmen forward, "grab the Chief, get him to the Doc."

"Aye Skipper."

Eric slipped behind the controls, checking the telltales as he reviewed the system displays.

"Engines and reactor are running a little hot, Sir, but within spec. We're good to go."

"Alright, Ensign Callow, take Ops," Reid said. "Michaels, get us lined up. Weps, take out those stragglers!"

"Aye skipper!"

"Skipper..."

"What is it, Callow?"

"Check out the signal from planetside..."

Reid turned his head, looking over the data from Ops.

*Jenn is in deep.*

"Helm, new tasking."

"Aye skipper. Standing by."

******

## Casino

"They're not looking to let us go!" Jennifer snapped as she rolled over the fighter/gunboat and tried again to gain altitude, only to be penned in by powerful beams from above her altitude and be forced to dodge back down.

"Contacts converging on our position, Ma'am. They're calling in more support."

"More!? Don't they have enough already? Goddamn it!"

While the beams were not as powerful within the atmosphere of a planet, and certainly their range was *far less*, that was actually working against her. At planetary ranges, the fighting was basically instantaneous, and dodging lasers didn't work unless you had at least a *couple* light seconds to move in.

*And, since one lightsecond is basically twenty **times** the diameter of the entire planet... this isn't good.*

Dodging not being an option, she could only react, maneuvering as quickly as she could once she felt the burn start. Her own body's instinctive reactions to pull away from burns had, thus far, kept her and the rest alive but there were limits to what her reflexive actions and the Neural interface could pull off. The damage to the armor was still marginal, but it would build in time.

Even being able to reflect back the energy efficiently had a limited application when the plasma from the *superheated air* the beam had passed through was flash frying the surface every passing second.

And, while it wasn't inherently damaging, she knew that each hit and even each near miss was going to be coating her armor in a carbon film. That film would degrade the beam resistant qualities of her armor, absorbing energy instead of reflecting it away. Given time, the Casino would burn.

*Damn it...* She thought just as the comms crackled to life.

"Casino, Bug Hunt. Heard you needed a CAP. Heads up."

\*\*\*\*\*

Eric grimaced as he stared through the blinding white light, his eyes burning as he manually killed the filters so he could see the raw imagery through the heat of their atmospheric entry.

"Target AO ahead, twelve hundred klicks, Skipper."

"I don't know how the hell you can see anything through that mess, Lieutenant, but I'll take your word for it. Weps!"

"Forward targeting RADAR is spinning up, heat shield retracting. LIDAR inoperable due to interference."

"Lock targets as soon as you see them," Reid ordered.

"Aye. We have soft locks from prediction systems preloaded, skipper. We're hot the second the heat clears."

Reid nodded, flipping a switch to gain access to the communications system.

"Casino, Bug Hunt," He said firmly. "Heard you needed a CAP. Heads up."

He killed the channel, nodded to the crew around them, "Alright. They know we're coming. Helm, Weps, it's your show. Punch a hole in that ceiling big enough to fly a starship through."

"With pleasure, Skipper," Eric said from the Helm, not looking back, "Weps, I've got you lined up for the initial punch. Watch for stragglers when we breach the perimeter, they'll try and swarm us."

"Got it, Lieutenant. Call the play."

Eric checked the periphery briefly, waiting for the heat shimmer to fade just a little more. The radiant energy of the reentry heat was dropping below the danger zone, and the enemy ships were showing up across the system.

"Casino location marked!" Callow called from Ops.

"Thank you," Eric said, "Weps, I'm lining you up. Fire as she bears!"

"Got it... firing in three... two... Fire!"

The ship's main beams lanced out, striking down into the Imperial formation. Ships burned as they tried to evade, but failed amid the surprise of the attack. Several burned up almost immediately, while others were singed enough to pull off wildly in a panic.

"You've got a hole, Jenn! Go for it!" Reid called.

"Roger, Bug Hunt. thanks."

Eric pulled hard back on the controls as they bottomed out their dive barely a kilometer above the ground, and still moving so fast as to make that less than a *second* away. The reactors of the old destroyer whined as they started to climb again, leaving a shockwave shaking the ground in the wake.

The sky ahead shook as the horizon again began to fall, the curve of the planet starting to show again as the Bug Hunt pulled for orbit while the Casino dropped into formation along side them.

\*\*\*\*\*\*

**Imperial Tower**

"I have summoned the guards," The entity rumbled out, "I would end you myself, but you may yet have some value."

"Man, or spirit, after my own heart... but I have some other plans," Gordon said easily.

"Your plans are of no interest to..."

The entity paused mid speech, looking confused for a moment.

"I... what?"

"Huh," Gordon interjected, checking his timer. "I was a

tad fast. I don't suppose you'd be willing to tell me how it feels, would you?"

He rose to his feet as the guards charged into the room from outside the throne room, their weapons directing right at him.

Gordon ignored them.

"What have you… done?"

"Not sounding so good, Majesty," Gordon said lightly as he extended his hands out to the side in deference to the guards surrounding him from behind.

It was a bit of an understatement, actually, as the Emperor's image glitched in and out, like some digital fragment of code that wasn't supposed to exist. The Imperial guards almost dropped their weapons as they saw the form appearing, apparently against the Emperor's will.

*Interesting.*

Gordon was leaning forward unconsciously, taking in everything he could manage. His eyes just flicked once to the tell tale light that showed the entire thing was broadcasting out to any Terran receiver in range.

"You… did… this."

"With help," Gordon nodded as he watched the Emperor shrink, slumping as he seemed to focus more and more on just remaining… intact. "Honestly, it's a little anticlimactic, sorry about that. You probably deserve more, what with being the Emperor and all that…"

He ignored the confused and shocked gasps from the Imperial soldiers as he stepped closer to the crumpled entity.

"But you killed my world," Gordon said coldly. "So giving you anything other than a long slow, *excruciating* death was never going to make me happy anyway."

The shadow of the Emperor looked up at him, "What… How?"

"You don't have the time," Gordon said, sighing. "You'll survive this, if that brings you any comfort. Haven't worked out how to *kill* any of you yet… but your memories? Those are just quantum bits, no different than any of our computer systems. I may not be able to destroy the computer, too many civilians live on it…"

He leaned in, getting as close to the image as he could, despite knowing that it really didn't matter. The pageantry of it appealed as Gordon whispered loudly.

"But I *can* wipe the drive clean." He hissed out. "May you rot in whatever hell accepts your kind, and may your next incarnation not be such a *raging asshole!*"

The entity glared, but there was a fearful tint to it all.

"You… die… too."

Rumbling in the tower could be felt before it was heard, coming up from far below them. The Imperial guards looked around nervously, uncertain as they had to fight to stay on their feet.

Gordon just shrugged with a cold smile.

"I died thirty years ago. I'd tell you to give my best to my daughter," The old spy said simply. "But neither of us are going anywhere near where she ended up. Good bye… *Majesty.*"

The Emperor raged as his image flickered uncontrollably before suddenly vanishing in a blinding flash. The rumbling around them intensified as the Imperial soldiers panicked and ran.

Gordon just took a seat.

*One last mission… accomplished.*

*****

### Bellerophon

"Watch it! We've got a breach in the line! Plug the hole before those beasts get through!"

The command deck of the cruiser was a chaotic mess, far from the normal discipline that Jason Roberts much preferred, but chaos was the way of battle and he knew how to adapt.

The Drasin were pressing in from all sides, the Imperial ships had taken the worst of it since they had opted to run straight into beam range, but the Priminae and Heroics weren't far behind.

"Sir! Transmission from the planet... it just cut off."

Jason half turned, "Gordon?"

The comm's officer shook his head, "Don't kno-"

"Skipper!"

"Sir!"

"Look!"

Jason twisted as everyone seemed to suddenly be clamoring for his attention.

"What the hell is..." He trailed off as he looked at the screens.

The Drasin were... falling back.

"What... what's going on?"

"The Drasin drones have withdrawn from combat, Sir," Bell said stoically. "They are regrouping and... leaving the area. Trajectory indicates escape velocity from the system."

Jason stared.

He knew what Bell was saying, he could see it himself, but he didn't believe it.

"Those things don't just *leave*," He said numbly. "What is going on?"

"The Imperial remnants are giving chase, Sir. Should we...?"

Jason shook his head, "No. Hold on. Get me Admiral Tanner. I think we need to have a long talk."

"A moment sir."

"Comms, better get me a full copy of Gordon's transmission," Jason ordered. "And anything else from the planet mission."

"Aye sir. We have questions from the others, should we pursue the Drasin?"

"Anyone with pulse weapons, harry from range," He ordered. "No one is to risk their ships, however. Let the Empire clean up their own damned mess, we were just here to keep the Drasin from jailbreaking themselves. I'm not risking lives to save Imperial ships."

"Yes sir!"

Jason left the command crew to their tasks and just stared at the screens showing the alien menaces fleeing by all rights, and couldn't help but wonder what the hell had just gone down.

*Gordon's mission. Did it succeed?* Jason looked to the side where the Imperial planet was shown on a screen. *Were they after the Emperor all this time?*

He felt numb.

*Are... were **we** ever the actual target? Or did we just get in the way? What in the hell is going on?*

\*\*\*\*\*\*

**Epilogue**

## Bellerophon

Jason Roberts was sitting in the Bell's conference room, Miram had joined them from the Bo, while Morgan had shuttled over from the Auto, and they had been joined by Tanner from the Priminae flagship. The hastily thrown together fleet was still in the Kraike system, and had basically taken full control of the Imperial capital's high orbitals while they worked out what the hell had happened and what they were supposed to do going forward.

Others had come in through the miracle of teleconferencing, and since they'd started talking the fighting had gotten hot and heavy. No one had any sympathy for the Empire, of course, but the situation had left them with something of a quandary.

Emotions were running high, both among the Terrans but also... surprisingly to him at least, among the Priminae. Jason had never really known them to be emotionally hot people, but they had been known to surprise even him despite that.

"The empire is in shambles! Now is the time to push our advantage," One of the Priminae captains was roaring over the network. "They're in revolt across the entire Empire. We push now, we can end the Empire as a threat for good, make them pay for what they've done... to us, and to you Terrans!"

There was a lot of agreement there, across both groups.

*Is it the right move, though?*

Jason wasn't sure it was. He certainly wouldn't mind taking the Empire out of play, but he was a soldier... not a murderer, and most of the Empire would just be civilians to the slaughter.

"Captain Roberts?"

Jason looked up, eyes locking on to Admiral Tanner.

"Yes, Admiral?"

"You seem to disagree."

Jason nodded slowly in the silence, "I think I do. Our history is a bloody one, as I'm sure you know. We had a war, we called the Great War. The war to end all wars."

He chuckled bitterly, "Arrogant of us, and stupid, but then that's us all over I suppose."

"The side that won that war enforced penalties on the losers, demanded reparations for starting the war, for all the damage… that sort of thing."

"That would seem reasonable," Tanner said hesitantly.

"You'd think so," Jason agreed, "but it was stupid. It ground them down, made them ripe for a demagogue, and the war to end all wars became just the prologue to a much larger one that followed."

Silence greeted him, leaving Jason the center of attention. He hated the fact that he could practically *hear* Eric saying the words he was speaking, but he supposed the man was right more than he was wrong.

"As I see it, we have three choices," He said, looking around. "I'm going to assume, however, that genocide is off the table?"

The faces of the others jerked away, shocked looks coming back on him. He smiled thinly as even Tanner stared at him with wide eyes.

"Yeah, unless you're willing to wipe them *all* out, there's only a couple options. We could leave them be as is, hope they don't come after us again…" Jason said wearily.

"Or?" Tanner asked hesitantly.

Jason saw the recognition in many of the Terran faces.

"We enact the Marshall Plan."

END

Printed in Great Britain
by Amazon

62140735R00218